Praise for Ted Krever's books:

Mindbenders

"...a storyline that takes hold in the first few pages and doesn't let go..."
"...really fast paced...I found myself unable to put it back down."

"...dialog that left me breathless."
"...[a] global, international conspiracy of corporate and governmental politics, mind control, murder and intrigue."
"OMG!...finally crawled into bed early hours of the next day."
"This is that rare piece of fiction based on fact in such a way as to make the two seem to blur."
"Mindbenders...will make you wonder if your mind really does belong to you."

Mindbenders 2: The Fiery Sky

"...a more than worthy followup to the 1st book, fast paced, well written and exciting!"
"...takes me places that were only in my imagination - I feel like I have been to that island in the South Pacific living on the water, and I've been parched in the Aussie desert - it's all real."
"...A complete thrill ride from beginning to end...great style and substance."
"...intense, memorable scenes..."
"...seamlessly weaves multiple storylines together, delivering a powerful punch of an ending."

Ted Krever

GREEN

"…not your typical romance…
"…a unique look into the mindset of men, rather than the typical
romance, which is told from the woman's point of view."
"… a smart, witty and wise look at love later in life…"
"I found myself laughing aloud more than once, only to shortly
thereafter find myself deeply touched."
"The descriptions…of Ireland are alone worth the price of the
book…"
"If you like reading about horses, Ireland, friendship, love in any
form..."
"Part a love story, part a political thriller, and part a satiric
commentary on life and politics…"
"Green is a charming book."

Howling at Wolves

"This book, simply put...is funny!"
"Keep your tissues handy as you won't stop laughing."
"Nothing is sacred..."
"…like Garp on steroids (or maybe Viagra?)

A Crafty and Devious God

"…a great read…"
"Weirdly excellent"
"[The] writing is very natural, loose and easy, yet deep and thoughtful."
"…an engaging character study… a tale of a man who's lost, looking for his way, and a girl who knows she is destined for great things and is determined to achieve it at all costs."
"I gave it a try. And kept reading, and reading, and reading. Just very well-written, scattered throughout with concepts that made me think (which I occasionally like to do)."

After

…short stories of New Yorkers trying to make sense of their changed world in the immediate aftermath of 9/11."
"These stories are emotionally impactful but they are not grim. Each character finds some measure of hope or understanding or, at the very least, adaptation to their circumstances."
"…a masterful job of depicting the surreal dream-like state that trauma survivors inhabit…"
"Intricately woven stories of despair and ultimately hope…"
"…a tender tribute to the survivors of 9/11."

Ted Krever

A Crafty and Devious God

By Ted Krever

Little David Publications
www.tedkrever.com

ISBN: 978-1-7327865-0-9

This is a work of fiction. Names, characters, places and incidents are products of the author's imagination or are used fictitiously. Any resemblance to actual places, events or persons, living or dead, is entirely coincidental.

Cover photograph by Jessica Schroer-Smalley, used with permission

New York Times, July 18, 1998:

Shares of Broadcast.com, a small three-year-old company that streams live news, radio, music and other programs over the Internet, more than tripled in value yesterday in frenzied trading—the best opening-day gain of any company in Wall Street history...

Investors have clamored for Internet stocks all year long...but even the underwriters who priced shares of Broadcast.com for public consumption failed to anticipate the ravenous investor appetite for them...

The shares had been priced at $18. Soon after they began trading, Broadcast.com shares shot up to $68 on the Nasdaq stock market, then soared as high as $74 before closing at $62.75, a nearly 250 percent gain that made Broadcast.com a $1 billion company in a matter of hours...

The [founder] of the company, Mark Cuban...is now worth about $300 million.

~~~~~

Preface

I'd love to say I knew she was trouble right from the beginning, but I'm not that smart.

After moving out of my marriage, I have this plan. Not much of a plan but just enough to keep me from throwing myself off a rooftop the first few nights.

I move back to the Jersey shore—Seaview, an hour's ferry from New York City. I grew up just a few miles away. I move into this little house a seawall away from the Atlantic Ocean, I run three miles a day up and down the beach and wangle myself as anonymous a job as I can find, repairing TV's and computer equipment for the only person on the Eastern seaboard who seems less interested in meeting people than me.

And on a breezy afternoon, a week or two into this orgy of denial, this girl comes into the shop and says, "Any of you guys know something about the Web?"

"Something," I say. "You having trouble getting connected?"

"No, I need a server set up at my house so I can host my own site. I need something strong enough to host streaming video. Live video."

"I can make you a machine that'll host video," I told her. "Multiple processors, if you want, lots of storage. You'll need a separate machine for the video server, in addition to your regular Web server. But I'd really recommend you hire an outside company to send out the video—let someone else do the work, unless you want to put in a generator and hire a staff to watch things 24 hours a day."

"You know who I could hire?" she asked.

"I can make a list of the usual suspects," I told her.

Her voice dropped half an octave. "Okay," she nodded. "Let's talk."

We went to the coffee shop down the corner and discussed what she needed. She agreed to outsource the video server, but she wanted a Web server built from scratch, and wrote me a check on the spot for half the cost of it. I took it to the bank and waited two days until it cleared. Then I bought the parts and put it together.

I was a technical manager at a television network in the city—first in traditional TV production and then, the last few years, in what is now called 'new media'. So I got to know machines. Cameras, editing equipment—and in the last several years, computers. I tinkered with them and fell in love with them.

I built a few websites, for myself and friends. I wrote a novel and put it up on the Web, a chapter at a time, with linked pages and little animations that illustrated the story. Nobody visited the site, but I got some satisfaction from it.

So while I'd never actually put a computer together, I knew what parts were needed and what to tune. I decided I could build it myself, and was delighted to discover I was right.

Once I was comfortable the machine was solid and fast, I called and told her it was ready.

"Come on up—I need it installed," she said.

I hesitated for a moment, wondering if I should ask for an installation fee.

"I'll pay you to do it," she offered, and I smiled the whole way over.

Her house was a severe two-story modern with windows all around. It was dusk as I reached the place. The lights were on inside—the glow leaked out the windows like a bell jar full of fireflies.

Almost all the living space was on the second floor, and most of it was wide-open glass, with a deck that wrapped around all four sides of the house. A living area filled most of the floor, overlooking Ocean Ave and the beach at one end, with a view of the river—looking over the roofs of some shorter homes—on the far side. There was a bar on the back wall, with three bedrooms behind and a sparse kitchen across from it, partitioned out of the living space.

"I've got everything cleared out for you," she said as we came upstairs. I set the boxes down and started unpacking my equipment—*her* equipment.

I tend to have tunnelvision when I'm working, but she kept parading back and forth, moving things around and then moving them around again in front of me, until I couldn't miss her. She wanted to be noticed. I hadn't looked at a woman since I left home. But now, I looked.

She was gangly a few years ago—it was evident in the self-conscious way she walked. But there was nothing gangly now— now she was just lanky. A little gawky swing lingered in her arms and legs, a funny, uncoordinated pulse that took the edge off her, made her funny instead of intimidating—made her more *real*, somehow.

There was exercise equipment in a corner, and it showed— her body was athletic and girlish, nothing extra, but all the right equipment in good proportion. Her flax hair picked up the red in the sunset. Her face was long, but the eyes were big and the whole effect of her was open, girl-next-door friendly.

Friendly, but at the moment, rather strange. She continued to straighten things she'd already straightened and strike poses that work in photos but never in real life unless somebody's working pretty hard.

Well, let her pose. I didn't get the sense she wanted me to do anything but watch. And watching wasn't bad. I got a rise out of it—it was nice to know how that felt again. To feel like a man, even a rusty middle-aged one.

Once I had the system set up, I called her over and showed off a little, playing some video from files I'd placed on the hard drive for demo purposes. She stood close to me for a moment. She smelled good.

Then she lugged a huge tripod from the other side of the room and said, "Okay, here's the camera." She pointed to a camera on the floor by the bar, and I knew we were in trouble.

"Whoa!" I said. "I thought you were talking about consumer camcorder stuff. This is a professional camera."

"I told you I needed top-of-the-line equipment," she declared.

"This *is*. The computer has a $500 video card. The next step above this is $3,000. Nobody makes professional video for the Web. It's a postage-stamp sized window on the screen, and you've got a $30,000 video camera here."

Suddenly she's uncertain. "This is too much?"

"It's a nuclear reactor to boil water," I told her.

She shrugged. "I'll return it. What should I get?"

Then we talked equipment for an hour. It was a fun conversation for several reasons, not least the fact that her nipples kept playing hide-and-seek through her sweater.

But after an hour, I'm fascinated by her. She knows six different ways to set up Hollywood lighting, to use machinery to get the right emotional effect. We have a ten-minute conversation about George Hurrell, the ancient Hollywood master who perfected cheekbones with Garbo and Claudette Colbert. She's got his techniques down pat, but somehow, she doesn't know how to plug a microphone into the camera.

I realize she's a good student. If she can get it out of a book, she knows all about it, no matter how difficult. But she's not worldly at all—obvious things, those not found in books, are out of her realm. She doesn't try to figure them out. She doesn't take a chance on being wrong.

"So you trade that camera in for a good DV machine," I advise. "The picture will look just as good, for one-tenth the money."

"I'll go tomorrow and get one," she says. "Want to come with me?"

"That's my consultant hat," I answer, feeling a little giddy from the nipples. "That's twice my computer handyman rate."

"Okay," she bites. "Tomorrow, 10am. Meet me here. Four hours, tops. It takes longer than that, I don't pay."

She starts straightening things and striking poses again. I take another good look at her and head home. On all counts, I'm on a roll.

Peapatch 4 West

I live in a house with a name—Peapatch 4 West. A name is an affectation for a house, usually reserved for those rich enough to properly display their affectations.

Mine, however, is just a little weathered plaque, paint flecking at the edges, fastened over the door by two ancient screws. The screws fasten to roof tiles bleached from the years and exposure to the sea air. Misaligned, chipped and torn at the edges, the tiles are an exemplar of the state of my house—the place is a wreck. Nonetheless, it comes with a name—when you're missing a compass, you don't turn down a weathervane.

When my marriage broke up, I moved down here. I knew a house like this existed before I'd ever seen it, and I searched until I found the properly diminished location for the next chapter in my life.

And here I sit, blanket on my lap, watching through the steaming window as the seagrass blows in that stiff autumn wind, and the spray flies over the seawall across the street. I slouch in my desk chair and write letters to myself, waiting for the sun to rise, the whistle of the radiator and the start of another day.

I call the house to talk to my son. Ring ring—no answer. His voice on the answering machine. I leave a message. Call me back, buddy, I love you.

I'll disconnect the modem before I shut down tonight—I worry that a bolt of lightning or a power surge will blow the computer out. T he power here sucks. I ran a test when I first moved in and found surges to 145 volts. So I'll unplug it—later, but not just yet. It's my lifeline to the world.

I spend a lot of time on the Video Voyeur pages. Kids eating pizza, watching television, reading the paper, getting naked. It's much like my marriage—lots of leading up to getting naked and very little actual nakedness.

I watch the fishcam, one of the first things I ever watched on the Web, and the coffeecam—an unblinking view of a coffee machine in an office in San Francisco. I can tell you by sight who takes milk and who takes sugar. One afternoon, I saw an older woman—a woman my age, I guess—get two cups at once, distracted by a pile of her own belongings she'd placed on the counter. Staring at her as she stared at her things, I realized she'd just been fired and had cleared out her desk—thus the pile on the counter. The wind doesn't only blow cold in my neighborhood. I've seen birds die in the aviary cam in Atlanta, and the crowds swell and dwindle at the Hong Kong zoocam.

And I've watched Kelly and LeopardGirl. Many nights in the past month, I've watched them fiddling with their blouses, sitting around in their panties and bras watching tv, and then watched them fiddling with themselves on camera.

Virtual sex is OK—not as good as real sex, but without the headaches. But I want to earn my orgasms. LeopardGirl makes you wait a while before she unbuttons her blouse. There's a little suspense, and that's how God intended voyeurism to work.

I jog morning and evening. I'm stubborn. The sand gets heavy this time of year, from the seaspray and the autumn air soaking in at night but still I run. Over the seawall, footsteps creaking on the wooden steps, then onto the thick beach. Watching the gulls, picking up shells and stones, smelling the air and stretching my muscles, such as they are.

There aren't many muscles in me that don't need stretching.

I told my wife I was unhappy; she told me there was nothing wrong. Then she told me that whatever was wrong was *my* fault—I was too angry, too loud, too argumentative, too analytical. So I became more moderate, quieter, gentler, less argumentative—analytical stayed, despite yoga and zen. But her complaints never lessened.

She was right—in that marriage, I really *was* a bad, mean person. But I realized somewhere along the line that, outside that marriage, I didn't have to be. The problem was not either of us; it was the two of us *together*.

So I left, in a spasm of optimism and now, every minute of the day, I curse myself a stupid fool for believing anything would change.

I hate...you name it. I hate the front door for sticking, I hate the neighborhood dogs for barking at me as I jog by. I hate the two gay guys across the street, who barbecue every weekend—even in this autumn weather—and play music I like way too loud. I hate my boss here when he makes no provision for my recent tragedies and for condescending to be nice to me when he does.

I haven't contacted anyone since I moved out. I'm not ready yet, I tell myself. I have a little money saved and there's a kind of healing I need no doctor can offer. I need to start over, to get my own footing. I have unfinished business with *me* yet.

Or maybe I've just reached a dead end.

My wife's last words to me as I walked out of our house were "You'll never see your son again." She said them knowing there was nothing that would terrify me so much. Every day I call without an answer, just his voice on the answering machine, those words echo louder and louder in the back of my mind, until the echoes are louder than any sound produced by the outside world..

Meanwhile, the people I meet remain proximate strangers— the grocery store owner, the mailwoman, the fat man next door with the grey hair and the collection of checked shirts, sitting on his front porch waving to the cars on Ocean Avenue all day long. I live among them, but not with them, running my penitentiary time up and down the beach, doing odd jobs that will never pay the bills, and sitting long into the night with cheap wine bottles, some old tunes on the stereo and the mesmerizing boredom of the web girls.

Dancing

I walk the mile and a half to Livy's house. She's perched on the deck as I pad down the street and, in the driveway when I arrive, warming up a yellow vintage Jeep. She is wearing sunglasses, a thin pink blouse tied above her navel, and shorts. My guy radar tells me there's no bra under the blouse, although two sizeable pockets in front obscure the proof.

I get in the passenger seat and we take off. She clearly doesn't like anybody ahead of her. She works around car after car, in a series of lurching moves, bursts of speed and nerve. We narrowly miss seven accidents—but we do consistently miss. As we bounce along, I can enjoy the cleft where the bottoms of her breasts meet her torso. You take your job perks where you find them, I always say...

When we get to the store, she takes my arm and drags me inside.

"Okay, Mr. TV—show me what I need," she demands, smiling.

They have a row of camcorders set up, sending pictures of a still-life—a vase of flowers with a thick-patterned tapestry draped behind—to large monitors overhead. It's a good display. I walk the row, pointing out the best models and how to tell a good picture from a bad one on the monitors. I can see her repeating the details as I feed them to her, watch the information entering her personal knowledge base.

"I'm surprised," I say, "that you don't know cameras. You were encyclopedic about lighting yesterday."

"That was *performance*," she says. "This is tech. I'm the director, not the cinematographer. I'm interested in anything that enhances the performance. *You* worry about the camera for me."

She buys two of the big cameras and two mini, top-of-the-computer types. I have to convince the kid salesman to search for a multi-box and switcher to plug them all into, so Livy can use them all on the site.

"I didn't even know we sold this stuff," the kid salesman says.

When we tote up the damage, she's dropping about $20,000 in equipment. Either she's using up her trust fund or has very expensive taste in hobbies.

As we carry it all back out to the car, I ask, "So what are you shooting?"

"Me," she answers.

Back at the house, I set everything up. She knows exactly where she wants it all—a minicam on the computer in the living room, another on the dresser in the bedroom, and the two bigger cameras on tripods converging in the living room.

I run cables and extensions all over, taping them to the baseboards, making sure the wires don't cross so the audio doesn't pick up an interference hum—all the geeky TV things I haven't done myself in years. It's fun.

"OK, let's run through," I say, once it's all connected.

I patch the camera output into the big TV on the wetbar, so she can see the picture from anywhere in the room. I hand her the remote control for the switcher. It's tiny—she can wear it hanging from her wrist and switch cameras with one finger action.

"You've got 4 cameras," I show her the keypad on the remote, "—Camera One on the computer, Two over by the kitchen facing the deck, Three by the deck facing the kitchen and 4 in the bedroom. Push the number on the remote, that camera shows up on the monitor. Pretty simple."

I approach new experiences cautiously at first. It's how I managed to grow up in the Sixties and still have a few brain cells left.

Not Livy. She starts pushing buttons, one after the other, watching the results in the monitor. Working without letup, as though her first impulse is to see if she can break something. She stands in the middle of the room, where the camera views converge, and stares at herself as each camera view clicks through, rapidly, in turn.

She rotates slowly, figuring the angles. It's *performance*, I find myself thinking. She's blocking out her moves.

After a minute of walking slowly about the center of the room, she grabs up a tripod and carries it five feet to a new location—a different angle. And a better one. Okay—she's got an eye.

Now she begins to move again, pawing the floor with a dancer's light step, toeing forward and backward, eyeing the cameras warily, switching from one to the next, as she moves. Turning them from adversaries to allies, judging from the look on her face—mastering their territory, channeling these electrons in the ether.

There's a pattern emerging in the way she switches shots, and it's not what I'm used to, not what I was taught. I learned traditional camera technique, where one angle is chosen as 'the best' for conveying the scene. For Livy, one angle works off the other; one view complements the next, and the story is told by the cacophony of images as much as by the content of any one of them.

She's halting at first. But gradually, something clicks in and then she's bouncing, flashing, around the room, twirling and switching from one camera to the next, faster and faster, lighter on her feet with each second, the shots banging kaleidescopic as she flies closeupflashingby, stretched head to toe, a dervish of motion...and beautiful. Beautiful and free and joyous.

Then I type her domain name—www.seaviewgirl.com—into the Web browser and a clean shot of the living room couch appears on screen.

"Voila," I exclaim.

"I'm in business," she says, smiling.

She has a funny smile, I notice now for the first time—a smile like two veils. There's a real smile somewhere underneath, and it's open and relaxed, the way she wants to appear—maybe, the way she wants to *be*. But there's another layer, a layer that isn't quite so open or relaxed, that always seems to be looking for the fine print, and that layer hovers in front of whatever is going on inside her.

The sun is bouncing off the windows on the far side of the street. Behind the stores, the darkness is moving in over the ocean, the eastern edge of sky, the darkness ready to take over so quickly this time of year.

She's beginning to move under the lights again, checking out the cameras online now. And I give in to the moment, to my stupid impulse to do the job right, to my endless dull conscientiousness.

"You know, we have to fix your lighting," I tell her. "You don't have it set up right for dancing."

I'd found myself thinking about it after I'd gotten home the other night. She'd concentrated her lights in just a few places around the room, to get dramatic effect for her close-ups, I guessed. That didn't leave enough in the central part of the room, where she did her dancing.

The result was that, instead of any detail, the dances showed a smearing, streaky movement, a *representation* of what was happening, instead of the thing itself.

So now, I start moving a few lights around to show her. To show her I can make it better.

"Don't do that," she says. "I like it the way it is."

I insist on showing her how it would look. I'll show her I can make it better. And the skeptical voice in my head says, I'll show *me*, maybe. I'll show me I can still do *something*.

She dances a little for me, once the lights are set up 'properly'.

The pictures are crystal-clear. They show every false step, every movement off the beat. They show the frayed edges of her shawl, the dirty dishes stacked in the kitchen sink and newspapers in a pile near the deck.

Then she plays back the tape of her dance the other night. The dim light is moody, mysterious. The shawl is a cape and jet exhaust. She cuts a ghostly figure, the smearing video tracing her movements and stylizing them all at once. I begin to see this isn't dance, not in any traditional sense. It is movement for the camera, and for a fuzzy Web camera at that. She has invented something that works for this new form.

"You're right—it's better your way," I say, and start moving the lights back where she had them.

She grabs a light, to help. Then she arches an eyebrow and says, "Did I tell you my first boyfriend was 18 years older than me?" and I nearly stop breathing.

Is this thing coming on to me? I quash the question instantly—there's no sense to it, on any level beyond my own vanity.

"I'm doing my first Webcast tonight," she says now. "Would you hang out and make sure I don't have any problems? I'll pay you for the time."

In The Light

The next thing I know, I'm sitting in a pile of Chinese takeout containers and wine bottles, spooning assorted dishes into plates for us to pick at.

She comes out of the bedroom in a red spaghetti strap dress, her hair brushed behind her ears, looking innocent, friendly and seductive all at once, just the look that got me married once and in trouble several times before that.

She pads around in front of Camera One and turns on the TV. She flops down on the couch and plays with the remote for a few moments, finding a channel she likes. She picks up a plate and eats, slowly, a bit at a time, for about fifteen minutes.

Then she stands up. One of the straps falls off her shoulder. She makes no effort to lift it again. She holds up the plate and says, "Can you give me some of the vegetables and plain rice?"

I spoon some out on her plate and she eats, again, slowly and very deliberately. For a skinny girl, there's no problem with her appetite. After a few minutes, she pulls a magazine off the floor by the couch and lays it on the table. She reads for a while—maybe ten minutes.

I can see her on the couch—and, if I turn my head, in the large monitor atop the bar. The camera is rolling, and, as they say in the TV business—*my* business—the clock is ticking.

Finally, I ask, "Um, is...this it? Shouldn't you do something?"

"Such as?"

"I'm not sure—you dance, right?" Then I gather the question together a bit more precisely. "What do you actually *do*?"

She laughs. "There—I laughed", she says. "That should buy me another ten minutes."

She sits a little longer, and now I can see she *is* aware of the camera. She's just biding her time, building to something, like Hitchcock showing us the field, the bus, and the distant neighbors, before the crop duster plane finally appears to try to skin Cary Grant.

Finally she gets up and steps lightly around behind the couch. She touches a button on the CD and music fills the room. She throws a glance at me and the audio console near me—is this going out? I adjust the level on the sound so I can see the green ribbons dancing on the console—yes, the music can be heard by anyone on the Web with speakers attached.

She sits on the couch again, but this time sitting up close to the edge. The strap is still hanging off her shoulder, the dress ' drooping a little at her breast. Now she begins to bop, just to sway to the beat, sitting on the couch.

Then she says to me, "Would you mind...sitting out on the porch? You can take food or whatever you want with you?"

This hits me in the face a bit. "Would you rather I leave--give you some privacy?"

"No—I want you here in case something doesn't work," she says. "But...could you sit on the porch? That would just really help me out."

She's very friendly and apologetic about it, but she knows what she wants. That seems to be the rule with her. I smile politely and take the red wine onto the porch.

There are two chairs out there. I take one over to the sliding door and sit.

She begins, once again, to dance. Lithe movements, stretched out, on the tips of her toes, lightly at first, and then with more emotion. Clearly, there's no choreography here. She's making this up out of the air—out of her gut.

There's a hunger, an urgency here that isn't necessarily pretty or comfortable to watch. There's a look on her face that is gripping and grasping, something that *wants*, wants bad. The same note is struck by her bounds and leaps, her body continually reaching for something just beyond her grasp. It isn't classic, but it's moving and very raw. Both the abstracted, smeared, shimmering image on the tube and the panting, athletic young woman crossing back and forth in front of it—the Siamese mirror twins of her.

My head swivels as she bounds around. Finally, she settles onto the couch again. She's disheveled and sweaty, but she tosses her hair and throws it over a few times and suddenly she looks terrific.

And then she starts peeling off the red dress. The straps come loose and she crosses her arms in front of her and peels it upward—that magical moment in a man's life—to reveal her breasts.

They are not large—just my taste—and exquisitely formed, conical and upturned, with a nipple like a dab of paint. The skin is soft but the shape is lovely. A sculptor could work a month on one of those curves and not get it right.

She stands, giving a delicious glimpse of a flat stomach and a lovely mound barely covered by tiny red panties.

She's motionless in front of the camera for a moment. Expectation and payoff, all at once. Then she reaches behind the couch and pulls out a cut-off t-shirt. She pulls this over her head, hesitates a moment—as if to say goodbye—and pulls it down over her breasts. The material is flimsy—her nipples push right through.

Now she gets up and goes over to the treadmill and begins to run there. She works it for twenty minutes, switching cameras to give several views. The view is very good.

So what's absolutely predictable now is that, while the view Livy's presenting isn't all that revealing anymore, the whole atmosphere is charged. All is sex; sex is everywhere. Those few seconds undressed have fired the whole evening with possibility.

She spends another half-hour on the couch, sewing a button onto a dark blue dress. Demure as could be, except no one—not me, not the audience, however few of them there are—can view her that way anymore.

And I'm having a real hard time with this, all of a sudden. An hour ago, sitting in the living room with her, if she had gotten naked, I would have enjoyed the view but I would have been working. Really. It would have been uncomfortable, but I would have understood my role as a business consultant. Now, sitting on the porch with an empty wine bottle, my Chinese containers and a glass sliding door between us, I feel like a peeping tom. Like the audience.

And I am feeling the cold, the evening September chill. I take it as long as I can, but my knees and ankles are protesting loudly. So I go to open the sliding door, to head back inside. I tug at it—locked. I tap on the window. Then I bang on the window. No response, even though she should be able to see me from where she's sitting.

Finally, I lower myself off the side of the deck, holding on for a moment to gauge the distance, and drop to the dune below. I head home angry and frustrated. I pull her up on the web and warm myself up for a time before falling asleep in my chair.

Unlocked

The next morning, I woke in a foul mood. If I had a cat, I would have kicked it. I would have gone looking for it, so I could kick it.

I ran and everything gave me trouble—my knees, ankles, feet, neck—all stiff, creaking, aching, binding. Old, old, old, old and old.

My run takes me by Sylvie's house. The world is still at that hour, except for Sylvie and the birds cawing and pecking. Forces of Nature at work. As I mount the dune below her place, pushing at the sand to get my footing, I catch a glimpse of her above, scurrying around like a crab in her light, stiff stride.

"Don't step on anything," she advises me severely.

Sylvie taught me about lacquering stones, and grouping them.

Sylvie lives right on the beach at the very edge of town. She says she remembers this place when it was show business refugees and gangsters, God knows how long ago that was. Sylvie showed me how simply painting on a coating of lacquer would keep the lustre of shells and beach stones. She's been making displays of them for years. I am beginning to photograph her collection. Maybe I'll do some myself eventually—it's very peaceful. If they come out well, I'll put them on my webpage. I'll dedicate it to Sylvie.

But the pictures won't capture the gentle movement of her gnarled hands, the way her eyes look squinting through those bottle-cap glasses of hers, as she demonstrates her technique. She makes the arrangement of stones in a bowl into art.

"I made a lot of money with these things, in the Sixties and Seventies," she rasps, moving stiffly to the counter to get some seagrass for a garnish. " Arthritis is hell. I just can't place things anymore like I could. The hell with cancer—once you get it, you're dead anyway. They should spend millions on a cure for arthritis."

"Ever hear of Advil?"

"Can't take pills—they powder your lungs. You take too many, soon you can't breathe anymore."

She is working on one of her projects. Pulling clumps of weeds from the top of the dunes, she has arranged them, fan-like, on the weathered blue decking behind her house. Then she adds what seems like a random collection of shells, crabshells and seahorses on top, and photographs them in the bright seabouncing light.

Once finished, she hefts the whole artwork as a piece and dumps it unceremoniously back out on the dunes.

She does this three times before muttering "Time to move on."

Then she disappears into her shed, a little tumbledown rectangle the same greyblue color as her enormous Nathaniel Hawthorne house. She emerges with a can of paint and a wide brush and proceeds to varnish the shed. Same color as before, but shinier.

She works the brush, bobbing up and down, putting her shoulders and back into the strokes. This way and that, up and down, sideways, filling the cracks, overpainting and painting hard, really laying it on with passion.

I find myself smiling, watching her and thinking back on her as I jog back to my Peapatch house. She does art like work, and work like art, I think. Not a bad approach.

I call home—no answer. My son's voice on the answering machine. It's Daddy—call me back. Please. Hang up.

As I said before: when I feel this way, I take action. The action doesn't really have to fix anything, or even lead to a fix—it just has to neutralize the hopeless feeling till it fades. In the past, I've gone looking for a new job on days like this. I've run ten miles. I've finally returned library books from 1975.

In this case, I decided to look for a girlfriend.

We're weird creatures, we humans. Any degree of lyricism we manage in this life comes wholly despite ourselves. Underneath all that civilized posturing, there's a set of scales—an incredibly savage, harsh, honest, shrewd, predatory level of judgment—judgment of ourselves. I was suddenly aware of a scale of self-measurement I'd never know existed before.

Without any forethought, I found I knew my value on the open market as a man. I knew it intimately, and impassively, as though it was in no way connected to me. Underneath all the other craziness I'd preoccupied myself with, I'd been keeping score.

I knew what I could afford. I needed a schoolteacher, or a legal secretary, or a ruffian artist with a couple of love children running around her studio.

I wanted someone with kids—I knew that in my life, I hadn't discovered my real feelings, or understood the real value of things, till Daniel came along. I wanted that in anyone I was going to spend time with. Besides, kids made it harder to get dates—I could probably get a prettier girl than I deserved if she had kids.

I'm not a cynical person, really. It was kind of astonishing to hear these thoughts rising so easily in my head, but I recognized that this sudden outburst of shrewdness was a pretty useful survival instinct at work. I was coolly sizing up my prospects for success. I had a goal, an objective. I was on a mission.

There was a good-looking woman of about 40 in the little market near my house. Ten year old kid—no wedding ring. A prospect. But she spoke with those Connecticut rounded-tones, and she threw seven live lobsters into the cart.

That ain't happenin'. Men may be shallow about looks — women are shallow about money. Women marry *up*, and I wasn't up for her. Hey, I didn't *choose* this reality; I just live here.

Slim thirty-five year old with dark hair and glasses at the video store. Foreign film section. So far, so good. Get a little closer. She takes off her jacket — her entire back is covered with a tattoo of Isabella Rosselini in black leather. The three videos in her arms are all lesbian themes. Not likely.

Fortyish woman with child at the laundromat — probably straight, or at least bi, though the child could be adopted, of course, or a test-tube refugee. Lots of choices out there. Leaves the laundry to be done, instead of doing it herself. That's a yellow flag already. Then she gets into an argument with the owner about how to divide the loads — which items *must* go with which other items — don't you know this *already*? I walk away. Not what I need at this time, thanks.

And then there are the 13 other lovelies that I fall in lust with, walking the several blocks to the store. Pretty, bright, optimistic, in good shape, with good jobs and money in their pockets. Haven't fallen on their faces yet in this life. Not a fit. I've fallen on my face recently — and not for the first time. I need someone who understands what that feels like.

And that's how it goes. Too old, too young, too pretty, too successful, too difficult, just plain too weird. Lots of choices, same result.

I go to work, speak to no one and proceed to repair five televisions and three impossibly confused computer problems in two hours. Frustration can be a great source of energy. But I get no pleasure from it.

At 1 o'clock, I go out for a sandwich. Livy is sitting on the bench along the street, in a very girlish slip dress.

"You didn't say goodnight, " she starts.

"It got cold on the porch," I reply.

"You should have come in."

"The door was locked."

She looks stunned. "I didn't lock it—did you see me lock it?"

"I'm not saying you locked it—I'm just saying it was locked and I was cold." I'm not sure if she's serious or not, and I don't give a damn either.

"Well, I'm sorry," she says, apologizing for something she didn't do.

"You did a good job," she continues. "I know that camera setup is complicated. But it still isn't quite right—will you have another look at it?"

She leans around to look me in the eye, since I'm childishly refusing to look at her.

"I'll make sure the door stays unlocked, okay?"

I nod, and we head back to her place.

It's sunny out, temperature in the high 50's. The sun blazes through the windows of her big room. I work out some glitches in the camera-switching unit. She stands in the corner by the bar, painting. Spreading paint on a large canvas, to be more precise—there's no artistic plan or passion behind it.

Then she shows me a radio transmitter she's bought for one of the cameras.

"You know how to set up cameras—can you *shoot*?" she asks.

"It's been a few years, but that's how I started," I said. "You don't forget."

"I thought maybe you could do some handheld camera for me," she says.

I blush. I'm not aware of it until I see her reaction. But she smiles instantly, and I know.

"Umm—of what?" I ask. It's an innocent question, really.

"I'm an actress," she says, answering the question behind the question. "I'm an actress, a dancer, and a painter. I'm going to share my life onscreen. I want to share my ideas and my creativity and my feelings and—just *everything!*—with my audience. I want it to be spontaneous—but the thing is—" she pauses, searching for the words, "—it's not enough to be spontaneous..." and she sputters out.

"They have to *know* you're being spontaneous," I say.

There's a sudden look of surprise on her face, and then an uncomplicated, unveiled smile.

"Yeah," she says. "And if you're trying too hard to show you're being spontaneous—"

"You're being contrived," I finish, and she actually laughs. I do too.

"I spent ten years doing documentaries—it's not as different as we'd like you to believe," I explain.

"Right. So we've got to figure out how to walk that line—if you want to try?"

"Well, again—what am I shooting?"

"I thought you could shoot me while I dance. And move around me while I move around."

"That sounds interesting."

"Do you dance?" she asks, looking me over. Looking me over, not an unreasonable question.

"I'm an enthusiastic, but very bad, dancer," I reassure her.

Her eyebrows go up, rueful. "Well, we'll try it."

She turns on some music—electronic sounds over insistent bass and drums. She takes a few steps. I move with her. She turns and moves the other way—I follow.

She stops.

"No," she says, "That won't do."

I see a look of concern flit across her face. It is just a moment, veiled, filtered, the same as all her expressions. But I suddenly realize she's worried I can't *shoot*! Hell, I've been shooting video professionally since she was...

I suddenly become *very* determined to show her what I can do.

"I've been moving *with* you," I say quickly. "That's no good; it tones down your movements. I need to keep taking an angle to you—then your movements get accented, deepened."

"Right," she nods, fervent, and her eyes open up for me again.

She moves forward, a few steps. I move across her arc. She begins to stretch out her body, pulling her torso at an angle to the path her legs are taking. I move around her and stretch the camera out away from my torso, so it seems like she's stretching, stretching beyond all physical possibility.

"Yessss!" she yips, and we're rolling.

Now the music cuts back, idling, a little vamp. Livy stands in one place, pulsing, swaying, eyes closed. I let go, and now I'm swaying too, waiting, expectant, along with her. Then she pulses bigger and I stay put but I start to move the camera--in and out, closer and farther, her eyes filling the frame, then her face, her head and shoulders, arms and legs snaking back and forth, hair bobbing in the air.

And then the music picks up and she begins to move and so do I.

I'm light as a feather all at once, moving around her, following my own breeze. Her eyes open, she sees me surrounding her and a huge smile breaks on her face and I'm smiling too. I cut across in front, and she passes and circles round me, me turning to follow her.

We're both laughing and grunting now, little yelps going back and forth, from effort and delight. She crosses my arc and I lift the camera overhead, shooting down on her as she passes.

Suddenly, she launches herself and grabs the camera out of my hands in mid-air. She dances a broadening, wobbly circle, spinning around the center of the room, the camera at arms-length facing her, the room a blurring ghost in the background, until she collapses to the floor in a happy, heaving, gasping mess.

I stand over her for a moment, not sure what to do next. Is she okay?

She is smiling like she's more than fine. She *looks* more than fine. Does she want me to take pictures anymore? Not that I care, cause I'm feeling pretty fine myself.

"C'mere," she says, and waves a hand at me from the floor, waves it like a limp rag, funny girl.

I sit down on the floor next to her. She has a goofy smile on her face and she's still breathing hard. I feel kind of goofy—giddy—myself. She waves her hand at me again—she wants me to come down further. I lie down on the floor next to her now.

And she leans over and kisses me. Not just a girlie kiss, either—a real kiss. A kiss with intent. I was a Boy Scout—'Be Prepared', they teach you, but I'm taken completely by surprise.

She's a good kisser, though. And she doesn't stop with one. We start kissing in bunches, and now I'm breathing hard too, both of us caught in the moment.

Then she grabs my crotch! Jesus! I jump like I've been shot. She squeals a laugh and flashes me a look that says, 'Yeah, I'm a dirty girl—so what?'

I can take a challenge. I put my hand purposefully on her breast and caress it, gently but firmly, with the bottom of my fingers and the palm of my hand. Hell, I've wanted to since the instant I met her, so why not? I shoot her a look back— 'I'll see your crotch grab and raise you a breast.'

She laughs again, but I don't remove my hand. Her breasts feel good, and I haven't touched a woman with intent in a long time—I'm not stopping until she tells me to.

Instead, she puts her hand back on my crotch, but now she's caressing me, and she stays with it. She means it.

It takes a second to dawn on me that I am actually going to fuck this beautiful thing. Since leaving Marla, I have spent a fair amount of time thinking about the first time I would have sex. I have certainly fantasized about women over the years, and about Livy pretty much continually since I met her. It's been fun, and it was all I had. But now, all at once, it is a little overwhelming to realize *you're there*. And then there is that manly concern—it's been years. I don't know how much I really have to offer, so to speak.

But before I have a chance to get too nervous about this, it becomes clear there is nothing to get nervous about. I respond to her touch but quick.

And knowing that, I throw my remaining concerns out the window and start working on instinct. I kiss her neck and her breasts and then my hands are under her dress and finding no underwear there to restrict them. And then her dress comes off and my clothes come off and I just plain stop thinking.

We make love for five hours. We lie around on the floor after successive batches of spasms for ten or fifteen minutes and then we're off to the races again. I just keep touching her in between, keeping her simmering, and then she gets excited enough to get *me* going again. We find out she can get me going pretty much anytime she wants to.

After five hours I know I'm done for a while. Like maybe a month. I drink half a gallon of water from the fridge. Then I join her, lying on the floor.

"I'll tell you what—you don't have to pay me for today," I say, and she smiles. Then she rolls over to face me and fixes me in a serious glance.

"We're not in love," she states flatly.

"Fine—great—no problem," I shrug. Like that's a problem…

"Well, I should be a little more comfortable with you watching me now," she murmurs. Then she rolls over and punches a button on the remote control on the floor next to her.

"Will you check the camera by the kitchen? It's jumping when I switch to it."

It suddenly occurs to me that this whole thing's been on camera. That would have thrown me for a loop if I'd realized it beforehand. But now I'm about as relaxed as you can get without actually snoring standing up.

So I go check the equipment, butt-naked, then lay down on the couch and fall dead asleep while she dances for the ever-present audience—for now, just a glowing red light on a camera across the room.

They got a lot more tangible very soon.

Magnetic Hypnotic

Okay, let's get this out of the way now:

Yes, I was screwing a girl who was way too young for me, by any standard. And there's no question but that even the *standards* that exist for these things are frighteningly lax.

Someone told me the standard for a man is 'half your age plus seven.' So, being 48, that would make a 31-year-old okay for me, I suppose.

Ha!

When you hear a standard for personal relationships that starts with 'half your age plus' *anything*, you know it's a con job. The guy who came up with this was obviously moonlighting from his government job, developing tax loopholes and straightfaced usage of the term 'civil service'.

And since the whole thing is such a joke to begin with, what's maddening is the fury that's been directed at me since this went public. I've been denounced for moral turpitude in Congress (who hasn't? and who are *they* to talk?), in churches, synagogues and mosques around the country and on television by Oprah and even Geraldo Rivera (*that* takes some doing).

Now where's all *that* coming from? Donald Trump almost ran for President a few years ago with the model-of-the-month on his arm and got merely a few sniggers. I demand to know--why was it okay for *him* and not for me? Because he's got millions and I don't? Because he's been married several times to shallow pretty girls half his age, so we don't expect anything better from him? How is *that* fair?

It seems to me I have the constitutional right to be as shallow as the multibillionaire down the block. I'm sure it's in there somewhere. This is America, after all. My grandparents came here so I would have the opportunity to pursue the shallowest of goals just like the *goyim*. And I have.

It bothered me some, being so shallow. I worried about it at night, lying in bed with her after coming 17 times. I thought about it a lot. And this is the conclusion I came to:

An absolutely gorgeous 23-year-old woman has offered her body to me, in the interests of science, to test the limits of an average middle-aged man's physical endurance and, more significantly, to test the philosophical quandaries of playing out an age-old and well-documented fantasy: great mindless sex with a woman young enough to be my daughter, who doesn't want anything else from me—illicit, dirty, inappropriate and totally unacceptable sex. Tastes great, *and* less filling.

Thousands of men—no, forget that, *millions* of men—around the world were dying to be in my shoes. Well, maybe not *shoes*, unless they have that fetish thing—but you know what I mean...

Men who'd never heard of us were dying to be in...my place. I was their stand-in, their proxy. It had come to me, through no talent or virtue of my own, to represent the fulfillment of a dream for these guys.

In short: I had a social responsibility, a historic mandate even, to fuck this girl as frequently and creatively as I could.

That was my conclusion. It came to me in a blinding flash, and I wrote it down on a napkin next to the bed as fast as I could.

Did I take any of this seriously? Of course not. It didn't *deserve* to be taken seriously. Livy was offering me the only kind of relationship I could have handled at that moment—anything with a second's worth of seriousness, I would have had to decline. I didn't have an ounce of sincere feeling in me that didn't scare me to death. All I was capable of at that moment was sensation.

But sensation kept me going pretty nicely for a while.

If it makes you feel better, I will say it was strange at times, and not *all* of it was totally fun. Most of it maybe—the largest part—well, almost everything, fine, but—anyway...

There was a real poignancy for me in experiencing her flesh. Just the feel of it, the taste of it, was so different, so new and perfect and low-mileage. Marla was a pretty woman, but I'd forgotten what a young girl really looked and felt like. I felt like a vampire, stealing some of her youth and sucking it into me.

And I really did feel rejuvenated, in a much more literal way than I'd expected. I woke up all at once in the morning — Eyes open, and I'm up!! — as opposed to the endless, slow thawing-out process I had gotten used to. The proverbial spring appeared in my step, I ran harder, things that always annoyed me didn't annoy me as much. I had a sense of perspective, all of a sudden.

All this, despite the fact that — after the first day's orgy — the sex wasn't actually all that good for awhile. That was a bit of a shock. It took me a while to admit she wasn't really that good in bed — awkward and uncomfortable.

First, I thought it must be me. I must not be satisfying her, I thought. Or maybe she's finally had a look at me and is turned off. But that's a man's shallowness, as I said — we worry about looks. Women are shallow in other ways.

What I realized was, she *was* an actress, one with the habits of a good student. She'd *studied* seduction — and honed it to the point of genius. I'd seen her that first night from the porch, and, I'll admit, several other times in the privacy of my home, and she could stop your heart.

But seduction was something she could master all by herself. Sex — good sex, at least — requires opening up to the other person, feeling their needs and getting back excitement by getting *them* excited. It requires trust and self-assurance, some confidence in your own attractiveness, and it shocked me to realize that she wasn't all that self-confident.

Once she had a blemish. It was the size of a dime, maybe, on one side of her forehead, but she spent the whole day contorting herself to keep it away from the camera. Of course, I was curious about what she was hiding—and she didn't want *me* to get a look at it either. We must have made quite a puzzling scene for our poor viewers that day—the two of us ostensibly making love, while all the while, she's twisting into a pretzel to keep one side of herself off-camera. Lovemaking by way of the WWF.

During a break after the fifth round, I caught her in the bathroom trying to put makeup on it and I burst out laughing.

Bad move—she thought I was laughing *at* her and she got pissed. She was about to stalk out or kick me; I'm not sure which. I grabbed both arms and said to her, "Nobody but you sees it; nobody cares."

She threw my arms off and hissed at me, "I *have* to be attractive." It was a lament.

"You don't know how attractive you are, do you?" I said. "Sweetie, you can have twenty blemishes and they wouldn't notice. You're beautiful."

"I'm not as beautiful as you think I am," she said. It was a harsh line, harshly delivered.

But it broke through the barrier. Suddenly, I could see the way she saw herself, and I understood a little of what she was going through.

Her face was long and her nose was long. They were in proportion, and they suited her, but she wasn't a classic beauty. Her lips were thin, not the Hollywood collagen style, and she had a little overbite. I thought it was cute. Her hair was straight and hung on the side of her head.

I found her both beautiful and overwhelmingly sexy—and clearly, we had a large and growing audience that felt the same way—but in a culture that tells women every month fifty new ways to remake their hair and tells them to learn how to make him *beg*, Livy was not immune to the fashion inquisition. She was mercilessly aware of every deviation from the ideal.

Sex appeal—*anyone's* sex appeal—comes from confidence and self-assurance. And at that moment, she had none. I was staring at a frightened kid in a woman's body. Over a blemish. I held her by the shoulders now and looked her in the eye.

"Livy, you're approachable. You're smart. You *like* sex. You have fun with it. You love that these guys are watching you, and they get off on the fact that you love it. You're sexy because of the way you look into the camera and *dare* them to turn it off. You say 'I'm going to bite off big chunks of life, chew 'em up and spit 'em out.' You can have a bad hair day or a blemish or put on a couple pounds—you just keep feeding 'em that attitude and they'll keep coming back for more, period."

She *liked* that. More important, she bought it, quickly. She went back out and ran the table the rest of the night. And that made me feel good, in a couple of different ways. It made me feel like there was some purpose I could serve, something I could do for her, and that gave me a surge of purpose and power.

The other way it made me feel good was that, once she bought it, she relaxed a little—and then the sex got amazing.

We made love in the shower, on the living room counter, the deck, the laundry room, every horizontal and several vertical surfaces in the house; we took a camera to the beach on a sunny day and worked the dune grass just off the seawall. We kept busy. Better than that, she was responsive now. I could play with her and she would play back. No thinking, no delay, no plan, just response building on response building on response.

The idea that I would be having sex with a woman in front of a camera was ludicrous—and not just because of my looks, either. I would have shriveled and died under any other circumstances. But she *believed* in it. Sort of. Maybe. In a way...

We're susceptible animals—when we want to believe in something really bad, when we need to believe in something desperately, we *believe*. And who can say—before, during or after—where the borderline is between truth and need?

Livy, at that time, needed the idea of 'life in front of the camera'—it was crucial to any self-respect this girl had for what she was doing—and I wasn't going to get in the way of that. I had signed on for the cruise, and if that meant I needed to learn to play shuffleboard, I would. Having sex in front of a camera was just the Livy Post Cruise Line equivalent of shuffleboard.

What made it okay, at first, was the fact that we had virtually no audience to speak of anyway, and however many they were, they weren't paying attention to *me*.

And so, with both of us relaxing, we reached a place where sex becomes magnetic and hypnotic, a trance where you're exchanging electricity, where you both feel what the other is feeling, instantly and continually.

I would roll my finger along her nipple; she would moan and I would know to rub the side of her breast with the palm of my hand, then to tweak the bulb with my fingers, and then send two fingers barely over the surface of her torso until she shivered. I could hear her moan, I could feel her breath, I could sense her pulse speeding and her hand on me, pulling and caressing, hushing me at one moment and urging me on the next.

We got to the point where we could excite each other almost without contact—I swear, I could keep her going with my hands right over her body, without actually touching. Just disturbing the magnetic field was enough. She felt it and responded as though my fingers were all over her, but it was the lightest, most teasing of touches, and she loved it, and I delighted in the fact that we could pull that deep state off.

We had achieved bliss—thinking about nothing. Yogis work for years to reach this destination, I thought, but *this* is the scenic route.

But lying next to her after she fell asleep at night, her statement kept coming back to me. I've learned to listen to any phrase that keeps ringing in my head, because it has a message. And this one ran true to form.

'I'm not as beautiful as you think I am'—I'd realized, when she said it, that her concern was not centered on *me*.

I might have been the man making love to her, but what I thought of her was not the issue. She knew she had me. She was thinking about *them*—the hungry eyes on the other side of the camera—she was worried about losing *them*. I realized, lying in that quiet room, listening to her breath, that she was *always* worried about them.

That was when I understood her ambition. I saw how big it was, and its hunger, the way it gnawed at her.

Strangely, I found that I liked the idea. That passion, that need—it made her more vulnerable, almost heroic. This was a *fight* for her. I didn't know what the fight was about, or why she had chosen it, but I *wanted* to know. I wanted to learn more.

Of course, as the yogi's say, watch out what you wish for...

It took a little while longer, but I learned *plenty*.

Alarm

Call the house to talk to Daniel. Ring ring no answer. His voice on the answering machine—leave a message.

I can't. I can't do this anymore.

It's been ten days. I'm going nuts. I'm sure nothing serious has happened to them—this is just Marla's willful payback—it *has* to be. But I can't take it anymore.

I get into my Honda Civic and start motoring up the Garden State Parkway to Staten Island. It's Saturday morning and it's early—the traffic is light. I drive about 85 miles an hour. I make good time.

I pull into the driveway, which is empty, and sit for a minute, stewing, trying to figure out the next step. They could have just gone out for a while. They might be back any minute. Or they might be on a round-the-world cruise, for all I know.

While I am mulling, I think about my socks.

I left the house in a rush, because Marla wanted me out the instant I told her I was leaving. I wanted to stay overnight, have us both tell Danny the next day, but she wouldn't have it. So I had to rush through the house, gathering my clothes in a bag—and I forgot my socks. I stayed at my mothers overnight before going to Seaview, and I am now wearing a lot of my (now dead 14 years but his socks live on) father's socks.

So I think: at least I can get some of my socks while I'm here.

Once I'd left, whenever I spoke to Marla about anything in the house, she would burst into tears. She would suddenly remember the quaint shop where we bought [fill in the name of the item], and what we ate for lunch the day we bought it, and the quaint brooch the old woman was wearing when she sold us that picture frame with the cat on it and that she was originally from Czechoslovakia, this old woman, and wasn't it a shame what was happening now to those poor people in what was once Czechoslovakia?

So I just couldn't bring up the socks and go through the story behind each individual pair—it was just too much for me. This was really an opportunity.

But as soon as I open the door, I hear the buzzer and know I'm in trouble. We haven't used the alarm system in the house in years. I run over to the red-lit panel on the wall and pop in my birthday. The light stays red. Oh shit! I was sure that was the password! I try *her* birthday. Red. Daniel's birthday. Red. Shit! Shit! I turn for the door—I have to get out before the damn thing goes off. But before I take a step, it's too late. The house is screaming like an electrocuted cat.

I go upstairs and get my socks. What's the difference now? For good measure, I find my camera and lenses as well, the ones she told me she couldn't find. Then I head down to the front door.

Standing there in all their splendor are Peter, our neighbor from across the street, and Peter, our next-door neighbor. Both of them hold rakes in their hands. It's like *American Gothic* except the models aren't as pretty. We stand for a long moment, staring at each other.

"Well," I say finally, " if there are any leaves lying around the house, I have nothing to worry about."

"Uh—hi," Peter Across stammers.

"Haven't seen you around in a while," Peter Nextdoor says, more insinuating. I size him up for a moment. He's curious, he's interested, he's not pleased I'm here in the doorway of my own home. Word gets around fast. Well, Marla's a good-looking woman.

"I moved out—we don't have to dance around it."

"Is she okay?" Peter Across asks. Why didn't I know she'd be telling the neighbors what a scum I am. Now he thinks I've come back to attack her?

"She's gone to her sister's for the week" says Peter NextDoor. Thanks for telling me, fella—interesting that *you* know that. Thanks to you too, Marla.

"Okay" Peter Across shrugs. "I didn't know it was you," he says and walks off to his house.

Peter Nextdoor hangs around—not exactly belligerent, but curious. He is one of those guys who's always outside puttering, never so happy as reworking the back yard or changing the oil on his truck. If he works, it's a sideline in his life. Not a bad way to go, I find myself thinking.

"So *you* wouldn't happen to know what the alarm code is, would you?" I ask him.

He steps back a bit, flustered. "No...no...that's none of my business," he says. God, he *is* interested. Good luck to her if *she* is. "You don't know what it is?"

"I thought I did," I answer. "She must have changed it."

"Why don't you call her sister?"

That's easy for *you* to say, I think, but I have to do something. With the sirens screaming bloody murder, I dial the number of her gold-digger sister at the house she shares with her rich (naturally) much older (naturally) husband in the Hamptons (where else?) and wait for the recrimination season to open.

"I need to talk to Marla."

"You have some nerve calling here."

"Carol, just let me talk to her please."

"After what you pulled? It's bad enough she still wants to talk to you."

"Well, thanks for your input here—can I--?"

"I've told her to see a lawyer. I know two or three really nice men who'd love to go out with her."

"Millionaires all, I bet."

"They have their own businesses—why do you say that?"

Because that's the only kind of men you know. " Just playing the odds. "Can I talk to her—please?"

She puts the phone down, and Marla comes on a minute later.

"What did she say to you?" she asks.

"She was charming, in her usual way," I tell her.

"What's that sound behind you?" I'm shocked it took *that* long for her to hear it.

"Did you change the alarm code?" I ask.

"At the house? Yes, I—are you at the house?"

In the background, I can hear Carol shrieking "YOU SEE? I TOLD YOU! HE'S PLUNDERING! PLUNDERING!"

" I came to get socks," I tell her. "And to make sure someone hadn't knifed you and Daniel in your sleep, since I haven't heard from him in ten days."

"I thought you took all your stuff," she says, coyly.

"I thought I did too. I forgot socks."

This upsets her. "You mean you were just going to take them and I would come home and find them gone?"

"What—have you individually named them or something? 'Omigod—he took Clive! My favorite argyle?' They're socks—I need them, you don't."

"I just think you should tell me when you're taking things."

"I'm taking my socks. Is that okay?"

"Yeah," she sighs. " That's okay."

"So will you give me the password so I can let the neighbors out of their misery?"

She pauses for a moment. Then I hear the doorbell ring—the doorbell by me, in our house.

"Hold on a second," I say. "The neighbors are restless."

When I go to the door, it's not the neighbors—it's the police. I smell the faint scent of Peter Nextdoor in the air.

"Yes, officer?"

"Are you residing at this location?" he asks. He is a young cop—black hair in a buzzcut, six foot and strongly built.

"This is my home," I hedge.

"Do you have some ID with this address?"

I produce my driver's license. I am thinner than the picture, but it's clearly me.

"Is the alarm defective?" he asks. Moment of truth—am I going to be smart or truthful. Truthful gets me half an hour of wrangling.

"I just forgot the code—I haven't used it in a while. My wife's on the phone—I'm getting the number from her."

"May I speak with her?"

This, I hadn't anticipated. But I don't have much choice now. I lead him upstairs to the phone. I start to pick it up, but he holds his hand up in my face and quietly takes the phone from me.

"Who is this, please?" he asks.

They talk for a few moments. He questions her a couple of different ways. I sweat with a fear I never thought socks could produce. The cop seems first concerned, then suspicious. Finally, he hands me the phone, with a snort. "She'll talk to you," he says.

"The password is 'marion'" Marla says—her mother's name. "Remember this the next time you do something that would make me want you in jail."

Friends

The doorbell rang. Livy ran downstairs in her jogging suit to answer.

It was almost noon. The deck doors were open and the autumn breeze had already scattered piles of papers all over the floor of Livy's big wide-open living room.

I heard the door open downstairs, and then a succession of squeals and laughter. I moved a lightstand nearer to the bar and then wandered to the stairwell.

Downstairs, three young women her age were clustered around Livy, all embracing and talking at once. She looked thrilled—and then she shot me a sharp glance.

I don't know why no one's proven telepathy yet. There are so many sharp scientists out there angling for grants that somebody should have nailed this one. It definitely exists, and here was more proof.

Somehow, from a glance, just a passing glance, I understood I had to move the cameras.

At the moment, there were several cameras on tripods set up around the big main room, and a few more in fixed locations on the ceiling. It would be impossible to miss them, and just as difficult to explain what we were shooting, just in case you didn't want to have to explain this. And clearly, she didn't, at the moment...

I didn't have much time. She wouldn't be able to stall them down there for long. The downstairs contained a garage, laundry room, a half-bath and a den filled with big stacks of unopened boxes she'd apparently accumulated over the years. When you came in from the garage or the front door, there was only a tiny foyer with a hat rack, a little bureau with a mirror, a closet, and the stairs. So they weren't spending much time down there.

The first thing I did was walk to the computer and minimize the chat window, taking it offscreen. I'd seen our midday audience go crazy horny watching Livy eat an orange. I could only imagine the kind of comments we'd get if we had four girls visiting for twenty minutes. This was surely not part of the online experience she'd want to share.

I grabbed the two cameras on tripods and stood dumbly, trying to decide where to go. There was no time to remove them. But where should they point?

The voices were coming up the stairs now. I carried the cameras to the art area, where Livy kept her paints and easels and art materials sprawled in a corner, the wood floor covered with a coarse-haired matt splattered with paint. She had spent some time there the first week I knew her, but since then she'd ignored it.

They reached the top of the stairs and saw the cameras right away—as I said, you couldn't miss them. I fiddled with a connection on the back of one camera.

"Is this the right angle on the easel?" I asked Livy and she smiled, the relief evident to me on her face.

"Are you doing a movie?" asked the tall red-haired girl in a black sweatshirt and jeans.

"This is Robin," Livy said, introducing the redhead first, "and Karen and Celia." Karen was shorter and more stocky than the other three, Celia dark-haired and bohemian in a very old-fashioned way, with a nose ring thrown in for currency.

"It's a website," Livy explained. "People can watch me paint."

"Oh, you're still doing your painting. I'm so glad—you're so good," Robin gushed. "Does it pay?"

"It's the Internet—nothing pays yet," Livy said.

"Except pornography," Karen offered, and they all laughed, Livy included.

"But there are new millionaires every day on the Internet," Robin pressed. "Every time I look at the paper, there's more. *They've* got to be making money."

Livy looked lost for a moment.

"They're selling stocks based on potential," I answered, unasked. "And people are *buying* them! Did you ever read about the California Gold Rush? Same odds of success."

Livy flashed me a look, but I just went back to fiddling with the cameras.

"So where can we see it?" asked Celia, though she was looking out the window at the moment.

"www.livypost.com", Livy answered. "It's experimental — it's not up full-time yet. But the paintings are there."

The four young women sat down at the dining room table and Livy ordered lunch in from the deli at the corner. She gave me a couple of looks, like she wanted me to take off, but I kept tinkering at my equipment. She hadn't introduced me yet, so I was damned if I was leaving. Her friends were cute.

And there was another reason.

When you're with someone — and having sex with them — as much as we were, you *talk*. At least, that's what I remember from before my marriage. You share confidences, preferences, fears, longing, your 10 best funny stories. You get to know each other, to feel comfortable in the same skin, so to speak.

Not us. From the beginning, every time I started down that path, Livy would change the subject. If I persisted, she would let me finish my story—and then change the subject.

Clearly, the way she felt comfortable was *not* sharing anything of her life before we met.

Which made the chance to see her with her college friends just about irresistible.

The first tipoff—though I almost didn't catch it at first—was that the others kept telling Livy how great she looked. I heard it four or five times before I realized they weren't just being friends—somewhere, there *had* been a transformation.

It was hard for me to imagine Livy being anything but stunning. But then, as I watched her sitting at that table, in that company, I saw the transformation happen again—in reverse.

Robin was doing the talking. At first, I assumed it was just her turn. But as lunch came, and I worked on the cameras, and then the placement of microphones and setting up the lights in more permanent (but bogus) positions, Robin kept talking. And I flashed back to high school, that wretched period of my life, and some of the girls' cliques I remembered from there.

They had a pretty rigid hierarchy, and here it was all over again. The leader was the real pretty girl, with her pretty, but plainer friend, and then the hangers-on; the girls who hoped to catch the boys hanging around the other two. And in this group, Robin was the leader—the prettiest, most vivacious, the driver of this car. Livy had the front passenger seat—the cute, but plainer, friend who makes it a team, but always takes the background role.

Livy, sitting next to Robin at that table, had visibly shriveled in a few minutes. She was the prettiest non-Robin in the group. There was no way Robin could hold a candle to the Livy I knew— but that Livy wasn't around anymore.

This Livy watched Robin talk, with eyes like gongs waiting to be rung. She responded to everything Robin said. When Robin told a joke, she laughed heartily. When Robin looked over at her while making a point, Livy nodded her assent vigorously. She was, surprisingly enough, a very adept second banana. The other two girls were along for the ride.

In this particular universe, they were all reflections of Robin. And, until just before I met her, this was clearly the universe as Livy had known it. She'd fallen right back into it as though nothing had happened, as though she'd never changed.

Maybe because she hadn't, I thought. Maybe this pale, shy girl was what Livy saw in the mirror every morning.

It would explain the panic at every blemish, every dress that didn't fit just so. It would explain why she was so insecure about her very evident charm.

My Livy—the laser beam, demanding, assertive, determined force of nature, driving hellbent for leather down whichever boulevard or rutted dirt road was going to make her a star—was an act. She willed this creature into existence every morning, and forced her to exist for the next sixteen hours or so, until she finally fell off, exhausted, to her rest.

It was, at once, a colossal feat of nerve and determination, and a terrible glimpse of a house divided against itself. Livy was creating this amazing pretense, day by day, but she was doing it by shutting out someone else inside her.

I had only the vaguest sense of who *that* person was, until I got home that night and checked out www.livypost.com. Then I found out.

There they were—Livy's earnest, expressionistic representational paintings—puffy-faced human ciphers without detail, with the most enigmatic expressions, set against an iconic landscape. Twenty variations on several major themes. $600 apiece, contact the artist by clicking here.

I spent a long night, looking at those paintings. They were a young woman's paintings, but they had vision and passion. And conviction. Someone inside her had believed in those paintings. Someone not on view every day at seaviewgirl.com—nor seated meekly next to Robin at the lunch table, either. More importantly, she'd done nothing like them since I'd known her. She hadn't come close.

If only there was a market for serious paintings in the world. Maybe there is, but not one big enough for Livy's ambitions. She'd abandoned herself to this new search, this new approach. She'd abandoned something inside herself—that came through to me, and touched me, hurt me, on some very personal level that I didn't quite understand.

I would come to understand it later, a bit later.

Pillow Talk

So Livy is lying in the middle of a tangle of sheets, hair a mess, no makeup, sunlight pouring in the window on every naked pore. She is ravishing. And for the moment, she knows it.

"So," she says, mischief in her eyes, "tell me about *Flash*."

"Flash?"

"Yeah," she sparkles. "I've heard you talk about it. Tell me what it does."

"It's a computer program. It makes animations for the Web."

"Animations? Pictures that move?"

"Yeah--?" Where the hell is this going?

"Do they move like this?" she says, and arches her shoulders and then her hips, into one fetching little pose, boy. Her breasts bob with the move—that sweet hairline between her legs sets at an angle as she rises off the bed ever so slightly. I begin to rise too.

"Or this?" Now she settles into the puffy sheets, rolling around in the soft spread of them. She rolls softly, enjoying the touch of it. She glances at me again, and yes, I understand the mischief in her eyes.

"Not quite like that," I say. "More like *this*," and I go into a manic staccato bounce, like the frames of film through a gate. Technically inaccurate, but clearly that won't be an issue in this conversation. She bursts out laughing, and I stop.

"No, Flash just lets you make pretty pictures that are really small."

She sits up a bit, and moves a little closer to me, a quizzical expression on her face.

"Small—is that desirable?" That smile of hers is growing again.

I smile too, trying—not very hard—to keep from laughing. "In this case, yes."

"Okay," she says, very quietly.

"They're *very* small." I move closer to her, speaking even quieter.

"*Very* small," she repeats, just breathing the words.

"Very. And once it's made these teeny tiny little movies, it *streams*."

"Ohhh," she sighs. "*Streams*—that sounds good." She's right next to me now, her shoulder touching the middle of my back, her breast rising and falling against my arm.

"It *is* good," I confide. "Because then Flash can send you just as much of the movie as you need at a time." She moves her hand over my shoulder. I touch her neck, running a finger down the slope of it, then tracing her collarbone. "Just a little bit, and then a little more and a little more..." my finger tracing the curve of her breast, just tracking the outer orbit, rolling my fingers around the edge ever so gently. My other hand is cupped on the underside of her thigh, moving up and down, very slowly.

"What if I need a little more than that?" she asks, her voice cracking a little bit.

I kiss her neck and roll my hand around to the inner wall of her thigh, moving toward her mound. "Flash has this ability" kiss the neck again "to check ahead" cup her breast "and prepare" trace the wrinkle where her thigh meets her torso with my finger verrrry lightly "in case you want something else," her hand between my legs "so that as soon as you" kiss on the mouth and down the throat, many kisses "let it know you're ready," both of us breathing heavy now "it's ready too." Muffled moans and cries from both of us for a while; then she comes up for air for just a second.

"I have to learn to program" she says, and dives back into action.

Who says geeks don't know how to have fun?

Community

It was around this time, during those first hazy days living between Livy's legs, that Sylvie hurt herself, in a fall outside the house.

The doctor said she would just be sore for awhile. She'd twisted a muscle, but nothing was broken, so she could function if she was careful.

That approach might have worked with someone less willful, but it did nothing for Sylvie. She was up at 5:30 as usual, straightening that endlessly messy house, watering the weeds she insisted would grow large and memorable in the pebbly sand. The predictable result was that she fell twice more that week, and the doctor said she had to stay put and have a nurse in.

"I won't have it," she said. "I'm not an invalid."

I tried to reason with her.

"It's a companion," I said. "It's someone to make sure you don't do things you don't need to do."

"It's a jailer to make me an invalid, since I haven't cooperated becoming one on my own. I won't do it."

I brought Livy over for a visit. Sylvie had asked to meet her. She had seen on my face early on that I'd met somebody, and she teased me mercilessly until she got more detail than I thought I would ever dare repeat.

"This is very interesting," she said. "I'm impressed with her open-mindedness. There are so many young bucks around, but there are advantages with a slightly older man."

"Thank you for the modifier," I said, "though it's inaccurate. Much older would be more truthful."

"Not too old for the job is the only thing that matters, to my mind," she said and smiled a wicked smile.

"You're a randy old bird," I sniped.

"I have my gentlemen friends who keep me warm," she responds. "I like good sherry now and then, I like a man now and then. I haven't forgotten what it's like." She smiled. "This is a good thing for you right now. Though I would say you shouldn't get too carried away—it's almost certainly just a flirtation. Even if it isn't, you may want to make sure your face is covered, in case you ever decide to try for Congress."

"The way things go these days, this might be an asset."

"That's true," she said drily. "But you would absolutely *have* to be a Democrat."

So she insisted on meeting Livy: "very interesting character—you must bring her around" So I did.

Somehow, I expected Sylvie to be discreet about what I'd told her. What got into me to make such an idiotic assumption, I don't know.

She hadn't been talking to Livy for more than five minutes when she said, "So I understand you undress for cameras in the house. Do you like having your own business? Doesn't the government drive you crazy with taxes and forms?"

Livy barked a startled laugh and replied, "Yes, they're a pain. But at least I'm only paying myself and my computer consultant over here. So I don't have a lot of payroll hassle, which is the big drag they hit you with."

I waited for the next line to follow from Livy's mouth. She waited just a beat.

"By the way," she continued, "sex is just how I *get* them there. I checked our stats for the week today — "

"That's the history of how many people looked at the site, what pages they looked at and where they came from, things like that," I explained to Sylvie. "How'd we do?"

"Well, we're still going up, and we're getting repeat visitors," Livy told me. "And we haven't done any publicity yet, so you can't expect big numbers."

I knew, of course, that she *did* expect big numbers. But there was no point saying it—she'd just go into a funk once we got home.

"The interesting thing," she continued, "is that I don't lose much audience when I'm cleaning or watching TV. They hang around regardless."

"Well, surely, they're hoping you will undress sometime soon," Sylvie chimed in, the voice of reality.

"Of course," Livy answered, "and I will. But I watch the chats when I'm painting or on the treadmill or whatever—when they don't think I can read what they say—and some of them are debating the artwork and the collages and all that. So I think maybe there *is* a way to work other stuff in there and keep them interested."

"What do *you* think?" Sylvie turned to me, eyebrow arched. "When a man is confronted with a lovely thing like this, and he knows she's going to take her clothes off, is he capable of debating artwork and collages?"

She smiled her shrewd little crow's smile. I had to smile back.

"Well, we have been domesticated, to a degree," I said. "10,000 years of living with women has made a dent. If I go out with a woman more than three times, I know the chances are she'll be taking her clothes off sometime soon. I've certainly learned how to admire her apartment and her paintings, if she's done some interesting paintings, while I'm waiting."

"But you're still *waiting*," Sylvie poked. Thanks a lot, pal.

"We're *men*," I said. "When we're with an attractive woman, there's this voice between our legs yelling, 'NOW! NOW! I want it NOW!!' But that's not all there is to it."

"What else is there?" Livy asked.

"I find women fascinating," I continued. "I don't understand them for a moment—maybe that's why they're fascinating. But I like women, too."

"Some of your best friends are women," Sylvie said, with a look that would curdle milk.

"Look—there's no doubt it's easier for me to find a woman fascinating—to pay attention to all the things that are interesting about her—after we've had sex and she's not competing with that loud voice all the time. But the bottom line is, with very few exceptions, I've never gone to bed with a woman I haven't found fascinating afterward. So there is some level of judgment other than the mere physical at work here. Or are you going to tell me you're all inherently fascinating?"

"I won't go *that* far," Sylvie said, taking a sip from her cup.

"There are sex sites out there that are on a schedule 24 hrs a day," I add. "Tune in; see a sex act. You watch Livy, you get long stretches of writing and painting, watching TV, running on the treadmill—if somebody just wanted a turn-on, there has to be an easier way of getting there."

"So you mean there's hope for your sex?" Sylvie asked, her eyes dancing.

"I won't go *that* far," I answered, smiling back. She must have been quite a flirt in her day. They'll say that about me, in about a month.

"Of course," I continued pointedly, to Livy, "it would be easier to get them involved if you were sharing work you really cared about. If you were doing painting that really got *you* excited, that really involved you, that would be more likely to involve *them*."

"I like my paintings," Livy said.

"I do too," I agreed. "But I've seen livypost.com—I think you were more involved with those."

It felt like I was bringing up another lover, some infidelity. She squirmed in her chair and stared at the table.

"That's a different style," she murmured. "It isn't me right now." And, for a moment, she was that shy gawky girl again.

Sylvie, wisely as always, picked up her hostess role.

"This sounds interesting," Sylvie said. "If you can really tune in to someone else's life, someone will eventually turn this into some fascinating new art form."

"That's me," Livy said immediately. "I'm going to do it. My goal, Sylvie, is eventually to have other people's homes and cameras up on my site, or at least sharing a start page, so people can come and see this community of people living separately but interacting. And I'm real interested in it being more than just people undressing, although I think you have to have the nerve to do everything in front of the camera in order for it to really be something new."

Sylvie watched her quite seriously now. "So this isn't just something you're doing to make money short-term. You have *aspirations* for this."

"Yes, I do," Livy said, eyes blazing. "I want to be known for what I can do. For *everything* I can do—paintings to acting to writing emails as performance art to having sex for the camera. My whole life as an art work."

"I saw some photos of Picasso eating lunch," I said. "He had a whole fish that he was filleting at the table. And when he finished, he looked at the skeleton that was left, glued it to the plate and added some paint around the edges and presented it to the photographer. Another work of art—and it really was."

"That's what the greats do," Sylvie said. "They can transform any moment. Anything can be special, looked at the right way."

"That would be Madonna for me," Livy said.

"We've got to work on some better role models for you," Sylvie cracked, and I smiled.

"No, I don't think so," Livy asserted. I knew that rising tone of voice—she wasn't going to be dissuaded here. "I know the others. I've studied art and literature, films and music. Madonna has perfected the modern art—turning her *self* into the artwork. She's relaxed lately, and she has a right to, but everything she did for a while was part of her art. She didn't have the greatest records or the greatest films but she had the greatest *impact*."

"Isn't that just self-promotion?" Sylvie asked. I stayed out of this discussion. I'd heard the Madonna analogy a couple times from very serious, intense 25-year-olds at work—I'd learned to take it seriously.

"It's self-promotion, but it's not 'just' self-promotion," Livy explained. "It's a media-run world. If you want an audience, that's how you get them. That's how you *keep* them, if you want to be more than a flash in the pan. And I want to be more than a flash in the pan. So she's like God to me." She turned to me. "I guess that would be like the Beatles for you."

"No, more like Neil Young, or Dylan," I said. "I believe in a crafty and devious God."

"What does *that* mean?" she asked.

"I don't know—maybe God rules the heavens, but on this planet, he's clearly left us to our own devices. And the people that do well here—and I don't mean they make lots of money, necessarily, but that they do work I admire—they don't seem to be real self-effacing, earnest people. If God made us in His image, he's a crafty and devious God."

"This is very interesting," Sylvie returned to the subject. "Share your life with the world. Share what you know, share your friends, your anecdotes, share your spare time and hobbies and all that. Share what makes your life meaningful."

Livy perked up. "Exactly. I want to make art out of my life. I want something real from my life to happen on camera and reach people. It's an experiment. I figure we have three years to find the form before the big entertainment companies completely dominate the Web with formula shit. Do you want to try it?"

Now Sylvie looked completely blank and, I'll admit, so was I. "What are you talking about?"

"Put cameras in the house here," Livy replied. "Show everyone your projects. Share your life story. You want to try it?"

"I won't put one in the shower," Sylvie said immediately.

"Fine—I'll keep the nudity franchise for now."

Sylvie began to make these little humming noises. "Hmm— could I? Interesting...I could...hmmm..."

Then Livy turned to me. "And you should have a camera in your place too."

"I have one."

"Then turn it on. Broadcast. Be my neighbor."

I looked at her as if she was crazy. "Come—let's get her some fresh coffee," she said and led me into the kitchen.

"Do you know how to make coffee?" was the first thing she asked when we got there.

"You don't know how to make coffee?"

"I don't drink it."

I made one of those single-cup things out of Sylvie's cupboard, while Livy explained to me.

"I really want to do this. She certainly isn't what I had in mind at first, but it's really a good idea. We'd have a real community, not just a girl taking her clothes off. Besides," she added, "this way we can watch her. If she gets in trouble or breaks something, one of us can get over here and help her out."

"You're getting awfully protective for knowing her an afternoon."

"I like her. Most people judge me—they look down on what I do, regardless of their age." She sighs. "I don't know—I just feel like it. Do I have to have an explanation for everything?"

"Sorry," I grovel. "It's a weakness of mine. I'll get over it."

"Do so," she says, and carries the coffee in, pretending she made it.

seaview.com

So the next day, I went into business for myself, so to speak.

I had already put up a little website, but now it became a scrapbook of photos and essays on whatever came into my head.

Pictures of my shell-and-stone collections, linked to Sylvie's—I'm not afraid of being second-best. Pictures of my little rented mansion, the neighborhood, the old man next door sitting on his porch watching his portable TV and waving indiscriminately at every passerby, pictures of the beach and the waves and the sailboats, the crab claws littering the sand at low tide and the birds pecking at them.

And essays, scrawled without revision or second thoughts, on whatever came into my head. And because I came to the keyboard every morning direct from bed, with the sleep still in my eyes and my dreams fresh in my head, much of what I wrote was about my marriage, my separation, my wife, my son and the hole in me that was nowhere near healing.

25 years ago, in college, I was in love with writing. I took classes and wrote like a fiend. I was discouraged pretty regularly,

because I wrote too plain a language—I didn't have the grace a writer should have. And you can see, from reading this, I'm not much for the music of words. But now I had something to *say*, something that was busting out of me, ideas that demanded to be freed of my body, whether or not anyone ever read them.

I wrote without thinking about an audience, because I'd never had one. It probably was the best thing that could have happened to me, because I found my voice pretty quickly, and got comfortable with the things I wanted to say, before they showed up.

And that was fortunate, because, a week later, they showed up almost overnight.

Livy put up a new homepage—seaview.com—with links to my site, Sylvie's and Livy's own seaviewgirl.com. seaview.com explained we all lived in the same town, and made it appear that the site *belonged* to the town, with the three of us coincidentally the only participants. And Livy put a link to the seaview.com page on her regular site—so suddenly Sylvie and I got an audience from her.

I was astonished when I logged on one morning and found 10 emails to the site from guys who'd read what I wrote and felt the urge to reply. Some of the replies were wrenching and heartfelt; some were vented anger and pain. Several writers just thought I was an idiot. But I touched a nerve in ten other human beings.

It had the strangest effect on me, seeing those words on the screen, appearing by magic from out of the ether, from other spirits among the machines. I was comforted just by the fact of them, by the simple fact of their existence now in my carefully enclosed world. And all at once, I became aware of just how tightly, how carefully, I had enclosed myself.

I wrote all ten of them back and asked their permission to post their comments. The only ones who didn't give permission were two of the guys who thought I was an idiot—I suspect they thought I was going to make fun of them. I was just trying to keep with the spirit of the Internet.

Anyway, I put up all the comments on the same page as my essay. Then I went searching around and found a free discussion board. Once I put that up, we had a place to discuss whatever we were feeling at the moment. Over the next month, it became a free-for-all about marriage, men's expectations and divorce. By that time, there were almost fifty men participating every week—and god knows how many 'lurking' in the background, reading without involving themselves openly.

I got a new email—which, on the web, is the equivalent of a new identity. safehouse@seaview.com was the name. It felt like I was providing a service, and somehow being subversive at the same time. Which is what my life felt like at the moment.

The traffic grew quickly, starting a few days later. Livy made a deal with a link-exchange service—owners of the sites put up ads for each other, the assumption being that, if you're interested in one, you may be interested in others. It took Livy a while to find a service she didn't find objectionable—she wasn't going to be associated with hardcore pornography.

"People may not see a difference yet," she said, "but they will."

A few days after the redesign, her first ad started appearing on other, more heavily trafficked sites. The traffic to her site increased by a factor of a hundred within four days.

And both Sylvie and I got some spillover. Suddenly we had a *big* audience, by our standards.

Sylvie was really the most creative of any of us. Without thinking twice, she was living the life.

She provided her endless imagination to the process. Collages of shells and seagrass, paint and paste, techniques for cleaning stains off old paintings, how to recreate seventy-year old woodwork for an old house, how to make soup from scallions and water and whatever else you had lying around the kitchen.

And more: why friends are more important than career, how much money it took to have a comfortable retirement, answers to questions on everything from dating to investments to art history to living a sane and meaningful life.

Remember: Sylvie was a page off of Livy's site. So her mail in the first weeks contained a puzzled, "Is she going to take her clothes off?" component. But almost immediately, the unseen crowd responded to her funny and cocky, touching and vulnerable presence. And by the second week, she already had a group of much younger people writing her for advice. And, always saying that she had little to offer, she was giving them quite a bit in reply.

She was absolutely unconscious on camera. She didn't question her own judgment like us younger folks, she had no false modesty or self-doubt. She spoke her mind. It was wonderful to watch.

While Sylvie was transforming everyone who came in contact with her, my spillover web traffic was transforming *me*. I put up a couple of essays about my marriage—offhand comments in a growing sea of words—but they started me down a path I never imagined.

SAFEHOUSE DIARY: MY BOY

So let's talk about that little boy of mine—not that he's so little anymore.

He's ten now, and about 4 inches shorter than I am. Huge, smart, funny and wildly, obsessively imaginative.

I was indifferent to the idea of having children. I agreed because my wife really wanted to have a baby, and then I fell in love with the first sonogram, when he still looked—literally—like a shrimp.

The first lesson he taught me was that there was a God—that there was something in this universe that responded to us.

My wife and I had a hard time conceiving. When she finally got pregnant, about 2 weeks after that first sonogram, we were told she had cysts on her ovaries and that, if they didn't disappear in the next week, the doctors would have to go in and remove them—and that would almost certainly destroy the fetus.

They said this in a tone of voice that made it clear they didn't expect the cysts to disappear.

I went home and prayed, for the first time in my life, really prayed. There wasn't anything else to do. I promised to believe, if we could have this child. And the next week, the cysts were gone.

In my own, typically skeptical Jewish fashion, I've kept my end of the bargain. I now know there's something out there.

The second thing he did, in a roundabout way, was kill the marriage.

Because of him, I discovered what it was to be open and trusting and caring about another human being, in a way I'd never understood. All those words finally had meaning. And I saw what was missing in the marriage.

My wife could never let her guard down. She could never let go, she couldn't trust, she had no faith—and neither could I, when we met. Maybe we were a perfect, neurotic match—we found someone else with whom we could be guarded and cautious, untrusting and yet married.

As much as he kept me in the marriage, because I couldn't imagine leaving him, Daniel made what was missing there a gaping sore.

The problem with all this understanding is that, somehow, it keeps pointing up how much exists about all this that I still *don't* get at all, all the feelings that I'm not in touch with at all. More evidence of the space that's grown up between me and me. A space I have to shorten up but good before I really come out of hibernation.

I put things like this on the site, and the email traffic exploded, from guys going through the same thing, and my little discussion group was really gathering steam.

And then, in that first week, I got a bonus I'd never considered. I got an email from my son.

Seeing Daniel

```
Hi Daddy!

    I saw your Web Page. It was NEAT!
I miss you. Will you come see me sing at
school Friday? I love yu, Daniel.
```

It turned out that, not only had Livy listed Seaview.com with the search engines, but she'd also registered and listed Sylvie's and my name there as well. So Daniel found his father on the Internet.

A quick phone call established that, indeed, he was singing in his school talent show Friday. It also established that Marla had no idea he had written me an e-mail. She hadn't seen my page either. I was grateful for that, although, when I thought about it later, I realized she would, and that was alarming. But at that moment, I had other concerns.

"Any reason I don't get to know about him singing?" I asked.

"I didn't think you'd care."

"Marla, come on. That's not playing fair."

"You left. You don't want to be with us any more. I don't want to get him all excited that you might be coming and then you don't show up."

"You could ask me first," I say. "You don't have to say anything until you've asked me."

"No I don't. But that still assumes that you'll show up if you say you will."

"Have I ever missed anything he was in?" I'm struggling here, to be polite, to keep my eye on the big picture.

"You missed the school play."

"That was the day after I moved out. Are you telling me I could have shown up without us having a scene?"

"I thought you didn't care about scenes. I thought I'm the one who's too concerned with what other people think all the time."

"You tell him I'm coming Friday. I'll be there. What time?"

"Two. I hope you will. It hurts him so much when you disappoint him."

I hang up and instantly the emptiness and anger flood all over me, sucking all the air out of the room.

'It hurts him when you disappoint him'—when did I disappoint him? She'll make a comment like that, with no basis in fact, and it'll be spinning through my head for hours.

It's fine for me to tell myself I've come so far, that I'm transcending the narrow boundaries of my old self. La la la la la la.

All it takes is a 2-minute conversation with *her* and all the old patterns come roaring back. I feel like I'm the only one interested in surmounting them.

When Daniel was diagnosed with a learning disability, something called Asperger's Syndrome, my wife–the good teacher that she is—brought home the literature. I read it and realized that he got it from me.

Hyperactive, hyperverbal, no understanding of social cues. Social cues: the kind of body language that people use to send messages to each other, the kind of polite hints we use when we don't want to say things directly. That stuff goes right over his head and mine.

The diagnosis explains why I'm so fascinated by—why I spend so much time dissecting—the way people act, their motivations and intent. It's knowledge I have to work hard to come by, whereas most people just 'get it' naturally.

Marla spends an endless amount of effort and time trying to deal with his symptoms—helping him learn how to learn; helping him get through school. It's invaluable, real effort and real exhaustion. But it's also aimed at the things she cares about; at keeping him from looking funny to others, to outsiders. Those stares from people she'll never see again, that terrorize her nonetheless.

I can't help him in the way she does—at least, I'm not as good at that as she is. I've tried to find things he can be good at and encouraged him to work at those, to help him feel good about himself, to show him he can work around those limits. I can't fix his outward manifestations—I don't even notice them, really. What's *inside* him, I get—and I care about.

Daniel wasn't the only place we saw things differently. Marla was comfortable with our marriage just as it was, because we were the only ones that knew how empty it was. As long as things looked alright to the outside world, she could go on ignoring what it felt like.

I couldn't.

When I realized that, I got the last big revelation—dead is dead. After a certain point, it doesn't matter whose fault it is. The only thing that matters is—you can't *fix* anything anymore.

You make a marriage *together*. The marriage is not about either person; it's about the effect you have on each other. And we brought out the absolute worst in each other. So finally, I was ready to move on to the next step. And the next step was to live again.

I got up the nerve to tell her I was leaving. I waited until Daniel went to sleep. I had prepared myself carefully—I had thought through the possible scenarios: she would either scream her lungs out at me for being such a son-of-a-bitch, or surprise me by saying, 'Thank God someone finally said it. I don't know how much longer I could have gone on like this.'

As always, she took the approach I didn't expect.

She cried.

After ten years of treating me like a non-person, of ignoring every approach, every entreaty, she cried like a faucet and said she thought things were getting better and had no idea I was that unhappy.

And after years of controlling every single aspect of our life—telling me which clothes were acceptable and to clean the hair up off the bathroom floor and that my friends made her uncomfortable and I shouldn't invite them over anymore, and having a smart retort for every complaint I had—and I had plenty—she simply sank into her chair in a veil of tears, and blamed herself.

All my preparation went out the window—I didn't know what to do with this.

I'd seen her lie to herself over the years. I have a cynical catchphrase about her: Marla lies to herself, and then tells you the truth as she sees it. But because she convinces herself of the lie, the hurt she *feels* is real.

So I couldn't ignore the tears. The crazy truth is, I respond to her feeling *anything*, real or not, because she spent so much of our marriage refusing to feel at all. So I was lost now in this jumble of emotion.

God, this sucks. I hate feeling anything. All those love songs that tell us what a glorious thing it is to feel?—those guys haven't left their wives in a while.

Anyway, the main thing I wanted out of our conversation was a cooperative relationship regarding Daniel. This wasn't easy, since she would start crying and flagellating herself vigorously every time I mentioned his name.

"Marla, I'm sorry, I'm just concerned about how we're going to tell Daniel. I think it's—"

"He'll be alright," she would say, whimpering but gallant, eyes dead, like Ronald Colman refusing the blindfold. "I'll take care of everything."

"I just want us to tell him together," I said. "It'll be so much less scary if he hears it from both of us. Then at least he won't feel caught in the middle."

"No," she said immediately, sitting up straight and wringing her Kleenex, like a general regrouping in the midst of battle. "I'll tell him you're working nights now. You're working nights, and he won't see you for a while. Then we'll see what happens."

"Marla, that's not a good idea. We're lying to him, which I don't like, and secondly, he's going to figure it out. He knows more about what's going on here than we do."

"I'm telling him you're working nights," she repeats. I know this tone of voice. This is the 'we're doing it this way. Your choice is to do it this way or start a huge fight' tone of voice.

One of my laws of life, hard-won knowledge from this marriage, is that the more unreasonable person always wins the argument. This is an absolute—by definition, it can't be any other way. The reasonable person seeks common ground; the unreasonable person won't settle for anything but victory. Who's going to win? Hands-down? This is a question?

So at 1145 pm, I'm running around the house, pulling clothes out of drawers and stuffing them in suitcases. I stumble around in the dark, trying not to wake Daniel because then Marla'll throw a fit and he'll be caught in the middle, which is the last thing I want.

And also because, if she insists on lying to him, I can't stop her—I've never been able to stop her doing anything. But *I'm* not going to lie to his face because she can't face the truth. I won't do that to him or me.

It's a good thing, too. Because, the next night, when I call from my mothers house to talk to him, his first words on the phone are, "When are you coming home?" and "Why are you staying at Bubbe's house? Our home is *here*." When I get Marla back on the line, I say cooperatively, "I thought you weren't going to tell him."

"He figured it out. All your stuff was gone."

"Uh-huh. Without it sounding like, 'I told you so,' because I don't mean it that way, can we agree it would have been better if we told him together?"

"Yeah," she sighed. At least she understood it.

The next day, I set off for Seaview. And she took off for her sister's—without telling me, of course. So I haven't seen either of them since, though I've talked to Daniel on the phone almost every night since she got back. She shoos him off the phone and tells me 'later' whenever I talk about coming to see him.

So now, Friday, I drive up to Daniel's school, my hands trembling with excitement and dread.

I get there a few minutes early, as usual. I was always early for things; Marla was always late. Now she is sitting stiffly towards the back of the room when I arrive. "They're going on any minute," she hisses as I take my seat. I immediately flood with guilt—I thought I was early, how'd I almost miss him? They actually start twenty minutes later.

The twenty minutes pass like death. She looks beautiful— tall and slim, chestnut hair cut at the jawline, in a casual off-white blouse and dark skirt, cut above the knee. Great long legs issue from the skirt and crowd the space between the rows.

I catch the scent of her perfume, and a glimpse of the beauty mark on the back of her neck. She smiles politely at me once I take my seat. Then she sits and watches the kids putting the finishing touches on the stage, never looking at me again.

"How was your trip?" I ask.

"Fine," she says, without looking over. None of your business, alien intruder.

I suspect that she's furious at me—it certainly wouldn't be unreasonable—but I can never tell with her. This is the way she used to act, day in and day out, angry or not. By the end of our first year of marriage, she kept her distance come rain or shine. I was convinced she was angry at me—why else would she treat me that way?—and get upset when she insisted everything was fine. If that's true, why don't you talk to me? And if it *isn't*, why don't you tell me what I did, so I can make it better?

Only now does it occur to me that she probably *wasn't* angry, half the time—she just ignores other people a lot. And, as much as I aspired not to be, I was always other people to Marla. Meanwhile, a lot of her conviction that I was an irritable, nasty guy came from *my* conviction that she was stubbornly refusing to explain what she was mad about.

A friend of mine, twelve years ago, was going through a divorce. Marla and I were already having problems. I asked him how you knew it was time to get a divorce.

"When you stop hoping someone else will run her over and you start thinking about doing it yourself, it's time to leave," he said. That turned out to be a pretty good description.

I remember that feeling now. But the main feeling I have is that horrible, tearing voice inside that's screaming, "Hold me! Love me! Don't you care at all?" I felt it all the way through the marriage, though I wouldn't admit it to myself until I left. I just stuffed it, like I stuffed everything else.

And I feel that gloom now, that pall that left me palateless, not enjoying anything, not seeing any other possibilities in my days, just work and sleep and pining for my wife to smile at me naturally, without posing, and put her arms around me. Now, it's almost a physical comfort to have that over. At least I *know* now she's not going to do that.

And then, finally, the show is under way and Daniel takes the stage. He is huge. He was already the biggest boy in the class, and he's grown in the past month. He is with a crowd of other kids, marching onto the stage.

The school is very big on performing skills—they speak long and hard on parent's night about the way it helps kids' self-esteem and success in later life. Not a place to be a shy person or a slow starter, though.

America isn't much for slow starters in general. Being one myself, I should know. I never had much ambition to do anything but write stories until Daniel was born. Then I spent ten years trying to climb the corporate ladder as best I could. Now, I'm back to writing stories.

He sings—it's a Broadway show tune, rewritten for the occasion, welcoming the parents and promising us a great time. He has an unusually high speaking voice—always has, from a baby—but his singing voice is clear and he has style. Somehow, as a shy 10-year-old, he knows how to sell a song. I thought several times, when I was at the network, that I might be making contacts that might someday help him, as he clearly loves performing. Now I wonder how long those contacts keep, once you're off the scene.

As the show goes on, he's clearly the star. He has two numbers that are virtual solos—the rest of the kids are the Pips—and a skit where he reads lines he clearly doesn't completely understand. Nonetheless, he sells the laugh lines. His earnestness carries him through—he's a likeable boy, and the audience embraces him.

When the show's over, we come out of our seats and work through the crowd to the front. We never make it, because he pushes through to us—to me. "Daddy!" he shouts and runs to hug me. Thank God. I didn't know whether he'd hug or shun me. I hold him and fight back the tears. If I start, he will, too, and that won't help anything.

"I missed you," he starts, and I say, "I missed you too." Then I switch quickly to "I got your e-mail. That was *great!*" and he beams.

We go for ice cream—all activities in his life are linked with food, preferably ice cream. He has a strawberry shake, I have a cup of low-fat. Marla has a banana split and makes short work of it. She has always been rail-thin and has always eaten enthusiastically, including lots of sweets. But she misses meals without noticing too, and never seems to gain a pound. When they get around to cafeteria choices in metabolism, I pick hers. I probably married her out of metabolism envy.

And then it's time to go, way too soon. "We have to pick up Grandma at the doctors," she tells him.

"Is she okay?" I ask.

"Just a check-up," she says, but again with a tone that suggests this is not my concern. And she's right, I suppose—it's just hard after fifteen years to stop caring about her family. I love almost all of them, other than her sister the evil gold-digger whore witch.

Daniel's clinging to me. "Next weekend?" I whisper to Marla, and she nods, reluctantly. It occurs to me now that she hasn't ignored my wanting to see him out of a desire to punish me. It was just her way of ignoring the fact that I wasn't around anymore—out of sight, out of mind. That amazing tunnel vision of hers. Now that I'm here, she bows to reality.

"I'll come next weekend," I tell Daniel, "and we'll go to a movie or something, okay?"

He looks up at Mommy to see—is this alright? She nods. Everybody knows the new politics already.

Daniel and I are both struggling not to cry.

"What movies are opening next week?" I ask him.

He tells me. He knows all movie openings and what star is guesting on every series on television. Anything with a commercial has prime real estate in Daniel's frontal lobe.

"We'll go see it, okay?" He pulls back a little from his tears. I get in the car quickly and drive back to the shore. It's a good twenty minutes before I stop boiling with pain and hurt.

I think about our house. Nothing fancy—a townhouse with a tiny back yard, butted up against other townhouses. But it took a year of work to get the money together for it. I had to finesse our finances, get a gift from my mother for the downpayment, and wrestle a team of bankers and lawyers to work it out.

Marla made it lovely inside. But I remember a day just before I left, sitting in the den looking into the back yard and wondering why we never planted a tree. The yard would have been a thousand times nicer, more friendly, if we'd planted a tree. It wouldn't have been as expensive as a hundred other things we did. She spent no end of energy trying to make the inside of the house pleasant and attractive and neat, everything in its place— energy to the point of mania. But no tree outside.

I decided that was how things were for her—there were things inside her area, and she took care of those, and things outside, that she just didn't notice or care about. Daniel made it inside. The house made it inside. Anything that was part of a lifestyle she wanted—SUV's, cellphones, brand-name clothes— those made it inside.

I didn't. No matter what I did, I stayed the unadorned lawn outside that never got the shade. That never got the attention that said, we need a tree here.

New York Times, July 13, 1998:

His Web site started slowly, but Mr. Brown, 34, a grocery store merchandiser who lives in Bridgeport, Conn., kept adding [Monty] Python memorabilia, sound clips, scripts and pictures. Soon the site took on a life of its own, and Geocities began promoting it as one of its 'landmark' pages.

By June, ... his site had attracted more than 100,000 visitors...

One they expose themselves to the world, Geocities members closely watch the count of how many visitors their sites attract, and they express glee at receiving an E-mail from a far-off place.

'I was a ham radio operator in high school,' Mr. [David] Bohnett {Geocities founder] said. 'It was exciting to collect postcards from people you talked to around the world. That is a lot of what the Web is about.'...

'We truly are a community of neighbors who help each other out,' Ms. [Sherri] Kaufmann said...'Recently, my father became ill, and I was overwhelmed by the letters from the friends I have made [online].'

~~~~

First Steps

When I got back, seaviewgirl.com was booming. And Livy was already pushing for more.

"The site grew 150% two weeks ago—last week was only 120%—we're falling backwards."

"We got the link exchange two weeks ago—you can't expect every week to be at fever pitch," I suggested, with a futile logic.

Livy wanted *every* week to be at fever pitch. The site was her life, her big break, her universe. Everything that could be done *must* be done, done as well as it could be done, and done *now*.

I worked to fine-tune the metadata I'd put on our pages. Metadata is information that is embedded in the page but not visible to the reader, information that explains the content of the site to search engines. If you write the metadata properly, when a person searches for the right kind of content, your site will show up at the top of the list.

I learned a lesson, writing the metadata. I had entered a wide variety of subjects—health, fitness, love, food, running, nudity, New Jersey, life, women, naked, painting, fun, undressed—do you begin to see a pattern here?

So now Livy came over to eye my work—she could see I was struggling with it. She looked at the list and, characteristically, cut right to the heart of the problem.

"There's no sex there."

"You keep reminding me this is not pornography."

"Well, thanks for listening, but we both know how I get an audience. The challenge for me is getting it to be about more than just sex once they get here—just another normal woman's life."

I typed in a few terms, with her looking over my shoulder now.

She eyed the list and ordered, "Add blowjobs. You forgot blowjobs."

I still hadn't gotten used to her mouth. Coming from that innocent-looking face of hers, it was still a shock to hear it.

She smiled, angelic, as though she read my mind and wanted to show me just *how* innocent she could look.

"Well, you like them, don't you?" she said.

"I *love* them," I moaned.

"Well—so do they," she said and I typed it in.

I looked back up at her and she smiled and said, "I'm a dirty girl."

She took such pleasure in being a dirty girl. She took such pleasure in being a baby girl too. She neglected none of her weapons.

We went to dinner at some local restaurant one night. I was used to the stares we got when we went out together. Mostly it was women, which surprised me. The men would look for a little while when we came in, and then would carefully, studiously, not look at us the rest of the evening. The women stared, though, stared long enough to satisfy themselves that we weren't father and daughter, that we *were* a couple. After that, they kept looking back, and the looks weren't friendly.

This night, the stares were even more hostile than usual. I wondered if I was wearing my 'cradle-robber' t-shirt or something—then I looked over at Livy and understood why.

She had put her hair in a ponytail as we got out of the car. She did that occasionally, especially in the morning when she got up, as a convenience. But now I noticed the rest of the outfit—white man-cut shirt, dark skirt above the knee, white sox and little pumps. She never looked like she wore any makeup anyway. Now she sat upright in her chair, chewing gum—where did *that* come from?—legs pressed together at the knee demurely and arms drooping gawkily all over the table, while she looked around with a totally bored when-are-we-going-home expression on her face. If I wanted to know where the looks came from, all I had to do was look across the table at my date, the 16-year-old parochial school girl with the attitude.

I bit my tongue. I had signed on for this cruise, after all. She *told* me she was an actress, and she needed, periodically, to have her fun. And, I suppose, for me to have it with her.

She would tell me things at times to try and shock me—the two boys she'd seduced together in high school, the lesbian affair she'd had. They felt like stories, and somehow, it never mattered to me if they were true or not. The more interesting point was her need to be wild. It was a nagging imperative to her, something important enough to keep working on—to be over the edge, just a bit out of control. Or at least to *pretend* she was—I never felt like she'd ever really let her life get out of control.

Anyway, after a few more child molester looks at the restaurant, I just couldn't keep silent. I just *couldn't*. I turned to her, with *my* most innocent look, and said, just loudly enough to be heard all over the room, "So—you want to go for the record tonight, baby?"

She smiled back.

"Seven times? Sure you're up for it, daddy?"

I looked at my watch.

"It's still early," I said.

They brought us the check quickly. I don't think I ever got change so fast. We didn't eat in that place again.

She was almost totally self-driven, and she drove herself relentlessly. I could see she really enjoyed sex—if she hadn't, the whole thing would have gotten way too weird for me early on. But her inner need to *prove* her attractiveness, over and over again, was obsessive, and the fact that she and the site were becoming more successful only seemed to be making things *worse*.

She would have fits of nerves. She would sit in the bathroom for half an hour, muttering at the mirror—her lips were too thin, her nose too long, her hips too narrow, her tits too small.

She must have done that from the beginning. But now, in a hundred ten-second whispered confidences, she was beginning to repeat those concerns to *me*. I've had these conversations with women before—I know my role is to reassure—but I also know that, as soon as it becomes necessary to *have* the conversation, the man's position is hopeless.

"But do you *really* like them?"

"They're gorgeous, sweetie."

"If you really meant that, I'd know."

"Then why ask me?"

"You're supposed to make me feel better."

"Well, tell me what answer will make you feel better and I'll say it."

"It won't mean anything if I tell you what to say."

You guys all know this conversation. It was just weird having it with this woman who was every sick wet dream I'd ever had. It would have made me feel really needed, if only I'd been able to make her feel better.

Now, I began to see her willfulness, that incredible drive of hers, as the flip side, the inevitable result of this battle she was having with herself, to master her fears, her insecurities. It didn't feel like she was just naturally so determined—it was the product of something bigger going on inside her.

Livy somehow *needed* life to be a struggle, and when it wasn't enough of a struggle by itself, she would create some layer of difficulty to make it harder. She had to have something to fight every day.

In that light, the idea that she would try to become rich and famous coming from pornography made perfect sense—it was the long way round the bend, the hardest possible first step in that journey of a thousand miles.

Most people go out of their way to avoid struggle and hardship. Livy ran at it headlong, day after day, shouting, "Think I'm scared of you? Take *that!!*"

She was punishing herself—for what, I had no clue. I'd known enough creative people to know that wasn't all that unique.

I also knew from experience, though, the kind of tab you racked up, and had to pay eventually, for that kind of bravado. You can spit in the world's face, but you're almost always spitting into the wind.

The more I come to understand this about her, the more my feelings for her soften. Spitting in the wind isn't exactly a hobby with me, but it's not an unfamiliar experience either. In fact, I realize I may have more expertise in this area than she does. Instead of making me want to run away, understanding all this just pulls me closer to her, makes me more protective, in a way I've never felt about anyone but my son.

I feel almost queasy at times, watching her battle the world in herself. It all matters to her *so much*. Every nuance of the audience's reaction, every tick of the day's numbers, is imprinted directly on her nervous system. She carries the score around with her, in all its variegated forms, intertwined with that painful, insistent hunger for attention and that need to achieve herself, the alarm clock that ticks in the back of her head all day, every day.

As much as it scares me, I want that hunger—for *something*. I don't know what can ever make me feel like that again. But after the jaded, 15-year slow-death of that marriage, just being near her, helping her try to get where she's going, gives me a chance to experience that depth of feeling again, if only by osmosis.

Need is a powerful thing—it makes every moment matter. But it also leaves you perpetually strapped to the mast, screaming at the crew to run the boat onto the rocks so you can hear those Sirens belt one more scatsong. Recognizing Livy's vulnerability without understanding where it came from, realizing what a puzzle she was to herself, I got hungry to know more. She was a mystery to me—and I love a mystery.

This was the moment I crossed over the line.

This was the moment I got hooked.

In Character

I show up at Livy's the next day and she knows something's up immediately.

"What's wrong?" she says.

"Well, there's a whole side to this that I haven't been thinking about," I tell her. "Truth is, I just haven't been thinking much at all. I saw my wife the other day, and I've been thinking about it ever since. We will be getting a divorce at some point."

I see the look of discomfort on Livy's face. "This has nothing to do with you," I say.

"I know," she replies. That was not one of the replies I would have hoped for, but oh well...

"Well, I've got to make sure it *continues* to have nothing to do with you," I say. "She called me last night and we worked out some money for me to send her so we can both get by for now. But I can see she's already looking for leverage. If she can show I'm working on a web pornography site—"

"This is not pornography!"

"I know that. But the distinctions are going to seem real thin to the jury in a divorce case, okay?"

"I don't care what people think."

"Livy—" I take her hand in both of mine and kiss it, just to get her attention, "for the moment, I *have* to care, just this much."

I can see, looking into her eyes, that she hates this. She hates having to give in to any imperative outside herself. I admire this in her, but, after recent exposure to Marla, there are some uncomfortable questions that I need answered.

"Livy, can you to play this one my way, because I need you to—because this is really important to *me*?"

Somehow, this gets through to her.

"Okay," she says, and I hug her to pieces, because she's just proven to me she's not Marla, that I don't have to make the same mistake over and over again. Thank God for at least making *new* mistakes.

"But we're not in love," she repeats. It's her mantra, and has become a repetitive joke between us. But she's reminding me now. "I can't fall in love until I'm famous."

"You have no idea how wonderful it is to hear that."

Now she's taken aback. "What do you mean?"

"Marla used to tell me she loved me at every appropriate and inappropriate moment, at all the places you're supposed to say that, and in such a habitual way, that it wasn't only meaningless—it actually came to mean the opposite. It meant, 'as long as we say this, we're locked into the lie together.' So I'm happy as a clam not to be 'in love', okay?"

"Okay," she said.

"So," I pause, thinking aloud, "I can't appear on your site anymore."

"What do you mean?"

"I can't. My son found my website. If he's found it, my wife will see it. Once she's seen it, it won't be long before she finds the other Seaview pages. And it isn't that big a stretch for her to start checking you out. If she can show I'm part of this, she could take my son away from me forever. I can't take that chance."

"So—are you saying I have to find another partner?" She says this coquettish—she's playing with me, but at the same time, we both know she wouldn't have any trouble finding someone else, if she wanted.

"Well—I just think it's interesting that none of the guys on my site—almost all of them came from yours—have recognized me with you."

"Maybe nobody's looking at your face here."

"Yeah, that thought occurred to me. And webcams aren't all that sharp, either..."

"What are you thinking?" she asks.

I shrug. "What if I was in disguise?"

"What?"

"Why can't I wear a wig and a mustache or something on your site? I know it's not what you had in mind..."

She frowns. "I've told you how important it is that I put my life on camera, openly."

"Yes—I get that. We can do the same things we've always done—I just don't want any *outsiders* to recognize me."

"You really think your wife won't recognize you, just because you've got a wig and a mustache?"

"Marla hates anything with sex in it. She won't watch the dirty scenes in R-rated films, she gets upset at Calvin Klein ads. She certainly wasn't like that when we were going out—if she had been, I wouldn't have gone out with her twice. But she retired as soon as we got married. Unless she recognizes me in the first half-second she comes to your site, we'll be out of danger."

"This really wasn't what I had in mind," Livy mused. At least she was thinking about it.

"We're a fun couple, and fun couples play, don't they?" I pressed. "Isn't playing also part of life?"

"Yes, it is," she admits.

"So let's *play* when I come over. I'll be the mysterious masked lover or the traveling salesman or some such, and we'll play. The audience'll get their thrills, you can still share the *rest* of your life with them and I won't have to worry about losing my son."

"Your timing is interesting," she says. She walks over to the computer and pulls up the chat group. She searches quickly down the list and opens one post. "This came in today, and I've been thinking about it all morning."

romeo27@aol.com: I hate to say this, because you're so passionate about it, but we really aren't interested in seeing real life online. Real life is boring most of the time. Real life is what we come here to *escape*.

It's a good post. I'd seen several recently making the same point, but this one had something different. Pithier, more trenchant, brilliantly realized, with a rare sense of wit and style. Let's put it this way—*I* wrote it. Always useful to have an extra email address when you need one.

"He's pretty blunt," Livy owns, "but I think he's saying what a lot of them are feeling. The numbers are stagnating—and we're stagnating. I can just feel it."

"Seduction is not real," I say. "It's fantasy and wish-fulfillment. It's riffing on reality, but it's still playacting. It's contrived and manipulative, and as long as both people are enjoying it, it's a blast."

She pulls a wig and a pair of big glasses out of a plastic bag.

"So you're into playacting?" she asks.

"Okay—just no whips or handcuffs or any of that stuff," I caution.

"No problem," she nods. "Don't get mad, but would you go out on the porch for a little while?"

"I thought we got over that."

"We did," she says. "I've just been thinking that I...enjoy having you outside, watching. I can sort of play off it...I can pretend. And then I'll open the door and you can come inside."

So I go sit on the porch to watch her.

"Put on your disguise, mysterious masked lover," she calls after me.

A few moments later, she comes out of the bedroom, in a simple yellow blouse and cutoff jean shorts. She sits for a few minutes at the computer, typing some written greetings for the chat boys.

Then she walks to the dresser in the bedroom and comes back with several hangers full of clothes. Several dresses, sheer and clinging, that she tries on, one after the other, in front of the camera, like a mirror.

She has as little underneath as usual, so the view is tremendous, and she picks a variety of angles to enhance the tease, starting from a rear ¾ view, then moving to a full-frontal, sharing all her curves and touching herself, priming herself, while she tries on the various outfits.

There's nothing coy about her tonight. She is a full sexual animal. I am having a great time watching. It amazes me to realize that, after having sex like rabbits for almost a month, it is still arousing just to watch her undress. Part of great seduction, great art, great sex, I realize, is to make mysterious that which everyone already knows.

Finally, after twenty minutes of changing outfits and strip-teasing the universe, she finds one she likes, a camisole that shows her off while looking as innocent as could be. She stands in front of the mirror primping a bit, adjusting the way it falls, accenting every curve, until everything is clearly implied but nothing is obvious.

And then she pushes a button on the table and starts, surprised by the sound of a doorbell. She steps over to the sliding door where I sit and opens it.

"Come in," she says. Now I'm surprised, but I get up and walk inside.

"So I know I'm late on the rent," she says, "but I just wondered if there wasn't some way we could work this out."

Ohhhkay—we're playing *this* one, are we? I focus my eyes directly on her nipples and answer, dropping my voice an octave, "I suppose there might be a way."

She leads me to the couch. We make a little small talk. I can see on the monitor on the bar that she has her legs slightly apart, flashing the universe, as we speak.

It's an odd moment. I am sitting across the couch from her, making reasonably normal conversation, while she has an intense sexual moment with the anonymous audience, who have a much more intimate view of her than I do.

Her eyes flash—she is enjoying this. Then she leans back into the couch and gives me the delicious view she's been giving the audience. "I would do anything to buy a little time. What is two weeks worth?" she asks.

"Two weeks is a lot of time," I say, dropping my voice and rasping out the words for dramatic effect.

"I've *got* lots of time," she answers and leans forward, dropping the dress off her shoulders. And then she motions me to take her on the coffee table. Being an obliging sort of guy, I do.

This is very different from what we've done before—harder, less friendly and faster. Sex in character. I've never done this before, but it's not hard to get into it. We are panting at the end, and spent.

She scrawls out a sign saying "We're safe for two more weeks—check out our advertisers," and holds it up, next to her naked breast, before shutting the cameras down. The site will hold that freezeframe until we start up again in the morning.

"That was good," she says. I wonder if she is critiquing the sex or my acting. "I think we can find a way for you to stay in character—or characters. "

I had no idea where this would lead. And probably just as well. Sometimes, you just shouldn't know.

Ms. Sylvie's Neighborhood

I walk the little sandy bluff to Sylvie's back door and knock.

"Come in" she says, opening the door and running back to her computer.

"I've got Messenger, or whatever they call it," she says.

I walk up behind her and look at the screen. The posts are flying by in the little window.

"I had a crowd this morning and somebody told me how to get this thing and now we're all having a jolly chat. It's amazing. I say a sentence and they all come back at me at once. But they're such a nice group." She looks up at me, amazed. "There's one from Guatemala—writes very good English—and a gay couple from New Zealand. How do they find me?"

"Most of them come from Livy's site, originally. They see the link there."

"Ohhh yes yes," she muses. "Well, it's good to have a variety of interests, I suppose."

"This is all wonderful," I say. "But why don't you take a break—"

"Why?" she asks.

I hold up the video camera I've brought with me.

"How about showing everyone the neighborhood?"

"I don't think so," she says instantly.

"Why not? You've always got these great stories to tell— why not share them?"

"I won't make a show of my life. I know Livy takes it all very seriously, but I draw a distinction between these things that I do and my life itself. I think a healthy life needs boundaries."

"Sylvie—"

"Besides, it's using up my 'intellectual capital', isn't it? I heard that the other day on some stock market channel— 'intellectual capital.' That *is* the way stockbrokers *would* think about it, as though you could hoard ideas like bullion. Lock them all up in a big concrete building—then the rest of us can all run around with no ideas at all, but the value of the ideas would appreciate by 275% annually," she snorts.

"We love to diminish things in this country," she continues. "This is their way of diminishing ideas, to my mind. So, to answer your question, I can't tell all my stories because I'll deplete my inventory and I won't be able to float my IPO in a few months."

She gives me that sharp bemused stare of hers. "I liked it much better when people like me knew absolutely nothing about the stock market," she concludes. "They don't even have interesting jargon."

I try to drag her back onto the subject, if any.

"Sylvie, you're the only one around who remembers some of the history of this area. I've met six people in town, and they all know you. Everybody in this town knows you, or they know of you. Don't you think you should set that knowledge out somewhere--?"

"Before I croak? I suppose there's a point there, but I don't—I don't like—I don't think it's time yet. I don't see the man with the sickle at the back door quite yet."

I want to do this. I want to convince her to— I haven't actually shot anything in years myself, I'm convinced she's a natural on-camera, and we'll get great stuff. So I persist.

"Sylvie," I ask, "how young is Livy?"

"My dear, you should know—she's a zygote," she says, and I must throw an expression at her, because she follows immediately with an explanation. "A *tabula rasa*, if you prefer. Nothing in life has left a visible mark on her yet, though I suspect there must be a few marks under the skin."

"Well, I guess what I'm getting at is—she's not what I would have considered to be 'your audience', so to speak."

"I don't have an audience," she says quickly.

I point to the chat window, which is going great guns, discussing a craft project she'd thrown together the day before.

A Crafty and Devious God

"I beg to differ," I say. "And Livy wouldn't have been that, in my mind. Too young, too citified, hip, etc. Choose your own word."

"I'll admit that—I agree," she says. "Though I think I'm as hip as could be."

"Okay. Well, Livy told me to come here and get you to do this, because she felt you were the best example of living a creative life on camera that she'd ever seen. She wants you to do it, so she can send people here from her site and get them to understand what she's trying to do. Because she thinks you do it better than she does right now."

Sylvie turned beet red, and I knew I had her.

"She *needs* you to do this," I told her.

Of course, she said yes.

Ten minutes later, we were on the street below her gray elephant of a house. The short street is only two blocks long, leading to Ocean Avenue. But this section of town is actually built on the beach, and possesses some of the most impressive houses in the area, most of them dating to the turn of the century. These are Victorian homes, and they point out the contradictions in Sylvie's house, the contrast of her even older, mid-18th Century style and the modern windows and doors, in its starkness actually looking very modern.

- 123 -

Sylvie stalks to the first of the gingerbread houses, right next door to hers. It's set lower, farther from the water, but it's just a walk through the backyard and over the dunes to the waves.

"This was built by Louie Kopplemeyer," she says, "the well-known gambler and gangster of the 20's and 30's. Gambler and gangster were synonymous in those days. You didn't have to hurt anyone to be a gangster then; all you had to do is break the law with regularity. Even our gangsters were more innocent than they are now."

She moves swiftly on her bird legs to the next house. It appears almost a copy of the first, but with more modern, less ornate trim, and painted in a much lighter palette. The two were built so close together that the roofs almost make contact.

"And this," Sylvie says merrily, " was built by Louie's brother Manny, and occupied by Manny and his wife, a Broadway showgirl—and a very nice woman—named Thelma Baxter. She was a big deal in the Twenties. The Follies. Seen with Jimmy Walker and Gene Tunney. Men committed suicide over her. A cocktail was named after her."

"Were you friendly with her?"

"Oh my yes, in the way a 10-year-old girl might be friendly with a 35 year old worldly beauty living down the block. I idolized her and she accepted my idolatry. She taught me how to straighten my hair—it was all the rage then. She let me try on her lipstick and her clothes and she painted my nails once. My mother would have been scandalized, but by then it was only my father and I. He smiled and told me I probably shouldn't become too close to those people down the block because they were—I think his word was 'unreliable.' At the time, I didn't know what a swindler he'd been himself."

"Did you stop seeing her after that advice?" I ask.

"Of course not," she chirps. "But I didn't let her paint my nails again."

"And then about a year later, I woke up one morning and the police were all over the street. My father wouldn't let me go outside and I didn't see Thelma again. She moved away shortly after. It took me a while to find out what happened—and several years before I actually *understood* what happened.

"Apparently, Manny Koppelmeyer was not the vibrant personality his brother was. Thelma being spirited, shall we say, she became...diverted by her brother-in-law next door. And that morning, Louie was found dead with a bullet in his chest, right *here*."

She deftly steps over a low row of hedges onto the front lawn of the property. With the arrogant self-absorption of television crews everywhere, I follow her onto the gray autumn grass, focusing on the spot she's pointing to.

"You seem very certain of the spot," I say.

"A young girl, especially of those times, didn't forget the place where she saw her first dead body, let me tell you." She says this with a look of absolute mischievous relish on her face. "Or her first naked one, but that's another story," she adds, blushing.

"You'll notice," she says, pointing upwards, "that Louie was found in just the spot he would have landed, if he had been standing on the roof outside Thelma's bedroom. And the fact that he was found on the lawn wearing only his trousers; no shirt, socks, shoes or garters—men wore them in those days—anyway, that made the story a bit more sensational."

"But since no one admitted having seen the shooting," she continues, "and it quickly turned out that there was no lack of candidates wanting Louie dead, the case was never solved. It was left in the hands of the gossips, of which I am now the only one left."

We step back onto the sidewalk and head on down the block. A face appears in the window of the next house, watching us, as though ready to intervene if we decide to march onto *their* lawn. But Sylvie just pauses, viewing the house like a string of pearls she's appraising in a shop window.

"Mrs. Dunst lived here. A rather brittle person, to my mind. Never very friendly. I think she moved here after her husband passed away or left her—people didn't talk about such things in those days. But maybe she felt so isolated that she made herself isolated, I don't know. Died of a stroke, many years ago. Don't know the new people"

She moves to the next house. "The Krinskys lived here. They used to dance in the back yard on summer nights, just the two of them, to Sinatra and Tony Martin. She moved to Florida after he passed away—he had diabetes and bad veins. I think she had cancer."

And the next. "The Lewises—they had two daughters my age—but they only lived here a short time. Then old Mr. Nash— nasty old fellow. Kept two big snapping dogs chained up in the back yard. He contracted scarlet fever and passed away suddenly. No one knew how he'd got it. He never seemed to leave the house. Nice couple live here now—I see their two girls playing on the block. I wonder sometimes how much you should know about the place you live—it's a mixed blessing."

We reach the end of the street, the empty lot fronting Ocean Ave. Sylvie stops and looks back on the block, eyeing, it seems, all that history, all those lives, in a glance.

"It's interesting, isn't it," she says, "that we look back on people we knew once they've passed on—people that smiled at us and said 'hello' and showed us some little kindnesses or shared a moment or an incident—and after they're gone, the first impulse is just to remember how they died. Our lives are an effort to make something that makes us feel good about ourselves and to make some sort of difference in the world, and then you die and people say, forever after, 'Oh yes, good old so-and-so—cancer, stroke, hit by an egg truck, left yolks all over the block'—*that*, they'll remember forever."

"Even your friends, your family, the lives that remain real to you, the ones you will always remember alive—they become fixed in memory. They can't surprise you anymore."

She folds her arms, as though annoyed suddenly by something I can't see.

"At this age," she says flatly, "my life is filled with ghosts, when what I need are surprises."

Playing Around

So, for a while, we *played* at sex.

I was the postal delivery guy, who appeared in uniform to drop off and pick up packages and ogle Livy in whatever she was barely wearing that day.

I was the lawyer, trying to straighten out various fictitious hassles with her internet company and the authorities. I used jargon we found on the Court TV website, and I overcharged wildly, so that I *had* to take advantage of the poor girl, just to make sure she didn't fall too far behind in her payments.

I continued my recurring role as the landlord, who also got some of his financial burden taken out in trade.

None of our little games were brilliant drama, obviously. But they did bring up the numbers. Each scene increased the number of visitors to the site, especially once we started replaying the days 'hot clips' every night at 8 and 11 Eastern time.

For subscribers, that is. We made some changes to increase revenue as the audience grew rapidly. The video window that had been up on the Web at the beginning was the output of the switcher—whichever camera had the best view went out live on the Web. Now that changed.

Now, the 'free' view was the camera on the bar. It showed the whole room, and gave the best view of Livy on the treadmill. But the rest of the time, other cameras were better. You could click on a link for the 'subscribers feed' but that only worked for a minute at a time—unless you subscribed. $19.95 a month.

Along with the better camera output, the 'hot clips'—the day's hottest moments, available anytime at the click of a link—only ran at half their length unless you subscribed. Otherwise, they shut down just before the good stuff. Livy quickly mastered the time-management skills of on-air personalities—I'd like to think I was a good tutor, having worked with so many far-less-entertaining examples in the past. She learned how to stretch things so you were unbearably horny just about the time the video shut down.

We could tell from the number of individuals coming to our site—and the amount of repeat traffic—that we had a good shot at a real business here. But we were astounded by what followed. In the first week of the new regime, we had 1,000 subscribers. Do the math—it was a nice start.

But, as usual, Livy wasn't satisfied with half a glass—she loved the numbers but she wasn't satisfied with the stories. "I thought it was going to be more fun than this," she lamented.

"Let's work on something requiring a little more choreography. You be the delivery boy, but come on a bit too strong."

"*Elvis* too strong—I think how hot I am?"

"No—*nasty* too strong. Push me—but look sharp," she warned.

We were in the downstairs room—that's where we went when we wanted to be off-camera. I carried my bag of groceries into the room and grabbed her shoulder as she passed me by. In a second, she pulled my arm and rolled me over her hip onto the floor, just like the movies.

I lay there, my back hurting. I looked up at the big grin on her face. "Round Two?" I asked.

We practiced several sequences of moves until we found a group that worked, without me actually breaking anything. She was good at it—I couldn't get a grip on her that she couldn't break, and I tried. I got into my delivery guy costume—a jean jacket from a thrift store down the street, t-shirt and black pants—and we were ready.

Just before she was going to turn the cameras on, I said, "What's your motivation here? I mean, your audience has seen you doing the nasty with the landlord and the lawyer to pay the bills. Why am I different?"

She turned to me, arched her shoulder and raised an eyebrow. "Because I don't want to," she replied, and started to turn on the machines.

I liked that. I like that more and more as it echoed in my head. And when we played the scene, as I picked myself up off the floor, about to leave, I turned to her in redneck New Jersey character, and shrieked, "Hey, what's wit' you? I seen you on the Internet wit' other guys. Why not me?"

There was only the tiniest hesitation, and then she fell right back into the pose.

"Because I don't want to," she repeated. It was lovely.

That night, the whole chat was transformed. A major discussion ensued about women coming onto men, their clothes and attitude, what was a turnon and not fair, when a woman had the right to say no. Livy was bold enough to put it plainly: Even an exhibitionist has the right to say no.

The discussion got heated, but it was a real conversation.

"And admit it," she said, "they would never have thought about this in this way for a minute, if they didn't start out with my hand down their pants."

That night, in bed, she turned the microphone in the bedroom off. It was the first time it had been off since we started out.

"This really works," she said. "The stories make a point better than the documentary approach did."

"Well, it's all part of your life," I said, trying to be charitable.

"Yeah, but the life part *doesn't* work. The numbers are different lately—there's more competition out there and we've raised the ante. Now, when I do regular things, they go away. They check back and stay if something's going on. So we'll lose them unless we keep pushing this thing forward."

"Don't limit yourself," I said. "You don't necessarily have to give up what you wanted to do. The creative path is usually the third one—the one you make up that goes around the original two choices you *thought* you had."

She looks sour for a moment. "I'm not giving up what I wanted to do," she barks. "My life is going to play out on camera—I'm just not naïve anymore."

I looked over at her—I guess my confusion was showing.

"You asked me if it's about sex—I said sex is part of my life, so it's about sex," she answered. "Well, manipulation is part of my life too. Don't you always manipulate the one you love?"

She paused a second, waiting for me to answer, but I had to consider that one. So she continued.

"I mean, look at tonight. We had about thirty seconds of thought-out material, and look what it led to. Those guys got really engaged in that discussion tonight. And we got there by calculation, by manipulation—they responded to it far more than they did to just showing 'the truth'."

I looked over to see if this upset her. But as she brushed her hair off her face, I caught a glimpse of the most luscious look in her eyes—unadorned ambition and determination to win, showing wide-open with no filters.

It floored me that she let me see it, naked like that. She gave her body easily, indiscriminately—it was her collateral, and she had several mortgages banking on it. But she tried to keep her inner fires more buried than anyone I'd ever seen. She was almost a totally submerged human being. This was the most open she'd ever been with me—maybe it was the most open she would ever *be* with me, and it thrilled me and chilled me all at once to see it.

That's when I stopped arguing. We were heading into the sea of storytelling, and no turning back. I have known a few other people like her before—capable of making a 180° turn without stopping or thinking twice—but not many.

"So we need juicier stories," she said, "and a way to build the tension, to keep them coming back. How could we exploit the chat for telling a story?"

"What do you mean?" I asked.

"I mean, can we plant comments in the chat?" she said. "Y'know—like have a couple of email addresses and send notes to the chat, pushing the rest of them to think about what's happening the way we want them to? Make them demand what we want to give them? Make them hungry—ahead of time—for what we've already planned? Make them think it's *their* idea?"

I couldn't help but think she would've made a great network news executive.

"What do you have in mind?" I asked.

"I don't know yet," she replied. "I'm just thinking about it."

The thought stuck with me as I headed home later, out on the street in the October night. There was a breeze—I could see my breath on the air. As I headed down Ocean Ave. towards my house, I looked at the carved pumpkins with the gargoyle faces and the spooks fluttering in the breeze.

And I had an idea. As Dr. Seuss said, I had a wonderful awful idea.

The Pale Guy

A week later came the first appearance of the Pale Guy.

We called him that for the Marilyn Manson chalk-white facepaint. I got him a grey coat that hung to the ground, with a tall hood and a long stringy-haired wig that stuck out around the edges. This was the Pale Guy.

He looked plenty eerie in the moonlight, especially on those foggy autumn evenings when the cold rolled in at dusk. I rigged a very small battery-powered light inside the base of the hood that shined up onto his face, and made him look absolutely sinister. But the right trappings still demand the right actor, and I had just the fellow.

"Lance Pacquett

The Kick-Boxing Plastic Surgeon"

"Whatever type of part you have, Lance Pacquett can play it! With a buffed, perfected 6'7" physique, a highly-trained speaking voice and an attitude that projects to the rafters, Lance makes a powerful impression."

"And with his experience in the high-pressure world of plastic surgery, you know that Lance can handle the demands of any shooting schedule or dramatic moment."

I had received the resume and glossy black-and-white headshot years earlier at the network, and kept it because I always found it hysterically funny. The headshot showed Lance in all his buffed glory. Dark hair and eyes set wide, a long thin nose and a pronounced chin—every feature outsized, out of proportion, cartoonish. Also prominent in the photo was his hairless chest and heavily muscled arms, curled leading to a menacing fist.

The list of credits glued to the back was split between acting and plastic surgery. Appearances on a few cable public-access martial arts shows, a one-line part in a Hollywood action film I'd never heard of, and the obligatory role of Harold Hill in a summer stock production of "The Music Man" filled out the list.

The other column was more impressive, actually—Johns Hopkins graduate, internship at Columbia Presbyterian in NY, hundreds of plastic surgeries, specializing in breast augmentation and liposuction. He even listed several former patients as references, complete with their home phone numbers.

I was working in the operations office of a network television news magazine—not exactly the most fertile territory for casting calls. Clearly, he had sent his sheet out to every address he could find with TV in the name.

However, I had to admit, he wasn't wrong, because now, years later, here I was, about to hire him.

I remembered he lived in New Jersey and guessed, correctly, that somehow he hadn't gotten much acting work from this unique resume. When I told him about the part, a stalker in a continuing thriller plot on the Internet, he offered to postpone a scheduled surgery and drive down to talk to me immediately. I told him the next day would be fine.

Lance proved to be absolutely fascinating. He spoke at length and articulately about the craft of acting, but he couldn't see the forest for the trees.

"I need you to stand on the deck and look menacing," I explained.

"Do I have any lines?"

"No. Not yet. Maybe later."

"Do I do anything?"

"No."

"I don't get it. How do I look menacing?"

"Lance, you're 6'7—what do you weigh?"

"290."

"290—you'll be menacing enough just standing there."

"Yeah, but I need to know where I'm coming from as a character."

I gathered myself. I remembered all at once why I hated working with actors.

"Lance," I said, taking a deep breath, "this part is about zen—it's about stillness. The less you do, the more menacing you'll be. In fact, when you move—and you should only move when absolutely necessary—you should glide. Nobody should see your legs or anything else moving—they should just see you in a different place."

"Ohhhh," he moaned, and I could see this would give him enough of a challenge to keep him churning for a while.

I told him to report two nights later, Halloween night. He insisted on walking the territory—the deck and back of the house—before he left and promised to arrive at least an hour early so he could do his stretching exercises and visualization.

I did some additional preparation. I got myself another mail account with another phony name—ROThornhill—if you need a phony name, Hitchock is always an appropriate reference. Then I posted some comments using the new account on Livy's chat for a few days, just getting the regulars used to my name, getting to be one of the guys. Getting ready for the big night.

The night was perfect—misty and bleak, the air a purplish haze. Livy was running on the treadmill in a light white tank top and panties. The Pale Guy sat in a corner of the deck out of camera range, with a laptop tied into the network connection.

As she stepped off the treadmill and took a drink of water, the Pale Guy appeared on cue on the deck behind her. The online cameras only generated about 10 frames a second, so he appeared in the background of only 100 frames or so, a blurred eerie presence. But the frames hung up on the Net long enough for the audience to notice him.

Not that I left anything to chance. As I saw his image appear on camera, I immediately typed a note to the chat group to make sure nobody missed it.

```
From: ROThornhill@Tipsy.net
To: Seaviewgirl.com
Re: Pale Guy
Who's that guy on the deck? Did
you see him?
```

The rest immediately chimed in. The few that hadn't noticed him now retrieved the last five frames—a cache of recent frames is a standard convention on sites like this—and flipped.

```
From: aol977799988@aol.com
To: Seaviewgirl.com
Re: Pale Guy
*Who the hell is THAT?
*Wacko? Call the cops!
*That's    nobody.    She    has    a
scarecrow on the deck.
*No—look at the frames—right arm 5
degrees higher frame 232 than frame 231.
arm is moving. It's a ral guy.
```

And then, after no more than two minutes:

```
*Guys—I've put the two frames into
my paint program and sharpened them up.
```

```
I've    put    the    frames    up    at
www.guildoctor.com/~arias/Seaviewpix.    I
think he's a Goth.
     *What's wrong with that?
     *No-like  a  serious  Goth,  a  Satan
Worshipper.
     *Let's call the cops!
     *We don't know where she lives.
     *Idiot!  She  lives  in  Seaview—it's
the name of her site!
     *Great—so    what?    Seaview    what?
Delaware?  New  York?  Massachusetts?  Did
she make up the name?
```

This rattled me a bit. I had assumed everyone would get into this as a Halloween prank. I had no idea any of them would take it seriously, though it now appeared they *all* did.

```
     *I  blew  up  a  section  of  one  of
last  week's  pictures—there  is  a  car
parked  outside  the  house  behind  her.  It
has a Maryland license plate.
     *Okay—I    got    the    number    for
Seaview, MD PD. I'm calling.
```

I calmed down for a moment—they had the wrong state. That bought me some time, but now that they'd raised the subject, I started thinking about how we could use this incident to greater advantage. So I motioned Livy to the shower, and sent Lance an email, telling him to stand by the bathroom window, right behind her.

As she got out of the shower, the Pale Guy was clearly visible in the window, just for twenty frames or so, and then eerily disappeared from sight.

I headed back to the laptop.

```
*He's there again!!
*Shit—is that a better picture?
*No. It's a shitty picture.
*there got to be something we all
can do. call the county sheriff?
    *Sheriff?  Where  are  you  from?
She's in Maryland.
    *Okay folk, just got off the phone
with the cops. They wanted my name and
number. I hung up but I think they're
trying to trace me.
    *Great! What happened?
    *I told them I was watching this
woman take a shower on the Internet and
we're worried about the Peeping Tom on
her porch. They didn't like that.
    *What are we supposed to do? Just
stand here and watch?
```

I was getting nervous now. These guys were very concerned for Livy, and that was touching. But all this nervous energy could lead to real problems if they tried other Seaview Police Departments on the East Coast. If they made that connection—and got that phone number—it might wreak havoc on my future plans for The Pale Guy. For, seeing now the radical effect he was having on the audience, I knew we would have future plans for him. And

I wanted us to be in control of any police interaction. So I had to find another way to channel our energetic horde of protectors.

This seemed self-evident at the moment. It seemed logical, necessary, obvious. I had no idea where it would lead. I was innocent, thoroughly innocent of what was to come, as we all are. Innocence like a baby. Innocence like 'Well, if Gen'l Custer says 'March,' then we march' and 'Nice of the Greeks to gift us this big horse, don't you think?' Of course, if we always knew where the road would take us, most of us would stay home, preferably hiding under the bed.

So now I wrote:

```
    *What about that guy?-the guy who
runs the other site on Seaview?
    *What guy?
    * whiny-sister divorce guy. Has
the other site on Seaview. Not the lady
with the shells.
    *he's okay.
    *Why don't we have him call the
cops! He's in the same town as her!
```

Worked like a charm. One of the guys emailed me, and— after tipping Lance to disappear—I actually did call the local cops myself. I told them I saw a peeping tom on the balcony at Livy's address. As soon as I knew they were coming, Lance and I bolted.

It was a great scene on camera. Two town cops arrived minutes later and were confronted by a fetching young woman in a very flimsy nightgown telling them she had glimpsed someone peeping in her window. Didn't matter that her description in no way resembled the Pale Guy—no one online heard the conversation anyway. We managed to lose the microphone for the moment.

But the boys online knew I had succeeded in calling the cops.

And the next day, a lot of other people knew as well. The story made some of the newspapers. The idea that a group of men saw a stalker on a Website and called the police was enough of a hook to get some national play. And instead of everyone realizing it was just a Halloween prank, the papers played it as some kind of bizarre irony that it happened Halloween night.

In the middle of the article, my name was mentioned as the guy who'd called the cops. And Livy was quoted as saying she was looking forward to thanking this fellow who'd 'saved her'. Our sitenames—Livy's and mine—were listed at the end of the article in several papers.

We were protected by the general ignorance of most reporters about the Web. How I knew the address to send the police was a question never asked—and a good thing too, seeing as I had no answer.

The article netted us far greater response than we'd anticipated—Livy's audience quadrupled overnight. We put up special links to the Pale Guy clips—the fact that they showcased

Livy, athletic and damp, didn't seem to hurt subscription sales at all.

And my site got a lot of spillover too. Most of the visitors were interested in Livy's offer to thank me—when I was going to see her? I got a lot of advice as to when to see her ('soon' was the leading choice), and what to do when I saw her (you can imagine the leading suggestion).

What I realized, when I got a chance to actually *think* about all this, was that it was the way around my worries about Marla. I was now a *character* in Livy's story. I had received emails asking me to help out a girl who happened to live in my town. What else, as a good citizen, could I have done? And now, she wanted to thank me—and I had fifty emails making sure I knew about it.

Suddenly, without ever having planned it, I had a paper trail inexorably leading me to this girl who just happened to take her clothes off on the Internet. I was acquiring a girlfriend without ever appearing to take an active role in the process. Whenever Marla dragged me into court, I would at least have an excuse to explain how I got mixed up with her. It was certainly a step in the right direction.

There was one other persistent, and ominous, thread in my discussion boards. Three separate posters wanted me to find the Pale Guy and attack him, vigilante style, and send them pictures of his dismembered corpse. Or, if I could find out his address, they offered to do it themselves.

And I also got one chilling note, a week or two later, from someone claiming to be the Pale Guy, warning me to stay out of his way.

Pale Games

paleguy@aol.com: OK safehouse—
watch you back! Keep out of my bizness.
Don't want you around. So don't be
around. Or it's just you and me—no cops.
No more cops. Got it?

The email address didn't actually exist. No way to trace it. Believe me, I tried.

It really freaked me out for a while. I wondered if I shouldn't publish the letter—maybe I'd get more publicity if the stalker had contacted me, as well as threatening Livy. But the local cops were already keeping an eye on Livy's house, just for fun—if it seemed like there was a real threat, they'd blanket the place and Lance wasn't interested in wearing the hood and makeup under those circumstances—for good reason, as we all found out later.

And then we'd have to lose the stalker, and that was unthinkable—he was hugely popular. Well, let me rephrase that a little—like any good villain, he made the heroine much more popular than she would otherwise be. Our traffic was through the roof, and Livy started getting interview requests from 'serious' media—if you consider Us, Slate, the Star and Nerve.com serious.

The articles turned out to be 2" blurbs on a This Week page. But it was a lot of play, all at once, and the articles were sympathetic to the plight of this heroic young woman who was trying to live her life on the Internet—each article included the obligatory paragraph where she got to speak her piece. Getting that out in mainstream publications was an achievement, at least.

Livy prepped our favorite couple of local cops with all the details of the Pale Guy's appearance, and they corroborated our story. I've been in the news business for fifteen years—give them two sources, they have a fact. Give them three facts and a pretty face, they have a story. So, it went swimmingly—for now.

I decided to do nothing, say nothing, to Livy, about the email threat from the 'real' Pale Guy—I would just keep my eyes open. He was probably just a freaky viewer.

We were barreling full speed ahead. Knowing nothing succeeds like more of a good thing, we were arranging for the Pale Guy to become a regular.

We had to make the game a little more elaborate to keep the cops out of it. Livy finally put shades on some of the larger windows. This made it easier for the Pale Guy to show up for just a few seconds in the background and then disappear.

Someone on the chat would catch a glimpse of him and e-mail her or me immediately. We would call the cops—at least *appear* to call the cops—and Lance would change into a cop uniform and show up in minutes, just missing the Pale Guy again.

The local constables were helpful by being predictable. They always showed up, patrolling the block, at the beginning of Livy's prime time show, or when we'd tipped them off that something juicy was going to be happening. They would hang out down the block for a few minutes and catch the view—after which they would have to get moving if they were going to stay on schedule. So we would then have fifteen to twenty minutes free. With the Pale Guy's visits averaging twenty to thirty *seconds*, it gave us plenty of leeway.

Some of the constabulary were viewers as well, and it didn't take long for them to start asking questions about Lance the Police Officer. Livy told them he was a security guy we'd hired and put into a rented uniform—"it is show business, after all. He has to look the part."

The police warned Livy these private security guys weren't all that competent, but she argued that it was necessary nonetheless.

"Just having him here keeps the stalker from getting too close," she argued. "Besides, would your wives like you appearing on my show every week?" That seemed to end the discussion but quick.

The seachange in the audience had a bigger effect on *my* site than on Livy's—hers was built for traffic from day one. My audience grew by a factor of 50 the week after the first sighting of the Pale Guy, and they were all focused on my relationship with Livy.

Some of the tamer messages:

```
        rasslemania: You gt her over there
and get her on tha couch and you don't
need no time limit on your camera, you
just take care of hr. on the table to is
good.
        raygun72: I think she doesn't like
those guys she's got on her site—I think
she could use something a little mor
romantic in her life. So when you get
her on the floor, maybe you could do her
with a rose in your mouth or something.
```

You get the picture. Some of the messages were such that I couldn't finish reading them. I committed the ultimate web faux pas by deleting them and then posting a message that I was not responsible for what other people put up on my discussion boards, but that if I saw something that offended me, it was coming down.

The traffic—both the amount of it and the change in tone— totally disrupted the things I'd grown to like about my little site. The guys who regularly showed up to talk about their marriages were turned off by the new guys, and the new guys had no patience for the regulars with marriage problems—most of the new guys knew how they'd treat the bitch if she gave them any lip. It was like being locked up in the NFL Husbands Therapy Group.

It bothered me, too. I was working some unhappy stuff out of my system on the site, with my articles and the contact, the back-and-forth, with the unhappy husbands club. All that, for now, was swamped in the tide of Seaview Girl and What You Ought To Do With Her mail.

It took me several days to get back on top of things. I separated out the marriage discussion, and set up a new discussion board just about Seaview Girl. Then I posted a message on the new board:

> I appreciate all the attention, guys, but let's not get ahead of ourselves. I haven't even met this girl yet, so I don't know if she's interested—or if I am. I certainly want to know if she's getting stalked. I'll be glad to get in touch with the cops or take action if need be. I know she said she'd like to meet me sometime soon, so I'll keep taking your suggestions—but keep them on this board, if you don't mind. Thanks.

The messages came every few days—Stalker at Seaview Girl's. I would dutifully drop whatever I was doing and head over. Again, he'd vanish in minutes, almost as if he knew I was coming. I would reconnoiter the territory and then head back home. Everything according to plan.

But plans—even the best-laid plans, as they say—have a way of developing a mind of their own.

Salon, October 28, 1998:

There certainly are plenty of sexually liberated women and academics who are attempting to change mainstream thinking about the porn industry. "I think what's changing that perception is money," says Pauline Albamar, who started the successful site Babes4U after receiving two master's degrees from NYU's Interactive Telecommunications Program. "Money is what defines things, and the fact that the sex business is making money online, the first industry to do so online, has really garnered a lot more attention and shift in attitude. Have people's ethics changed about sex? I think it helps if people like me, relatively young and intelligent women, have no problem making money off pornography -- then it does change people's perceptions."

~~~

Morphing

Livy was moping again.

"I'm tired of being their 'ho," she said. "I want to be their *girlfriend*."

"Well, you started down this road," I warned her. "They're used to counting on you for...stimulation."

"I don't mind that," she whined. "I'm reliable, that way. I'll get them off. But there has to be a way to build something else too, to include something more than just sex, doesn't there?"

"Well, truth be told, you've probably gone about this the way most men would prefer—sex first, then a relationship. Much easier to concentrate on the woman's personality once you've gotten all that horny energy out of the way."

"But doesn't that prove a woman's point? If you give it to them too early, you can't get anything else."

"Is that the problem?" I asked. "Or is the problem that you haven't demanded anything else?"

Ooh, she didn't like that.

"What's that supposed to mean?" she demanded.

"Look—I think you enjoy taking your clothes off. It turns you on, getting that attention from them—you just don't like having to do it on a schedule. You don't like calling it pornography, but I think *you're* convinced that if you don't do it frequently enough, you'll lose them."

"That's not true," she said.

"What percentage of the audience dropped out in the half-hour following sex last week? What was the average?" I demanded. "C'mon—I know you know."

"35%," she muttered.

"And how do you know that?" I pressed her. "It doesn't say 'sex act', and 'following sex act' on the Webtrends report, does it?"

"No."

"So you keep track of what time we had sex, and you check—you see how big the audience is before, during and after. And you worry about the fact that they fluctuate."

"Of course I do. It's my business," she said.

"Well, but then you've defined your business—even in your own head—as being about the sex. And the little 'stories' we're telling—the landlord, the lawyer, blah blah...are those great drama? Would you tune in to watch them if they didn't promise a turnon at the end?"

"Of course not," she admitted.

"So why should they take you seriously? If you haven't demanded they think about anything else, they're men in a pack—

they won't. Right now, you're having sex with them, but you haven't given them the whole 'I like flowers and long walks on the beach and how come you never talk to me about Nietzche and the state of humankind' conversation—complete with the 'if you don't start taking me seriously, you're going to screw up this good deal you've got' ending. And what else have you offered them? What other reason should they have for looking beyond the surface?"

She took this in. I could see she was thinking about it. But she walked away, staring out the window, and I got the feeling she was just going to stand there until she could walk away from the conversation, altogether.

And that was emblematic of the bigger problem, the one *behind* the one I'd brought up—and the more crippling one.

The question in her head was: What else do I have to offer?

From the moment we met, she'd displayed herself to me. The first time we worked well together, she had sex with me. As soon as the audience fluctuated a little, she'd bailed on the 'life in front of the camera' thing and taken her clothes off. She really *didn't* see what else she had to offer.

"Who painted those paintings—the ones at 'livypost.com?'" I asked.

Her whole face pursed—the eyes darkened, her mouth tightened, her cheeks sucked in.

"That was a pretentious little girl," she said. "That was somebody who didn't get the way the world works."

"Oh? I just thought maybe whoever that girl was, she might have some interest, she might create a little competition for the sex part. At very least, maybe she'd create another side that they could pay attention to in between the sex parts."

"That's what respect is?" she asked. "What happens between sex?"

"No. But right now, there's *nothing* between sex. Start somewhere."

She turned back to the window. "Let's stop talking nonsense, okay?"

"Okay. Second thought—not as good as the first, but how's this? Let's start dating."

Now she looked confused.

"Huh?"

"I've been thinking about this for a day or two. You owe me the 'thanks' you promised to give me for calling the cops on the Pale Guy the first time, right? So how about, instead of it being sex, I show up and we have a date? And we want more dates?"

She stepped away from the glass, her eyes totally gone inside her own thoughts.

"We'd be really acting *scenes*," she said. "Not the skits we've been doing." She clearly liked the idea, but just as clearly, it worried her.

"Do you think we can pull it off?" she asked.

"We're playing ourselves," I answered. "How hard can it be?"

"So they'd have the experience of *seeing* me as a girlfriend," she murmured.

"Right. I could even be a little puzzled about the difference between the exhibitionist on the site and the sensitive, shy girl I'm dating. That would give you a chance to tackle that question head-on."

"What sensitive, shy girl?" she demanded. "I'm not *that* good an actress."

I hadn't consciously thought through what I'd said, but now it came out of me all at once.

"The terribly sensitive, terribly shy girl," I told her, "who's afraid to look anything other than commanding and determined all the time—the one that's always in control , that laser beam who's always pushing everything along at warp nine, and the one who's always quivering in front of the mirror alone in the morning. The one you don't want to let out—in front of me, in front of them, probably in front of you, though I'm damned if I know why."

She was staring at me real hard. I stared right back.

"I know she's in there," I said.

And then I saw something I hadn't seen before. I *saw* the fear. There was a wound, visible in her eyes, that went straight through her, and now straight through me.

"It's the next step," I said.

I wanted to add, 'You have to take it,' but I didn't. I knew her well enough to know that if I said that, she'd move heaven and earth to prove me wrong.

And the reality was, I didn't have to say it. Our own hearts are our ultimate destination—the quest that never ends, the question that's never fully answered. Anytime you can glimpse a bit of a signpost on that journey, you *have* to follow it.

The only question was where this would lead.

Pat & Mike

The plan was ready, but Livy was nervous, and her testiness ended up putting things off an extra day or two:

> madog@hot.net: TITS!
> seaviewgirl@seaviewgirl.com:
> BALLS! I want to see you put up a site where you show your balls, and we'll compare how many people come to it, okay? We'll get there—have a little patience. This is my life, not just your playroom.
> madog@hot.net: I'd love to show them to you.
> seaviewgirl@seaviewgirl.com: Well, sorry—we haven't opened the audience participation area yet. Right now, it's a one-way street here.

The next Pale Guy sighting was planned for the next night, and that was supposed to lead to the two of us meeting for the first time. Lance was all prepared. But, that evening, Angel240—one of the regulars—was giving Livy a hard time. Angel240 is probably my age or better (worse?), and clearly not a happy guy. Every couple of nights he would log on and whine about Livy's taste in clothes, politics, religion, a laundry list of complaint we all took for granted by now. The regulars on the site would egg him on to show how rude and gross he could be.

These were the same guys who routinely typed "get necked (naked) for me, honey" forty times a night—sometimes when Livy was *already* naked. These were the guys who wrote Livy in endless detail of the specific methods by which they would service her. She always shrugged it off as part of the territory.

But this night, Angel240 got ugly. He called Livy names and got very graphic, describing acts most people couldn't even imagine and some that would make it impossible for you to ever purchase insurance again.

Finally, she blew.

She just stopped typing and yelled "Oh SHIT!!" She stood up—stark naked at the time—looked into the camera and said, "Angel, that is truly disgusting. I'm tired of this shit. If you can't think of some nice way to do it with me, there are lots of other women out there you can harass—don't do it to me."

And she walked off for five minutes, causing no end of flames to Angel240 for having lost the audience their view.

When she returned, in a ratty old green bathrobe I'd never seen before, she looked right into the camera eye and *yelled* at it.

"You know, I sit here trying to figure out what you all will like. It's not like you want one thing—I get twenty messages at a time telling me to do this and that and everything else in between. And I have to figure out what will work and what I'm willing to do. I'm a real person, not just some blow-up doll you can do anything you want with. If you get gross, you turn me off and then I don't feel sexy at all. So you treat me with some respect or I'll just shut you down."

And she put a sign in front of the camera, taking us offline for the rest of the evening.

"You sure you want to do that?" I asked.

"I've done it," she said. "It's done."

"You sure it's a good idea?"

"It's the one I have. If you have another idea, I'll consider it."

So much for any thought of our meeting *that* evening. And, as with so much else with Livy, it turned out to be a very lucky turn of events.

The next day, there was a knock at the door. When I opened it, a little weasel-faced young man with a thick rug of hair and no chin handed me a thick legal paper. Livy was being sued by a lawyer—a subscriber—for failure to perform contractual services, in that the site contained notices suggesting we would be 'live' 8p-2a Eastern time, and Livy had shut us down, in her pique, around midnight.

Livy was concerned at first.

"We're not making enough money to afford lawyer's bills," she moaned. "They'll bleed us dry."

"I don't think someone can sue for that," I said.

"I don't care—even if it never goes to court, I still can't afford it. *He* can—he's a lawyer."

"Yeah, and they stick together. Then again," I thought aloud, "they also travel in packs."

"Huh?"

"I have a thought," I said, and went to the phone.

I called the law firm the guy worked for and asked for the press relations department.

"This is a law firm," the woman on the phone responded. "We don't have a press relations department."

"Well, if you were going to be mentioned in a nationwide press release in connection with an internet pornography site, is there someone you would choose to respond for the company?" I asked, all innocence.

She stammered. She wanted to know if she could take my number and get back to me. I said I'd hold. It didn't take them long to find someone.

"Stephen Bardwell" came the crisp voice at the other end, a few minutes later. Just from the way he spoke, I've decided he spelled Stephen with a 'ph' rather than a 'v' in the middle. He sounded like the kind of guy who would count the letters.

I explained, as briefly as I could, that one of their firm's lawyers was threatening to sue us and we thought this was great publicity for the site. So we just wanted to know who the firm's press contact was, so we could put this in the press release. Bardwell asked for the name of the lawyer, and I gave it to him.

"And the basis for the suit?" he asked next.

"She wasn't naked long enough," I answered.

He sat silent on the other end for a long moment. Then he asked, "Can you be a bit more precise?"

"The owner of the site, Livy Post, decided to shut down her various...activities, which include nudity and self-pleasuring (I tried to think of a term that sounded lawyerish) early that night, because she took offense at the comments of one of the patrons — and of course, I'm not suggesting that patron was your attorney, by the way."

"Oh—uh—no, no, of course not." Now *he* was stammering.

"Well, your attorney felt he hadn't gotten his full value for the evening, and is suing for failure to perform contractual services. So I just figured, once the story hits, you'll be getting a lot of calls, and I figure you'd rather have one person field them than have your entire staff of lawyers trying to figure out what they want to say to reporters. You know how reporters get."

Another long pause. I knew I wasn't being subtle, but I was pretty sure my point was getting across.

"There won't be a suit," he said finally.

"Excuse me?"

"There won't be a suit," he repeated. "Mr. __ was just joking."

"Well, we did receive a notice, delivered by email this morning…"

"It was all in fun. There won't be a suit," he said again. "Is there anything else I can do for you?"

I got the spelling of *his* name. And then, just to be an asshole, I put out the press release anyway. But it worked—as the man said, there wasn't a suit. The lawfirm denied it ever happened. But we had the papers.

The story got good play over several days—the webcam girl who refused to be treated like a concubine got some ink. Between the suit and the Pale Guy, Livy was becoming known on the gossip pages of America, putting her on an even footing with Meg Ryan, Brad Pitt and Henry Kissinger.

So *now* it was time for us to meet. A few nights later I got a message on my boards—stalker at Seaview Girl's.

I went running outside, carrying a new nightvision camera we'd purchased, now that we were successful capitalists. It ran on an infrared wireless hookup to the server, so the picture would go out live on my website. This is another piece of technology that would have seemed miraculous to me ten years ago. Standing in a pitchblack closet, the picture looks like daylight.

So when the stalker was sighted, I searched the neighborhood. I looked around the side of houses, behind the corner store and throughout all the vacant lots in a two-block radius. I acted nervous and cautious—carefully checking out an area before I ventured into it, as though I had no idea where the stalker might be hiding.

Of course, I knew very well. At that point, he was in his car, changing into his policeman uniform. And as soon as he was finished, Lance would knock on Livy's door and take her statement, as he had numerous times before.

But this night, she met him outside the house, under the garage camera. And when I showed up, having searched the area, Livy walked right up to me.

"You're the guy who called the cops," she said.

I nodded.

"Thanks," she said, put her arm around my shoulder and gave me a shy, sensitive kiss. Not the amorous kisses I was used to getting from her, on or off camera, but a girlish, friendly, convincingly shy and grateful kiss.

"You want to come up—have a drink?" she said. She stammered a little.

"Okay" I answered, shy myself now, in response to this sweet, tentative character I barely recognized.

She led me up the stairs. She was wearing some scoop-neck short-sleeved thing, with a nice skirt cut above the knee. Standard flirty-girl stuff, nothing daring at all. And the body language was that kind of friendly informality Americans have perfected and taught the world—the textbook behavior when you've just met someone you like or are beholden to.

We went into the living room, and then the kitchen. She pulled out two fluted wine glasses I'd never seen before, and gave me that brand-new shy smile. "White or red?" she asked.

"Red, thanks," I answered, like I'd never told her before. She poured me a glass from my bottle, which sat on her counter, and pulled a bottle of white from the fridge for herself. Then she motioned me to sit on the couch, the couch I'd spent so many nights on already, and took a seat demurely across from me.

"So how long have you lived here?" she asked, and I just drifted into space.

It was eerie. I'd been sleeping and eating with Livy for six weeks already and now I was answering questions about what kind of wine I drank and how long I'd lived in the area.

I'd already played twelve silly roles on her site. But now, I was playing *me*, and it was plain weird.

What made it even stranger was that we were making the kind of small talk couples make when they first meet—which is something we'd never done. We'd blown right by that stage, going from technical advice to fucking like rabbits in a matter of minutes.

So I answered her questions, but I felt really out of place, second-guessing myself at each step. I was also walking a bit of a tightrope between what would sound right when Marla dragged me into court and what wouldn't contradict what I'd already said on my website. With all this going on, creating the character of me didn't come very easy at all.

I tried to see Livy as though I'd just met her, to try to go back to the first excitement I'd had when we first met, to channel Lee Strasberg or Stanislavski or Nijinsky or *somebody* that could help.

I was floundering but good.

I was answering questions by rote, not even paying attention. I could see in her eyes—flits now and then—that she wanted more from me. I didn't know what to do. I felt totally out of place.

And then, all at once, I just went blank, and everything got better. I somehow lost myself—I can't really explain it any better than that—and lost all the thoughts about what Livy was doing, about the way she was playing herself as a character, about the things I had to remember, the things I wanted to be careful about it. And I started channeling Spencer Tracy.

I might not know how to handle this situation, but Spence would. I knew the attitude he would have in this situation—his amusement at the wide-open girl now acting so prim, and looking even sexier for it, his self-assurance that things, though a little unorthodox, would work out the way they were supposed to. That kind of self-assurance that human beings not appearing in Hollywood films never possess.

And then our little scene just flowed. It wasn't brilliant, but it got better all at once, because, suddenly, I was coming from confidence. I might not have much confidence in myself as an actor, but I've got loads of confidence in Spence. And the audience agreed—the chat made it clear after that they wanted more.

We were off and running.

With Daniel

I had Daniel with me that weekend.

For the first time.

It took some doing to get him. Marla kept saying, "He's scared of going anywhere overnight" whenever I proposed the idea. If she'd been willing to reassure him, she could have allayed those concerns, but of course she wouldn't.

So I was left to bring it up myself, crudely, bluntly—the only way I know, not the standard of behavior Marla approves of.

Tough.

I went over on a pre-arranged Tuesday night to take him out to dinner, and I knew it was time to bring it up. I waited until the end of a nice evening.

He was hungry to play as soon as I picked him up. The boy needs to pretend, to let those voices out of his head, like most people need to eat and drink. I was just the same at his age— socially inept and immature, overflowing with energy and voices inside demanding attention.

We play Flintstones (I am Barney), Yogi Bear (Boo-boo), James Bond Jr. (I am M and Q and the bad guy) and Birdnet (a great version of Dragnet he's created, with him as Gannon and me as Joe Friday as portrayed by Tweety Bird—"thith ith the thity: Loth Angeleth, California...").

I try to find out what's actually going on in his life but all he wants to do is play. ET Part Two—ET returns to find Elliot a teenager and moved to New York. "And no government men," Daniel warns me. He will not tolerate anyone really bad in any of his stories.

It gets crazy sometimes—it becomes a real pressure, this constant need to play. I run out of energy long before he does and I struggle to keep up, to understand, not to become indifferent. We go to a deli for dinner—somehow they managed to drag a subway car into the middle of the place, for the patrons to eat in. A couple comes in with a 4 year old; he is scared of the train, that it might pull out if he gets in. The father keeps saying to his wife, "Just ignore him." I think to myself: Ignore your children and they'll grow up to be people who think it's okay to ignore their children.

Finally, we get home. "I love you," he says. "I love you too, buddy," I tell him, with a hug. It's painful to hold him. I know I have to let him go. I feel the hole in me—I've exchanged the hole that Marla left in my life for the one Daniel leaves. It's almost easier when I don't see him so often, but that's no answer to anything. He needs to see me, and I need him. He's the only reason that anything feels real to me.

Marla comes to the door—my door, the home we bought after I pulled every string I could think of to make the mortgage match our bank account.

Now's the moment. "Daniel, I would like you to come stay with me for a weekend. I have an apartment near the ocean."

Marla's immediately angry—she feels I'm manipulating the situation. Of course I am—the same way she has. There's no way to play this that doesn't do that somehow.

"Is it ten minutes away?" he asks. He's always been afraid of getting away from home. He hates holidays, when we go to family, and vacations if we're not home. He's spent all our vacations saying "When do we go home?" and then saying "That was a great trip" as soon as we get back.

"No," I say. "It's about an hour away. It's near the ocean, and you would have to sleep with me on a fold-out couch."

"A fold-out couch?" he asks, suddenly thrilled. Marla and I both know instantly that I've won.

"Yeah," I say, my nerves settling. "There's a mattress inside the couch—you pull it out to go to sleep."

"You don't have to if you don't want to," Marla says, both an out and a subtle suggestion. If she thinks I'm letting that go unchallenged, she's nuts.

"I have an idea," I say immediately. "This weekend, I'd like to bring you down there. You can look it over. If you don't like it, you tell me and I'll bring you right back home." I turn to Marla. "I don't want to coerce him. I want him to be comfortable."

She's defeated and she knows it. He hasn't said a word yet, but the way he's looking at her, it's clear he wants to go. It's also clear from his expression that she's already made it clear, in some subtle way, that he *shouldn't* want to. I squash the bitter thoughts that are flirting around the edges now. No time for this. Maybe later, but now I stay focused.

"If you want to go," she says to him softly," you can go." He shouldn't have to wait for her to say that—I'm his damn father. But as soon as she says it, he hugs me—and hugs her. I have my shot.

That Friday, I pick him up from school. Marla wants me to take him after dinner, but I insist—he'll be less antsy seeing a new place in daylight.

When I get to the school and he's there and runs to the car and we drive away, free and clear, just the two of us, I feel a swelling in me that's almost indescribable.

We drive down—and we play. He pours out new stories, combining characters from cartoons, game shows, Regis Philbin (very short distance required to turn this guy into a cartoon character) and Albert Einstein. Einstein becomes a superhero—he can fly and figure things out, knows karate to beat the bad guys and talks like Ludwig Von Drake. Which, I realize, is probably who Ludwig Von Drake was supposed to be anyway, so things come full-circle here.

As I see this need of his—it didn't seem so desperate when I lived at home, maybe because we tapped the well every day—I recognize my own.

Those stories in my head—the ones I'm pouring out on my website now—I need them, I need to get them out of me, the same way he does. The need is visceral—and apparently, genetic.

When I met Marla, I gave up wanting to write. I told myself I was through playing, that it was time to just grow up and make a living.

I made a living—and continued writing, fitfully. I wasn't ruthless about it, protective of the time and solitude needed to make it work. Which was good, since Marla just tolerated it. She never understood all the time I devoted to this enterprise, time that would have been so much better spent buying things or on another job to enable us to buy more things. And in the back of my mind, I felt ashamed I was letting her down—I knew she was more real, more practical than I was.

Only now do I know she was wrong. Now, looking at Daniel and his stories, I see how central it is to my happiness. And I see the price in anger and frustration—at myself, and at her—that I paid in denying it.

We park alongside the house and Daniel scopes out the seawall and the river at the two ends of the street. Then he goes inside.

I'm no fool; I open the fold-out couch immediately. He insists on opening and closing it three times.

"We get to sleep *here*?" he yelps, and I relax.

Finally we close it up and survey the rest of the place. Other attractions turn out to be the stall shower—all seagreen tile!—and the new computer I've built with a DVD player that plays movies!! He loves this—and he shows a frightening interest in Jennifer Lopez' Website. I haven't given a moment's thought to the traditional father-son talk, but maybe it's time...

We sit on the porch swing for a few minutes. He snuggles up to me—I put my arm around him. He says, "I love you, Daddy." Heaven's got nothing on this. Then he says, "You smell *good*." And again, as seems to happen to me so often in this place, I remember my father.

I remember staying at home alone with him one weekend when my mother was away somewhere. And he wanted me to sleep in the bed with him, because he was lonely without her. It was one of the few inklings I had over the years of his feelings for her, because neither of them showed their feeling real easy. My mother adored him and was devoted to him forever—she refused to even date another man after he died. But she was never the type of person who found it easy to show her feelings, and I think—

with him being as emotional and bighearted as he was—that it frustrated him as time went by.

But I remember his smell, lying in that bed watching him snore—I remember it still. A sweetish smell, not strong but definitely there. I remember how close I felt then, just from the smell of him. And now here is Daniel with me. I've worked so hard to make sure our relationship is very different from mine with my dad, but clearly, some things don't change.

We sit for a while, in simple peace. This is something I can't remember doing—ever. He is usually fidgeting with fifty things he wants to do. But now we sit, in bliss.

Eventually, it ends, of course. He says, "Let's go to the beach!" and jumps up. Early October and it's still hot as hell. Somewhere, George Soros is hording the world's freon—once he gets it all, *then* the politicians will admit there's Global Warming.

We change into our suits and trudge across the street and over the seawall. He loves the seawall. A typical 10-year-old boy, he sees it as a fort from which to fire imaginary bullets down on unsuspecting pedestrians. After picking off 10 or 15 innocents, we clamber down through the sand to the water.

It's low tide. The waterline is way out. We walk the dense wet sand, littered with stones and shells, down to the green roiling f0am.

We dive into the cold water and swim out a little ways. Daniel's been swimming since he was nine months old—he's a good strong swimmer. He knows how to handle the waves, and they aren't strong this time of day.

About twenty feet out, we stop and stand—it's only about four feet deep. Daniel splashes some water in my direction and I splash back.

With both of us laughing, I look down to splash some more and stop dead. I'm trying to figure out why the water is black. At first I think it's oil in the water, but as I move, it moves—*they* move, I realize.

"Daniel—look at the water!" I exclaim, feeling a shiver up my spine.

"What is it?"

"Look—fish!"

We're standing in the middle of a school of fish—millions of them. Silver fish, no more than five or six inches long, moving by us in a dense pack, enough of them to turn the sea black and shimmering.

Daniel looks into the water. His eyes widen. At first, he's frightened. Then his interest grows.

They flutter around us, the stream pulsing with the waves, constantly moving, constantly replenished, so endless it seems as if they're not moving at all, just hovering in place. They dart away from us when we stick a hand in the water—but the stream continues undisturbed, moving just a foot farther away—and slewing between us when we step a foot farther apart.

"Daniel?"

"What?"

"I've been coming to this ocean since I was a lot younger than you. I've never seen *anything* like this, ever."

"Wow!" he says, and he means it.

We stand in the same place for fifteen minutes—an eternity for this hyper child and his hyper father—the fish pouring between us, around us, until the stream finally lightens and we leave, amazed.

"I can't wait to tell mommy about this," he says. I nod—this is something to share. Then he continues, "I can't wait to have kids so I can tell them about it."

"Uh-huh," I nod slowly. We're definitely going to blaze new trails in the traditional father-son talk.

From that point, things go beautifully. We swim the next morning—another unseasonably warm day—like fish. Underwater half the time, then riding the waves, body-surfing for me, boogie-boarding for him.

Then I make lunch—I learn to make chicken nuggets in the oven, a new culinary step for me. I barbecue on a desk-radio sized hibachi I've bought, hot dogs and hamburgers, and even a little strip steak one day. In the afternoon, we go to a little children's museum, we rent DVD's and watch "Ghostbusters" or "Beetlejuice" or whatever gross film he wants. Or we go to the movies.

And we go to Sylvie's. I take him the first time because she begged me, wistfully, the night before I picked him up. "I love other people's children," she says. We go back because he instantly falls in love with her.

I'm shocked how quickly he takes to lacquering shells and pasting them onto masonite, painting colors onto the background first. He has a wonderful time, and insists on going back every day, much to her delight.

At night, we watch television—even with the site roaring, I'm not willing to break out of my Spartan regimen and buy cable. I'm stunned he survives.

I read him a book—he loves "Little Toot," about a tugboat that the other boats laugh at, who proves himself one day, of course. And then he goes to sleep around 9:30, leaving me several hours a night to work on Livy's site and mine, from my computer.

Sunday afternoon, we head back to Staten Island to drop him off. We pull up to the house at 5:59 pm—right on the money—and everything falls apart. She's not home—no car in the driveway. I pull over to the curb and try to settle him down.

"Mommy'll be home soon," I say. "No big deal."

He dissolves. He's in tears in seconds. "We have to go find her," he says, his voice cracking.

"It's okay, buddy, really—" I try to assure him. "She set this time up with me—she was real specific, so I know she'll be here any minute. Is mommy ever on time for anything?"

"No," he admits. I wasn't even sure he knew this about her.

"So she's a little late—no big deal." I take a quarter out of my pocket. "I'll bet you this quarter she's here in fifteen minutes." He looks at the quarter for a moment, but then he breaks into tears again. "I miss my mommy" he bleats.

Just tear my heart out, why don't you? Even before I had kids, I couldn't bear to hear a child cry—the purity of feeling was just heart-breaking. And now, to hear my own boy this way just chops me up. I put my arm around him, trying to smooth things over, patting his head and smoothing his hair. Not that it does a bit of good.

She shows up an hour later. As hysterical as he was before, he's even more now. He runs into her arms, and I carry his stuff to the door. He kisses me goodbye and snaps "You can keep your 25 cents" but I know he isn't angry at me—he just needs her. He needs us both.

Any kid in this situation has to have a fear—especially at first—of being abandoned by either parent. Let's face it—I put that fear there. I feel that one, in my stomach, for a long moment.

But then, I see the satisfied look on Marla's face as she leads him, crying and distracted, to the stairs. Not the look you'd expect from a concerned parent, but a look I've seen before, at times when I would get angry and she would be able to tell me what a creep I was for losing my temper. That familiar, totally inappropriate look of triumph I've seen before.

She wasn't just late getting home. She was an hour late on purpose, whether she'd admit it to herself or not. If he's going to go off to daddy's for the weekend, next time let him have the fear in the back of his mind that she won't be here when he gets back.

I am raging in the car all the way home, driving like a maniac, cursing every driver in front of me all the way back down the shore. The fact that she has it in her to do this to her own child—the fact that I *married* her, and she has it in her to do this. The fact that there's nothing I can do about it—and the fact that she probably doesn't know, and never will acknowledge, even to herself, that she did this at all—it's all too much for me.

I hate manipulation—it drives me crazy—and it has always been second nature to her, powered by a complete lack of self-awareness and therefore a complete lack of conscience.

I'm up late into the night, churning. He'll come back down here with me in two weeks, I know he will. She won't stop him— she'll just keep making it uncomfortable. At some point, this battle between us will come to a head, and I'll have to find a way to deal with it. But not yet.

Right now, I just miss my buddy. Lying in bed at night, I hear my own voice, with that same tone with which his voice tore into me, crying out for *him*. We're all trapped in this cycle of need and denial. If there's anyone that thinks there's justice in this world, he should be struck dead by lightning right now.

Safehouse Diary: The Marriage

I do not feel charitable toward my wife.

She separated me from my child. I no longer wake up with him having climbed into bed with me. I no longer hear him calling "Daddy!" when I walk into the house at night. Except on certain weekends and occasional weeknights when we've been able to arrange it, with the ceremony and security concerns of a state dinner.

She forced me to leave her and live in a leaky windy shack in a no-account town like this, wanting just as strongly as I can to forget everything that ever mattered to me a year ago.

She would deny any and all involvement in this. After all, I left her. As far as she's concerned, I'm insane, or suffering from a self-destructive preoccupation that keeps me from appreciating what I had.

So let's remember.

Marla is where I learned about unselfishness as a profession. Marla spent at least the last decade being noble about me. I got angry about things. I got angry when she lied to me. I got angry when she was heartless and uncaring. I got angry when she spent us into bankruptcy and even then didn't stop throwing money out the window.

When I got angry, I raised my voice, I broke mirrors, I threw things, I told her exactly what she had done to pissed me off—and I didn't apologize for being right. These were all unforgivable sins.

Marla was halfway through her second decade of selfless, loveless nobility when I validated it by leaving her.

And does she thank me? No.

Our whole relationship existed because of my feelings. That is so simply because she felt nothing. Without me, the void would have been obvious, and she might have had to deal with it.

Luckily, I was an out-of-control mess, which allowed her to put up with me. This became her continuing act of charity and nobility. She allowed me to live with her and be imperfect.

And now, in leaving, I've thoughtfully provided her the opportunity to be a deserted wife and mother, and that clearly has been even more fruitful and enjoyable for her than being married ever was.

The thing is, looking back, I'm not sure it isn't what she wanted all along. How else to explain things? When I started telling her I was miserable, that I wanted someone to love me back, she did nothing. When I found things we could do together that made us both happy, she did them when I provided them and got no pleasure from them. Or, if she did, the pleasure ended the moment the activity ended. Meanwhile, anything I did that annoyed her lived forever. She wouldn't give me the chance to fix any of these annoyances. She would just suffer in silence.

And I sat there, like a brainless schoolboy, trying to please her, asking her questions and getting no replies or grunted half-sentences and never admitting the truth:

that she had no interest in fixing anything.

That she was prepared to have a dead marriage and tear up our son and me and any prospects of happiness because she was so comfortable in her noble, unselfish isolation.

And that I hadn't realized any of this when it was obvious to anyone with half an eye open.

And that I hadn't acted on what I knew was true, even when all my senses were screaming it at me.

And so now, as I'm starting to develop new relationships, new friends, a new life, I realize why I get nervous about it. I've got an unreliable, dangerous, demonstrably stupid partner to deal with in this relationship.

Me.

~~~~

Bridge Out at the Rubicon

While I'd spent the weekend with Daniel, Livy had puttered around the house on camera, looking a little forlorn, not getting naked very much and commenting about me regularly to the guys on her chat.

Monday night, I logged onto her chat. She was nude at the moment, but still had the towel she'd used to dry off after her treadmill session sitting around her neck.

```
        MeekmanJ: I like you best on the
table. How bout getting on the table for
me?
        Safehouse: Hey, Seaviewgirl! How
was the weekend?
        SG: Hi Safehouse. Nice to hear
from you.
        Lottastuff: Yeah, the table is
good. Can you do a headstand?
        Safehouse: How about moving that
towel and giving me a good view of your
clavicle, baby?
        MeekmanJ: Get this guy outta here;
he's ruining everything.
```

```
    Seaviewgirl:  You  want  a  better
view, huh?  The  view  isn't  good  enough
for you?
    Safehouse:  The  view's  great.  But
I'm  dying  to  get  a  little  clavicle
action here, girl—how about it?
```

Now the clavicle—the collarbone—is not generally considered a terribly exciting part of the body. But I was feeling kind of silly, and she'd picked up on it. So now, Livy proceeded to do a brilliant parody of a striptease. She worked the towel back and forth a little, showing a little of her collarbone, just a flash here and there, lifting the edge of the towel for a moment.

```
    Safehouse:  Ooh,  that's  good.  Show
me a little more, please.
    Seaviewgirl:  C'mon—you  gotta  beg
for it.  Otherwise,  all  you  get  is  the
usual T&A action.
    Safehouse:  No,  not  that!  Please!
Give me that clavicle, baby!!
    Lottastuff:  Yeah,  baby—show  it!
Show it!
    Seaviewgirl:  I  told  you—you  have
to beg.
    MeekmanJ:  If  she  did  a  handstand,
we could all see it.
```

She kept up the collarbone tease—otherwise stark naked— for five minutes, until the whole chat had turned into a chorus chanting 'Clavicle! Clavicle!" It was a great moment.

> Safehouse: I had a real good time the other night. Want to do it again?
>
> Lottastuff: Hey, guy, the lady's gotta make a living, y'know?
>
> Seaviewgirl: Love to.
>
> Safehouse: Amazing what you can do with a towel. Have any other tricks?
>
> Seaviewgirl: I *can* do a headstand— want to see?
>
> Lottastuff: Hey, can we get a word in jhere?
>
> Safehouse: Can we see the blood rushing to your head?
>
> Lottastuff: She hasn't become transparent yet, buddy.

(Livy does a headstand on the floor right behind the table. With the keyboard on a long cord on the floor in front of her, she continues typing.)

> Seaviewgirl: Okay—if any of you guys can do this, I'll start coming to *your* chat.
>
> Safehouse: How's the bloodflow? You see the weasels crawling on the walls yet?
>
> Seaviewgirl: I don't get weasels on the walls from blood flowing to my head. I think you're just remembering the Sixties.
>
> Safehouse: In the words of David Crosby, if you can remember the Sixties, you weren't really there.
>
> MeekmanJ: Where are the weasels? I don't see em.

```
        Seaviewgirl:  Is  this  the  way  you
romance all your dates?
        Safehouse:  Only  the  ones  doing
naked headstands online.
```

So we went out again. I arranged for us to go to Rodrigo's, a nice little Spanish restaurant with a terrace along the ocean. Lance came out and shot us, on handheld camcorder with the wireless hookup. I had run through a few tests with him beforehand—he was a decent shooter if you didn't ask him to do anything fancy.

We got to the place just in time for the sunset to begin creeping across the sky. She looked gorgeous in a white slipdress, her hair pulled back behind her ears and little silver globe earrings, all tinted redgold in the autumn dusk. I wore the New York special—black shirt, black pants—but nobody, including me, was paying much attention to me.

We came out onto the patio, along the ocean, the waves licking the sand and the blue and purple bands bleeding across the sky. She wrapped her arm around mine and we walked down to the table together and it suddenly occurred to me that this was the kind of romantic time we'd never had before.

We ordered wine, a salad with shrimp in a green sauce and some tortilla chips. I watched her across the table. Her hair shined and flowed in the breeze, her green eyes shone like beacons. She was luminous.

She reached over and took my hand and there was the electricity again—the same electricity we had in bed, but now confined to our hands. I wanted to make love to her right there on the deck, but I just sat and enjoyed the breeze and the waves and the wine.

The pleasure didn't last long.

The next step was plotted out. We were just playing ourselves—as I said before, how hard could it be? All we had to do was chat politely and get through the evening, and we'd be a couple. Then everything was possible. Livy would be acting on the site as a girlfriend, we'd have a wealth of storylines we could play out over time—romance, sex, splitting up, boy loses girl, boy gets girl back, etc. She'd have the chance to establish herself as something more than a striptease, I'd be a boyfriend in the eyes of any future court dates. We'd be swimming along.

That was the plan.

"So, uh—what do you like to do?" I said, and stammered, dropping the words in the middle.

"Huh?" she said.

"I'm sorry—stupid question," I said.

"Why?" she asked, flustered for a moment.

"Well, I guess I know what you like to do, don't I? Watching you on the site and all..."

"Well, no," she said, getting visibly unhappy all at once. "That's not all I do."

"I didn't mean it's *all* you do," I responded immediately, trampling on her words. "I'm sure there are other things..." and my voice trailed off.

"Did you see that 'Frontline' show last night about adoption counseling?" she said and I nearly fell off my chair.

"Last night? Yeah, I saw it," I stuttered. I didn't see *much* of it, because I was busy doing handheld camera with her while she danced and painted, removed her clothes and made everyone happy, with that sober-sided PBS documentary droning on in the background.

"That kind of thing drives me crazy," she continued. "All these politicians droning on and on about legislation to make things 'regular'. Things *aren't* regular.   Just commercialize adoption and have some standards. The government can set those. But then get out of it."

"Commercialize it? Sell babies?"

"What's the other choice? Endless bureaucracy and a false sense of security for the rest of us? We all run around thinking these kids are taken care of, while the government can't get out of it's own way."

"But don't you think the government protects the kids somewhat? You want them just up for the highest bidder?"

"Kids don't care who raises them," she said flatly. "At least this way, they get the advantages of money."

It was an astonishing conversation. First off, I couldn't believe she'd actually heard the content of that broadcast—I couldn't remember a word of it. But, as we went on, it became clear that our views on things of the world were so different that it was hard to find much of anything to discuss without an argument. One or the other of us would state an opinion and a long silence would follow.

And that's how it went, the whole rest of the night. We didn't like the same films, or TV shows. I tried paintings, but she wouldn't touch the subject. We headed back to the apartment, and I put some music on that I liked—that I loved with all my heart. She laughed.

"Those guys can't sing," she said about the Band. Cut me with a knife, why don't you?

The problem was, we had really skipped the romance part. We never had a romantic evening. We started working together, we had sex and continued to work together, for the betterment of Livy Post, a limited liability corporation. We had shared that driving goal, and the sex. But the reality was, when it came to anything outside that, we had no chemistry.

When she'd kissed me goodnight, limply, and shut down the cameras, I came back upstairs and she exploded.

"What happened? You always have things to talk about. You never shut up. How come you didn't talk?"

"I tried. We just didn't connect," I protested. "Maybe we were just nervous—it was a real first date."

"Nobody would go to a second date, after that one," she said, accurately. "If we can't talk about anything, how the heck do we have a relationship?"

This had to be a serious problem, if she'd stopped cursing.

"We do things together," I told her. "We don't make small talk, either of us."

"Great—a couple of misanthropes, whose success rides on being charming on camera. There's a business plan."

She marched around the room. I could hear the drums in the background, just watching her.

"They don't have to find us interesting," she said, "But they have to believe we're a couple. How do we do that?"

I stared at her blankly for about thirty seconds until I realized the way she was looking at me. It wasn't a rhetorical question—she expected me to have an answer.

"I don't know what to tell you," I admitted.

"You *have* to," she said, and suddenly she was more vulnerable and alone than anyone I'd ever seen. "I *need* you to."

I threw my hands up.

"What do you want me to do? How should I know what to say? Who knows what they want?"

"*You* do," she said, forcefully. "You *have* to."

"Why *me*?" I barked back. "Who the hell am *I*, that I'm such an expert on them?"

"You *are* them," she said simply.

Alison

Lately, I've found myself daydreaming about Allison Stark.

It is proof of how far I've gone over the edge—or how disordered our relationship has become—that I can be sleeping with a 23-year-old exhibitionist thousands of guys stay up nightly panting over and I'm daydreaming about some middle-aged woman who might have died in 1976 for all I know.

In my life, she's always been the one that got away. More accurately, the one I let get away. Six months haven't gone by since I left for college that I haven't thought about her.

Allison was my wife's best friend in high school. Or actually, Marla was Allison's best friend—Allison definitely came first.

She had honey-blonde hair to the center of her back, long legs issuing from the shortest skirts I've ever seen, before or since, and the kind of offhanded innocent sexual aggressiveness you only possess before you've had much sex, when all you know is the fun, without the real-life mess of complications and mixed feelings.

I knew she would never go out with me—I knew this with the frightening certainty of a misfit sixteen-year-old. She was gorgeous, and friendly, easy with people in a way I still haven't mastered. She probably wasn't as popular as she seemed to me— she was too thoughtful and ironic to be in the pantheon with the jocks and cheerleaders—but nonetheless I knew I was never going out with her. The laws of teenagerdom are painful but not complicated, and I stuck by them, even when she laughed at my jokes and threw her own zingers back. She enjoyed my company, but I was too clueless to realize it.

That summer, I'd just started driving. I took my dad's car and drove down to the beach—this beach, actually. I drove from nearby Monmouth down to Seaview.

I want to say I drove down to meet girls, but that wouldn't really be true. I just went to the beach to be miserable, *wishing* I could meet some girls.

In the movie in my head, I am wearing a white t-shirt without logos—this is just before people started paying good money to advertise products on their own time—and blue jeans, with no patches. Patches as a fashion statement also came just a few years later.

I had summer friends in Seaview—the children of two families that came down from Brooklyn—Michael, Tommy and Becky. They sat, fully clothed, on the rock breakwaters that jutted out into the ocean. They smoked cigarettes and talked tough, but we got along for some reason. We had endless discussions about God's existence, the meaning of life and whether we were just a ping-pong ball on some intergalactic gaming table. We talked in deathly earnest about this stuff, and we thought it really mattered what we decided.

It was a scary and magical era, all at once. I had several friends just a year or two older who'd been sent to Vietnam and one or two who hadn't come back already. The fact that it was the kids with less money that were going was not lost on us, though we didn't know quite how to confront that fact. Except that it made us want to go to college real bad.

But it also was an era when everything in the world changed, every year. Styles of music, haircuts, slang, fashion — you'd wake up one morning six months later, and it all had changed. And another six months would go by and it would happen again.

Drugs, sex, Eastern religion — all these things started appearing on the radar screen of kids at these lazy New Jersey beaches. The drugs ranged from pot to speed, LSD to reds — amphetamines — all of which I was too scared to try, for a while.

While that world was frightening and unstable in a way I've never experienced since, there was still a feeling we could make our mark on it, that *anything* was possible — a feeling I've never experienced since, either.

With Michael and Tommy and Becky, this sense of possibilities took the form of an improv group. We started improvising scenes—other kids at the beach would throw situations at us and we would make up a scene, beginning, middle and end. We had no training, but we were just having fun, making it up as we went along. I got into character easy and fast and I was funny. Funnier than I realized, at first, because sometimes they were certainly laughing at me, not with me. But who cared? Suddenly, I was *good* at something.

Like all good improv groups, we had several savior bits, places we could take the scene if we were flailing, surefire endings. But we didn't use them much, since most of the audience was the same kids and they would have beat us heavily about the face and neck if we'd gotten lazy.

So we got to be beach celebrities. It never got us any money, but it knit us together.

I was sitting on the rock pier one day, playing improvs in front of a small crowd, when I looked up and saw Alison towards the back of the crowd, watching.

She had big round sunglasses and a two-piece bathing suit that was pretty racy then but wouldn't raise eyebrows in the lobby of the Plaza Hotel now. And she was watching me with a look of surprise and delight that is burned into my memory to this day.

Somehow, I didn't choke. Maybe because I realized she'd been watching for a while, there was no sense getting nervous.

Instead, I got a bit giddy, and we really took off, giving a great performance.

When it was over, I tried to be nonchalant for about ten seconds. Then *she* walked up to me.

"That was really good," she said, and any attempt at cool I'd had just fell apart.

"You think so?"

"It was really funny. *You* were really good. Why don't you do plays at school?"

"I don't know. I just don't fit in there."

"Well, you did great here."

I was flying. I wasn't used to success, especially with girls I wanted looking on. The experience was dizzying. I was so loose I wasn't thinking at all about what I was doing or saying.

"Thanks. How'd you get here?"

"I took the bus."

"You need a ride home?"

"Sure," she said without hesitating. If she'd thought about it for just a moment, I probably would have realized what I was doing and fainted. As it was, I was just acting naturally, without any thought at all—something I just didn't do at that age. Something I'm just learning to do now.

"I'm hungry," I said, as we headed for the parking lot. "Have you had lunch?"

"Nope."

"Wanta go to Toddy's?"

"Okay," she smiled.

It was only once we'd gotten into my father's car and pulled out onto Ocean Ave., heading for the local diner, that I realized I'd asked the girl out on what might be construed as a date—and she was going!

Normally, I would have frozen at that point, but we were past the danger zone—she'd already agreed to go, and she was looking at me like I was George Harrison or something. So I relaxed, we went to lunch and had a really great time.

We talked and joked and laughed and then I took her home and that was it. I didn't call her. Didn't have the nerve. Figured it for a fluke, and did nothing to make things otherwise. The following year, we had no classes together and I didn't see her very much. I would have had to take a chance on actually blatantly, openly, asking her out. So, of course, I didn't.

When we graduated, we all ran the halls the last day or two, getting signatures and remembrances in our yearbooks. I still have the book—it was in a box I had in storage. Marla dumped several of them on me when I picked up Daniel last weekend. I went through them slowly, after I'd dropped him back home on Sunday. In my yearbook, Alison wrote, "I'll never forget that wonderful week we had."

We had one afternoon. I remember acutely the pain I felt, the first time I read that note and realized what a fool I'd been.

I went on to college, thinking there'd be other romances. And there were. But Alison was always there in the back of my mind, and several years later, I came home looking for her. Alison wasn't around, but Marla, her best friend, was. I saw Marla to pump her for information about Alison, and found that Marla was interested. We started going out, she was eager, Alison wasn't around and we ended up married a year later. In our fifteen years together, we never spoke about Alison once.

But she remains, as she always has, in the back of my mind, with her light step, ready at any moment to emerge from that crowd of remembered and barely remembered faces, with that quizzical bemused look still on her gorgeous face. And I know, somehow, that seeing her in my mind's eye means no good for any other woman in my life at the moment.

Rough Waters

It is another Daniel weekend. I pick him up Friday afternoon at home.

I don't even see Marla. I honk at the door, he comes out a moment later with his stuff and we take off.

I'm elated—this is too easy—every other weekend has demanded at least a quarrel at the door, while she lays out rules and conditions for that dangerous two-day period when he's outside her sphere of influence.

As we turn from the main drag near the house onto the highway, there is a green Taurus wagon about five cars back that makes the turn as well, going the same way we are. I notice it. I keep my eye on it.

How does the mind work? What is the ticklish instinct that says, 'Pay attention to *this*'? Not a question I can answer, certainly. But for some reason, that Taurus has my attention.

So, as we drive south and play Daniel's stories on the highway, I glance at the rearview mirror and confirm that yes, the

Taurus is still there. I slow down a little, and he doesn't get any closer.

And again, still there when we turn off for Seaview. There's a long bit of highway before we actually reach the bridge onto the little peninsula, and the Taurus stays with us—always at a respectable distance, several cars back—almost all the way down. Then, as we mount the last hill before the dive to the shore, it turns off into a strip mall.

Idiot. You make yourself crazy over nothing. I plunge into one of Daniel's tales, where he is a Junior X-man in training, developing claws and controlling my mind.

And then, at the bottom of the hill, way back in traffic, is a green Taurus wagon.

Is it the same one? How can I tell? He was never close enough to read the license plate, assuming I'd had the presence of mind to think of that.

Now I'm humming pretty hard. Once I see him cross the bridge, I'll be pretty sure he's not friendly, whoever he is. But by that time, I won't have much room to maneuver. Do I really want him to know where I live? I have to decide: either I go over the bridge and head home, or I turn off onto a side road now and run away from him.

But then a little sanity intrudes on the paranoia. If this guy meant me harm, we've just driven long stretches of Parkway with no one around—he could easily have forced me off into woods or marshes if he was determined to do so. He doesn't want to hurt me—he wants to know where I live. And I decide it might be better off if I let him.

If I just go home, and show no sign that I've picked him up, I'll know what to look for. The streets are small and short—he'll have to park nearby. I'll be able to see him coming. If I alert him that I'm paying attention, he might get more clever and I'll be the one caught out.

So we head home.

It's a strange weekend. I have been nursing a cold for a few days, and the next morning, it turns into flu-like symptoms and then, when I actually go to the drugstore and buy a thermometer, a temperature of 101°. I call a doctor and get an appointment squeezed in at 3 that afternoon. I scan the streets nearby—no Taurus anywhere in sight.

Daniel wants to play—is desperate to tell his stories, as usual. But they require me to be engaged, to participate, and I am way underpar here.

I tell him I'm sick and not feeling well. I explain that he has a lot of energy and I can't keep up with him right now. I tell him he's 10 and I'm 45, roughly. My age is slipping backward as I get older.

He listens—he cares. He wants to understand. Then, as soon as I finish talking to him, he shoves a toy in my hand and says, "*Now* will you play with me?"

And then I bark. "Daniel," I snap, "You're being very selfish now and I don't like it. I'm sick and you have to think about something other than *you* once in a while."

He gets mad. "It's not fair," he says and stalks off. "You *never* want to play with me."

I follow him into the other room. I shouldn't, but I always do it anyway.

"What did I do the last three hours?" I demand.

"Play with me," he answers, honest to a fault.

"So what's your problem?" I wait for an answer.

"I—I—" He raises a little plastic screwdriver I bought him, part of his toolkit, as though threatening me with it. I stare him down. He puts it back on the table. He wouldn't hurt a fly, I hope. But this is not the first time he's raised a tool, or his hand, as though to strike.

"This is what you've got to work on, buddy. You get angry and you say things you don't mean. I know what that's like—I did it with mommy, and it led to a lot of our unhappiness. I don't want you to make the same mistakes I made."

He's still mad at me. He looks at me, sullen for the moment, and simply says, "Jerk."

It stings, boy. I blink a few times from the blow, and he sees it.

"I'm sorry," he says, repentant instantly.

"That hurt," I tell him.

"I'm sorry," he repeats.

"I don't care if you're sorry. First you hurt, then you say you're sorry. It doesn't make it better. You have to do fewer things that you're sorry for."

He dissolves into tears, and now I'm instantly repentant. "I'm sorry, daddy," he oozes.

I grab him, and pull him to me. "I know you are," I say. And I know he is. I know from being there.

I am doing the same with him that I did with his mom — lashing out with my tongue. Putting him in his place. Being right. Diminishing him when he badly needs reasons to feel good about himself.

With him in my arms, I realized I can't lose him, at least not yet. I'm still his Daddy, for now. My flaws are overwhelmed by his need. But that won't last forever. I don't like his behavior, but I also don't like that guilt, too easily roused and too powerfully stored. Someday, and maybe not too far down the road, there'll be a reaction.

"Listen buddy," I tell him. "I'm not feeling great this weekend, and I get afraid that you won't want to be with me if we don't always have a *great* time. So maybe I over-reacted a little. You understand?"

Zip! The sound of words going right over his head. But at least now *I* understand it. He's my son—he tolerates Daddy foaming at the mouth—it's nothing new. He starts to cry again. He melts into my arms and says, "I don't want you to die."

Huh? "What are you talking about?"

"You're going to the doctor. You're going to die."

"I'm not dying," I tell him firmly. "Not for a long time, buddy. No way. I'm just sick—I'm going so I can get better."

"Oh, okay," he starts laughing, nervousness subsiding.

It's such a short time that they so badly want to be just like us. And we want so badly for them to be something so much better.

"I love you, buddy."

"I love you, Daddy."

He does, too.

Generations of Pain

I sit on the porch with my journal book, in the middle of the night, listening to the rain drip off the tin roof.

Trying to get tired, afraid to get tired. I've done this all my life, listening to rain, rocking on the porch, trying to relax, trying to escape.

I have nightmares I can barely recollect. I sleep, but get no rest.

I can't remember the nightmares, the details, no matter how hard I try. What little I remember leaves no clear impression, except they were about Marla and Daniel. About leaving them. About being bad.

Marla's demanding marriage counseling now. After years of refusing to go when I begged her, now she's raking me over the coals if I deny her this 'chance to make everything right.' She's made it clear this is a phase I'm going through, she understands I need to get it out of my system so I can return to her. I made the trek north last night, to drop Daniel off and talk about it. Instead of denying every complaint I ever had—as she did for fifteen years—she now admits they were all true and wraps herself in guilt.

The truth is, I don't care. I don't trust her anymore. I don't believe what she says. You can rekindle passion, but how do you get trust back when it's obliterated? The fact that she can make a 180° turn in a month and a half only makes it harder to take her seriously. She wants me back, and she'll do whatever she thinks it'll take to reach her goal. That's the same way she got me to marry her—excuse me, learned that lesson, sweetie.

But there's no triumph in that knowledge.

The optimism has burned off, the thrill of being on my own has died down. I am saving myself—at least I'm trying to—but I am abandoning Daniel, forever. Leaving him to live with Marla and me to live on my own. No matter how much I see him, he'll be hers, with me as the second parent. And as soon as she finds someone else—and knowing her, that won't take long—maybe not even that.

I'm saving myself—and I'm ashamed of it. And I don't know what else I can actually do.

The rain pours down in sheets. I listen to the sound—and find that I'm listening to the sound of rain on a roof five miles away, farther down the shoreline, the house in Monmouth where I grew up, where I sat on the porch as a child and learned to listen to the rain. My room was on the ground floor, right off the porch—my grandparents lived upstairs—and when it rained and I couldn't sleep, I would climb through my bedroom window and sit on the porch and just listen to the sound, until it soothed me enough to get back to sleep.

It was my father's house. Somehow, without my ever meaning to or even consciously thinking about him, my mind in this place keeps returning to my father. Everything that happens, particularly when I'm with Daniel, or dealing with Marla, seems to come back to him, and I'm damned if I know why.

My dad was not a big man, but he carried a big impression around with him. (My dad was 5'8", but his impression was 6'4", 260.) Everything about him was outsized—his anger, his affection, his need to be right and his competitiveness.

I always lived in fear of disappointing him, and I always disappointed him.

My father was a salesman—he had a mattress store on Rte. 9. He never tried to sell a customer something they couldn't afford. But he worked hard, he had routines concocted, to find out exactly how much they had to spend and to make sure he got every penny of that and a little more (because people always had a little more money than they originally planned to spend).

He did well enough from this little hole-in-the-wall store to have two homes, a good vacation every year, money put away for the future and to put my sister and I through college.

His only other interest—not surprisingly—was buying stuff. He and my mother would go on antiquing expeditions, carting home plates and plaques, ashtrays and lamps with stuffed squirrels wrapped around tree trunks. These would be carefully placed around the several wings of the house, and then forgotten. And then they would go out and buy more stuff.

He nursed a lifelong grudge against Franklin Roosevelt for sending him to war. I've been tempted many times to make light of this—to pretend he was joking. But I know he wasn't. It was particularly strange that my father, the committed Jew who built several synagogues and decorated the house with menorahs and religious paintings and sat devoted shiva for his father for a year, objected so bitterly to helping crush the Nazis. But somehow, Roosevelt had interfered with his life and that made him angry— just like drivers who made moves he hadn't anticipated and waiters who didn't come quickly enough and customers who couldn't make the decision to buy and buy now.

Being frustrated and angered by these things came out of my father on an almost atomic level. I thought for a long time that he had a genetic need to get annoyed. It was part of the fabric of life that others disappointed him, didn't live up to his standards, didn't do what he thought was good for them (which had an uncanny correlation, most of the time, to the things that were good for *him*).

His anger was fierce, frightening. He would yell and his face would get red and he would become completely incoherent. He would spout manifestos against the offenses that had set him off.

At times, these could be truly profound flaws, serious concerns for mankind or simply for people he knew and cared about—he cared an awful lot about a lot of people—but other times, he could summon the same anger over tiny slights or things people hadn't even done yet but might do in the future and that would offend him mightily if they did.

And I found, when I got married, that I carried that anger in me, and that it popped up again, torturing both Marla and me, early in the marriage. It took me years of working to get it under control, and by the time I started getting it, it was a hollow victory. Marla was gone—physically in the house, but just not there anymore. No matter what else happened, I made the first breach in the wall, and Marla couldn't—or wouldn't—get over it.

And now I have nightmares...again.

I woke up in the middle of the night once years ago and was able to remember a snatch, just the tiniest bite of a dream—a nightmare. And I knew, without knowing how, that I'd been having the dream over and over again for years.

The piece I could remember was a singsong voice—my own voice—chanting "You'll die in the gutter. You'll die screaming in the gutter." My theme song, apparently.

It's been ten years since that evening, that awakening, but I still hear the sound of that voice. It's still inside me. It's the sound of me pulling against myself, and it scares me more than anything else I can think of.

I can see the gutter yawning very close by. It's a fight to stay out of it, and I'm fearful that in wrestling with me, I'll find that the evil is the stronger twin. That all this creative stuff I cling to is vanity, that Daniel will stop caring about me eventually and I'll be left with nothing, really nothing.

In my minds eye, my father steps out of a warehouse. He is young, in a sepia tone picture—young and thin and with that curious half-smile of his and his impossibly wavy hair. All at once, I can see his exuberance and his frustration, the conflicts, petty and major, with his business, with my mother and her distant way of expressing herself—and certainly with me. He seems like a boy to me at this moment, always demanding, always dependent on approval.

All at once, it hits me. He wanted *my* approval. Always. He intimidated me and scared me, he blustered and yelled and fought. He was fighting with himself. He was frustrated because we didn't love him back—he thought. I adored him, and still do. He's my Daddy and will be forever. With all my fear of his anger, I never doubted that he loved me with all his heart and would have done anything for me if he could. He just couldn't show it, and I reacted to what he showed, forever denying him the approval he was after.

Marla was the same deal. She couldn't show what she felt, and she is so afraid of disappointment...that she creates disappointment over and over. Just like my father. Could that have been in the back of my mind when I met her? Could I have known, in some part of my psyche that never has to answer a roll call, that she somehow, in some crucial part of her, reflected my Daddy?

And now I think of *his* father. My grandfather married a prickly woman who ran an exacting household. When he was 71, he developed cancer and she threw him out of the house. He lived with us for two years until he died. I'll never forget that, and I'll never stop being haunted by it. I thought of it constantly when I decided to leave Marla.

I'm suddenly overwhelmed by the pattern, the history, the thread of need and denial that has passed through three generations of the men in my family. My grandfather and his distracted wife, my father choosing a wife who loved him endlessly but showed it cautiously—and me. I chose a wife who continued the pattern. But that's where the trail ends—where it *must* end.

You can't make someone love you more than they do. You can't make them show it more than they can. But sometimes it's necessary to say, I'm not getting what I need. I know you're doing the best you can, but I need more. Even if I wrecked it, even if it's my fault that you can't feel anything more for me, I need to grow past that mistake. I need to do better.

I need a lot, and I need to have it, to hold it, to know, for sure, that I'm loved back. I need hugs and kisses and someone who'll be transparent with me, hiding nothing, trusting me and earning my trust. Maybe I'll get there and maybe I won't, but it's the only place worth trying to get to. And I have to get there, not just for myself, but to stop infecting anyone else—Daniel—with the same pattern, the same frustration. I've got to show him some better alternative than love as frustration or as an eternal tease. These generations of pain have got to stop *here*.

I sit up in the chair, startled, as though waking up all at once from anesthesia, and take a deep breath. I feel like I haven't been able to breath for years, and now I can. All at once, I get the pattern, I understand the nightmares—I know what I'm afraid of.

Just keep going, boy. One step, then another. Eventually you get somewhere. Maybe not where you wanted to go, but where you're meant to go. Just breathing, trying to get back to sleep, listening to the rain on the roof. The roof here and the roof down the highway, down the highway through the years. The soothing, peaceful sound of rainfall. That's the point.

At least, I thought that was the point when I sat down and started to write.

New York Times, August 13, 1998:

...statistics on Web use show that women are slowly closing the gap with men in terms of their interest in sexually explicit on-line material...

'I have a lot of trouble finding sites created for women by women,' said Jane Duvall, whose site, Jane's Net Sex Guide, reviews sexually explicit content of all kinds. 'And that's a pity because the Net lets you be anonymous and look at material from the safety of your home. So it's tailor-made for women—who wouldn't be caught dead in an adult video store, say—to work out the sexual inclinations.'...

'Women are interested in exploring their sexuality on line, but what has clearly been lacking is adult entertainment on the scale of what is found for men,' said Anne Semans, co-author of 'The Woman's Guide to Sex on the Web'...

~~~~

Turning the Screw

I showed up at Livy's the next morning steaming with ideas.

"We have to regroup," I said. "It's time you did some interviews. I know some people; I should be able to get you a national magazine—you'll just have to be a good enough story to get a couple of pages, instead of a couple paragraphs."

"Uh-huh. You have a story that will get me a couple of pages?"

"Yup. 'Erotica you can bring your girlfriend to.'"

I said it once, and watched her soak it in. A smile came over her face, and she nodded. "That's pretty good," she said.

"*Pretty good*?" I protested. "What guy wouldn't want *that*? A place to get your sweetie horny *with* you? That's not just 'pretty good'—that's the holy grail."

She kept nodding now, eyes staring into the distance, thinking it through. "Okay—that's a done deal. We're doing it," she said.

"And I have another idea," I continued, "to make sure the interview gets some play."

She made me explain it, naturally. Livy doesn't trust anything when it comes to her career—she'll make the decisions, thank you. But twenty minutes later, we were set, ready to begin the next campaign. sI had decided that she didn't mean what she'd said, about me *being* the audience. It didn't matter anymore anyway, I told myself, but I also knew it wasn't the whole story.

Her comment had sent me into a funk at the beginning, because it was just close enough to the truth to be scary. I was probably about the age and background of the regular members. Certainly, what I liked was probably what they liked. And she was obsessed enough with them that she could have chosen to be with me, just to know what they wanted.

But somehow, that's not what it felt like. Somehow, as I thought about it, it felt more like the rationalization hiding the real craziness inside. The neurotic tic you admit to, in order to keep hidden the even more neurotic tic underneath.

It took a few days to set up the interview. I knew some producers from my TV days who were now magazine writers, and 'erotica for the whole family' put us in *Rolling Stone*—Livy agreed to several photos, as nude as they'd allow, and they agreed to show some of the tamer webcam pictures.

Roling Stone was a big 'get'—a big audience, a magazine always willing to be a little disreputable—we'd get a photo of her in there that would never make *People*, for example. Not that we were big enough for *People* yet. But the *Stone* also had Gap ads. We coveted Gap ads.

The writer, Karen Shimkus, was going to spend two days with Livy, watching her work, and doing the interview while Livy was online, so she could get reaction to her questions from the chat group as well.

Karen was a good friend. She agreed up front that I was not to be named in the article, just identified as a 'romance Livy is beginning with a local middle-aged former tv executive, that is being played out online, like everything else in her life.' Okay, so she exaggerated my position—I was a middle-level guy, not an exec—but magazines do that with everyone.

Karen seemed genuinely impressed with Livy, which didn't surprise me—Livy's passion was touching and affecting to anyone who's ever wanted to be somebody, even if most of us don't admit how strong the hunger is. Livy does, and I knew Karen would be honest enough to respond to it.

But I caught Karen looking sideways at *me* a few times. This was not the kind of enterprise she expected to find me in, based on our days at the network. I had to admit, it wasn't the kind of thing *I* would have expected of me either—but I was all the better for it, I felt.

That night, Livy was supposed to do a full evening's erotica—art, treadmill, striptease and chat—with Karen and a photographer. I figured it was time for the coup de grace—I arranged for Lance to show up in costume.

"I was wondering when you were going to call," he said when I called him. "You can't wait so long between appearances— if he gets too desperate, you can't tell *what* might happen."

"'He?'—Who's 'he', Lance? The Pale Guy?"

"Yeah, you don't know what he might—"

"Lance, he's a character we made up. I can tell *exactly* what might happen, because I write the story."

"Sure, sure," Lance mumbled. "But he won't like it. Anyway, the fans won't like it."

"The *fans*?"

"Yeah, I have my fans," he answered, in a tone that dared me to be surprised by this.

"Where do you get in touch with your fans?" I asked, trying to figure out how this was possible.

"I took the name 'PaleGuy@hotmail.com'—you should see all the mail I get."

Be calm, I told myself. Pretend he's your ten-year old. Think of something to say that doesn't start with 'You ignoramus.'

"Lance, let's try to focus here. You have fans of the Pale Guy writing you at hotmail—is that correct?"

"Sure. They think he's really cool, and I really got to understand his motivation and stuff, talking to them."

My lower lip was going to bleed if I bit it any harder.

"Lance, what if—just for argument's sake—the police decided to take our little game seriously? Like tomorrow night, for example, when you're supposed to appear in front of a writer and photographer from a national magazine. You have to give your real email address to hotmail, don't you?"

"Oh come on—I'm not an imbecile," he said, unpersuasively confronting the foremost question in my mind. "I use my friend's old free email—he died in a store fire last year. They can't trace it to me."

I gulped hard and moved on. I mean, this is the 21st Century—Andy Warhol is old hat already, conventional wisdom—why shouldn't the Pale Guy have a fan club?

"Lance, you don't have any other email addresses, do you?" I was still a little freaked about the email I'd gotten from 'the real' Pale Guy—it couldn't be Lance, could it?

"No. Just mine and his," he mumbled, absently enough that I believed him. Lance was beyond weird, but, despite his size, there was nothing really threatening about him. I couldn't imagine him writing those notes.

So we started preparing for the nights extravaganza. We would have a decent audience—Livy had told the regulars she had a photo shoot that night, so they'd go online for that—and we'd have a national magazine witness to the dangerous stalker who was menacing the plucky Webcam artist.

Lance and I painstakingly worked out the mechanics of his appearance. I had rigged up a harness on the flat roof of the house, that would allow him to lower himself down onto the deck behind Livy, and then raise himself back up to the roof again. Once on the roof, he'd work his way across to the spare bedroom, get into his policeman's uniform and go outside to take the police report. It was—literally—too neat to be true.

That night, we're all in the living room—me working the cameras, Karen and the photographer coaching Livy through the shoot—and the Pale Guy suddenly hovers down onto the deck in the background. I kept one eye on the chat groups and the posts exploded when Lance showed up.

Karen saw it too. She was asking Livy questions and taking answers from her and the chat group, and she saw the first couple of Pale Guy sightings and swiveled around in her chair, looking to the deck.

"Who the hell is *that?*" she exclaimed. Just like in the script.

Lance moved, moved his shoulders and his arms, pulsing, as though trying to grab at Livy through the glass. Then he *glided* across the deck.

I'd suggested it to him originally just because he'd insisted on some motivation, something to work on as an actor. But he actually got it down, and it was positively bizarre to watch. He glided as though his feet never touched the ground. I could hear the harness scraping slightly on the roof above, but no one else seemed to notice.

Livy and Karen stepped back from the windows, toward the kitchen. Karen looked more frightened than Livy. This was going just according to plan.

And then the stupid photographer decided to get heroic. I'd seen that he was enjoying his work, shooting Livy. He'd been flirting all day, and she'd been flirting back—that's one way to make sure you get good photos: seduce the photographer. Livy couldn't help but seduce every man she met anyway—this was just one more. But now he decided the scene needed a pointless act of heroism, to impress the girl.

Before Lance could get back in position to hover up to the roof again, the photog barged through the doorway and tried to tackle him. Visions of doom raced through my head in that one split-second as the photographer hurtled toward my monster.

Lance shocked me by sidestepping lightly—the photog went hurtling right past him. Then Lance lifted him bodily off the deck and deposited him upside down in a tall planter we'd intended to put a tree in someday. While Karen was calling 911 and I was thanking God, the Pale Guy hovered back up onto the roof and disappeared.

Karen turned around and saw Lance's feet flying up above the deck windows and yelped, "Where is he *going*?"

"I'll check the roof—you stay here and protect her," I yelled and ran for the guest bedroom.

Lance was inside, gasping for breath and clutching his chest. "You didn't tell me about that!"

"I didn't *know* about that! He's a freelance—he's on his own. We've got to get you out of here!"

"You mean I don't get to be the policeman?" Lance complained, between wheezes.

I could hear the sirens on their way. "I think we're going to have some *real* policemen here in a few minutes. Get out of that costume and get down on the floor in the back of my car—now!"

I waited long enough to see him clamber down the stairs and hide. Then I opened the door and yelled, "I see him! I'm going after him!"

"Let me come with you," Karen called back.

"Somebody's got to watch Livy, just till the police arrive," I yelled, and slammed the door behind me.

I hurtled down the stairs—I had to get out of there before the police arrived or Karen was able to follow. I pulled the car out of the drive and around the turn—I could see the flashing lights a block away. I drove at a nice moderate speed until we made it to the highway. Then Lance and I had coffee for an hour and I dropped him back at his car, three blocks from the house.

When I got back, everyone had had a few drinks to calm their nerves. Karen said, "What happened to you?"

"I almost caught him, a couple of times," I answered. "He kept ducking through backyards and when I got around to the other side, he was just gone—vanished. I caught sight of him three times, but whenever I got close, he would disappear. The guys *magic.*"

"He lifted me like a loaf of bread," the photographer said. Livy was bandaging the bump on his forehead where he'd been dumped into the planter.

"This guy is really scary," Karen said to Livy. "You should think about a full-time bodyguard."

"That's a good thought," I agreed. "We'll have to look for somebody."

"Well, I've got my alarm squad," Livy said, pointing at the now-black monitor flickering at the table. She'd turned off the feed for the night, claiming upset and exhaustion—but the chat group was moving a mile a minute, the exhilaration of a Pale Guy sighting juicing the troops. "Those guys won't let anything happen to me.

Date 3

The *Rolling Stone* article hit the next week. It was a sensation. We doubled our hits overnight. Subscriptions were up by 50%. Livy was once again a happy girl.

Three nights after that, we had our third date.

We had no choice about it, and that was mystifying. The previous date had felt like a total disaster, to both of us 'on the ground' in the middle of it.

But no one in the audience seemed to have noticed. Or, tantalizingly, it seemed that our miserable date had actually worked in our favor.

We'd had a dull date. We hadn't connected at all. In a Hollywood film, that would have been the death knell—the audience would have been streaming into the other cells at the multiplex, getting free looks at the also-rans.

But this was the Internet—and everything on the Internet looks like real life. Not only was a mediocre, uninspired date not a shock in real life—it actually seemed to have fired up the audience about us as a couple.

Livy was getting dozens of posts from women, who suddenly seemed to relate to her, now that she wasn't this infallible guy magnet. The vulnerability that was all too obvious in real life had found a way through the screen.

And my site got a huge spike in users again, but the tone was different—now they were determined to help me be a good boyfriend, a better date. The goal was still the same—it always is—but the approach was more subtle.

The details were interesting, but the message was clear—our audience *expected* us to get together again. Some of them thought I was okay, some thought I was a dork, others that I was way too old for her—but everyone had an opinion. Which meant they cared. Which meant we were on the right track.

But we were scared to death about it. Livy was nearly twitching the afternoon before. She told me she was throwing me out at 1pm, so she could 'prepare.'

"We can't have two in a row like the last one," she warned me. "We got lucky once, but it won't do a second time. I've been reading their posts. They're going to be watching, and they expect something hot. It's our third date—they're expecting sex."

I shrugged.

"I mean—you know, I'm always willing to make sacrifices for the cause."

"Yes," she said, "I know you are. But we need a storyline, something to keep the interest up."

"Okay, I'll see what I can think up," I said.

"No, I've thought of one," she responded. "Just be prepared for anything."

She invited me over for dinner. I arrived at 6 O'clock to find the place lit by candles, the lights low and soft music.

She was in a wonderful filmy blue and aqua dress. Her hair was pulled back behind her head, exposing little loop earrings. Her eyes shined through the dim light. She served grilled salmon with bok choy and rice. It looked and tasted great.

"You cooked this?" I asked—I couldn't help it.

"I paid for it—doesn't that mean I can take credit for it?"

"Absolutely," I laughed.

We ate. We drank wine. We smiled. And suddenly, for the first time on one of our dates, I had a genuine feeling.

I found myself genuinely enjoying the moment, the silence, the pleasure of her nervous, guarded, filtered smile, those eyes that so desperately wanted to be happy. Somehow, from this totally concocted, artificial situation, came a genuine gratitude. I'd come from so much sadder a place than this.

"I haven't done this in a long long time," I said. "You know, the lights, the music, dinner—the whole deal."

"I don't know if I've *ever* done this," she answered.

"Why'd you start tonight?" I asked.

"I thought maybe you'd appreciate the traditional approach."

"You mean, being old and traditional like I am."

"Yeah," she nodded and smiled openly now, that wonderful mischievous smile of hers.

"Thanks a lot," I said and laughed and she laughed too. And suddenly all the tension and the expectations, all our determination to make the night go well, just evaporated. The mood lifted and we went with it.

I'd been thinking about it for a long time, but I finally asked, "What the hell do you see in me anyway?"

"I see somebody who knows who he is—or at least he's willing to find out. You know a lot of things, you're generous with what you know and your feelings—"

"And I look just like Harrison Ford."

"I was going to say that," she returned instantly, bless her. She lifted her glass. "What do you see in me?"

"Someone who's fearless. Guts. Joie de vivre."

"What's that?" Which proved her guts, just asking.

"French—love of life."

She lifted her glass—we clinked a toast to each other. Somehow, when we stopped looking for them, we found the words. We found the feeling. It was the most romantic moment we'd ever had. Actually, it was probably the *only* romantic moment we ever had.

After dinner, we settled on the couch. I knew the script—I knew I was going to get lucky tonight. It didn't matter—I was trembling, giddy, nervous as a schoolboy.

I now understood what I'd often read—Romance is just deprivation. Sitting so close to her, having been denied her for a week, not being able to touch her—yet—was exquisite torture. It was a *date*—millions of guys go through this every weekend. I don't know how we survive—it's probably why we die first.

Everything was heightened now. The music was heartrending, her perfume made me dizzy. I felt like I'd forgotten everything I knew about her—and about *me*. I felt 23 myself.

We kissed for a long time. I read a quote a while ago, something to the effect that sex was just an excuse for kissing. I don't know if I'd go quite that far, but the writer had a point. She was delicious. I devoured her.

Finally, at one point, I began to pull at the strap of her dress, and she held up a finger to pause me. She moved to the camera behind the bar and wrote a note saying "This one's private—see you tomorrow" and put it in front of the camera. Then she pushed a button shutting down the monitors in the house.

But we both knew—I'd rigged the equipment—that the cameras were still live. This was a twisted kind of subterfuge made necessary by Marla, because I was taking no chances with my visitations with Daniel. I'd told Marla that week that I wanted a divorce, and Daniel came to see me that weekend, so Marla was still being civil. But I didn't want to ask for trouble. Being able to say we thought we'd turned the cameras off was just enough cover to make me comfortable.

When Livy returned, I started pulling at her strap again and she moved away. "I want to do something else," she said.

"What?" I said, panicking at the thought she was going to call it off. I was beyond ready.

"I want to watch you first," she said. "I want to watch you get excited."

"I am excited."

"Good. Let me see—and you can watch me."

She pulled the dress down and exposed her breasts. She began to touch them, caressing the nipples. It was wildly exciting to watch her this close, to be teased so explicitly.

After a few minutes, she wriggled out of the dress and sat there, inches from me, in tiny blue panties, rubbing her breasts and moving her legs around, and then with her hand under her panties, moving up and down, around and around.

I followed suit, though I was so excited I had to go slow to keep from losing it all immediately.

Her fingers worked between her legs, rhythmic. The skin there glistened in the candlelight.

"I am going to explode," I said finally.

"No, you're not," she said and moved to me, and suddenly I was running at her rhythm, the electricity flowing between us again, as it always had. I caressed her ever so lightly, working off her moans and breaths, the two of us perched on that line, past thought, in that blissful, unconscious state.

And then I bent between her legs, for the first time in an eternity. I was there a long time, and she made lovely noises and moaned and groaned and trembled and shook and I felt her gasp and release and then again, several times. After just a second's rest, she was between *my* legs, pumping and teasing and driving me insane. I just flew and flew until I gave it all up and lay there spent, holding her, happy and completely empty.

We lay there a long time. I could feel her breathing smooth out, as did mine. I could feel the breeze through the room. It was hard to imagine life being any better than that.

After a while, she raised her head and looked into my eyes. And I knew she was up to no good. I knew that look—I'd seen it before, and it meant mischief, at least.

"That was very nice," she said. Laying in the weeds.

"Uh-huh."

"How long has it been for you?" she asked, all innocent.

"What do you mean?"

"How long since you got divorced?" she said, clarifying.

I thought about that for a moment. I'd been quite open about being a not-yet-divorced man on my own site, so I couldn't really lie about it here, not that I wanted to.

"Well, I'm not *legally* divorced yet—but if you're asking the last time I had sex—"

"What?" she yelped, shooting up in the bed. "When were you going to *mention* that you weren't divorced?"

It was eerie, looking back on it. I found myself struggling to remember if, in real life, we'd ever spoken about the divorce. I was sure we had, but I was too flustered at the moment to really be sure. She seemed angry as hell.

"I—I didn't think it mattered," I stammered.

"Well, I'm not worried about the piece of paper," she barked back. "But if you're not bothering to tell me something like that, what *else* aren't you telling me?"

I was still scrambling here. She'd told me to be prepared, but I wasn't—not for *this*. I was just running on instinct, and what came out, instinctively, was the truth.

"Excuse me, but have you told me one detail of your life before we met? I assume you came from somewhere before setting up a household full of cameras, but I've never asked questions—"

"That's right," she said. "You didn't *ask*."

"OK, I'll ask," I countered. "Where did you go to college? What did you study there? Were you the same person? Did you work your boyfriends the way you work me? Were you the wildest girl on campus?"

"You bet I was," she said.

"Really?" I asked and looked her purposefully in the eye. "The people who were your friends there—*this* is what they expected you to be doing a year later?"

I knew the answer, and she knew I knew it. I'd met her friends—I'd seen her paintings. I'd seen the way she ran from that whole aspect of herself, from those feelings that got too close to the bone. She faltered for a moment, and I knew I would pay for it.

"I—I don't know. What's that got to do with anything?" she demanded.

"I'm just saying, *neither* of us asked questions before. You can't get mad when you haven't asked a question."

"It's a question about how truthful a person you really are," she insisted. "How much of yourself are you really sharing with me?"

"Fine," I responded, and I could hear my voice raised in anger. "I'll answer that in detail—if *you* will."

She stared at me blankly. I'd hit home.

And just at that moment, it occurred to me that this was just a game. At least for her, it was supposed to have been just a scene, a way to juice the audience again. And I'd carried it over the line.

"Well, excuse me if I wasn't clear on the ground rules you have for romance," I said, hopping for the door as I tried to get my pants on and then slamming it behind me.

I arrived home to find 300 people of both sexes in an animated argument about our date on my discussion boards. I could only imagine the number on Livy's chat. There was no consensus of any kind—some felt that Livy was off her rocker, some felt I was a fool for telling her the truth in the first place, some felt I was too old to be having sex on camera, a view I heartily agreed with.

One of the most striking things about the evening was the variety—I'd never had women on my site, but now they were swarming there. I received ten marriage proposals from women around the country, and forty nude photographs (only 2 or 3 of which I would ever consider looking at again, much less doing anything about).

I was up till 4 in the morning, dealing with the tumult. Then I fell on the couch and was asleep in a minute and a half.

The next few days were a blur. Apparently, a reviewer from Nerve.com was planning a story on us, and was watching that night. She was wildly taken with not only the action of the evening, but the fervor of the audience participation afterward. "It was astonishing," she wrote in the article, which appeared the next morning, "to see these two couple and then fight, with all the gritty power those activities can summon in the real world—and then see them pouring out their state of mind—justifying, rationalizing, and trying to figure out *what* they felt—to their audience in the wee hours of the morning. It showed the power of the Web to make us all participants—it made other forms of storytelling seem suddenly remote and abstract."

That same night, a couple of writers in the CNN newsroom were watching us on their monitors while working on other stories. At one point, one of them decided to call their Web editor and suggest we might be a good story. So there we were on CNN, the same morning as the Nerve article.

And that started the snowball. In the next week, *MSNBC*, *Rolling Stone* followup, *US* magazine, *Salon.com*, and, the following week, a small mention in *People*. The next week, (Good Lord) *the New Yorker*.

Big time, big time.

We spent the next several days defending ourselves on our individual websites. Daniel was over for the weekend and got very annoyed at the amount of time I spent online while never leaving the house, but we had to keep the fires burning. At one point during the second day of the feud, I decided to take offense at something Livy'd written on her chat and jumped on it, giving my side of the story. She responded and we went at it hammer and tongs for half an hour. This made every story that went out about us the latter half of the week.

The New Yorker: "...the exchange carried the eerie feeling of being a fly on the wall during one of Gwyneth and Ben's periodic spats, except that in this case, Gwyneth is almost permanently nude and Ben is an attractive but not extraordinarily fit man, old enough to be her father."

I'm thinking of having a nametag made up for myself: *Nationally Recognized Attractive but Not Extraordinarily Fit Man.* Might get me some dates someday.

It was too much to hope that, in the midst of all this publicity, somehow Marla wouldn't find out. As I say, it was too much to hope.

Visit from Marla

I went out for my run the next morning. No big deal—just a run. You pound down the road, thinking about nothing but your stride and the potholes, and twenty minutes later, you suddenly have ideas from out of nowhere—from a refreshed consciousness. At least, that's how it usually works.

This time, as I turn back toward my apartment, who's sitting in the mouth of a sidestreet looking lost but Marla, in an expensive new Honda.

There's no way to avoid her—she's blocking a street I have to cross to get home. The only alternative is frontal assault.

"Top of the mornin', young lady. Dazed and confused? Need directions?"

I can see with her first glance that nothing good is going to come of this. It's one of those rigid angry laser looks that I know so well, and that still scare me to death.

"I found your website," she says, each word dripping with anger. I get a chill up my spine. "You're fucking some bimbo who strips on the web."

Have you ever had an automobile accident? I was in two when I first started driving. Time really does slow down—I still remember watching, detached, as the hood of my car folded up in front of me in slow motion. That's what started happened, listening to Marla. My mind outraced real time by lightyears.

How do I respond to this? I spent my entire marriage telling Marla the truth and regretting it, over and over. My life and feelings were never as neat and orderly as she wanted them to be.

Marla never told the truth if a lie sounded better; more colorful, neater, more heroic, than real life. The truth is never as tidy as she insists it should be, to the point that she always feels the need to dress it up.

With that in mind, I begin ticking off my options. Does she *know* I'm fucking her?—it could just be a phrase.

"Marla, she's a baby," I say. It's a non-denial denial, but maybe she's not in Woodward and Bernstein mode yet.

"That's a non-denial denial," she says instantly.

Okay—Plan Two. Tell a Big Lie and Tell It Decisively. The Bill Clinton/Josef Goebbels defense.

"Marla, I've got a website in town. Most of the guys who come to my site found me through her site, and I helped her out once when she was being stalked."

"You're fucking her," she says. "The tape is on the website." Shit! Big Lie goes up in flames! Okay, Round Three.

With my back to the wall, I fall back on the defense that never works with her: I tell the truth.

"Look, Marla, my website is actually making money because of her traffic. I need to make money to send you money, right?"

"Damn right," she says. Good, good—we're segueing—keep going, Marla. "You had a perfectly good job in the city," she continues. "You're on a leave of absence—you could always go back there."

"You know I wasn't happy there, Marla." Keep it going, keep it going.

"Don't change the subject," she says. Damn!! "You're seeing a stripper, while our son is visiting you. I'm going to court—I'll take him away from you so fast your eyes'll spin."

"Marla, that's not true. I have nothing to do with her when Daniel's here. He knows *my* website, but he doesn't know anything about her, and she knows I can't see her on the weekends I have him."

"He's never seen her? He's never met her? You're not planning on getting his approval, she's not somebody who's important in your life? "

Now it gets clearer. She's jealous that I'm going to *marry* Livy. Don't bite, old boy—parry and deflect.

"She's somebody I'm seeing, Marla. She's a nice kid, and she's made both our lives easier. I haven't had to plead poverty with you, and tell you I can't pay you what you want every month. You should be her biggest fan."

"You'd *better* pay me," she says. "You're going to pay me bigtime, whether you ever see him again or not. Don't think you're going to get out of taking care of him."

All of a sudden, whatever little strategy I had goes right out the window. I'm mad as hell.

"Marla, I've *been* taking care of him since I left. You told me what you needed to make the bills. It was a hell of a lot more than the law says I owe you, and I've paid you faithfully, with no agreement on paper. Meanwhile, since I left, you've bought a cellphone, an expensive car lease, a big screen TV, DVD player with surround sound, and a pool club membership for the summer. I am certainly getting by, because of the success of this website, but you're living better than when we were together—so don't complain to me about not taking care of him. I should ask for an audit, to see how much you actually spend on *him*."

"I'm keeping up our house," she counters. "He lives there—he gets the benefits. I can't just let it go to seed, just because you're not paying the mortgage."

"I'm paying for the mortgage. I'm giving you about 40% of my income, instead of the 17% the law demands."

"You should be paying the mortgage separately, in addition to the rest."

I've made my point. If I were smart, I would stop now. Do I? Of course not. I'm sick of her demands—I just want to shut her up. She should be grateful I'm not one of those husbands who's refusing to pay anything and stocking his money in an out-of-state bank. I've met plenty of those guys.

"If the house is such a problem," I say, "you can just walk away from it."

"What?" She exhales like I've stuck her with a pin.

"Marla—remember we went bankrupt two years ago?" I clarify. "Because you had 75 credit cards up to the limit? Remember the lawyer told us he didn't reaffirm the house, so that if we needed to, we could always walk away from it?"

She pulls herself rigid in the carseat, eyes wide, and I know what the residents of Pompeii felt that morning, watching Vesuvius in a bad mood.

"You want us to move out of the house?" she rumbles.

"That's not what I said. I'm saying if you're going to keep complaining about it—"

"You would put us out on the street, to save yourself a couple of dollars?" She is almost physically expanding, like a bullfrog filling its lungs before immersion.

Time is not running slow anymore. I am very familiar with this stage of Arguments with Marla. I have failed. She is either going to spontaneously combust or make me spontaneously combust. One way or the other, we're both going to be found in a charred crater in the middle of town—and I left the air conditioning on when I went out running. When they go to collect my worldly goods, they'll curse me for wasting electricity.

"Marla, you're making a big deal out of a stupid remark."

"Don't think you can just slough this off," she threatens. She's really good at threatening—she's developed this powerful look of contempt, honed over the years to a keen edge. If I weren't so used to it, it would be withering.

"Look Marla, I don't have anything new to say and neither do you. So why don't you just email me when you do, or leave me a message on the phone."

"Do you live here?" she demands, sitting at the controls, engine idling. "Let me come in. We'll talk."

I remember the night I told her I was leaving. She had gotten so vehement, so desperate to keep me from going, that when she went into the kitchen at one point, I got up out of my chair and stood on the far side of the dining room table, without realizing why. When she came back out, I realized why. In case she'd had a carving knife in her hand, I was going to have some distance between us. I had never thought of her as being capable of anything like that, but I was spooked by her reaction, and now that came back to me very clearly.

"No. I don't live on this block, and I'm not going home with you. If you have something new to say, I'm listening. If you don't, you can always call me when you do."

"You can't walk away from me," she insists. "We have to talk."

"Talk!" I return. "If you have something new to say, say it! I'm not stopping you."

"How could you suggest I give up the house? What kind of feeling do you have for your family?"

I close my eyes.

"This isn't a conversation. I have no place to go here," I say, sounding out each syllable like it's a foreign language. "I'm done. I'm leaving now."

I start to turn down a side street, back in the direction I came from, away from the house, away from her.

"You can't leave," she says.

"I already have," I say and mount the curb on the other side. This momentum lasts three seconds. Marla guns the engine and drives her new car up onto the curb directly in front of me. She comes so close to the fence that I can't squeeze between it and her car.

"You *have* to talk to me" she says.

"I *have* been talking to you—I *will* talk to you—when there's something to say," I retort. As I watch her, her expression wilts, from bug-eyed determination to dismay. I turn my head to follow her glance. A female police officer is walking up to us, out of the driveway ahead.

"Okay, please step out of the car," she says in that brusque, commanding tone of voice they must teach at the Acme Police Academy.

"Oh God," Marla moans.

"Step out of the car please," the officer repeats, pulling a pad out of her pocket. She has a nightstick and a revolver in her belt, I note. I guess it's not *that* sleepy a town.

"He abandoned me and his son," Marla whines, leaning out the window. "He won't talk to me."

"Abandoning means not paying," I say back. "I'm giving you 40% of my income. And I've done nothing but talk to you since I left."

I can read the officer's glance. By answering—and Marla's sudden lack of response—I've just gone from deadbeat dad to domestic dispute with two sides in the eyes of the law. Marla, however, is still sitting with her nose on the curb.

"I said step out of the vehicle," the officer says again, much more forcefully, and Marla complies. She looks as though she's going to swoon, and she gives me a hateful look.

"Thanks a lot," she says.

"For what? Making you drive up onto the curb?"

"He's threatened me for years," Marla protests, as the officer fills out paperwork.

"Well, if he had said a word here, honey, you would've had him," the officer tells her. "'Cause I was watching the whole thing come down. He didn't put a foot wrong."

Marla slumps up against the car. Her keys scratch the paint along the windowsill, the kind of thing that will drive her crazy later. She doesn't even notice. The officer asks her some questions, gets her information off her driver's license, and then turns to me.

"I'm going to give you a copy of this paperwork. Is there anything you want to say? Do you want to press charges? Is she threatening you?"

"No," I say. "I have nothing to say."

"Alright. I would suggest," she tells Marla, "that you confine your conversations to the telephone or letters or email or whatever. You can go now."

Marla remains standing by the car.

"I said you can go now," the officer says. The implication is, go now or I'll find something more serious to do with you. It's amazing how we all get the unspoken police threat without ever having been in trouble with the law, as I know Marla never has.

She gets in the car, thoroughly wrung out. I feel sorry and guilty—I made her this upset. She drives off.

The officer finishes the paperwork. She hands me a copy.

"Now that she's gone," she says, "is there anything you want to tell me?"

"No," I shake my head.

"We have a domestic officer at the station. He's a *guy*, if that makes things easier for you," she says. I get the implication here too.

"Thanks" I say and she walks off to her cruiser in the next driveway.

Half a minute later, an ambulance drives up and they take the 73-year-old grandfather in the house off to the hospital, breathing through an oxygen tank. On such coincidences, I think to myself, life flows its twisty course.

I have no idea just how big the coincidences will get before this tale shakes itself out.

New York Times, April 6, 1998:

Late last year, Timothy C. Draper, a West Coast venture capitalist, found himself listening to a pitch from two 20-something entrepreneurs who were insisting that their computer networking 'company'—basically a good idea in search of early-stage financing—was worth a whopping $15 million.

'It was outrageous,' Mr. Draper, the managing director of Draper Fischer Associates in Redwood City, Calif., recalled recently. 'They were just starting out.'

But not long afterward, the two young men, whom Mr. Draper declined to identify, did find other investors who agreed to buy a big share of the company based on a valuation of $20 million. The punch line: The entrepreneurs and investors then together sold the company to a large corporation for $30 million.

~~~

Show Business

Livy put the phone down.

"Well, we're a real business now," she said.

"Why—they're trying to sell you the deluxe copier/fax/printer/coffee machine with the 24/7 support guy who actually *lives* here?"

"No," she said. "They want to buy me out."

The fellow's name was Roger Donnelly. He had a variety of business interests, he told her, and he was real interested in taking over the business. She was going to meet him for lunch.

"Where should I meet him?" she asked.

"The Biarritz—it's the only place around here expensive enough for a proper business lunch," I said. "But are you comfortable going into a meeting with one of those sharks? Don't you want your lawyer there?"

Livy had a very nice, courtly lawyer named Martin who appeared every couple of weeks with a stack of papers and a bouquet of flowers. She always met him undressed. This would have been an opportunity for him to see her with her clothes on.

"I don't think we need him yet. You can be my shark repellent, if necessary."

"Me? You want me to come?"

"Oh, you have to," she said, and handed me a piece of paper with a flourish. "You're the stockholder."

The ornate certificate identified me as the owner of 100,000 preferred shares of Seaviewgirl Enterprises.

"Thank you," I said, and I truly was touched by the gesture. She'd always paid me well—at the contractor rate I'd made up on the spot a few months before. I was actually making slightly more money than I had at the network. But I'd never considered myself anything but a hired hand, at least in a business sense.

"Martin and I set up stock for the company months ago," she explained. "I figured it was time somebody finally got some." she said. "You built the damn site, after all. If my ship comes in, my friends get to cruise with me."

"Thank you," I repeated, and smiled to convey my gratitude for this gesture. Later, though, I looked back and realized she knew far better than I what an act of generosity it really was.

We met at the Biarritz a few hours later. Roger Donnelly had that Pat Riley look—the look perfected by the Lakers, Knicks, Miami Heat coach: tall, reedthin, slicked back hair that had been cut no more than 2 days before, nails manicured to perfection, just enough of a shadow to show that he shaved, and a suit that probably cost as much as my car. He was around my age, but his face showed his age without making the slightest concession to it. I'd seen guys like this at the top of the networks—in fact, with rare exceptions, it was the *only* kind of guys you saw at the tops of the networks. That look said success simply because no one but a success could spend the 35 hours a week in the gym that it took to look like that.

Donnelly stood when we arrived, though he eyed me for a moment before sitting down. He got right to the point.

"You're an artist," he told Livy. "You're not interested in paying the taxes or arranging promotions or setting up interviews. You want to be performing. I'll take all the boring stuff off your hands. I'll buy the business from you and hire you to work there— at, say, $1.5 for the year?"

That's not a misprint—he said "one-point-five." Not "one-point-five million" like a person, just "one-point-five." Like we were on intimate terms with ten thousand dollar bills. I already didn't like him.

It didn't matter. Livy needed shark repellant like a fish needs a bicycle.

"I figure I'll beat that projection by next summer," she said immediately. "And I'm not interested in being hired. Are you interested in investing in the company, or only in a buyout?"

"Well, I think there are real advantages in consolidating operations. There's no reason for you to maintain a backend— credit card processing, tech support, etc.—when I am already supporting ten sites. We could merge those and save you some cash."

"Okay, I outsource those, so that would be a good deal for me. Are you interested in investment?" she repeated.

About this point, I just settled back to watch her. I knew I wasn't going to have to do a thing.

"Yes, I'd be interested in 90% of the business."

"Would you be interested," she asked, "in 35%?"

"We can talk about it," he smiled, though less happily than before. "But there really would be advantages to your joining my stable."

And now I saw something in the smile that I'd been waiting for—a hint he was also interested personally. Not a shock, certainly, but I had a sort of pool going with myself to see how long it would take to show. He came in pretty much on time.

"I'm a show horse," Livy said. "I don't really want to be part of a stable."

"I didn't mean it that way," he said quickly.

"No, that's okay," she replied. "These 20 sites of yours—are they similar to mine?"

"Yes, same genre," he said.

I could feel it coming, right about then, but this poor Joe didn't have a clue. He'd obviously been finding girls who'd put up their own websites and was buying them up for a song, collecting the money, giving them an advance and doing the taxes. And maybe collecting a little gratitude on the side. And now he'd put Livy in that company. Bad idea. As I said, I could see the path she was leading him down.

"You do the back-end for your sites," Livy continued, "and the women take care of--?"

"Entertaining the customers," he said.

"Pornography," she said.

"Adult entertainment," he instructed. "That's what we like to call it."

"Do these women you own—do they make art on the site? Art that they sell separately, as another revenue stream? Do they have chat rooms full of men and women discussing their next date, the soap opera of their lives?"

"Not...exactly," he said, and maybe he could see the canoe beginning to tip here.

"Have they been written up in *Rolling Stone*? The *New Yorker*?"

"Um—no," he said, and the light went out of his eyes.

"Then I'm not sure I'll be able to share the advantages of being part of a stable with them," Livy said. "I'd be interested in a deal that made some concession to the uniqueness of this site as a business, and I'm interested in investment. But, if you want to do something substantial, now's the time to lay your cards on the table, so to speak. I plan on doing an IPO next fall."

Once I'd gotten up off the floor, I could see Donnelly sweating in that expensive suit of his.

Everybody and his brother was doing an IPO at this time. Every morning paper carried a new article touting the latest hot thing, and kids were becoming billionaires overnight. So why not Livy? At least, that was what she was saying now. I had no clue whether or not she was serious.

"Uh—I think you're right to have such faith in your own talent," he said. "But an IPO is complex, and of course it's only a good deal if you're set up to attract investment."

"I'm forming a Board of Directors," Livy said. "I have a formidable management team, and a very lean organization," and didn't I know *that* was the truth.

"Well, and of course," Donnelly counseled, "an IPO is really only attractive when the market is going great guns like it is at the moment. But that can change."

"Excuse me?" Livy snorted. "I read *Wired*—this market'll go up for the next thirty years."

"Well, I recognize that you have a valuable property here," Donnelly said. "If I haven't bowled you over with my offer, maybe I could come back with something more attractive in a few days."

"The timing sounds right," Livy countered.

Donnelly began to eat his lunch.

I would have done the same—it looked good—but Livy suddenly stood up and said, "I think we should go" and headed for the door. I thought about grabbing at least part of my sandwich, but I left it there regretfully and followed her out to the parking lot.

She walked at a good clip, and when we reached her Jeep, she threw me the keys and said, "You drive."

We'd gone a block before she threw up the first time. We made it two more before she found a paper bag in the back and threw up again.

I asked her if she wanted to stop, but she waved me on.

We reached my place first and I pulled up alongside.

"Come on in," I said. I got her a drink of water and a bucket. All the amenities of civilized living.

She sits. She drinks the water. Then she says, "Okay, you have to plant this with some business writer. You know any business writers?"

"A few," I say.

"And then we're going to need to hire a few more girls."

"Excuse me?" I say.

"I'm damned if I'm going to sell my company to some slick-back dude," she concludes. "If he owns it, he'll want to run it. Nobody's running me. I'll buy him in a year and *then* we'll have some efficiency. But not until I can run the table."

She looks up at me with that hunger I've seen before.

"We're going to build an empire," she says.

New York Times, December 28, 1998:

When investors sport a category leader, there is no limit to what they will pay to own the stock.

The main lesson of 1998, said Keith Benjamin, an analyst with BancBoston Robertson Stephens, is 'just don't fight the tape.'

It's fruitless, Mr. Benjamin has concluded, to try to find rational explanations for the astronomical Internet stock prices sliding across the ticker. The fact that, in the stock market, America Online is worth almost as much as Walt Disney and that Yahoo is more valuable than CBS is simply not relevant, he said.

~~~~~

Empire Building

Either Livy hadn't heard Rome wasn't built in a day, or she wasn't going to be intimidated by such an old model. We flew headlong into empire building.

The numbers only spurred her on. After all the recent publicity, we signed as many subscriptions in a week as we had in the previous month. And we had women taking subscriptions in astonishing numbers for an 'adult entertainment' site. Livy led another round of interviews, pointing out that that fact alone made Seaviewgirl.com a new class of erotica for the Web.

We bought five new servers, in managed facilities on both coasts, to carry the volume. Considering we'd only had two computers for the whole operation before that, we were riding high.

Howard Stern wanted Livy on, but she did a telephone interview and refused to undress for him—he insisted she should get naked, even if it was over the phone. She said he could watch an hour later and she'd be naked, but not now.

Why not?

"Because I don't feel like it."

And she made him *like* it.

Some of the old names disappeared off the chat, replaced by a much larger, different group—one that might have been here for the same old purpose, but were both more polite about it and more reverent of Livy as an artist. They were actually a little too reverent, I thought—I found myself missing the earlier, more raucous group at times.

She was running around like a broker at the closing bell— painting and dancing, running the treadmill and stripping, giving interviews and planning more publicity.

I set up the interviews, and made the contacts for a lot of them. We had a lot of media requests for video clips, which I edited, had duplicated and sent out. I spent half the day interviewing other girls for the site. That probably should have been fun, but it was flat-out bizarre. When a young woman has to convince you she has some personality and can act—Livy was determined that we would make up storylines for each of them, tailored to their personality—and that she looks good naked, and you have fifteen minutes each to do all this, it gets pretty weird pretty fast.

And that's all the time we had. We were both going full-speed now every minute. "What's the next step?" Livy demanded fifty times a day, especially when I didn't have an immediate answer.

Evenings were spent going over the girls I'd interviewed and planning out potential storylines. Days were a frenzy of activity.

"Livy, why don't we consolidate this success first—just the two of us—before adding more people?" I suggested, rubbing my eyes and feeling totally wrung out.

"It's Internet time, remember? Everything moves so fast—we've got to be thinking of the next step all the time. Besides, this will make all the stories better—the threads will run together, we can criss-cross everything, one will feed off the next. It's going to be great!"

"Sweetie, who's going to run all this?"

"*We* are!" She was bouncing from excitement. The doorbell rang—at 5:15 in the morning?

"That'll be Sylvie," she remarked, dancing to the door.

It was Sylvie—the world's other early riser. Now Livy almost lifted her bodily and carried her to the table.

"Sylvie's going to be our office manager!" she exclaimed. Sylvie arched an eyebrow as though her stomach had suddenly curdled.

"I'll have Earl Grey, with a little Scotch please," Sylvie muttered.

"No, seriously, you'll run the office," Livy insisted. "You can do the books—it's not that hard. And we can do art projects together. And you can kind of be the den mother for the other girls—keep them in line, organize the time schedules, all that stuff."

"Now hold on, my dear." Sylvie told her. "I'm not bad with figures, when I have to be, but this is a lot of responsibility, and I don't know if I want to take it on."

"Sylvie—you told me you could use some money. You're not going to take a loan from me—I know you won't. Here's a way you can earn some. And if I'm going to have someone hanging around here every day with us, I'd be most comfortable if it was you."

I'd known Sylvie longer than Livy had—she'd never mentioned any need for money to me. It was another indicator of a dependency, a friendship they'd developed quietly over time. At first I thought Livy needed it more than Sylvie, but now I saw Sylvie enjoyed having someone to worry over and protect.

Sylvie pursed her lips, thinking it over. After a long moment, she piped, "Three days a week. I'm not working more, not to start with. Let me see if I can stand it."

"Deal!" said Livy.

We already had an outside accountant that the books went to—all Sylvie had to do was keep track of the bills, enter them in the accounting program, then check over the accountant's numbers when they came back at the end of the month. So the job wasn't overly taxing.

But the other storylines concerned me, and I cornered Livy about it in the kitchen later.

She had thought it all out. "Look, we're doing fine now, and our story is working out pretty nice. But we're going to have to keep having fights and such, to keep us apart, so we can string things out—like a regular love story. And how long can we keep that up, without the numbers falling? We have to be able to switch the focus, take the pressure off us."

"But it's just *more* pressure on us," I said. "Unless I missed the writing staff hidden in the den downstairs. Someone has to come up with these stories, and once they start going, it'll only get more complicated. We'll have personalities to deal with. One'll want a raise, or more time on screen. The next one'll get sick at the worst possible moment. Meanwhile, you'll have the usual requests for publicity and photos to shoot and—where's it all going to come from?" I asked. "Why not put the same energy into telling a more interesting story with us?"

"Why should I think small?" Livy demanded. "Don't you want to go for the brass ring? Shouldn't I try to be everything I can be?"

I felt a chill down my back. I'd had the same thought just weeks before, thinking about how much I regretted some of the things I hadn't gone after in my life—a thought I'd bought into with few reservations. Now I found myself arguing the opposite position and, realizing the contradiction, I lost my focus.

"Yes, be everything you can be—but do it within the context of what we know works," I said. "Stay the course. Keep your sails starched. Shiver me timbers."

"You're babbling."

"I know," I admitted. "I'm not sure I know what I mean. It's just—I'm afraid of losing us."

"If I fail—or succeed? Are you just afraid of success?" she asked, and it hung in the air, sounding like a good question all at once.

It took me a moment to answer, but the words came out without my thinking first, a stream of feeling let loose.

"Either way, we lose. Right now, we're having fun—just you and me. We're learning how to play out this story and we're figuring out where to take it on the spot, how to bend our plans because the audience doesn't like something we're doing or because one of us has a good idea in the middle of a scene and we just want to go with it. That's pretty amazing stuff, and we're just relying on *us*, so we have that freedom.

"As soon as you go after something bigger, *this* gets lost. If you succeed, we become a factory. If you fail, you're frustrated and this becomes a consolation prize. Right now, it's the right size. I have this nasty feeling that this is as good as it gets. I think that's the paradox God offers us—you can have everything as long as you don't ask too much."

"So how is that different from being afraid of success?"

"I don't care about success—I want to be *happy*."

"This is America," she instructed me. "You have to do *everything* you can; that's the way it works. If I can do this with me, I can do it much bigger with 2 other girls."

So I worked with Sylvie on the books—it didn't take long to get her up to speed. And she had a great idea for an immediate project—she and Livy set up a huge canvas in the middle of the deck on a sunny day, with a huge dropcloth all around it. They placed pins in the canvas at regular intervals. Then they chucked paint-filled balloons at it and made a painting.

Afterward, Sylvie listened patiently to my endless concerns.

"She's young," she told me. "She gets to think everything is the way she wants it to be. For a little longer yet, she gets to think that way."

"What scares me," I told her, "is what she said about '*having* to do everything you can.' Like she had an obligation to get bigger because she *could*."

"Well, that's America," Sylvie said, echoing Livy. I stared at her, surprised. "She's no hippy, my boy—that was *your* generation's delusion. She wants success. A lot of success is better than a little. She's not content to be Marilyn Monroe; she wants to be Darryl F. Zanuck, too. Is that too old an example?"

"No, I follow you. She wouldn't, but I do."

"Well, I don't know if she'll make it, but this is her time to try."

In the next week, Sylvie restructured our web hosting deal—we had 1000 times the traffic we'd had when we first signed up. She got figures from 3 competitors and used them to hammer down our provider. It netted us a good amount of change every month.

Livy threw herself into our expansion—purchasing new equipment, supervising construction in the garage so each new girl would have her own place online, designing new subscription packages and new ads, second-interviewing the girls I thought were worth considering.

This was her moment, and she was determined, as always. Determined to make a big splash, determined to drive as far forward as she was capable. She worked day and night, without respite. She seemed to be thriving on the driving, the never-ending driving toward her destination.

She drove herself right into the hospital.

Hospital

One afternoon, I was late.

I'd gone home in the morning to tend my website, and that had taken some time, so I showed up a little later than usual.

Just in time, in fact, to see the ambulance pull away.

One of the things about a small town is that everyone knows everyone else's business. I was shocked to find that the whole town pretty much knew Livy as 'the Internet girl'. They all knew what she did. Some approved, some didn't, some didn't care, but there was a funny, disinterested acceptance of her role in the town's society.

I came to see it as one reason she chose to do her show in suburbia, instead of the city—in a strange way, it was more normal. She was the village character, not a celebrity or a freak, not a distant figure to be demonized or idolized. She was granted no special treatment in Seaview—just the local show-off, the girl who took her clothes off on camera, usually at home and sometimes at the supermarket. She evidently found being the local character more sheltering, more comforting, than being a city celebrity.

Anyway, the neighbors all knew Livy and me, and I was quickly told that she had collapsed and was being taken to the hospital in Monmouth.

I sprinted to my car and headed hard down the main road towards Monmouth General. I knew the hospital—it's where I lost my grandfather and my father, 25 years apart. Both of them died of lung cancer, both of them suffered for years before succumbing. I spent a lot of hours on ratty chairs in the lounges and wandering the white paint and brushed aluminum hallways. Just the smell, as I entered, took me back in a visceral, very physical way, to memories I'd managed to blot out for years.

"I'm here for Olivia Post," I told the desk lady, huffing and breathless.

The nurse was both helpful and sympathetic—another reason to get sick in the suburbs, folks. She wrote me a pass and pointed me down the right hallway.

"Room B-36, Mr. Post" she said, and I hurried down.

Livy was in a private room, with what seemed like a dozen tubes sticking out of her and a mask over her mouth. She seemed misshapen, all arms and legs protruding from the hospital gown and from the tangle of tubes and metal boxes surrounding her. Every breath she took was amplified, dramatized, supported by the ticking, clicking, and humming of the machinery arrayed to keep her 'comfortable,' as some doctor would surely call it.

The attending physician appeared a few seconds after I arrived. He had to be an intern or resident or whatever — he looked to be about 16 years old.

"She seems to be alright," he confided in a whisper, speaking as though there was actually some useful information in that sentence. "Is there any family history of strokes?"

I was just about to swoon into the nearest chair when Sylvie appeared out of nowhere and immediately got in his face. "As I told you, she is an adopted child. There is no family history that anyone knows of."

The kid looked crestfallen, and then blurted, "There's no evidence of a stroke. I just wanted to get a comprehensive history." As I rose to punch his lights out, he dropped the chart on the next bed and headed out the door quickly.

Sylvie returned the chart to its place on Livy's bed and turned to me. "She's fine," she said in an amazingly calm voice. "She must have been dehydrated or over-stressed. The doctor — you understand that was not the doctor — "

"Thank you God — "

"The doctor said she should see her physician as soon as she gets out. Does she have one that you know of?"

"No. Has she been awake?"

"Yes, she's fine. She's just sedated now."

I looked at the figure on the bed again. The bandages over the IV needles, the tubes and mask and the plastic bracelets, the sounds of the carts rattling by in the halls and the smell of disinfectant—I knew she wasn't going to die, but all my senses were registering death and pain and sadness, all the readings off the charts.

I turned back to Sylvie.

"Did you tell them I was her father?" I whispered.

"I told them I was her grandmother and I was expecting her father. Did you want her to wake up with no one here?"

"You told them she was adopted? What if her family shows up? Shouldn't they be notified?"

"Do you know anything about them?" she asked. I realized I didn't.

"Well, I do," she said. "We've talked about it. I've left her mother several messages on several numbers—I'm not sure what continent she's on, except it isn't *this* one. The girl was raised by her grandmother, who's dead now. The father died before she was born. So no one is showing up."

"You told them I was her father?" I was casting about—I was shocked she knew so much about the family. Livy had avoided the question, the few times I'd asked.

"Should I tell them you're her lover? They won't let you in then…"

"No, I suppose not," I murmured, disturbed by a tone of disapproval I sensed in Sylvie's voice. Or maybe it was my *own* disapproval I heard.

Somehow, lying in the bed with all the tubes in her, she looked younger and more fragile than ever. In this place where my father died—hell, the halls all look the same, it could have been in this *room*—all the feelings came back that flooded me when he was gone, the worthlessness and impotence that follow in the wake of the Reaper.

I realized that, looking at Livy right now, I felt protective—I again felt *paternal*, which made some of the things we'd been doing incongruous, if not downright unnatural.

She started to stir. It took a while for her to come around, and Sylvie called a nurse, who called the doctor.

The doctor was a man more my age, with a more reassuring presence.

"She'll be fine," he said. "But you have to make sure she gets some rest."

"You'll teach me how to tie her down before I leave, okay?" I said, and he looked at me with the uncomprehending gaze of the permanently serious.

They took the oxygen mask off, and she seemed to be breathing fine. Her eyes opened, and she looked at Sylvie, then the doctor, then me.

Her eyes were distant, half-comprehending. Her voice croaked something, far off and indistinct. But she was talking to me. I leaned in to understand. I wanted to reassure her, to let her know everything was going to be okay. I knew how frightening a place this was, and how frightening it was to realize you'd pushed yourself so hard you'd ended up here.

"What is it, Livy?"

"Are there any photographers?" she asked.

"What?"

"Did I get any photographers—here at the hospital?"

"I didn't see any."

"Damn!" she rasped. "If I was a *real* celebrity, there'd be photographers."

I nodded, and looked at the doctor, who seemed to have overheard the conversation.

"I'll need really strong knots," I told him.

Reality 101

The doctors made her stay in the hospital overnight, and she hated it.

The problem was, relaxing made Livy nervous. She was used to being engulfed, at the center of a rough sea of choices, all instantly demanding attention, decision—her hunter's intelligence was set at that level of alert, and she had no idea how to function at a walk.

She had a thousand unanswered anxieties and no ability to do anything about them. She kept reaching for a cell phone that wasn't at the bedside, she kept demanding numbers I wouldn't give her. She was not satisfied that the 'best of' clips I was running were still drawing our usual audience.

It became clear she was not going to get any rest this way. Finally, I offered a deal.

"You'll be home tomorrow, out of the reach of the doctors. Whatever you can do then, I'll help you do. But tonight, you have to *relax*. Just one day…please."

She rolled around on the bed, rubbing her ankles and toes as though they were the problem, mewing with every move, and groaned, "I *need* something."

"Like what, sweetie?" I asked, moving next to her and rubbing her neck.

She bent to my touch for a little while and then pulled up.

"I need a *real* massage," she said. "I need somebody to sit and listen to me whine about my aches and pains for an hour without ever thinking about how *their* day went—I need a glass of tequila and someone I can ignore without getting them upset. Dammit—no offense?—I need a *wife*."

"It's nothing against you," she added, to be polite. "It's not like we're in love or anything."

I didn't react at first, when she said it. I felt something let go inside me, but I declined to identify it, or dwell on it. I just made sure she took her medicine, and that she finally fell off to sleep.

By the time I allowed myself to feel hurt, that emotion arrived simultaneously with the awareness that I really had no reason to *be* hurt.

We never said we loved each other. "We're not in love" was her mantra, after all, and I welcomed it. I never pursued any sappy illusions about us staying together forever or being willing to sacrifice for each other. I don't even know if I *thought* she loved me. We were adults; we were enjoying ourselves and our time together. We were living, fully, in the moment. Which was, after all, what I kept saying I wanted.

But now I felt a little dazed and parched by the words. I realized I'd always assumed we at least *wanted* to be in love, or that we would be, someday—that at least we hoped to discover some real feeling hiding underneath it all.

And clearly, there *was* some real feeling there for me, just a fingernail's depth underneath the skin—lots of mixed, but real, feelings for her. The real connection that comes with sustained, manic lust. The pleasure that comes from being familiar with someone else's craziness. And sometimes, maybe even some of the same feelings I had for Daniel—an almost parental regard for her well-being that kept creeping in around the edges, and that made me far more uncomfortable than the lust for a woman half my age.

Maybe our unspoken code of conduct (every relationship has one) required me to keep all this to myself. And maybe it hadn't been necessary to confront it yet. But now that it had come lurching into the light, I could see that I always hoped to be *more* open about things like that as time went on, not less.

But I hadn't insisted on what I wanted. As usual, I had counted on things just working out somehow. And, as usual when you just count on things working out, they hadn't. Or maybe the time for that had just passed.

For now, it just plain hurt. But there were other concerns that, for better or worse, had to take precedence.

The doctors said Livy was suffering from exhaustion. They insisted she needed rest, and a bunch of it. But, now that a thousand years of medical research has been subordinated to 'what the insurance company will pay for', Sylvie and I were left to try to get her to deal with it.

She grudgingly stayed in bed the first morning, reading books, while the at-home nurse was around. I put up tapes of our last date on the site, and started looking over the list of girls to see who I should call in.

That afternoon, I headed for the bedroom where she lay, holding headshots and my notes.

"I've got three that I think are okay," I said. "We don't really have storylines nailed down yet, but I'll think of something."

Livy attempted to get out of bed, I suppose with the intent of coming out to the main room. Not a good idea. She wavered like a reed in the wind for a moment, then turned white and did a slow slide back under the covers.

"Are you okay?" I asked, rushing to the bed.

"O-okay," she mumbled, holding a hand up to let me know she was capable of movement.

"That was dramatic," I said.

Her eyes focus, all at once. It's that old look I've seen a hundred times on her face, that laserbeam I'm-making-a-decision, get-out-of-the-way look. I haven't seen it since she came out of the hospital. It's good to see, but I know there's work attached — there always is.

"Bring the cameras in here," she says.

"You want another camera?" I ask, not understanding. The room already has the one overhead camera that's always been here.

"Bring them *all* in," she demands. So, of course, I do.

And she proceeds to be exhausted, on camera, for three days. She refuses to bring in any other girls.

"I'm not starting that as a stopgap," she says. "It's an *expansion* of our service, not an excuse for lack of programming."

So, for three days, what you see on six cameras on the site is Livy in bed. Reading, watching TV, drawing sketches every once in a while, getting soup from Sylvie and medicine from me, sleeping for long sections of time, complaining with regularity.

The site traffic goes down, of course, but when I analyze it, the numbers are fascinating. The number of 'uniques'—the different individuals visiting the site—hardly changes. Our regulars are still coming, just checking in, like mom leaving the webcam on at home so she can check on the kids. They don't stay as long, of course, but a fair number of them write get-well messages. And we sell several paintings, though some of the buyers are just gambling that Livy'll die and the price will go up.

I mention this in front of her and she immediately says, "Any way we can say I died for a couple days, sell some more paintings and then bring me back?"

"Do you want to be considered a science fiction or a religious site?" Sylvie asks.

The second night, sitting in the kitchen with Sylvie while Livy sleeps, it hits me.

"She made it," I muse.

"What in particular do you mean?" Sylvie asks, carefully dipping the silver globe containing her tealeaves.

"She's achieved her goal," I explain. "She's living her life on camera. Nobody's asked her to get undressed. She still has an audience, and they're showing up to check on her. It seems like they'll be back when she's ready. They're really interested in *her*— she's more than a webcam girl."

Mom

The next afternoon, I arrived to find Sylvie trying to drag a huge cardboard box of dishes and silver up the stairs. I took the box from her and carried it up to the dining room area.

She began immediately unwrapping the stuff, removing the newspaper and laying the pieces on the metal and glass dining room table.

"What's the occasion?"

"She didn't tell you? No, of course, she wouldn't. Her mother is coming to visit. She got my message about Livy in the hospital—it took a couple of days for her to get it—but I spoke to her last night and she's on her way."

"Oh—uh—when is she arriving?"

"She should be here this evening. So Livy asked me to find the good dishes—she wants her mother's nicest things out when she arrives."

I wasn't listening to the conversation now. Livy's *mother* was coming. At an earlier age, this wouldn't have concerned me at all, but after fifteen years of marriage, the complications of a woman's relationship with her mother are well-trodden territory. So this mattered.

"What do you know about her?" I asked Sylvie.

"Oh, she sounds like a very *interesting* person," Sylvie said, drawing out the 'interesting' until it bled. "She's a travel writer. Speaks several languages, been everywhere."

"Uh-huh. So what don't you like about her?"

"Who says I don't like her? I don't know her at all," she chattered at twice her usual tempo. "Haven't even seen a picture. Just know what I've heard from Livy."

"And what don't you like that you've heard from Livy?"

"She won't talk about her, beyond what I've told you. Not a thing."

"Sylvie—" I stationed myself in front of her, cutting off her scurrying from box to table to box. "I know you. You've developed some kind of attitude toward Livy's mom for some reason. I'm going to be dealing with this woman, who's not going to love the fact that I'm probably close to her age and sleeping with her daughter. I trust your judgement. So would you share your thoughts with me—please?"

"Well," she muttered, "she *did* abandon her daughter, didn't she?" And she goes back to unpacking.

This was a point. I stood around, thinking about this for a moment, then reached into the box and start unwrapping things myself.

"You think I should make myself scarce?"

"Oh no, Livy won't have it. She told me she wants you here as usual."

"As usual. Her mom knows what she's doing?"

"That," Sylvie answered, pulling another dish from the remains of the New York *Times*, January 4, 1976, "remains to be seen."

Now Livy emerged from the bedroom, naked, and proceeded to a huge plywood box backed with canvas, a camera hanging from the ceiling directly overhead. She picked up cans of paint crystals and scattered them into the box. Then she lay down inside and rolled around, contorting herself, making shapes and patterns and—not coincidentally—spreading the paint all over her body as well.

After five minutes of this, she jumped up to the computer, sitting on a chair she'd laid a towel over.

"Okay boys," she barked at the screen, "what am I bid for this work of performance art? You get the painting and the tape of me making it. What's it worth to you?"

The bidding started at $15 and moved rapidly to $1500. Now Livy got up and walked over to where I was eyeing the new work of art.

"It's quick-drying paint. We can put plywood over the top and ship it out tomorrow morning."

"Ah good—then we can show it to your mother when she arrives tonight."

She looked at me, a bit crosseyed, like she wasn't sure whether to reply or not.

"Is there something wrong with my mother coming?"

"Of course not. You just didn't mention it. Do you want me around?"

"Of course. We're together. She should get to know you. You'll like her—you'll probably have lots of things to talk about. Lots of older folk things."

"Thank you—I'll have my walker brought around."

She smiled.

"Sylvie is putting the good china out," I said. "Your mom loves the fancy stuff, huh?"

"No, she hates it."

"Huh?"

Livy fixed me with a laser beam glance. "My mother kept this house, but she hasn't stayed here in years. She sees me for a weekend every year or so and then gets back to—" dramatic pause—"The World."

"She's always traveling," Livy continued. "She wants to be free to blow with the wind. She has no use for anything like good china."

"So why are you putting it out?"

"To piss her off."

Sylvie had placed the last piece on the table. She lifted the now-empty box and said to Livy, "Enjoy your reunion, dear. Just remember—you had the type of parent most children long for."

"What type is that?" Livy sneered.

"Absent," Sylvie replied, heading out the door.

Livy returned to the piece of floorboard and eyed it again. "I hope this thing sets right," she said.

"Shouldn't it be free to blow with the wind?" I asked.

She gave me a smile with a lemon in it, and said, "I'm taking a shower."

"Want company?" I asked.

"Is it okay for me to get back into action?" she joked. "I'm not paralyzed anymore?"

"You seem to have made a miraculous recovery. You're not only walking around without swooning, but you're creating naked performance art. I take that as a good sign."

"Well, fine," she said. "Let's celebrate."

"What do you have in mind?"

"Well, first of all," she said, "you should know the paint is edible."

We always enjoyed our showers. The camera was set up on the opposite wall, but because the shower had a sunken tile floor, we had never put a curtain up and just let the water run down the drain—it didn't spatter much, and the patrons so enjoyed the view.

And this day, in celebration, we enjoyed ourselves to the point that we weren't really paying attention to anything else. I was still smarting a bit from her crack the other night—call it love or any other word you like, there was a connection here, and I wanted her to feel it.

I made her feel it, if I say so myself. I took my time. We both got very wet. She got *very* clean. Clean down to the last molecule, you might say.

Of course, certain areas of the body take more effort than others, and I was expending that effort between her legs at the moment, kneeling like a penitent before the altar with a fat green bar of soap in my hand. Livy was just telling me—panting—that, when we finished, she was going down to the local church and *marry* the bar of soap, when the door opens and a voice calls out, "Livy, are you decent? I'm early."

"Mom!" says Livy, and tries to stand straight, but her legs just aren't working too good yet.

MOM?!! Oh God…

All I can see from my vantage point are Mom's long legs, through the gap between Livy's.

Isn't there a place I can hide?

Too late!

Busted.

I rise as quickly as I can, to try to make this picture a tiny bit less graphic. Want to spare Mom's feelings…

Then I realize, with my first moving impression, that she doesn't *look* a lot like the Mom picture I've got in my head. She looks an awful lot like Livy—pretty glamorous for a Mom. The same build, filled out the way a woman fills out, of course, but very nicely. My eye follows the lovely proportion of her hips, waist, torso.

As I stand, Livy—still a bit unsteady from cleaning—shifts in front of me. She is clearly shaken, and shaking her takes some doing. I'm actually a bit amused at her reaction as I reach to put our pet soap bar in the dish.

That's when I finally see Mom clearly for the first time, head to toe.

I drop the soap. Time...stops...

She is a tall lithe woman about my age—actually, exactly my age—with ashen hair, cheekbones and haunting—I'd forgotten how haunting—green eyes.

Livy's mother looks right past her, directly at me.

"Hello Tom," she says.

"Hello, Alison," I reply.

The Screw Tightens

It was a joke, of course, the kind of cosmic joke that only happens to those who tweak the noses of the gods, the kind of punishment that fits the crime.

When I took up with Livy—when I had sex with her the second time, once it became a choice of mine—I knew full well she was too young for me. I couldn't tell you what was wrong, but I knew in my heart that there was something unreal, unnatural, in it. I knew she was *somebody's* daughter. That was part of the fun.

I was breaking all the rules. By comparison to the practical, stolid life I'd been trapped in, I was being gloriously irresponsible. And why not? Who was being hurt? We were two adults enjoying ourselves.

At every step along the way, I'd been presented with this gorgeous dish on a platter and in every case I'd chosen to gorge myself.

But the gods are mischievous creatures, as we all know, and the moment had now come for the waiter to arrive with the check and the news that my credit card was tapped out.

I stood in Livy's shower, butt-naked, my privates at full cry, feeling the water pour down my face as her mother looked me over. Her mother, Alison Stark. Her mother, the woman I'd dreamed of, and despaired of ever seeing again.

Well, now she was seeing me—and Livy—the two of us— naked together.

The woman I was fucking, the girl who was someone's daughter, was...*her* daughter.

And so I laughed. I bellowed. I brayed like the jackass I was.

They both looked at me like I was crazy, and I couldn't help but wonder the same of *them*—how could anyone miss the exquisite, terrible humor of this moment?

Livy seemed to have been struck dumb. Having her mother walk in on a moment like this would unnerve anyone—but she clearly also caught the stunned greeting between the two of us. She didn't know what it meant, and she clearly didn't know how to approach the subject, just yet.

She stepped across to the counter and pulled a towel around herself. Then, with her mom still giving me the once-over, she tossed a towel to me—with the shower still running. I turned off the water and tried to figure out where to put it.

But, as soon as I managed to get myself under control, I found myself fascinated by how Alison hadn't changed in all this time.

In a second I realized that wasn't what I meant. Of course, she'd changed—we all had.

But clearly, over all the years since high school, as I'd gotten married and had a child and watched my marriage decay, as I'd watched Marla and I get older, I'd always had Alison in the back of my mind. And back there, I guess I'd added the years and the mileage, the experience and the seasoning—always gracefully, for she had more grace than any woman I'd ever known—and now, confronted with the real thing, I found I wasn't far off.

Her hair had gone from honey blond to ash, the dark sections had melted away and the hair had gotten wilder and more electric, till it formed a halo around her face. She had always resembled a fox—the long tapering face, thin nose and wide mouth, always hinting at a smile. That look was still there— clearly, she still laughed a lot. But now, the years had added a web of lines and creases that testified, in powerful relief, of a pain and sadness, some deep hollow, inside. Anyone who reaches our age without some deep sadness and disappointment just doesn't get it. She was beautiful and scary and inspiring—everything I could have hoped for.

I held the towel dumbly in my hand for a few moments. Finally Alison said, "Well, if I've ever wondered what you looked like—now I know."

I put the towel on right quick at that point. I tried to think of something helpful to say, but all I ended up with was, "I wish you'd found out a long time ago."

"That might have made *this* even more uncomfortable," she said, gesturing toward Livy, who was getting dressed real quick, "so it's probably just as well."

Livy looked like someone in the front row of a tennis match—her head going back and forth, back and forth, between the two of us.

"You know each other?" she finally blurted.

"We went out in high school," I answered. "Once. But we danced around it for a year."

"*You* danced," Alison said.

"Yeah," I nodded, "and I'm a lousy dancer."

"Yes, you are," Livy agreed. She was dressed now. She put her arm through mine and dragged me out to the living room and shoved me through the bedroom door. "You get dressed and then you can join us for a while. Mom and I have to catch up."

"OK," I said and she closed the door. She came back a few minutes later with my clothes, which was good, since I was too embarrassed to go out and ask for them.

The rest of the night was plain spooky. Livy kept assigning me cameras to move around, setting different angles for the night's show. I tried to get her to explain the new positions to me, but she just insisted she needed them moved, "because those are the angles I see in my head, okay?" She got testy when pushed, so I just followed my own judgment.

While I moved cameras around, she was talking with Mom, and didn't want to be disturbed. This frustrated me more than a little. I wanted to join in—to make sure her mom knew I was a valuable contributor to this enterprise, while Livy was minimizing me, making me the hired hand I hadn't been since the second day we knew each other.

It wasn't till evening before things settled down—a little. Livy was painting a canvas, with a brush. Like a regular artist. She seemed to be really trying, the way she should have from the beginning.

While her audience was used to following whatever she did, they got restless after a while for some action—they'd had her in bed alone for three days, after all—so she was catching it on the chat line, which I was quietly monitoring.

At one point, I logged on and let them know her mother was visiting. Livy saw my post and got furious. I could see it on her face, though she didn't say a word. But I wondered if Alison – who could not see the chat line from where Livy had seated her – could still read her daughter's face.

Alison nestled in the couch by the deck, watching Livy intently, her eyes moving from her daughter to the image on the big screen – and occasionally, looking over at me.

I was past the point of thinking. All thought was hopeless and useless in the face of this situation.

The woman I had dreamed of for twenty-five years was sitting a hundred feet from me, throwing a glance periodically in my direction. My lover, the girl who pulled me out of a pit of darkness three months earlier, was painting a few feet away and not looking at me at all. Mother and daughter. My *wife*—hell, let's not leave anybody out of this—Livy's mother's old best friend, was sitting about an hour away watching television with our son in the home I'd left her. And me, I'm the Beaver.

I don't have to tell you that the world's most eminent psychologists would have given up a lifetime of vacations to have been in that house at that moment. I went back and forth, trying to figure out a sensible approach to the situation, though Gandhi and Freud together would have been challenged by this one.

So finally, I just made a decision. I walked over and sat down next to Alison. I did it abruptly, simply because I'd been paralyzed for an hour and actually doing anything took an outsized effort.

Alison was taken by surprise, but she smiled at me and the years just melted away. We were a long way from high school, but the things you share at that crucial time just never go away. We'd traveled a long distance, but we'd come from the same place, and that mattered.

Out of the corner of my eye, I could see Livy staring—glaring, really—at me. She *really* didn't want me sitting there. I settled back into the pillows – hell, after twenty-five years of wondering about Alison, I was going to have a conversation with her. Especially considering that Livy and I weren't in love anyway.

"She's very talented," I started, of course. I've always found that, if there's one topic I desperately don't want to talk about, one topic too sensitive or dangerous for discussion—like my intimacy with my dream girl's daughter, for example—it's always the first thing that comes tumbling out of my mouth. This is one of the virtues that has made me the success I am in life.

"Yes, she is," Alison agreed. I listened to that light voice of hers, feeling the memory of it wash over me again. It was interesting—we were both whispering. It was like being in the living room of mom and dad's house, like it would have been the last time we'd seen each other. "She has an audience?"

"Oh yes," I answered. "She's got a devoted following."

I could see Livy leaning subtly, trying—and failing—to hear our conversation. Tough.

"And they sit home at night and watch her paint?" Alison continued.

"Uh-huh" I nodded, very seriously.

Alison sat for a moment, watching her daughter. Livy was working at the colors and the patterns, working hard at texture and layout.

"When does she usually start taking her clothes off?" Alison asked finally.

She flashed me a glance—I instantly remembered it, but was taken by its sharpness—that said 'don't bother snowing me.'

"Usually well before this," I said.

She nodded and smiled, to me and to herself. The smile was worth millions to me. She had shown me about five different smiles in the past few minutes. That's four more than I'm used to getting from anyone. Most people's smiles are social—standard responses to a situation. Alison's were real, transparent, straight through to the heart.

"I hope my visit doesn't lose her too much business," she said. "I'll have to talk to her about it. Or maybe I should just take my clothes off, too."

I found myself panic-stricken at the thought of this. Somehow it was okay—liberating and exciting—for Livy to undress for the camera. But somehow, it would kill me if Alison did the same—and I had no idea why.

She saw my reaction immediately. "Just kidding," she said. "But it might be interesting."

"Only under the right circumstances," I replied.

Now her eyes flashed at me.

"You're my daughter's lover," she said. "I assume she can take care of herself, so I haven't thought a lot about just how appropriate it might be, or what it says about you that you're seeing a 23-year-old. At least leave me the illusion that you're not trying on every *other* woman you see."

"Wait a minute," I stammered. "Whoa. That's not—"

"Okay, I hope not," she interrupted. "I hope not."

I was going to explain, but she just cut me off. "Let's not discuss it further," she said. "Time to move on."

And that was my unhappy start with Alison.

That night, Livy insisted on my staying over, and she made unusually loud noises as we were making love. I was very uncomfortable with this, and I knew it was because Alison was in the house. I didn't want sex that night—but Livy would have been incensed if I didn't.

And she would have had grounds. All the time we were making love, I was thinking about her mother. After maintaining Alison's illusion in the back of my mind for 25 years, she'd come back into my life, and lived up to every romantic dream I'd held onto. And now, sweating between Livy's legs, I was in the worst position to romance her that anyone in the world could have been.

Tea Service

I woke in the middle of the night and, in a fog of half-sleep, heard rustling in the living room. I got out of bed dutifully, threw on a sweatshirt against the night chill and opened the door to the living room.

It was like looking out the window a second time and confirming that yes, those little green men with the saucer were still on the lawn.

Allison Stark was in the kitchen, pulling and unwrapping objects from a box that had clearly seen many miles. The box was held together by habit: cardboard with a few words stamped across the side in blue ink that had long since faded to a memory, 12 different kinds of tape cushioning the corners, tears and dents and holes everywhere. From the packages inside, she was carefully unwrapping a teakettle, a service of cups and ceramic spoons and sifters. A tea service—looked oriental to me, and familiar somehow, but I'm no expert on such things.

I came out into the room and closed the door carefully behind me. Allison was rinsing the pieces, drying them, and placing them neatly in a corner of the kitchen counter. It was 3 am.

"Tea won't help you sleep," I said, trying to sound friendly and casual. Truth is, my heart was pounding so hard I could barely hear anything over it.

"Some tea will," she replied, not seeming surprised to see me. "But I don't really use this set."

"What do you mean?"

"This is home," she said, moving the cups around until they formed a nicely spaced semi-circle in front of the kettle. "I got these things the first year I was away, out of the country. I was in India, and I was just appalled and unsettled by what I saw. The casual filth, the way death and disease are part of every day, every block—it depressed me, it crushed me. I got very homesick. And I knew I wasn't coming home for a long time.

"So—" she bursts into a raucous laugh "—I went *shopping*! Actually, I didn't intend to buy anything, but I found a little shop with probably 200 tea services and this one looked like the teacups at the Chinese restaurant—remember the one on Ocean Avenue?"

"Oh sure—we went there the night of the Cuban Missile Crisis," I laughed. "My father said 'if we're going to die tomorrow, we're having Chinese food tonight.'"

"Well, these reminded me of that place. Don't they look just like the ones they had?"

"Oh God, Ally I don't know—I never remember things like that."

"No? I do. I don't know why—but sometimes the little things really stay with me. Anyway, this service reminded me of them—of home. So I bought it and placed it on a corner of the dresser in my hotel room. Every hotel room, every dresser, for twenty-some years now."

She reaches into the box, running her fingers around the edge and pulling out an old photo. She places it on the counter just between the kettle and the ring of cups, so the little girl's face is the centerpiece of this little display. It is museum, bookmark and shrine, all at once.

"Wherever I go, this gets set up, just so. It's my home for the moment."

"Livy?" I ask, staring at the little blond in the picture.

Allison nods. "You think she'll mind me taking up the corner here?"

"I've never seen her use it," I say. "She's not much of a cook."

"That runs in the family," Allison smiles—yet another incandescent smile. Flitting, swift, thoughtful and distracted, filled with a weird mixture of delight and an unexplained—maybe unconscious—discomfort, I *remember* that smile. As soon as I see it, I'm standing in the hall in high school again, fascinated and entranced. It has stayed with me all these years. It's amazing how touched I can be by a momentary expression.

Alison reads my face—I've only recently learned how transparent my expressions are. And here comes that raucous laugh again.

"I don't remember that laugh," I say.

"I was very ladylike when you knew me" she replies. "I wouldn't have had that laugh."

Then she looks me over like a butcher sizing up a side of beef. "I'm not used to your quietude. You were such a..."

"Loudmouth?"

"I wouldn't say..."

"Obnoxious motormouth, never shut up, never let you think, run all over you in a minute without a moment's conscience...? You mean like that?"

She bites her lip. "Well, that's kind of...hard. I *liked* you."

"Well, bless you for that, m'dear. Nonetheless, I was a loudmouth."

"Somehow," she says, pursing her lip, "you manage to make humility an ego thing."

We both break up. We crowd the far side of the kitchen, against the cold windows, to keep our giggling from waking Livy.

I step to the deck and pull the door open. The waves are pounding at the beach. Snow is swirling in the air, drifting atop the dunegrass. Gulls stand in groups on the poles pounded into the dunes as anchors. They stand huddled like little old men shivering in their overcoats, their wings folded up around their plump midsections, flapping wildly when a gust of wind threatens to blow them off their perch. The moon leaves a brilliant silver overlay on all this, on all of us.

I look up, to get Alison's reaction. But she isn't there; not really. All at once, her face is distant, distracted, her eyes locked on that endless internal landscape we all start from.

"What about you?" I ask.

"Huh?" she starts. God, she was really gone.

"What led you to become a travel writer? I don't remember you ever talking about anything like that." It's not really the question I want to ask, but it's the one I know how to ask.

"Oh, uh…I don't think I ever planned to be a travel writer — I just became one," she mumbles. She picks up one of the teacups and somehow keeps it suspended in midair, hovering between her hands, which do little spasms over the surface.

"I met Dennis at Penn. I didn't know he was in a military program then. He was really brilliant, handsome, funny, he wanted me, he wanted to get married right away. I wasn't as sure as he was, but he was so sure that I went along. I stumbled into marriage."

"We got married after freshman year — his parents attended, reluctantly; my mother arrived at the last minute. We got an apartment — we both worked after school. And then after sophomore year, the rules changed and they called him up."

"Jesus."

"We fought about it for a while. You know how anti-war I was. We talked about Canada; we talked about everything. He was very good that way—he would listen to what you said, but then he went his own way. He was a good American kid. He respected my opinion, but he felt that if other people were going to fight, he had no right not to."

"And I realized pretty quickly that it was one of the things I loved about him. He was a throwback—he had no cynicism; he still believed in all those old verities. And I wanted to believe in them too, even though—especially because—I really didn't. "

"I left school and we went to Fort Benning. They promised him an engineering unit—he was interested in architecture, so he thought that would be useful. But as soon as we got there, they put him in an infantry division."

"I heard lots of stories like that."

"You couldn't do anything; they were the military. They did what they wanted. He was pissed about it, but he was there and he was going to do his best. That's just how he was. I mean, I guess we were all too good to be true—we were so idealistic—but I wouldn't have been as good about it as he was. I would have gotten thrown in the stockade a couple of times, at least," she says, following it with that throaty laugh.

"So I became a good Army wife. It's kind of amazing how social the whole army thing is, for the wives—you want to be a successful army wife, it's sort of like being a politicians wife except you're doing it without him most of the time. I gave parties for the other wives, they threw Tupperware parties and picnics and all that."

"At that point, being antiwar and a college student seemed like another world, because here were these nice young women with their families and the military life, which is just all-encompassing—at least it was back then—and it just enfolds you in the mindset, that way of thinking, till you can't understand why those other people don't get it."

"But at the same time, I knew I *wasn't* an army wife, that I didn't like what we were doing over there and what the military stood for—I just loved Dennis. And I kind of got lost there somewhere. I had a sense of who I wasn't—which included everything in my life at the time—but no sense anymore of who I *was*."

"So finally we got word he was being shipped—to Vietnam, of course. By this time, I'd found a couple of other Army wives who were anti-war, and we were secretly involved in organizing some demonstrations in the area. But Georgia wasn't much for anti-war, and word got back to the post."

"Apparently, a delegation of officers came to talk to Dennis and the other husbands. He came home, just before he shipped out, and we had a rip-roaring fight about my role as wife, supporter and handmaiden to the warrior. It didn't go well, but I sucked it up and made up with him—I agreed to do whatever he wanted. He was going away and the military was taking care of me—and the other wives. We had homes on the base and benefits and checks coming in and none of us had any family or friends around there, and we were young..." The sentence just drifts off.

"I found out I was pregnant six weeks after he shipped out. I sort of buried myself in thoughts of the baby and what our life would be when he came back. I read all about childcare and all that, but I was also reading everything else decent I could get my hands on. I would ride the bus to Macon once a week—it was like a full day on the bus—just to go to a decent bookstore. I guess I was finishing my education, in a sense. I was a very unhappy girl."

" I got letters from Dennis, talking about the job they were doing. I could hear a little doubt in the things he wrote, once he got over there, but he was still that good son—that good son that attracted me—and he was going to do his duty, dammit, come hell or high water. And I was trying to be a good daughter."

"But as time went on, I could see he was really straining to keep up that sense of duty—he told me less and less of what was going on, and when he did, his explanations became more and more surreal. He wrote once that he didn't see how he could pacify the countryside unless they sent him a lot more flamethrowers."

"The rebel wives had drifted apart after the incident, and the other army wives had sort of excommunicated us, so I was really on my own for months. Livy was born in the fall, and I was ecstatic with her, making her room nice and getting her baby clothes and living in this fantasy world of mommyhood. I had given up on everything outside of her room, her strained peaches, singing to her and feeding her and changing her."

"Four months after she was born, I got a letter from Dennis saying he was going to have a leave and I should meet him in Manila. I got so excited! I bought new clothes, I bought him some tapes that he would know I bought for him, because he would like them and I would hate them—"

"That's a good spously thing to do—" I smiled.

"I thought so," she smiled back. And then the smile bleeds off her face. "Three days before I was scheduled to leave, I got the telegram—they still had telegrams, but they didn't deliver them anymore. They read them to you over the phone. I remember the woman started reading it and clearly she hadn't seen what it said till she got there. She must have been new, not to have had many casualty telegrams."

"Killed in action?"

"That's what the telegram said, but they left out the details. I'd lived on the post over a year, so I'd seen more of those telegrams than I needed to—and they always had some details of the action. I spoke to everyone in the company bureaucracy and they all mumbled some bullshit reply and then found a reason to get off the phone. I knew there had to be *some* action because there wasn't enough of him left to bury, though we did, for his mother's sake. But the embalmer at the funeral home recommended cremation because it would only take a second."

"Phew — sorry."

She nods.

"Finally, one of the other officers who was wounded when Dennis was killed came home and was shunned by everybody — the army, the wifely society, the whole place. And the story finally came out — they'd been fragged."

She paused for a moment and looked at me, an infinitely sad smile on her face.

"You know what fragged is, right?"

I knew. Murdered by his own soldiers. Usually a grenade in the tent, or in the sleeping bag while on patrol. One of the dirty not-very-hidden secrets of the war. There were over 300 cases documented — those were the guys they *caught*. In this case, it sounded like they took no chances. Evidently, somebody in the outfit didn't want to be as good a son as Dennis.

"All this — from the time I got word to the time I found out what really happened — took 3 days. So it was the day I had my tickets to fly out. My mother was there to watch Livy, and now to help me. I cracked open the suitcase, to put away the things I had planned to take to Manila. And then I just stopped. I just stared at that neatly packed suitcase, for like twenty minutes."

"It was just like I didn't exist, like I was some hollow thing just taking up space. My uncynical man had just gotten cancelled in the most cynical way possible. I had no life. I hadn't finished school, I had no trade, I would be out of the army life now that he was gone—I had nothing in the world."

"Livy seemed like a child's dream, all of a sudden. She wasn't, of course, but the way I'd been living—based around her—was a dream, and I had no way to separate the two at the time. My whole life had evaporated. I kept staring at the tickets and the suitcase. Then I closed it, and called a cab. I went downstairs, asked my mother if she could watch Livy for a while—I had to go away. I guess she could read it all on my face. She just said 'yes' and I went to the airport. And flew to Manila."

"When'd you come back?"

"For a weekend? I've been back every year. For good? You saw me. This afternoon."

She picks up the cup and puts it back in formation around the kettle. She comes over and pecks me on the cheek.

"It's been nice seeing you again," she says, and treads off to her room. I stand with my head spinning, staring at the gulls and the wind whipping the snow in the fantastic moonlight.

Plans

The next morning, winter was announcing its arrival—the air was brisk and clear, the wind stiff and refreshing, snow scattering itself all around the landscape. A beautiful day, spoiled only by the certainty that this beautiful day would be followed by months of bitter, biting, bone-chilling, wet, windy, beastly weather.

As I woke, I saw Livy scurrying around the room, putting together clothes to wear. Jeans, a hooded sweatshirt, socks and sneakers. Usually, she came out every morning to check the chat in one of her flimsy nightgowns.

"You're getting dressed?" I asked.

"You got a problem with that?"

"Well, you do have a public—that outfit's a long drop on the thrill-o-meter from what they're used to. How long do you plan on keeping this up?"

"Until *she* leaves."

"That could be a problem."

She was in the middle of pulling on the white sweatsocks. She stopped, without looking up.

"Why do you say that?"

"Last night, she told me she was home 'for good.' She made a point of it."

"Shut up!"

I shrugged. "I'm not certifying anything. But that's what she said."

Livy sat teetering on the edge of the bed for a moment.

"She didn't mean that," she said, as though repeating it would help her convince herself. "She can't do that. She'd *better* not." She started pulling on her sneakers.

"Why not?" I asked, and immediately realized I should have just stayed quiet.

"Because I've been on my own my whole life, and now that I'm using this house for something useful and don't need her *at all*, she'd better not decide *now* that she wants to come hang out. That's not happening. Not. OK?"

"Fine with *me*," I say.

She stared at me for a second, clearly mulling a question. And I was immediately certain she was playacting a bit, that the question had been simmering awhile, and she was elaborately pretending it had just come to her.

Finally, she said, "Whose side are you on?"

"Does there have to be a side?" I asked back.

She started to shudder, like a teakettle about to whistle.

"Okay," I said immediately and moved over to sit next to her. "Let's talk about this. I knew your mom a long time ago. It was a shock to see her, especially under the conditions we met. But I'm with you, right?"

"Right," Livy said, and then waited for the rest. She seemed quite clear on the fact that I should have more to say.

Of course, I was trying to say as little as possible. I'd already lied, just with that one statement. I had no idea where I stood between these two women. And I sure as hell didn't want to be tipping things one way or the other. Wherever we all ended up, we had to get there in some natural way. And there was absolutely *nothing* natural in this entire situation.

"You had a nice conversation last night?" she asked.

"We caught up on things a little."

"So whose side are you on?" she repeated.

"Does there have to be a side?" I asked back. If you're going to keep at it, so am I. The reality was, I didn't know what else to say.

"Never mind," she stammered after a moment's hesitation, and she disappeared out into the living room.

I jumped up and threw my clothes on.

I padded through the living room toward the bathroom. The two of them were sitting at the kitchen counter talking politely. Both pairs of eyes swiveled toward me in unison as I came through. Livy kept stealing glances at her mother as well, while Alison remained pleasantly smiling, focused on me. I felt like a moose in the crosshairs—actually, I felt like the unfortunate gifted moose that *knows* he's in the crosshairs.

"Good morning," I said brightly and they both said something perky in reply. Smiling and deferential, the two of them, feeling each other out like rams staking out territory on a ridge.

I felt the weight of the situation all too heavily in that fraction of a second—and then I heard the words "Why don't we all go out to breakfast?" coming from my throat.

They both jumped, like I'd wired the seats with a small electrical charge.

"Great!" Alison answered, a split second before Livy barked, "I don't eat breakfast...out...usually," the line dribbling off, sickly, at the end.

I put on my best phony smile—I hate situations like this— and said, "Well, I 'm taking a shower—you two decide what you want to do about breakfast."

I was in the shower just long enough to get drenched before Livy showed up.

"What do you think you're doing?" she demanded.

"What do you mean?"

She was about to light into me—I could see it in her face. But then she leaned stiffly against the counter, a totally unconvincing replica of someone relaxing. I noticed that the camera on the far wall was off. I wondered if they were off all over the house, or only where we were talking. Either way, it was a noteworthy occasion, the first time a camera had gone out since she shut down the house in anger at Angel279.

I'd beaten myself up about how artificial our relationship was, from my side. We started with sex and I never had to compete for her. Which was good, since the odds of my success would have been pretty long in that case.

But now I realized that went for *her*, too. Now she was feeling like she had to compete for *me*—compete with her *mother*, no less, for my attention. And that was plain weird, from every angle.

I had to wonder if she hadn't chosen me in the first place knowing she wouldn't have to compete for me—what other prospects did I have at the time, especially that would compare to her? Certainly, it could have fed her confidence level. And now, the shoe was—or at least, appeared to be, from her point of view—on the other foot. And it was driving her crazy.

Crazy enough that, Livy being Livy, the thing foremost on her mind was not to *show* it. And, of course, that just made us a good match, at the moment, for one another.

"Well, my mom has plans," she said now. "I'm sure she has things to do."

"Fine. If she does, she should do them," I replied. "I just felt like going out for breakfast, and I didn't want to exclude her. She is your mom, after all."

"Well, that's very considerate of you," she responded. "But I just don't think you need to make arrangements for us. I don't want her to feel obligated."

"No, I don't want her to feel obligated. I just thought maybe—"

Do I have to go on recounting this dialogue in detail? We've all had these types of conversations—where both parties are lying through their teeth, saying exactly the opposite of what they mean.

I wanted to spend every possible minute with Alison, and Livy wanted her to go away as quickly as possible.

I wanted Livy to be happy with her mother, which was completely impossible at the moment.

But I wanted Livy to be happy, too.

And if I had to choose between those imperatives, I was going to be *really* confused.

I grew up absolutely hopeless in these kinds of conversations—fortunately, 15 years of marriage to Marla had sharpened my skills, so I could now hold my own.

"Well, she *does* want to go," Livy finally admitted. "To breakfast, that is."

"Look, I don't care," I said, knowing from vast prior experience that God in Heaven would not actually strike me dead for this. "Why don't you two go? I don't want to get in the way."

This go-for-broke approach goes so far beyond lying that you usually stun your opponent into giving you what you want. It never worked with Marla—not once—but it bought me years of job security at the network.

Livy took the blow well, dammit.

She looked me straight in the eye and said, "Who do you want to go to breakfast with?"

This was, of course, a direct question that actually reflected her feelings—a total breach of the rules. Section 27, Line 12, subclause b-32. Check, and mate.

As the master, Mister Twain, says: If you tell the truth, you don't have to remember anything. So when my back is to the wall, I usually follow the Master's advice.

"Both of you," I admitted.

She looked at me for a long moment; then she went back out to the living room. I shampooed quickly and ran to get dressed. When the bell rings, you've got to be there, and this bell was ringing off the charts.

Tea In The Sahara With You

Livy drove. This guaranteed a memorable morning.

She was a fast and not particularly attentive driver, and the roads were narrow and full of traffic. This made for a few nailbiting moments.

But she *was* fast, so we were quickly at the Biarritz, the scene of our fateful business meeting only a week earlier, a darkwood bowl of a place with a good view of both ocean and river, not far from the state park.

I felt at the periphery of the conversation—seated at the table, but miles away, as far as the two women were concerned.

"This is nice," Alison started. "Do you come here a lot?"

"No," Livy replied. "I eat cereal at home mostly."

"Well, it's nice," Alison said. Long silence.

She continued, "I wonder if people still park in the lots around here and walk over to the park, to beat the toll at the gate."

"They have a guard in the parking lot," Livy said, and went back to drawing rings in the coffee at the bottom of her saucer.

Livy looked like my 10-year-old when I ask him how he's doing in school. Determined to avoid any meaningful exchange of information, sullenly pretending to be interested in anything other than the conversation at hand, but not providing any alternative. She sulked at her coffee, and then went to the buffet to assemble a plate.

Alison sighed. "Do you think she'll talk to me eventually?"

"You'll have to wear her down. Prepare for a long campaign," I advised her.

She stared at the table and nodded slowly. Then she got up and went to the buffet.

I wasn't very hungry. It was painful watching the two of them. I wondered if there wasn't something I could do to help bridge the gap between them. And then I could move on to India and Pakistan, or the Korea twins. I collected half a grapefruit and a muffin, along with my orange juice.

When I returned to the table, Alison turned to me.

"Did you ever go out with Captain Jack?" she said.

"Oh, God, yes," I said, turning to Livy immediately. "Captain Jack was this guy who had a fishing boat out of Seaview. He would take kids onboard to tie the lines and stow the fish and bring drinks up from the hold for his paying customers. If you happened to be hanging around the docks early, he'd offer you a job, give you a few bucks and all the beer you could drink." I turned back to Alison. "I didn't think he took girls."

"Oh yes," she said. "He also had a habit of groping us, though I didn't find that out till after I'd agreed."

"We played a dirty trick on him," I said. "My buddy Barry and I signed on and drank everything we could get our hands on—then, before he'd gotten far out, we dove off the ship and swam back in. After that, he wouldn't hire us again."

"I don't blame him," Livy said, humorless.

"Oh, I don't blame him either," I admitted. "We just thought we were being funny. We were kids."

"I think my generation is a little more mature," Livy continued.

"Absolutely," I needled her. "From the time you're ten, you're preparing to make your first million. Kids in college have far better investment portfolios than I'll ever have. But I got to be Huck Finn for a while, and you didn't."

"I don't remember you being quite such a snot before," Livy sniffs, and I repent immediately.

"Sorry. I'm not contemptuous of you—you *will* make your first million soon, and many more, and you'll deserve every penny. But every college kid in America is convinced they're going to, and the odds don't work that way. Besides, it shouldn't be the thing that 17 year olds are thinking about."

"What should they be thinking about," Livy sat up from her cup, "—love, peace and Woodstock?" And, for the first time, the anger and frustration, the whatever—it was hard to define what was boiling up inside her, but for the first time since Alison showed up, you could *see* it on her face.

"We believed in justice," Alison says, finally joining in. "We believed that people would treat each other well, given the opportunity. We believed that love could transform your life."

"Wow—*that* was off." Livy laughs.

"Says you," I mutter.

"We never articulated much of an alternative, except to say there should be one. We were very naïve about the fear of the unknown," Alison said.

"We were very naïve," I repeated.

"Very," Alison nodded. "But we believed in something. Don't you believe love has power? To transform everything? To heal and cure and remove obstacles?"

It was very brave—and, again, very naïve—to throw a question like that to Livy, who had been the cynical child of the Millennium all morning. But Alison was clearly trying to break through to her.

Livy, predictably, played this true to form.

"I think love is great," she said, "once you've accomplished what you set out to accomplish."

"You don't want to be loved?" Alison asked. It was so naked a question that I winced when I heard it.

Livy didn't wince.

"I want to be famous," she replied. "I want to be recognized and respected and outrageous and courageous. Until I get there, I'm not *me* yet. Until I'm *me*, I can't really give myself to anyone, because I'm not the person I want to be—that I *have* to be."

"But you're just talking about the way you appear from the outside—the way others judge you," Alison persisted. "What about inside? What do *you* want?"

"I'm the child of the hippies," Livy said, the contempt now plain in her voice. "I want to realize myself."

"That's what you guys got wrong," Livy continued. "You figured if you made yourselves more enlightened inside, it would fix things. You didn't realize you have to *do* something about it, not just *be* it. Otherwise, all you're doing is patting yourself on the back. Once I *am* that person—once I've done something—then I can share myself."

"Oh, you're wrong," Alison moaned.

"No, she's not," I said, surprised by my own voice. They both stopped and looked at me.

"Everybody at this table believes in self-improvement", I found myself saying. "Nobody wants to be a wife anymore— meaning, nobody wants to take a back seat and support someone else's dreams anymore. We all have *our own* dreams."

"Well, is that wrong?" Alison asked, looking very vulnerable all at once.

"Not as far as I'm concerned, no. But how do you have a society where everyone goes after their own dreams, without it turning into a free-for-all? I think that's one reason marriages don't last anymore—people are used to an old transaction that doesn't work anymore, and they haven't figured out what's going to replace it yet."

"Look at me," I continued. "The guy Marla loved was an operations guy at a TV network. That's who she married. Problem is, I didn't really want to be that guy. Getting that job at the network was giving up for me—giving up on the dreams I had for myself. Like Livy says, I wasn't satisfied with me. So, once we were married, the more Marla got comfortable, the more I felt trapped, being someone I didn't like. As time went on, and I started becoming more of the guy I liked, she wasn't comfortable with *him*."

"So what's the answer," Alison asked. "How do you care—how do you have something that matters—if everyone's in it for themselves?"

Livy sat, actually paying attention, but not looking as though this had anything to do with her.

"Well, you can't," I said, for once actually knowing what I wanted to say. "I've thought about this a lot since I moved out. What the hell is love? Is there some objective definition, some bottom-line test you can give it, so you can say 'Yeah, this isn't just infatuation, or lust, or whatever'? And I think the lowest-common denominator is: If you love somebody, you want them to have what *they* want."

"That's where Marla and I went haywire—we didn't want the same things, and we didn't love each other enough to work for the other person's happiness. And that's where Livy's right, I think. Until you've become someone you're comfortable with, you can't know what you want, which compromises you can live with and which ones you can't. And if you don't know *that*, I don't see how you can be happy with someone else."

"I don't know," Alison said. "You seem to be saying no one should do anything until all the questions are answered. Sometimes, you have to take a leap of faith—about yourself or someone else."

"All I know," Livy interrupted roughly, "is you should find yourself *before* you have a husband or a kid depending on you, that can get hurt by all those self-centered leaps of faith."

And that, don't you know, was the end of breakfast.

Traces

That night, after Livy falls asleep, I wander into the living room and there is Alison, as I'd hoped. Silently, without even talking about it, we walk to the deck and close the door behind us, bundled into sweatsuits and winter jackets. We've found our private place.

If we'd romanced, as we should have, in high school, each meeting would have been a search for privacy—all dates are, before you have your own place to go. A search for a place to talk, laugh together, to kiss and touch. Back then, the fear would have been our parents. Now, it's her daughter.

"She put *us* in our place, didn't she?" I start.

"I have a feeling she hasn't started yet," Alison said. "She's mad as hell at me, and she has reason."

I watch the light bounce off the ocean into her eyes, and suddenly I feel like I can ask any question I want. So finally, I ask *the* question.

"What happened? Why didn't you come back?"

She looks out over the rail, the wind blowing her hair in clumps around her face.

"I don't know," she says, "and not for lack of trying. I've thought about it constantly, and I still don't know why I didn't *make* myself come back."

"Actually, it's that thing we were talking about at breakfast," she continues, looking down on the beach and the waves and the end of the world, out beyond the water. "I had to take a leap of faith. I had to decide that I could be a mother and *be* somebody—a writer, a painter, a carpenter, anything—somebody I could feel good about. At first, I was lost. Then, as I found myself, bit by bit, I didn't think I could do both those things together. And then, every month I stayed away made it harder for me to come back."

"I was so ashamed for being gone—I hid from it by getting another assignment, writing another article. I would come home for a week, intending to stay, and the first time something uncomfortable would happen—Livy would get sick or demanding or my mother would make some comment about my lifestyle—I would take off. I was so afraid of being in a cage, I wouldn't take the chance that maybe I could break out of it."

She shakes her head. "By the time I decided I didn't care anymore—that I had to know her, come hell or high water—she was grown up."

She stops, purses her lips. "I guess the crisis came when my mom died. And I couldn't face it. I didn't come home for months—

then I visited for a couple days and left again. Then I couldn't finish my next assignment. I knew I should have been here. I knew it, but I needed *another* excuse to come back. And then I got Sylvie's telegram, and I came."

We sit for a while. I don't hear a sound—not the waves, not the wind, not the breath in my mouth. Nothing. Actually, that's wrong—I *do* feel. I feel a void, a lacking, the absence of a necessary substance, the lack of a molecule in the air or a mineral in the alloy.

"I'm sorry," I say finally. "It's real presumptuous of me to say this—but that's not a good enough answer, is it?"

She looks at me—Thank God, without anger.

"You always want answers. You always think there are answers," she says.

I shrug.

"When I look, I always find one," I say.

"Do you? Do you find one—or twenty?"

I stop for a moment. I know the answer immediately—it just takes a minute for me to be willing to admit it.

"Every time I look, I find an answer," I say. "It's not always the same one."

"So where does all your questioning get you?" she continues. "How do you know which answer is the right one?"

"It's easy," I say. "They *all* are."

She stares at this.

"They're all *right*?" she asks. "You never mislead yourself? You're never just plain *wrong*?"

"The answers that are wrong go away," I assert. "You forget them. The ones that keep coming back have something going for them."

"That's *it*?" she cries. "That's the end of the epic search for truth and beauty?"

I throw my hands up.

"That's the best I've got now. You keep searching till you die. I'm not dead yet."

"Okay," she says. "Well, I don't know why I left, and I don't know why I stayed away. Maybe if I spend the rest of my life thinking about it, I'll figure it out. I have the feeling that, as Livy might say, it's more important for me to *do* something about it— you got a problem with that?"

I smile. "Nope. No problem."

"Okay," she smiles back, and then the smile drains away. "Then help me. I have to get through to her. Whatever I did, I have to start over now. Help me make it better."

"You assume she listens to anyone," I say.

"She cares about you," she breathes. "She'll listen if you tell her something."

It is one of the most excruciating moments of my life. Here is the woman I want, telling me I can help her, because her daughter cares for me. Her daughter: my happiness—the obstacle to my happiness. Take your pick.

"I'll try," I promise.

The Law

I headed home. It was around 2 in the morning, and a cool night, another member of winter's entourage.

I headed along the beach wall, watching the stars and the waves rolling in. I could see planes descending toward JFK, and in the distance, the lights of Manhattan glistened.

I felt buoyant. Somehow, just having Alison around—even having her around arguing with me—was incredible, a miracle. Literally, my dream come true. And proof, I suppose, that you must be careful what you wish for.

I thought about it for another moment and then decided to stop thinking. Later. Tonight was a time to enjoy, not to consider.

I got to the house and fell fast asleep, without even pulling out the couch, without even taking off my clothes.

In the morning, I was awakened at 7 am by a knock at the door. It was a young pimply-faced man with curly black hair the texture of steel wool.

"Is this you?" he asked, shoving a paper in my face.

"Yeah, that's me," I answered, reading my name on the paper.

"Sign here," he said, and threw a clipboard up for my signature. I signed, and that's how I found out Marla was ready to go to court.

I assumed she would make an attempt to negotiate terms first. But that's not what these papers said. Court date, about two weeks away. She must feel confident.

When I got back to Livy's, things were shaping into some kind of routine. Livy was working the chat, wearing a spool of saran wrap onto which she dripped paint from tubes of many colors. After the paint had dripped sufficiently, Livy would roll around on a board on the floor next to her, then cut away part of the plastic and lay it down there. The mobile camera had a good view of it, and the audience was voting on which way they wanted the pieces to go together.

Alison was watching all this from the kitchen, and as I came in, she offered to glue down the pieces once the vote was tallied. Livy agreed without enthusiasm, and introduced her mother to the team. They responded, predictably, by both questioning how a mother could stand next to her daughter while she exposed herself on the Internet and telling her to take off her blouse. Livy let this go on without comment. Alison ignored it, going to work with the glue gun.

Sylvie was seated at the dining room table, working the books. I sat down next to her and watched her pump through the bills, one by one, scrutinizing them with that hawklike gaze of hers. It was almost restful to watch her.

Finally, Sylvie put her glasses down on the desk. She looked over at mother and daughter by the bright sunlit side of the room.

"They're a sad case," she said. "The young one needs to make a few mistakes."

"What do you mean?" I asked. I was well used to Sylvie's way of starting into her subject without preliminaries.

"Her mother made a mistake. A big one, no doubt. But she's here now. She clearly wants to heal the breach, and Livy won't let her."

"She's getting back at her," I shrugged. "Pretty simple stuff."

"Ummm," she breathed, staring at them some more. "But she's *playing* at it—she thinks the opportunity will keep coming again." She fastened that hawklike gaze on me. "And we know that isn't the way of things, don't we?"

A hundred things flashed through my mind at that moment—Alison, me, Alison *and* me, Daniel and me, Livy's rush to stardom, Marla and me. But I had come to Sylvie with one purpose, and now it pushed itself to the forefront.

"Sylvie, I need a lawyer."

"Oh? Federal, state or local? Misdemeanor or felony?"

"Divorce. Licensed to practice in New York State. Not an asshole."

She stared over her glasses at me for a moment.

"That is the entire list of qualifications?" she asked.

"I've known a few lawyers over the years. My experience is that they fall pretty neatly into the asshole or not-an-asshole categories—and damn few in the latter."

"Well, I know someone," she said. "Unfortunately, you're not the first friend of mine in these straits." She scribbled a name and number on her scratch pad and tore off the sheet for me. "Tell him I say 'hello.'"

As I was about to get up, she said, "You *want* a divorce, yes?"

I nodded.

"I see it," she ended. "You're much more purposed now than when we met. You were all at odds then. Wherever you end up, it'll be better for you."

"You don't think I've ended up *here*?"

"Here?" she sniffed. "This is a waystation—always was. You're invaluable for what you've done—but you'll move on, when it's time. I think everyone knows it."

"Livy?"

Her eyes narrowed. "She's the least sentimental of the bunch," she said. "The rest of you old folks are the romantics. She's enjoyed every minute of it, but she reads which way the wind is blowing before the rest of you get out of bed in the morning."

"And she gets up later than the rest of us, so that takes some doing," I retorted.

"I meant—Ohhh, go call your lawyer," she sniped, waving her glasses at me.

The lawyer's name was Nat Turner, which gave me an ominous feeling—being named for the leader of a failed slave rebellion was not the image I wanted to carry into court—but he was amiable on the phone and had an opening that afternoon. I made explanations to Livy and took off to see him.

"OK" he said when I presented him with the document I'd been handed. "Where are the other papers?"

"What other papers?"

"The complaint itself. The separation papers."

"This is all I got."

He looked over the page again. "I see—they've got another few days to serve you. They're waiting till the last minute to give you as little time as possible to prepare. You should run up to Staten Island tomorrow morning and make a copy—the court clerk will have it."

"Ok," I said, making notes on a pad.

"I should tell you that, since you've been served with a court hearing, I will have to charge you a $10,000 retainer."

"What?"

"This is a court proceeding now, not a negotiation. I doubt any lawyer will charge you less."

"Then I'm going to have to go without a lawyer. I haven't got anything near $10,000. I'm the one stupid husband who wasn't socking money away in an out-of-state bank account for months ahead of time."

He considered this for a moment.

"I'm sorry. I have to maintain my fees—I hope you understand."

"I do." I understood, but it wasn't doing much for that sinking feeling in my stomach.

"Look—you're a friend of Sylvie's. Why don't you sit a moment and let's just talk about your situation, alright?"

"Okay."

"First of all, as a lawyer, I recommending you *get* a lawyer. You understand that? You will be in much better shape with an attorney representing you."

"I *want* an attorney. But if you're right about them wanting $10,000 down, I haven't a shot."

"Well, then let's talk about that contingency. You'll be a pro se—that's what they call it, representing yourself. Pro se's sue the courts way more often than people who are represented by lawyers, generally because they do a pretty lousy job of it." He paused a moment, looking at me sternly to make sure I got the message—which I did. The only effect was to increase the bile level in my stomach.

"But, because pro se's sue so often, the courts bend over backwards to protect your rights. So you'll have a favorable atmosphere there. What is the main issue between you and your spouse? Distribution of property? The house? Any assets?"

"That won't be an issue. She can have the house. We have no other assets—we went bankrupt a couple years ago. Adultery, maybe, though it isn't true."

"You aren't seeing anyone?"

"I didn't have anyone when I left. I am seeing someone now—I started working for her, and having a relationship with her, shortly after I moved out."

"Well, if you had met her this morning, it would still technically be adultery—you're still married in the eyes of the law. But I haven't seen a case where adultery figured in twenty years— no one cares anymore. What else?"

"What I'm really concerned is that she'll try to make a case that I'm an unfit father."

"Does she have a case? Are you seeing your son?"

"Every other weekend and every Tuesday night for dinner."

"And how often have you missed it?"

"Never."

"No, seriously—" He clearly wasn't used to this answer. Unfortunately, from my discussion groups, I'd seen how often fathers who were freed from lousy marriages turned their backs on the kids as well as the ex-wife.

"Never. Every time since we agreed to a regular schedule, I've had him."

"Does she have financial problems having to do with your son?"

"I've been paying her about 40% of my salary voluntarily since I left. My son has a learning disability," I explained. "So I'm paying half the tuition of his private school and babysitter costs."

He looked down his nose at me now. Clearly there was something wrong with this picture, and he didn't see it yet.

"Okay—I'm at a loss. How is she going to say you're an unfit father?"

"I'm seeing a young lady. Emphasis on 'young'—she's 23. She runs an internet exhibitionist site—she's the exhibitionist. We've had sex online numerous times in the past few months. The tapes are available for download."

Turner's lip turned up a little bit, but he controlled it—he might have been biting his cheek pretty hard, though.

"That's a pretty creative problem," he said, but then his expression turned stern again. "Is your child involved in this exhibitionist website?"

"Absolutely not."

"Can she say that he was?"

"Never. He's never seen it, he doesn't know about it, I don't go to work when he's with me. He's only met the young woman once in passing."

"Are there photos of the meeting?"

"Not unless someone was across the street with a telephoto lens."

"Well?" he asked. "*Was* someone?"

I stopped at that. I remembered the night I thought the green Taurus was following me, and for some reason I thought about the emails from the 'real' Pale Guy. They'd started up again recently, after that long pause, and they seemed intended to rattle me. I couldn't figure out their purpose, but now I wanted to go back and reread them, with the thought of Marla and a private detective in mind.

"I don't know" was all I could say.

"Well, that could certainly be an issue. You're entitled to find employment, and if you've developed a relationship, that's pretty common human behavior. But if she can say your son might be mixed up in this thing, she could make it hard for you, if she wants to."

"She wants to."

"You know that for a fact?" he asked.

"I know her history and her tendencies. She's viciously angry at me for leaving—not that she doesn't have a right, I suppose—and she's never been above using him for leverage for what she wants."

"What do you think she wants?"

I had thought about this quite a bit actually, without thinking I had an answer. But now, it came out of my mouth without thinking.

"I think she wants to cripple me, to punish me for leaving. I think she wants to make sure I never have enough money to get by, that my life will always be dominated by her. If I'm not going to be married to her, I should never be able to get away from her anyway. And she'll do this by making me pay every cent she can wring out of me for his learning disability, and making me fight just to get joint custody."

His expression changed immediately.

"You're *not* looking for joint custody?" he said.

"Of course I am."

"No, you're not," he told me. "New York State, unlike New Jersey and much of the rest of the country, has a specific legal prejudice *against* joint custody."

Now my stomach sank through the floor.

"What? How?"

"Their argument—and, after you finish getting angry about it, one that has some merit—is that they will only give joint custody if *both* parents ask the court for it. If you can't agree on *that*, they figure, you're not going to agree on anything else and the child isn't served by having two adults at loggerheads all the time."

Everything felt dull now—the whole world had gone gray for me.

"So what do I have left?" I asked.

"Visitation. Liberal visitation, if you can agree on it, or visitation on a schedule, if you can't. You've been seeing him regularly, so that's a guide for proper visitation.

"But, if she wants to cripple you," he continued, "and she knows about your involvement in this website—"

"She knows I'm on it. When she sees my papers, she'll know I'm employed there as well."

"In a technical capacity," he pointed out. It hadn't even occurred to me that my employment could be construed in other ways.

"In a technical capacity, absolutely," I agreed.

"Then she will certainly be able to make it interesting for you. Once again, I'm advising you to get an attorney. Payment plans can be arranged."

"I hear you," I said. "But I don't know if I'm going to be in this job a month from now, or *where* I'll be. And I won't take on a bad debt."

"Then remember—by state law, you'll owe her 17% of your salary, less some taxes—though the fact that you're paying more will surely be introduced."

"My son has a learning disability," I repeated. "So I'm paying half the tuition and babysitter costs, over and above the 17%."

"I see you know the formula," he said. "You've seen a lawyer already?"

"Yeah—when I finally decided I was moving out, about a week before I told her, I went to see a lawyer on Staten Island. *Her* lawyer, in fact," I chuckled.

He didn't chuckle. "What do you mean, her lawyer?"

"The lawyer she retained. The lawyer who's representing her on the court papers."

"How long ago did you see her?" He was very interested, suddenly; he was sitting bolt upright in his chair now.

"About—four months ago now."

"You had a confidential discussion with her about your marriage?"

"Yes—I had to know where I stood legally, though she didn't tell me about the custody thing. I didn't think much of her—that's why I didn't retain her."

"Do you have any proof of the meeting?"

"I paid her $100 for the consultation."

"Then there's your defense," he said conclusively, bouncing his fingers on the desk in delight. "You disqualify her."

"What?"

"You consulted with her. Somehow, she missed it. You have attorney-client privilege with her—legally, she *can't* represent your wife. If you bring it up in court, the court *has* to disqualify her."

"Okay—" I was uncertain about this.

"Don't you see? She gets thrown off the case, your wife has to start over again with a new attorney. That's a new retainer and a bigger one, now that she's instituted court proceedings—and she's set back months. It puts you in the catbird seat."

"Okay," I said. Yes, it would be harassment, but it would certainly scuttle Marla's plans. And Marla hated having her plans scuttled. Maybe it would throw her into disarray and we could just negotiate things ourselves, the way I wanted to in the first place.

"Thank you," I said, shaking Nat Turner's hand. I walked out of the office with plenty to worry about, but at least I had a plan.

Dreams

Alison is sitting on the porch, in the middle of the night, overlooking the beach, as has become her habit since she arrived. I come out and sit next to her on the bench.

"Isn't it funny," she says, "how this beach makes me feel five years old? It just cuts through all the years and the miles. I drove to Monmouth yesterday. It just looks like a suburban town. I barely recognize anything; it brings back no memories. *This* place just gets to me in an instant."

"Every place I go here," I tell her, "I keep flashing on my father. I remember feeling close to him here in a way I never did anywhere else, and he keeps coming back to me. That doesn't happen in Monmouth."

The waves are crashing onto the beach, the sound mingling with the roar of a Harley on the street below. A tanker tracks the horizon, cutting through the moonglow on the water. It makes no sound at all, and soon, with the Harley gone in the distance, all that's left is the pulsing of the waves again.

"When I found out I was pregnant, I hated myself," Alison says. "I didn't know who I was, and I didn't want to be pregnant and I was ashamed I didn't want to be pregnant. It's funny, I feel how empty and alone and desperate I was *now*—I don't know if I let myself feel it then. Then, I just blamed me.

"And I called my mother. I was stunned that she listened. She was concerned and cared and I found myself talking to her—I thought, like an adult, but God…" she shakes her head, "I was so lost. And I think she knew it. And at one point, she said 'All the time you were a baby, I kept thinking I had no idea how to be a mother. It wasn't till it was over and done that I knew I did. You'll figure out a way.'

"And I remember thinking; I just don't have that optimism. I just felt like the world was corrupt, that we were failures and frauds—nothing was up to my standards, I guess."

"But I think," Alison continues, "that when I left Livy with my mom, that I was trying to do right by her, and rebuking myself, at the same time. I really thought I had to live up to those impossible standards."

I remember that time so vividly—but so rarely. I so rarely want to remember anything about those years—I spent them so frightened, so uncertain about *everything*.

"Y'know, it sounds insane to say this, but our parents had it easy," I tell her. "They had the Depression and World War II to deal with, but at least those were clear, tangible problems.

Everybody could see them, everybody could band together with some common purpose—and they were the kind of problems that would yield to hard work and effort. And they did solve them, God bless them."

"We didn't have it that easy. They handed us a world way better than what they remembered and said, 'Okay, now go out and make something really great, now that we've taken care of the big shit for you.' And we wanted to—we felt we were supposed to. But our satisfactions were different. We didn't have an enemy in jackboots or on Wall Street. In order to get what we wanted, we had to change things *inside*. 'We have seen the enemy and he is us.' That's a different kind of battle-and it's a lot harder to tell whether or not you've won."

"Maybe," Alison thinks, gazing at the waves. "But I gave up on my daughter—"

"She's still here."

She smiles at me—a sad, sad smile. "She's as impossible for me to reach as your father is for you now."

"I would dispute that," I say lightly. "Where there's life, there's hope, and other appropriate clichés."

"Well," she muses, "I certainly am not going to be able to get close to her and you at the same time."

God, it's wonderful—and painful—to hear her say those words. She *wants* to get close to me, despite the insane situation we're all in. And I want it too, so badly.

But we've been so truthful, so open, with each other. We've sat together now for what seems like many nights, without caution or pretense or any agenda beyond the bounds of this wooden deck, other than Livy. It's been the way I've wanted to be with someone for as long as I can remember.

And, that said, I have to tell her the truth, even if it does me no good.

"Don't make the same mistake twice," I hear the words coming out of my mouth. "We don't get to choose *everything*. We get lots of choices, but *everything* isn't on the list."

After a moment, she nods. The smile on her face is thin, but she knows what I'm saying. We both know, far too well.

"Let's go for a walk," she says.

It's a clear, dark night—Manhattan's towers and the million stars overhead all look close enough to grasp and hold. The beach is mottled with spray from the waves and a cluster of crabs track up and down in their weird impatient scutter.

Alison is investigating. She wanders the beach, drawn first by the thrumming tide, then by a crab shell decaying and the overturned hull of a sailboat awaiting its owner. Every item gets a glance, a touch, due diligence. Every moment gets its due. Moonlight becomes her.

This is the woman I wanted. I was right about her, from the beginning.

She catches me looking at her and smiles—she's taking *me* in, too.

We walk close together down the beach. I reach for her and then pull back—for a moment, I am once again that gangly thirteen-year-old at a dance. Not today's thirteen-year-olds, mind you—they are having group sex and day trading on their cellphones—the kind of hopeless thirteen-year-old *I* remember being.

She glances at me, her face flickering a question and then turning away. Fool! She wanted the arm around her shoulder. I'm a prisoner of my own uncertainty, my own doubts.

I feel the anger rising in me—anger at me, at my inability to do anything without thinking it to death first.

"A million nights I dreamed about this," I hear myself say.

"About what?" she asks, expectant.

"Walking a beach—this beach—with you. Seeing you again."

She smiles—she relaxes. She needed to hear it—I needed to say it. Thank God I finally did.

"I thought about you…a lot." She laughs, then goes wistful in an instant. "I thought about you all the time."

She looks around, that sharp glance of hers taking in the whole universe of sand and stars and waves crashing in and rolling only a few feet away. That glance brings out every line in her face—she's spent a lot of years skeptically, quizzically sizing up the sights of the world. The lines are beautiful, poetic, well-earned.

"I felt, sometimes," she says, "that my life got warped because of us."

"What do you mean?"

"We were meant to do something, to mean something to each other, back there in high school," she explains, and I know in a flood of feeling exactly what she means.

"We were supposed to love each other in high school," she says, "and then grow from that. Maybe it would have lasted, probably it would have blown up. How many people—at least people with imagination—ever stay with their first love? But we got blunted, because it—we—didn't happen, and I think it unbalanced a lot of things in my life. It's like a sailboat in a high wind—you've got to hang off the boat on the high side, to keep it from tipping." She grins at me—another new smile, an uncomplicated grin. "Once you've done it—once you've hung over the side—you know how. Then you can do it again if you need to. I was supposed to learn how from us—but we didn't sail."

I pick my arms up, to reach out to her, but they just won't go. I pull them back down, trying to disguise…whatever stopped me. Whatever made me uncomfortable.

Too late. She's seen it. She smiles bigger.

"Good for you," she says. "No, you can't. You've fucked it up big-time, my darling. My dream. You're my daughter's lover. You can't put your arms around me."

"Jesus," I hear myself moan.

"Yes, well, I'll give you credit for realizing, somewhere in there, that you can't come after me. You're the man I hoped you were."

"We don't love each other, she and I. We've said so." It sounds weak as soon as it comes out of my mouth.

"Sorry—two points off for that one," she says.

"Now, hold on. Let me try it again." I'm wagging my hand in front of her, beseeching. She seems willing to grant me another moment's indulgence. "What I'm trying to say is—man, this isn't going to sound much better..."

She's amused by my confusion, dammit! Like she knows I won't be able to talk my way out of this one—and, at the same time, like she's hoping I still might.

"First of all," I say, "I'm not what Livy needs. She needs someone to break through that wall of hers, to undermine all her excuses and make her let go, to just *feel*. The reason she wanted me was because she could never really feel romantic about me."

"And *I* want," I continue, "with all my heart, to find someone I can love for the rest of my life who'll love me back. That wasn't Marla, and it's not Livy. It might be you, and I can't just let the chance pass by without trying. Can I?"

She purses her lips and runs her hands through her hair, in a way I suddenly remember from high school. Every movement is deep in feeling for me now. I've fallen off the edge—I'm engulfed in sensations I haven't had in decades, thrilling and dizzy and frightening.

"But you *have* to, don't you?" she says again. "You chose the wrong girl for a fling. You can't come and put your arms around me, can you?"

She stands in front of me, six feet in front of me, her arms open at her sides, almost beckoning me, challenging me. She's right—I can't. I know I can't, as my heart sinks through the sand and the rock below it.

She walks out on a jetty, all the way to the end. The waves are strong, felt in a shudder underfoot and the spray filling the air. At the edge of the jetty she stands, letting the force of the wind and water envelop her. I stand behind. I watch her in wonder.

Then, after a long moment, she drifts back down the jetty to the beach. We end up sitting on the overturned sailboat, looking at each other like a prom couple.

"What are we going to do?" one of us says. I'm not sure who. There is no answer, and then many minutes of silence.

Finally, she starts talking, almost to herself, in a whisper.

"I got the letter from my literary agent that my mom had passed away," she murmurs. "Livy was about to graduate college, so it wasn't a practical issue as far as she was concerned. But it did away with my last pretense, that there was anyone else to care for her who might be hurt or diminished by my coming back. Or who might have made *me* feel diminished, maybe. Anyway, I started feeling it was time. Almost time."

"And one night, I was walking on a beach, staring up at the Southern Cross, and I thought to myself 'I can see the same sky at home.' And the next day I got Sylvie's message and I got on a plane and came back."

"That isn't true," I say.

"What?"

"The same sky'. That's the southern hemisphere. All the constellations are different."

"It doesn't matter," she answers. "If you want to see stars, they all look beautiful. It was time for me to see the ones from home."

"'I came to Casablanca for the waters,'" I quote.

"'What waters? We're in the desert,'" she plays along, getting the joke.

"'I was misinformed.'"

We smile at each other like safecrackers after a good nights work.

We head back to the house, and I find myself thinking this is how life goes. I find the adventurous woman of my dreams just at the point that she wants—needs—to settle down, to stop being adventurous, or at least wants to be adventurous in a different way. I hear my own words echoing: loving someone means—at very least—that you want her to have what *she* wants.

Standing in front of me is a woman who's been part of my life for years. If, as ancient cultures believe, taking someone's image means stealing a piece of their soul, surely I have stolen many many pieces of this woman over years of longing and dreaming. My dreaming has taken much from everyone whose life has touched mine. It's time to give something back, I think.

And I know what Alison wants.

Self-Respect

I wake in the morning with a word on my lips: self-respect. My eyes open and there it is, hovering in the air in front of me.

Not a big word, is it? But it hangs over every piece of my life, as far back as I can remember.

For months since leaving Marla, and almost a year before leaving, I've been peeling back the layers of the onion. I've seen Marla's distance, her coldness and her grasping for things, instead of feelings. It's never a problem for me to pinpoint other people's weaknesses.

I came to see the anger and frustration I'd gotten from my father, not a physical, genetic inheritance, but a handoff, a pass-the-torch of tendencies and expectations.

But now, as the snowfall creates a hush outside the window, I look back over all this, and the big picture finally seems to fall into place.

Everything I've been doing—all the wondering and analyzing, the mixed feelings and confusion, my frenzied efforts writing for the website, the divorce group, trying so hard to help

Livy get what she wants—it's all been about one thing: How do I learn to trust myself? How do I gain confidence that I can do better in the future, that I won't wreck the next relationship I get into?

I haven't had a good answer, though every morning at the keyboard has been a new attempt. Now, suddenly, I do.

I treated Marla badly because I gave up on myself. I didn't stand up for the things I cared for in my own life, and I took my frustrations out on her. If anything is to change, it has to change in me first. I have to feel good—at least, I have to feel satisfied—with who I am. Like Livy said, I have to be someone I'm comfortable with before I'll have something to share.

And, if I'm going to be comfortable with me, I can't let Marla threaten my relationship with Daniel. Not happening—I won't let it. I'm going to take down her attorney and beat her in court with no attorney of my own.

And I'm somehow going to get Alison and Livy talking to each other again.

These are goals I could never have set six months ago. But now, somehow, I see that I *can* do things. I've decided I'm competent and smart and ruthless, the child of a crafty and devious God.

The world is *everything* at once—hopeful and hopeless, painful and exhilarating, gutwrenching and cruel and sublime. All those aspects are out there, and if you walk the path, you have to walk with all of them. I've been tiptoeing on the edge of the path, hoping to avoid the ruts, crying "please don't hurt me" when confronted and nodding with wizened resignation when I get hurt anyway.

No more. No more. Now I'll walk the path, and God help you if you get in my way. I'll play fair, but no more than fair. I've bent far too much in my life for people who gave nothing in return. Now it's time to collect the tab.

Defense

The crickets were having a convention outside my window that day. A rising chorus of chattering came with the dawn and continued as I got dressed and ready at a uniquely early hour.

Then I headed north, to Staten Island and court.

I had to go to two locations before I found the papers. But finally, the court clerk provided the folder, which I signed for. I was allowed to copy anything I wanted — all a matter of public record, of course.

I started reading, and everything in my life changed at once.

At first, I was amused. Then I was amazed. Then I got angry.

According to Marla's divorce petition, I left two days after we 'discovered' Daniel's learning disability. I refused to pay for his therapies. The papers implied that I was trying to run out on him. I could feel my jaw tighten, as though possessed by the spirit of Clint Eastwood. But it wasn't funny, not for a second.

She never mentioned the money I'd been voluntarily paying her, more than twice what the state called for. She listed 2 bank accounts of her own, showing a pathetic balance in each—but failed to mention the third account in the bank statement I'd seen on her desk one night while picking up Daniel. Obviously, the account with the *money* in it.

After I'd made copies of her brief and driven home, driving way too fast and paying way too little attention, I sat down at the desk in my house and started reading it over again, point by point.

The first thing that became very clear was: she wasn't kidding. She was going after me hard, no quarter. She wanted as much money as I had. She had a whole list of therapies that the 'experts' recommended, all of which would be hideously expensive, all of which she said I wasn't willing to pay.

I had no problem taking care of Daniel, but this was a land grab. I was right—she wanted revenge. She wanted to make sure I never lived another independent moment in my life. If I wasn't married to her, I would be crippled by her, financially.

And she had a lawyer, and I didn't.

At first, this almost shriveled me, all by itself. Then I started looking at my email.

The computer I'm writing on now is mine—I bought it the previous fall, to host the web novel, and added a lot of trick stuff to it. It was daddy's project, but it was also a quirky machine, so Marla and Daniel used the old computer. For everyday tasks, it was actually more reliable.

So this machine had my email from four months before I left until now. And, because I'm a completely disorganized mess, all the messages were still in my inbox, or my Sent Mail box. And now I started going through them.

I found an email from Marla from six weeks before I left, telling of the raise she was getting a month later—a raise not reflected in her divorce papers.

I had all the emails that had gone between us every month, confirming that I'd transferred money into her account.

And then I found an email confirming that I hadn't seen the report on Daniel's disability—and the recommendation for therapies—until weeks *after* I'd moved out.

The report had come about because Marla had a brainstorm, a really good one. We were spending a lot of money on Daniel's education, sending him to an expensive private school. But even there, it took a lot to convince the teachers to work with his limitations.

Marla told me one night that, since the city of New York had no program for Asperger's kids, if Daniel was diagnosed by an unimpeachable source, instead of just our pediatrician, and if we could get him accepted into a special program, the city would have to pay for it. Which, considering our finances, would really help us out.

Getting the reports done took time and money. Marla was at the helm. She was a teacher, and knew what the Board of Ed needed to see. She made sure we got the right recommendations.

Marla finally gave me a copy when I saw Daniel at school that first time after I left. She handed it to me and said "Here are the reports on Daniel—you should read them."

So I read them, eventually, not that I saw any need to. I already knew the results, as she did. He needed a special program for his disabilities, with therapies as part of the special program. All the things clinicians say when they want to convince a government bureaucracy to pay attention.

It wasn't until a month later that she started hectoring me about the therapies.

"I need more money to pay for his therapies," she would say.

"What therapies?"

"The therapies in his report. Didn't you read the report?"

"Yes, I read the report. It was written to get him into a proper school and get the Board of Ed to pay for it. It was done because we were running out of money, not so we could end up spending *more* money on therapies."

"But it's in the report—he needs them now. And you have to pay half."

"The reports don't even say he needs therapies *now*—they say he needs them as part of a coordinated program."

"He needs them immediately. They're crucial, and if you're not going to pay for them, then I will."

Meaning her sister the gold-digger whore paid for them. I could smell that one in the background, the sweet scent of self-righteousness o'er the landscape. Marla was using Daniel to whip up family sympathy—his disabilities, the mean father who'd left and wasn't paying for his son's therapy.

I realized now, looking at the document on the table, that this wasn't a story her lawyer had concocted—this was the story she'd been telling her sister, and the rest of the family, to get sympathy and money out of them, for months. Knowing Marla, she now believed it was true.

But at least I had the emails. I could see that, if I kept digging, maybe I could show a pattern, a pattern of Marla behavior I knew all too well.

It was a start.

New York Times, August 31, 1998:

The question is probably: What was going through [Mark Cuban's] mind on July 16 as he watched the stock price of his company shoot from $18 to $74 before settling at $62.75, the best first day for an initial public offering in history?

'Oh my god, this is really, really cool,' he remembers...

~~~~~

Everest

When I arrive at Livy's that afternoon, she's sitting on the floor in the corner, talking excitedly on the phone. Sylvie is at the kitchen table, shuffling papers. Over by the deck wall, our new webgirl, Shoshana, is going through kungfu moves with Alison— Alison in a sweatsuit, Shoshana in a olive drab camaflogue tank top and military shorts.

Finally, Alison waves her hands, huffing and puffing a bit, and Shoshana ends the session. She walks to the camera and undrapes a bulletin board with a map of the Middle East on it.

"Okay," she says, dropping a strap off her shoulder and hefting a pointer in the direction of the West Bank. "Let's talk about tactical operations along the Galilee."

Alison pads over to the table, water glass in hand, perspiring, winded and clearly enjoying it.

"You're on-air talent now?" I ask.

"I told Livy if she wants to come up with a storyline for me, I'm open to the idea. So long as it's not too racy."

"I'm not sure that will benefit the business plan," pipes Sylvie. ", I, on the other hand, will perform a strip-tease on the balcony this afternoon at 12 and 3."

"What did Livy say?" I ask Alison.

"She said she'd think about it, but I don't think she intends to." She sighs. "It's pretty chilly around here."

"Who's on the phone?" I ask, watching Livy, who never ignores anything for long, talking rapidly into the instrument, her back to everything.

"Don't know," Sylvie answers. "She picked it up, got very agitated and carried it into the corner there a half hour ago."

At that moment, Livy hangs up. But she doesn't move—not for another two minutes. She just stays in the corner, motionless, staring at the floor with an expression guaranteed to keep anyone from interrupting her.

Finally, she stands and walks over to us, purposeful. You can see the gears turning. The phone lays in the corner, forgotten now. There is a sly smile on her face as she reaches us.

"So how does the cover of the *New York Times* Sunday Magazine sound to you?" she says.

We erupt like the last pitch of the World Series, whooping and hollering and jumping up and down. *Sylvie* is jumping up and down, for God's sake.

"It's not a done deal," Livy shouts over the din. "The writer has to sell the idea to her editor. But the headline would be 'The New Adult Web: Family Entertainment?'"

"Oh man," I coo. "That's a home run."

"That's Mount Everest" Livy agrees.

"Did they promise you the cover?" I ask. Ten years of media training—I know the questions to ask.

"She said she couldn't promise anything—only the editor could do those deals—but she wants me to be the focus of the article and said no one else in it would be more than two or three paragraphs."

"Those are all the right assurances," I have to admit. "Wow!"

"Now we need something big," Livy says. "Something—"

"Something bigger than sex," Alison interrupts, and everybody stares at her.

"We're bigger than sex *already*. I got sick and they stayed with me," Livy protests, with a tone of 'don't tell me my business.' "The writer said that's the focus of the article."

"That was then," Alison states flatly. "I've written a lot of articles over the years—take my word for it. You want something to happen *while she's here*."

I nod, vigorously. Livy stands silent. But she's listening.

"Something" Alison continues, "that says you have a more involving story, layers of stuff that go beyond sex, built around your characters."

I find myself wondering if Livy's gift for seduction isn't genetic. She is being seduced now by her mother, though clearly she doesn't want to be. She doesn't want to agree with anything her mother says. But—she *has* to...

"Okay," Livy says, with that breathy voice she gets when she *really* likes something a lot, really *wants* something a lot. "Yeah. It has to be character-driven. And not—" she is spooling up now, the idea catching fire in her head, "—maybe not even mostly about *me.*"

"A subplot," I offer.

"Something to establish that you are an *auteur* here, period," says Alison.

Bang! *Now* Livy's nodding.

When she's this hot for something, Livy will fairly consider any idea—even ideas she hates. So I have a thought, but I hold onto it for a few minutes. Better to let the conversation percolate, until we discover that a good subplot won't be that easy to come by. I know I have the right idea, and I know it's one Livy won't go for until she's backed firmly into a corner.

"Shoshana and I develop a friendship," Livy offers, "and she has some tragedy—a boyfriend dies or something."

"Peace might break out in the Middle East," Sylvie says, "and we'll have to miss all these instructive military lectures."

"The audience doesn't care about her yet," I say, impolitely. "It'll look like we brought her in to have a tragedy. That won't work."

"Sylvie gets sick and I nurse her back to health," Livy tries again.

"Been there, done that," Sylvie mutters.

"We've just done that one—with you," I agree.

"What else?" Livy asks, and, as she does more often than she wants to admit, she looks at me. "You've always got answers for everything. We've gone on dates, had sex all over the house and argued like cats and dogs. What else is there?"

"The obvious plot is right in front of us," I say, "and it's about as powerful as a storyline could be."

"What's that?" Alison asks. Livy already has a wary look in her eyes, like she's read my mind and doesn't like it one bit. And I know she won't.

"Mother comes back after years away and wants to bond with angry, resentful daughter," I say. "It's a classic."

I knew I was going to say it; I knew it was going to have an effect. But that one sentence just sucks the air out of the room.

Livy looks like she's been slapped. Alison's eyes grow a half-inch in circumference and she seems to go concave, ever so slightly, at the shoulders. Sylvie—Thank God for Sylvie—Sylvie's eyes widen, like a hawk sighting a rabbit, and she dives right in.

"What a story!" she cackles. "They already know your mom is here, and they can see you haven't spoken much. You have a confrontation of some kind, and each of you can spend time at the computer, telling the audience how you feel about each other."

"And," she adds, maybe because I am the evil soul who's concocted this idea and therefore has to be punished, "it would put *him* in a great position, since he's *stuck between the two of you.*"

I've always known Sylvie is the Voice of the Gods, but now she's proved it. Those are the words we've all been trying to avoid to that very second, and now there they are.

There's been an unspoken agreement between the lot of us up to this moment, that I am just some guy who hangs around the house, who just happens to know everybody. When I speak to Livy, we have our conversation, and when I speak to Alison, I am speaking to her, period. It's totally phony, but it maintains the peace. And now it's gone. The whole peacekeeping apparatus— Jeeps, Humvees, American and token British troops and Short Takeoff and Landing Aircraft—has now in a matter of seconds been unceremoniously packed up and shipped back to the UN garage.

There follows a brief period of insanely tense foot-shuffling and floor-staring—it may be one minute or twenty, for all I can tell, my mind having glazed over like a chainstore doughnut.

Finally, I look at Livy and say, "I'm sorry—I know this is uncomfortable. But I've been monitoring the chat, and they're certainly curious about Ally."

"They know Sylvie and me," I continue. "We're not going to come up with a radical plotline about us, and if they cared about us that much, they'd be at *our* websites."

"But this—" I gesture between mother and daughter, daughter and mother, "this is a pain anyone can relate to. We all have parents, and that's always a difficult relationship—and many of us have children, and that's just as hard. If you were going to keep to your original premise—telling your life on camera—this would be the meat in the sandwich. This is powerful stuff."

Alison still looks like she's watching the bomb timer tick down. Nonetheless, she clears her throat—twice—and croaks, "It certainly would carry your character to another level."

"I think my character has *a lot* of levels," Livy snaps and then instantly starts rubbing her eyebrows. Nobody says anything for a while.

Finally, I remember Spencer Tracy. I say to Livy, "This *can't* be real, you understand—it's a story."

"What?" she says.

"It's a story," I repeat. "This can't *really* be about the two of you. If you've got issues to deal with, that's your problem—deal with them on your own time. I need you to act out this *story* each day, *pretending*. If you have a fight on camera, you're not mad at each other afterward. If you have a girly-girl huggy thing on camera, you don't necessarily love each other as soon as it's over."

"We'll need to invent the details," I conclude, "and invent the issues—the problems between you—and play it out between now and the *Times* deadline."

"Or maybe it *won't* work out—that's always a possibility," Livy says.

"Right," says Alison. "It's a story."

"Right," Livy agrees. "A story."

Making Plans

It was quickly decided that Alison should be Alison—several of the audience members had already recognized her from her book jackets, and it would give the story, whatever it was, even more weight. And, while protesting it was just a story, I wanted to keep things as close to reality as possible.

But the devil, as always, was in the details. We all sat around the table for an hour trying to make it work, while in the background, Shoshana detailed the proper use of rubber bullets for civilian pacification, and worked off her thong while diagramming troop movements around Hebron.

Livy and Alison tiptoed around each other, saying only nice things, creating stories where blameless, well-meaning people got caught in unpleasant circumstances through no fault of their own.

After an hour of this, I finally had had enough.

"You've got to stop this," I said. "I'm going to throw up. This is not what happens in life, and it's the kind of thing that no one cares about when it does happen. If this story is about more than teenage rebellion, someone has to have made big mistakes and need redemption—and it isn't going to be the child."

To Livy's evident surprise—though not to mine—her mother agreed immediately.

"That's right," Alison said, "that's how it has to be."

"And the daughter is going to have to realize that her mother's really trying, and if she doesn't connect with her here, there may not be a next time," I continued.

I could see Livy's eyes narrow, the pupils shrink—she didn't want to get what I was saying. But I could see she did, nonetheless.

While the three of them, with Sylvie moderating, continued to discuss how to play out the tale, my thoughts wandered back to the divorce.

"I've got some personal business I have to look into. I'll be back before prime time," I told Livy.

"Okay," she said, still looking trapped. "But you've got to be part of this, you know. I've gotten an awful lot of comments about you on the chat lately. Everybody saw Alison come in—they heard you say you knew each other, and that you went out. They're real interested. That's got to resolve itself."

"Okay," I said. You got *that* right, I thought to myself—but I sure couldn't see how.

As I head home, the wind is kicking up. A winter storm is clearly visible, rolling in off the ocean.

When I reach the house, there's junk all over the place. Styrofoam cups, candy wrappers and split envelopes littering my postage-stamp back yard.

I walk from one end of the property to the other, picking up the junk and dumping it into a plastic bag. I quickly reach the far side of the house, by the old man who waves at all the cars on Ocean Avenue and keeps a 13-inch black-and white TV on the porch hooked up to a satellite dish in the back yard.

As I make my way between the houses, loading the garbage into my bag, he leans over from the porch, attracted by the sound. He's got a round head and a mane of gray hair like Friar Tuck—in fact, his hair seems to match the color of the sky exactly. We've never actually spoken up to now, but clearly, he's about to change that.

"Hey there, young fella!" he barks. "You'd think those garbagemen would pick up after themselves. They pick up after us and then leave the leavings all over the place."

"Yeah, well, I guess it creates employment. They drop it, I put it in a bag and they get to pick it up again."

"Heh heh heh," he cackles, but not as though he has the slightest idea what I'm talking about. "So tell me—you need any help on your TV show?"

I figure he's talking about Livy. I'm surprised to hear him call it a TV show, but then, he doesn't seem like the Internet type—maybe he just doesn't distinguish.

"I mean—it isn't much to look at," he continues. "You really ought to show something more—you know, outside of the house, windows; outside of the house, windows. Maybe what you need is a next-door-neighbor character to spice it up a little."

I stop picking up beer labels and cardboard boxes. "What are you talking about?"

"Your show," he says. "Channel 14. I've got great reception. Come look."

I climb the rickety steps of his porch. He leads me inside, through a warren of old TV Guides stacked in eye-height piles from one end of the house to the other. Seinfeld covers here, Batman there, Jack Benny on top of the corner pile. The decrepit wing of the Museum of Broadcasting.

He leads me to his ancient console set in the living room— thirty years old at least. Walnut console, with round analog knobs and ornate squiggles cut at the corners. He switches to UHF and then starts fiddling with the old manual dial, turning it back and forth in the range between Channels 13 and 14, just out of the normal broadcast band.

And there it is—a nice clear picture of my house. First a wide shot of the whole place, taken from overhead, on the sidestreet; then zooming into the bedroom window. Stays there for several minutes, then zooms out. In on the kitchen window, then out. Then the wide shot again.

I watch this for a few minutes, calculating the angle of the camera and the view of the house. The camera is located where it can see three sides of the house pretty well—everything but the side leading to TV Guide Wonderland over here.

This is pretty amazing. Nobody else in the world would be fiddling around on this channel, but my neighbor the Obsessed. Only a set that old would have a manual adjustment that would allow anyone to see it. Maybe my karma isn't all that bad.

"How long have you been watching the show?" I ask.

"Since yesterday," he says. "Since it went on."

He probably has it pegged too, I think. This is the kind of guy who would routinely scan every channel every day.

"Well, maybe I do need you to play a part," I say, and he perks up instantly. "This is a spy story. I need to come and go without this camera seeing me. Can I cut across your lawn?"

"Oh sure," he says. "Too bad the ground is sandy, so you can't dig a tunnel."

"Yeah, that is too bad. So I'm going to go into my house now, and later I'll come out the side window and cut across your yard. Okay?"

"No problem," he says, snapping to.

I head back to the house. I glance around quickly as the kitchen door bangs shut behind me. I can see the little black box on the phone pole, where the camera must be. I would never have caught it without his warning.

I sit in the mostly-empty living room for a while, just thinking. If the issue between us was going to be adultery, Marla wouldn't need a camera here—she'd have all the information she needed downloadable from Livy's site. I know she can afford the $19.95. So what does she want to see here? What could happen *here*?

Then I remember Nat Turner's question—had anyone gotten a picture of Livy and Daniel together at Sylvie's house? Obviously no one had—if so, Marla wouldn't need spy cameras trained on my little bungalow here. The issue is Daniel—she's hoping to catch Livy here with him.

I don't think she really wants to separate us—for all the anger between us, she loves Daniel and she'd break his heart if she did that. It's a blackmail tactic, for more money, like everything else in her papers.

I wonder—why broadcasting? Why doesn't the camera just go to tape? That would be the cheap way. You put a tape in the box on the phone pole, taping at the slow speed and pick it up twice a day. But that gives two opportunities a day to be found out. She's determined to catch me.

I start thinking like the news operations guy I am. If they're not taping it at the box, then there has to be a receiving station nearby—within a few blocks. With people sitting in it, taping the signal. That's expensive—she couldn't afford it, even with her sister's money, for more than a few days. It doesn't make sense.

I nearly fly out of the chair as the phone rings. I breathe deeply once and pick it up.

"Hello."

"Oh! You're home!" It's Marla—isn't *that* interesting timing? "I was going to leave you a message."

"Okay, well, just pretend I'm not here," I say.

"Um—I was wondering if you could watch Daniel for a few days. Four days. My aunt Audrey is very sick—you remember her, we visited them in Tampa?"

"Uh-huh. I'm sorry. What's wrong with her?"

"Uh—she has cancer."

"Wow. I am sorry." I really am—I like Audrey. Damn Marla to hell if she's lying about this, and I'll bet she is.

"Well, she may pull through. But I have to go down and I can't afford to take Daniel and my mom wants to go see Audrey before anything happens. Can you take Daniel?"

"Starting when?"

"Tonight? Tomorrow morning?"

I calculate a few things briefly. "Tomorrow morning would be better. 10 O'clock?"

"That's fine--thanks," she agrees, trying to hide the triumph in her voice as she hangs up. Uh-uh, sweetie, known you too long for that.

I pick up the phone again and dial.

"Nat Turner," comes the strong voice on the other side.

"Hi. I had a question left over after our talk yesterday—can I overstay my welcome that much?"

"Shoot."

"If you were hiring a private investigator around here, to check up on your husband who you were trying to get something on, who would you hire?"

He gives me three names and addresses.

Now I know what's up, and my blood is flowing pretty fast. Daniel will be with me Tuesday-Friday—prime territory for Livy's site, all our biggest primetime evenings. Marla figures she's got me: Either I go over there with Daniel, or Livy comes over here and meets him—either way, Marla has her blackmail. 'Exposing the Child to the Wicked Exhibitionist.' Or I can just stay off the site for four days in a row, do no work, make no appearances. Which hasn't happened since I got involved with Livy.

I could just leave him with Sylvie for a few hours a day—she could break away from the site that long. Daniel already loves her, and she'd have a ball with him. But my conspiratorial mind is going. It occurs to me I may do better by appearing to give Marla at least some of what she wants.

I take one chance—I figure she won't be paying for all this costly surveillance until I pick up Daniel. So I walk out the back door of the house and get into my car.

As I motor off, I keep a close eye on the rearview mirror, looking for cars that linger there too long. As I make turns in the narrow winding streets heading inland, there are a couple candidates, but they fade away, and I'm home free—not being followed, stalking the stalker.

Naturally, it's the last name on Turner's list that does the trick. A two-story building right along one of the small rivers that cut through the landscape. In the parking lot are the old green Taurus, a white Chevy Impala—former police issue—and an electric blue Chevy van with a cheesy rectangular porthole cut in the rear quarters and a small receiving dish on the roof. All the windows are smoked. I can probably recite the inventory of video equipment inside.

'Don Czinsky—PI' says the sign on the second floor landing. That's my man. PI—probably has pictures of Bogart and Tom Selleck on the wall of his office. Now I know what they look like—at least the cars, which in this case is all I need.

I head for a phone booth and make a few calls to Staten Island.

"Pediatricians"

"Hello—this is Tom Norman, Daniel's father."

"Yes?"

"I need a printout of his history."

"Okay. We'll have to run that overnight—you could pick it up tomorrow morning."

"That's great—thanks."

I drive back and stash the car two blocks from the house, where I can get it going out the window and across the neighbor's yard.

I am stunned by the calm with which I'm carrying all this out. I've never been a schemer or a gambler in my life, but I'm being both now.

This isn't about feelings, or justice, or truth or reality—it is a game, a game being played with our child as the prize. A game I am determined to win.

Taking Chances

I walk into Livy's that night feeling there isn't enough time for all the thoughts in my head.

"So what've you got?" I ask her immediately.

"Alison is here for a story. She's writing something about the Jersey Shore. So we're going to get together and hash things out between us," she says.

"No," I say, "that won't do." It's my old, blunt, TV voice— the voice of the guy who knows he has ten minutes to get a seven-minute story about the earthquake done before air.

"Excuse me?" She isn't used to being challenged like this—I haven't used that voice in a while.

"When's the Times woman coming?"

"She'll be here Thursday and Friday."

The last two days I'll have Daniel, I realize. The last two days of detective stakeout round-the-clock watch on me.

"Okay—Why do you and Mom have to get together *now*? You want the story to peak while the writer's here. With your storyline, if it doesn't work out now, Alison could just come back some other time. What can be happening where she has to deal with you *right now*? Where she can't leave and you're both under a deadline?"

Livy is watching me bubble. She gives me a little time to boil over, and I do.

"How about this? Your mom is here because, all of a sudden, she's developed a fear of flying. She can't go anywhere, so she's come home. She doesn't want to admit it, but you finally drag it out of her. She's planning to stay until she can figure this out. And she, Ms. Independence, resents being dependent on you and being grounded here and not being able to do her job. And you, Ms. Independence Jr., resent her coming back now that she's needy—because, when *you* were needy, she was never around."

Livy stammers a bit. "Well, I never felt—that isn't how—"

"It's a story, Livy," I remind her.

"Okay," she says. "Yeah, that's more dramatic." And that's it. It's the Livy I've seen in a hundred other contexts—the one who makes decisions and switches gears in an instant. I love that one.

"Okay—now there's a couple of other things we have to talk about," I continue. "I can't be here the next four days."

"What? Remember—we've got to work on your story too! You can't just drop out!"

"I can't be *here*," I repeat, and explain without details about Marla and Daniel. "I'll hook up my webcam, and I'll set it up so you can capture my page and put it in a window on your page. We'll have conversations every night by webcam."

"Do we have to wait till he's asleep?" Livy asks.

"No—but you have to be dressed if he's awake."

"Why don't we just have Sylvie watch him?"

"Marla has to know about Sylvie—Daniel talks about everyone he meets, and he loves Sylvie. So I think she's expecting that—'the old lady watches my son while he cavorts with the exhibitionist'. I have another idea."

"What?" Livy wants to know.

"I'm not telling."

"What do you mean?"

"I have an idea," I tell her, "and it'll play better if it's a real surprise—and it'll come down one of the nights the *Times* writer is here. So if you bear with me, I promise you a big finale for your article, and a happy ending—an ending I can live with—for my marriage."

Livy stares at me for a long moment, sizing me up. Trust is not an easy thing for her, especially when her precious site is involved.

"You *promise me*?" she repeats slowly.

"I *promise*," I reply, nodding.

"I don't think you've ever promised me anything before," Livy says.

"This'll be a big one," I say, and she nods her assent.

Then it's time for she and Alison to go on. I sit in the far corner and watch Livy go over to the table and sit, checking the chat.

After a minute or so, Alison comes over and sits next to her.

"So is there anything I can help with?" Alison says.

"I'm working," Livy replies, speaking with exactly the same I-don't-give-a-shit-what-you-do attitude she's had all week.

"You're just answering chat," Alison persists. "I thought —"

"I'm on camera right now," Livy answers and Alison sits up, back on the chair. If she's acting — she certainly knows where the cameras are by now — she's doing a good job.

"It's no big deal," Livy continues. "You can be here. Whatever's part of my life is part of the show," she sighs, as though dying to be through with this. Whether *she's* acting or not is an open question.

"I just thought maybe there was some art project you would be working on," Alison persists, soft-spoken and passive. Not herself. Olivia DeHavilland? Meg Ryan?

"No, I figured I would get undressed and masturbate — I don't think you can help me there," Livy snaps, and Alison sits up again. This is a bit uglier than I expected.

"I could give you some pointers — I have a lot more experience at it than you do," Alison responds, her eyes glinting, and now Livy is taken aback for just a second. Touché!

I pick up the phone, keeping my eye on the monitors as always.

I call one of the lawyers I knew at the network. He's a good guy and has been a discreet friend at times when we had sensitive matters of federal and state law at stake on our shows. But the main thing that puts me on the line with him is his encyclopedic knowledge of Federal communications statutes.

"How are you doing?" he practically yells into the phone. "I heard you took a leave—is everything okay?"

"Marla and I split up. I just have some sorting out to do."

"Sorry to hear. Occupational hazard, as I'm sure you know."

"Oh yeah," I say. "Listen, I've got a question that I think goes to your area of expertise."

"Go ahead."

"Is it legal for someone to use the broadcast band—either VHF or UHF—for surveillance camera use?"

"It might be legal for a government agency with a warrant," he says. "You might be able to fight it—"

"If I had 400 lawyers and unlimited money, like the network."

He laughs. "Well, yeah, I suppose."

"But for a private investigator, on a divorce case--?"

"Oh, hell no—what are you up to?"

"There's someone monitoring the place I'm staying with a microwave camera setup on the phone pole across the street."

I can almost hear him sit up over the phone.

"Well, I'll tell you—not only is he in violation of Federal Communications Statutes, but I'll guarantee you the phone company will sue too, if you can nail who's doing it," he tells me. "I've got friends at their legal department—they *love* stuff like this."

"Are they close enough friends to write a threatening letter and then forget it if necessary?" I ask.

"As long as it doesn't hang around long enough for the boss to know, sure," he says.

"And if I need you to explain communications law to a local chief of police, would you be able to do it? Like, say, Friday night?"

"Is it important?" he asks.

"To me? Very," I tell him.

"Fine—you'll have to call me at home."

"I've got the number," I assure him. "Thanks guy—I owe you one."

"Don't worry—I'm a lawyer. I'll make sure you pay up."

As I hang up the phone, I can see Alison on the monitor. I'm used to watching a monitor, instead of a real person across the room—TV practice, but I'm also convinced, after all these years at it, that I can what's going on *inside* someone using that magic screen. In this case, it takes no magic to read her unhappiness.

"—it's my house; I just wanted to come back and visit," she says.

"You haven't been back for more than a weekend in years; maybe ever," Livy rebukes her. "Why now?"

"I just felt comfortable coming back."

"You don't *seem* comfortable—you don't seem comfortable with anything," Livy badgers.

She is harsh, relentless. All the effort she's put into being charming and seductive on screen may be going down the tubes all at once, because she doesn't seem capable of controlling her anger. Alison is shrinking in the face of this onslaught.

"When do you plan on leaving?" Livy asks now.

"I—I don't know," Alison answers.

"A couple of days—a week—a month? You have to have thought about it?"

"I—I don't know," Alison repeats. "I haven't made plans."

"Why not? You always did in the past."

"I *can't* leave soon," Ally stammers. Her confusion and frustration seem very real. The effort of keeping her story straight, while battling her daughter's very real anger, is actually very convincing.

"Why not?" Livy demands.

"I can't—" Alison looks up, humiliated, and it all spills out. "I can't *fly* now, that's why. I can't—I'm...*scared*...to fly."

Livy regards her for a long moment. Alison looks like she's going to shake apart any second.

Finally Livy says, "Well, I don't want you here. There are lots of places you can get to by train."

And she goes back to the chat and the camera and removing her blouse, while Alison gets up from the chair and flees to the deck.

As I step outside, Alison is crying against the railing. I head over toward her but she stops me with a look, a look of naked pain and defiance.

"What made you blurt out that stupid idea?" she demands.

"Acting together?" I ask.

"You mean you had *other* stupid ideas today?"

"Ally—when you arrived, she wouldn't speak to you at all."

"Right—and now she's tearing me up."

"Well, what did you think? You'd walk in and she'd have her arms open? You're *talking* now. If there's any chance to put it behind you, this is it."

"But it's fiction," she says. "I can't talk about what's really getting to me—I have to talk about that stupid fear of flying thing of yours."

"What's really the issue between you?" I ask.

"What do you mean? My leaving her alone for twenty-five years, that's what."

"Okay—and what did she talk about just now? It wasn't fear of flying. *You* had to remember your story, but *she* just said what she's been feeling. And if we hadn't told her it was just a story, she wouldn't have let herself go enough to say what she felt. I promise you—any 'fictional' conversation you two have will lead back to your real problems. There's not a chance of avoiding it, no matter what you do."

She turns for a long time and looks out at the beach, which is clear and calm tonight. I've yet to find an emotional state that won't benefit from staring at waves in the moonlight—it helps anything and everything.

"You really think this will work?" she asks, sounding weary enough to die right here.

"I have no idea," I admit. "Just keep coming back, keep talking to her. She wants it to come to a head by Friday night—be ready."

Counsel

I head home, trying to sort through all the threads I have to draw together by Friday night.

The next morning, I head off to pick up Daniel's medical history—and Daniel.

The doctor's office is almost empty when I come in. It's a little past 9 and they've just opened. I ask the attendant for Daniel's records and she hands over the heavy printout.

I thank her and head for the door. Then I stand on the stoop and rustle through the papers, looking for the information I need.

The only notation having to do with Aspergers is 5 months ago—before I left, but not by much. My paranoia sets in—Marla works with our pediatrician's partner; she's the nurse at her school. Are they skewing things to help her?

I walk back inside.

"Is Dr. Marx in?"

"I'll see if he's available." She disappears behind the door to the examination rooms.

Soon he appears, relaxed and friendly as always. My paranoia dissapears.

"Hi Don."

"Hi Tom—how are you?"

"Fine. I just got a copy of Daniel's records, and the only mention of Asperger's is 5 months ago—I thought he was diagnosed a lot earlier than that, wasn't he?"

He looks briefly at the pages, scanning through quickly.

"You're right," he says. "I must not have put it down."

"Well, there's a legal issue," I say. I don't know how specific I want to be—do they understand what's going on? "I really need the records to be accurate."

"I'll make the change. Just give me a minute."

He goes in the back. Five minutes later, he comes out and the records are pouring out of the printer.

"That'll be better," he assures me, and shakes hands before disappearing again.

I take the papers from the nurse and head out onto the landing. Quickly, I search the stack of papers. Now the records place the diagnosis 4 years ago!

I know that's not right—we knew Daniel had Aspergers a year and a half, maybe two years ago—but not 4. Now he's been overly generous. Why? Doesn't he know about the divorce?

And then it hits me—he doesn't. He doesn't know a thing about it. I suddenly flash on when I call Marla at work—they still ask if it's 'her husband.' I *am* still her husband—but if they were aware of the divorce, they wouldn't ask the way they do.

She hasn't told anyone. Her desperate concern about what people will think of her—her obsession—she hasn't told a soul. So now Don, I'm sure, thinks he's helping us both out. And, though he may be exaggerating, he *is* telling the truth—we both knew about Daniel's disability long before I left. Marla should rot in hell for ever suggesting otherwise. And I intend to send her along on that trip.

She doesn't show her face when I pick up Daniel. Just as well—I honk and he bounces out the front door with his suitcase and a bag of toys.

"Hi Daddy!" he yells as he throws the stuff in the back seat.

"Hey Buddy—how're you doing?"

'Great!" If you put a pin in him, he'd fly around the inside of the car for four or five hours, he's so juiced.

"Great!" I answer back, laughing at his exuberance. I give him a big hug, and he hugs me back. No, this is *not* going to be the last time I pick him up for 'liberal visitation'.

The ride south is a lark. The sun is out, it's a crisp winter day, there's no green Tauruses in sight. Daniel has invented a new spy, Scott Dagger (a really good name for a spook, I think) and we're playing out his first adventure, saving the world from terrorists with nuclear bombs. It occurs to me he really has no idea what a nuclear bomb is—it's just something that sounds vaguely scary from old James Bond movies.

When we get home, I surprise him with a VCR I've picked up—and cable TV!! He's in Nirvana now—Nickelodeon, tapes and a fold-out couch! What more could a boy ask?

We go miniature golfing, take in a movie and then stand on the beach throwing a Frisbee as the sun goes down. *Trying* to throw the Frisbee, actually. He continually throws it into the sand. He's easily frustrated, so I shift to a big beachball and we throw that back and forth, getting fooled by occasional gusts of wind, laughing and yelling. When we finally stop, both of us sweating a little from running after the ball all over the beach, I can't ask for anything else.

Then we go out to dinner. He orders a cheeseburger and fries, as always, and then munches on my salmon, letting the cheeseburger go cold, as always. I guess he just wants the security of knowing the cheeseburger's there, in case he doesn't like what I've ordered.

We head home and I introduce him to "Abbott and Costello Meet Frankenstein." Who said the joys of high culture have to wait for adulthood? Then we pull out the couch and I read to him, from a child's version of 'The Count of Monte Cristo.'

He's groggy. He rolls over and snuggles down into the covers.

"That was scary—Edmund Dantes being in jail," he says.

"Yes, but do you see what happened? Even in prison, he learned all about the world from the Abbe Fariah—and when his chance came to escape, he knew what to do with it!"

"Uh-huh," he murmurs and rolls over and is snoring like a chainsaw in thirty seconds.

Well, it may not have meant much to him, but it meant something to me.

We've been in bed long enough that I'm getting groggy myself. I get up and pad around the house for a couple of minutes, long enough to come awake again, and then head over to the back room and the computer.

I fire up the webcam and send Livy an email that I'm online. She pushes a button on the switcher and voila! we both appear in a split screen video window on the Website.

"Hi," she says. "Where are you? I'm missing you." She has that pouty French maid thing going, and a nightgown that's slipping slowly down her lovely shoulders.

"I miss you too," I say quite honestly, eyeing the skin of those shoulders. "My boy's with me."

"Oh—during the week?" she says, playing along.

"Yeah—his mom asked me to take him for the rest of the week—she's going out of town."

"So can't we get together?"

Shit! What is she doing? Anything we're putting out can be recorded, if you're determined to keep it. And shown in court, if it's germane to the case. She knows that, doesn't she?

"Not till he's gone, I guess," telling the truth while I try to think if there's a reason I shouldn't. "Unless you just want to have lunch out somewhere together."

"Can't you get a babysitter?" she persists.

"He's with me for four days," I say. What's gotten *into* her? "Isn't it going to look kind of pathetic if I can't go four days during the week without leaving him for a date?"

"This girl has needs." Cut me like a knife, why don't you?

"I doubt the divorce court will want to consider those," I tell her. "Sorry."

Now I see her hesitate a moment, before plunging ahead — and taking me with her.

"But what about after the divorce? Can't I ever spend time with him?"

"Of course you'll get to know him," I answer. "I *want* you to. It just has to be outside the office, so to speak."

"Why? Hasn't he been to your wife's office?"

"Yes, sure—" Why is she doing this to me? She wants another quarrel online? Maybe... but the timing is very bad. "But my wife is almost always *dressed* at her office."

I force a chuckle here, to try to mute the challenge. This has always been where Livy gets up on her hind legs and growls at me. Not this time.

"I thought that's why you like me better," she says, smooth and quiet, and now I laugh for real, and she smiles too. Amazing how chemistry can carry over copper wire.

"Well, that's certainly true, sweetie," I assure her. "That's one of many reasons. But it's not really appropriate for him yet. By the time he's ready for you, you'll be the Queen of Hollywood."

She nods and smiles again. "Okay," she says. "I guess I understand that. I still miss you though," and she lifts her leg onto the chair, taking the skirt up with it.

"Oh, I miss you too," I say again quite honestly.

"Well, here's a forget-me-not," she offers, and my half of the split screen disappears, leaving her alone onsite. She then spends half an hour in a delicious strip tease just for me—and the other hundred thousand guys online.

Clever girl, I realize after logging off.

She's now committed me publicly to not seeing her when the boy is around, and done it in a way that shows quite clearly what I'm missing by making that decision. If it ever gets shown in court, it'll be testimony for *my* side. Thanks, sweetie—I'll try to return the favor.

Conniving

The next morning, the emails start again.

> paleguy@aol.com: Hey safehouse—
> stay away from my girl! I got plans for
> her this wk while you busy, late at nite
> when she got needs. I got my i on u.
> Keep you distence!

There are two more, all sent overnight. So he's baiting me. At night, late at night after Daniel's asleep, he promises to menace Livy. I should be there, to protect her. He knows from my past behavior—at least my past behavior as shown on the Web—that I love to, need to, protect her.

I'm convinced it's the detective sending the emails. He's trying to get me to bring Livy over to my place or Daniel to her place, so I can protect her. To make Marla's case that I'm a lousy, irresponsible father.

I spend a few hours early with my divorced men's group. The members seem to be mellowing a bit, at least the old regulars. Several have found new partners, most of them with new and interesting quirks, and those that haven't seem to be just fine on their own, thank you, at least for the moment.

Daniel gets nudgy near lunchtime—even Nickelodeon loses its charm sooner or later.

"Let's go for a walk," I propose, and he agrees. He knows Daddy runs most days, and this sounds easier. We get bundled up in our coats and knit hats, and step outside where our breath hangs crystalline in the air.

He's expecting the beach, but this time I propose a game. Each street in my section of town spans maybe two or three short blocks. I'll stop before each block, and he can go down it and hide someplace, and I'll try to find him.

He loves the idea. He's old enough now—and cautious, in the family way--that I don't have to worry about him getting lost or doing something dangerous or stupid. And looking for him gives me the chance to scrutinize every block within microwave range of the house.

It only takes five minutes to bag my prey. It's the electric blue van I saw parked outside Czinsky's office, with the little dish antenna on the roof. I see it instantly on rounding the corner, two blocks from my house. I fix the location in memory. I'll be back.

Having found it, I don't have to spend any more attention looking it over, at least not now. I look for Daniel and find him; that's one out of two—and we move on to the next block.

We walk all the way into town, and I take him to the diner for lunch. This is a big adventure—the diner is a converted Elks hall, with animal heads on the walls and a big mural of The March Westward, heroic pioneers and all that. No one seems to have considered that the entire United States is pretty much West of here. It doesn't matter—the place has cheeseburgers.

As we're walking out, Alison is coming in, carrying a load of newspapers and magazines.

"Hi!" she says, taken by surprise.

"Hi. Daniel, this is Alison—she was in school with Mommy and me."

"*Really*?" Daniel is always impressed by survivors of the Jurassic Period.

"Yes—I was a good friend of your Mom and Dad's."

She holds out her hand and he gives her a studied, practiced handshake. Marla's therapists are making sure he knows how to do all the social amenities correctly. If there was ever a disability more suited to Marla's worldview, I can't imagine what it would be.

"I've got to talk to you," she says, and motions to the now-empty table we've just abandoned. We sit back down again, Daniel with that 'when-is-this-going-to-be-over' look of his.

"This plan of yours just isn't going to work," she says.

"What's wrong?"

"She's not talking to me at all. I can't get her to see anything differently if she won't even talk to me."

"No—that's a problem, I'll admit. Just go home and relax," I suggest, like the home-visiting doctor. "I'll fix it."

"How are you going to *fix* it?" she asks, openly skeptical.

"That's *my* problem. You worry about what you're going to say when the time comes."

Daniel and I walk home via the beach. The angle is good—I get a clear glance down the block with the microwave truck. It's sitting in the same place it was when we passed it on the way into town—they weren't spooked by my appearance. Good—they're confident. Let them stay that way, for another day or two.

When we get home, Daniel pops "Abbott and Costello Meet Frankenstein" into the VCR again, and I head into the back room and pick up the phone. I dial the New York Times.

"Trish Garay."

I got a message from the feature writer, the one who's writing about Livy. She wanted to interview me, as the boyfriend, and she was unhappy I wasn't going to be around while she was writing the article. She asked that I call her at the office, to answer some questions now.

I do my duty as a servant of the media empire—I answer all her questions dutifully, repeating the company line about how Livy and I met (my heroism with the Pale Guy), what it's like dating a woman guys everywhere want (strangely like dating anyone else, except you have to forget the cameras) and whether age really matters (sure—she's not as wise as I am, but I'm prepared to overlook that).

As soon as there's a pause, I mention, "I've got to admit— you're very thorough. I didn't think you'd want to talk to me at all."

"Why not?" she responds. "Your romance has really made the site different."

"Well, maybe," I own. "But now, I would have thought that Livy and her mom would be the big story."

"Oh?" Of course, Livy hasn't mentioned this to her at all. Thinks she can ignore the program, eh? Uh uh...

"Sure—Mom comes back from traveling around the world for years, wants to re-establish herself with daughter, who won't even speak to her." I drop my voice to a conspiratorial whisper. "But then, I guess you shouldn't get into that—it's kind of private."

"Well, she does say her whole life is open on the site," the reporter says and I know I'm home free.

"I know—she's an idealist," I confide. "I keep telling her she should reserve a little more privacy, but—well, you've spoken to her, you know—she's an open book."

"Yes—it's interesting she didn't mention it," she says. "When did her mother get back?"

"Last week. Yeah, you know, I can see the subhead: 'The Internet Girl with Nothing to Hide Finds a Skeleton in her Closet.'"

I can hear the pen scribbling on the pad over the phone.

"Well, thanks," she says. "I may want to speak to you again. Is that alright?"

"Sure," I say cheerily. "Sorry we won't get to meet." As she hangs up, I think: until Friday night, that is.

Later, we head over to Sylvie's—she's called me twice to ask 'when are you bringing my young man over?'

"Sylvie!" Daniel yells as we're halfway up the dune path and he runs up and hugs her. Then I'm surprised to hear him yell "Alison!" and she emerges from behind the shed and gets a hug from him too. Now he's seen her twice, so she gets a hug—that's Daniel. Alison's taken by surprise, but she melts into his embrace in a second, the smile growing on her face.

"You're very strong," she says.

"Oh, he's my lumberjack," Sylvie cracks. "Remember we broke up that wood pile last time?" she says to him.

"Yeah—you have any more? I can do it even *better* now," he bubbles, miming breaking a board over his knee.

Sure enough, Sylvie has stockpiled some more wood that she's found on her morning strolls up and down the beach. Daniel and Alison form a little wrecking crew, she handing him the boards and him breaking them up. I stack the pieces against the backside of the shed, so Sylvie can get at them for her winter fireplace.

Alison picks up each board with a comment: "Here's a good one." "This one's thick—be careful." "Look at the knot on this one."

She's feeding on his energy, his smile. There's some hole in her that's so visible, that so visibly *needs* to be filled. And he responds to her, feeding that energy back.

When we're done, she wipes her brow.

"Phhshew! Do you ever get tired?" she laughs.

He laughs back. "No!" he says, and giggles even louder.

She picks up a board and pokes him lightly with it. He's easing into a giggling fit, where almost anything keeps him rolling down that hill. Now she's laughing too, which makes him laugh, and finally he leans into her and she puts her arms around him. And then he gets the hiccups.

"Hiccups!" he yells. "Water!" and runs into Sylvie's kitchen for water. This is our hiccup fire drill ritual.

Alison stands on the dunetop, looking at me with a face full of mixed longings.

"He's amazing," she says. "Thanks for letting me borrow him for a while."

"He's got lots to give," I say.

"He loves everybody, doesn't he?"

"No—there are people he doesn't like. But if he likes you, he assumes you will care for him. When kids his age are mean to him—kids he thinks are okay—he is always surprised, and always assumes they won't do it again the next time they see him. I think he knows better but just won't admit it. He is always rewriting movies we've seen so the bad guys are nice now. He doesn't realize that it kills the story, and he doesn't care."

"He's got a big surprise coming," she says.

"I know—but not yet. Hopefully, not too soon." I fix up the last of the boards.

"I'm pretty sure Livy will want to speak with you tonight," I tell her. "I think I fixed it."

"Oh? Thanks. How'd you do it?"

I wave my hands, dismissive. "I think it's done, let's leave it at that. Do you know what you're going to say when the time comes?"

She smiles, that rueful half-smile I found so familiar on Livy's face so many months ago.

"My eyes glaze over every time I think about it," she says. "It'll have to come to me when I get there, I guess."

I nod.

"Good luck," I say.

"Thanks for getting me there," she says and kisses my cheek softly.

Daniel comes out of Sylvie's backdoor now, a peach in each hand. The one in his right hand is half-eaten—the juice covers the lower half of his face. He offers the left hand tentatively in my direction.

"Sylvie has peaches," he says. "Want one?"

"You want it, don't you?"

"Uh-huh," he nods.

I smile. "You keep it," I say and he smiles back a thousand times brighter than I'll ever smile again.

He starts heading down the dunepath. "I'll be the Wolfman and you be Dracula," he says.

"I guess we're going home," I say to Alison and Sylvie, framed in the kitchen door, and we wander down the path toward our little beachfront estate.

Split Ends

That night, after Daniel falls off to sleep, I log on and, sure enough, there is Alison, lurking in the dark behind Livy as she answers chat.

Livy's still ignoring her. Damn! I was sure the writer would call and start asking questions, which would *make* Livy pay attention. Maybe she didn't call? Maybe she couldn't get through?

Alison stands by the windows, looking out, then turns for a moment and looks at her daughter. The looks are furtive, brief— inconspicuous, as far as the audience is concerned. However, in reality, Alison knows Livy can see her on the monitor, so there's nothing inconspicuous about it.

Livy is typing answers to the chat, but now I notice something odd—her hands are moving an awful lot for typing. Up and down—she's *banging* the keys. Banging them hard.

She *did* get the phone call. The writer *did* ask.

Livy is being defiant. She didn't want to get into this storyline—it's the first time I've ever pushed her, or tricked her, into anything she didn't want to do—and she's resisting all the way.

Finally Alison finds some sort of stain or something—I can't see what it is, really, if indeed it's anything at all—on the window directly behind Livy. She starts rubbing it, to get it off the window—but the only thing that comes across online is the sound, the squeaking of nail on glass. This goes on for twenty seconds, until Livy explodes.

"*What* are you doing?"

"Sorry—just a stain," Alison says.

"But why are you lurking there?" Livy demands.

Alison takes her cue, and in a lightfooted second, she's sitting next to Livy on the couch.

"I don't understand—how does it all work?" she asks, pointing at the screen.

Livy is dumbstruck.

"It's the Internet," she says.

"I've spent most of the last ten years in remote vacation resorts," Alison says. "And I'm never anywhere long enough to really learn something like this. How does it work?"

Livy looks at her, and then at the screen, and then back at Alison. Her face hovers halfway between laughter and pity. Then she sighs and begins to point at the screen and explain.

"These are the guys. They're logged onto the site and they're writing me their opinions and what they want me to do and what they think about each other, the headlines of the day or the kind of weather we're having. Their messages come up here, and I can type my replies here."

"Uh-huh. And what's that?"

"That's the switcher. I get to control which camera here is going out on the public feed—the one the general public sees. Although members get to pick whichever camera they want."

"And how do people get to your...site?" Alison says, pleased to have come up with this jargon.

"Either they've read about it in a magazine," Livy says, "or they look on a search engine."

"What's that?"

Livy shows her a search engine. Alison starts looking at the categories, asking to see this and that, and then, all at once, you can see the light go off, when she realizes the size of the universe in front of her.

"You mean, these are all pages like yours that people put up?"

"Uh-huh," Livy laughs now. "Maybe not *exactly* like mine..."

"No—I didn't mean it that way," Alison laughs too. "But how do you make sense of it all?"

Livy looks at the screen, as though she's just seeing it again for the first time. Then she shrugs.

"I guess you can't. You follow up on the things that interest you, and leave the rest alone."

"Don't you always feel like you're missing something?" Alison asks, wide-eyed. "Like, no matter where you go, there are a hundred other places you missed?"

Livy looks at her and says, "You just have to make choices."

Alison looks at her—does she realize what she's said? Then she goes back to the computer.

Alison stares at the screen in wonder. She clicks a link, sees the page pop up—Livy shows her how to use the 'Back' button to go back and click another.

"I missed so many things," Alison says, looking at the screen and then looking at Livy. "So many things."

Livy catches *this* line—she looks down at the floor for a moment. Trying to ignore it, to make the moment go away, maybe. But it's too late. The question is hanging in the air now, and she can't avoid it. She *can't*, I tell myself.

I feel like I can't breathe. There's a thousand pound weight on my shoulders. It's the crucial moment—the moment they tell every salesman about. My dad told me about it at the store. Once you've made your pitch, once you've put the deal on the table, the next person that speaks—seller or buyer—loses.

The silence is endless, years of silence echoing over the phone line from Livy's house to mine, to the houses of all the others watching, to the offices of the New York *Times*, and the Bombay *Journal*, for all I know.

"Why did you stay away?" Livy says finally.

Somehow, now that the bell has rung, Alison is ready for it.

"I was ashamed," she says.

"I left because I had to become myself—and I really *had* to," she explains. "I would have died—my whole life would have been a death—if I hadn't done that. You were far better off with your grandma than with me, the way I was then."

Her face drifts now, the eyes turning inward and the words pouring out of her, autopilot. No more thinking. No acting at all.

"But once I found me," she says, "I was ashamed for leaving you. I knew who I was, finally, but I didn't..." she drifts off for a second, then taps her chest with her fingers, lightly, "I couldn't *forgive* myself for my mistakes."

She wheels around in her chair now and looks Livy in the face. "Y'know, it wasn't even really a mistake—I *had* to do it. I couldn't forgive my *weakness*."

Livy's listening, and thinking. But her face is hard—she hasn't given an inch yet, from anything I can see on the monitor.

"But even then, you didn't come back," she argues, quite rationally.

Ally gives off a rueful smile. "Well, I did—a weekend at a time. And you were distant, or angry at me—and then there was your grandma. I could see how *she* needed you—and that she was doing a great job with you. And I felt funny breaking in on that."

"If you wanted to be with me, you wouldn't have let that stop you," Livy spurts all of a sudden. "We could have still been with Grandma."

Ally shakes her head.

"I know," she says.

"Somehow, you could never give up anything you wanted for me," Livy says, almost whispering.

"I know," Alison nods.

The two are sitting now in darkness, their blonde hair and light skin glowing against the dark, indistinct room like a Vermeer.

"Livy," Alison finally says, "I didn't come back because I felt I needed an explanation that would make it alright. I felt I had to be able to explain what I did without hurting you."

She's looking hard at Livy's eyes now, but Livy isn't there. She's looking away, at the floor, at the monitor. If she's trying to find a distraction there, it's a futile search—even the chat has stopped dead. No one is writing a thing.

"The reality is," Alison continues, "you want an explanation—you want a *reason*—and there isn't one, anywhere. There is no reason—if there was, I wouldn't have done what I did.

What reason can a parent have to abandon her child? Only a *lack* of reason."

"Look at *you*," she continues, speaking very gently, very soft, like a mother to a very small child who's fallen asleep in her arms. "Is this site—what you're doing here—the only choice you had for artistic freedom? There's no way you can convince me of that. This is rage—rage at me, rage at the world, rage at yourself—rage at *something*. That's where it all comes from. It's raw feeling being changed into something else, something you can't resist. Human beings can always resist reason—there are a hundred reasonable ways to resist it. But there are other things in us that we can't resist or understand or explain and somehow, those are always the things that take over."

Her voice is deepening now. There's not much left in her, but what's there is raw bone itself and she starts pulling it all out and laying it on the table. Go, baby, go.

"I'm not saying I'm a virtuous person," she says. "I did things I hate, looking back, but I know I had to do them. And now, I don't have a reason or a good story or a good excuse. I'm just hoping we can get past the big mistake I made a long time ago and that I spent a long time not being willing to face. Because my life isn't over yet, because I can do something today that I couldn't do yesterday. Because I can do *this* today, that I couldn't do yesterday. And because that moment—that one morning, years ago, when I decided to close the suitcase and go to the airport, instead of unpacking the suitcase and putting my clothes neatly in the bureau and going downstairs to have tea—that doesn't have to be the story of the rest of my life. I'm hoping you can find some room for me in *your* life, because I need to be with you again. I need to be your mother."

And she sits back, finished—drained.

Livy sits motionless, staring at the floor. Then, after a long moment, she looks at Alison as if for the first time and takes a deep breath. I find myself taking a breath too.

"Well, your timing stinks," Livy says. "I don't think I need a mother anymore."

She gets out of her chair and walks off camera. Alison is left alone, in the middle of the empty screen.

Hide and Seek

I go back into the living room and watch my son sleep all over the fold-out couch. Daniel is the corollary to an old rule of business: he expands to fill the sleeping space allotted. Somehow he's stretched from one end to the other, arms and legs crossed and tangled.

I've learned over the months that I will have to get into bed and push him, using my shoulders and legs, push him hard, before he will give any space back. None of this will wake him. Nothing wakes him until the sun comes up. Then he's instantly awake and ready to power Toledo again.

I watch him breathe peacefully amid the tangle of covers, and then I do something I've never done since he was born: I leave him alone for a few minutes.

I put a note on the bed saying, "I just went for a little walk. I'll be right back. Daddy." Then I slip out the living room window, the one facing my neighbor, the proprietor of TV Guide World.

I pad quickly around, skirting the front of his house, where the camera can't see me. Then I duck down his street to the river, and then across the planking river wall for two blocks.

The van is parked on a sidestreet, so I can't see it from the river end. And they, hopefully, can't see me. The house along the river looks deserted—the garage is open and no car in it. Better yet, it has a fence, and the van should be just on the other side of that fence. I just want to know it's still there. I don't want any surprises *tomorrow* night.

I step quickly but very lightly across the narrow gravel at the end of the street. A boat is moving slowly up the river—the sound has reached here before the spotlight on the bow; hopefully, it will muffle my footfalls. I step onto the damp grass of the lawn and duck behind the fence. I mouth a silent prayer that the seemingly empty house doesn't have a dog. But all stays quiet as I make my way past the hammock and the standing clothesline to the fence in back.

I can hear the engine humming as I reach the fence— goooood. It takes me a few seconds to find a crack between the planks that I can see through, but then I get a nice view of the van. I can see some glowing light blotches through the small window cut in the side. There's no one in the drivers seat, but the engine is humming along—gotta keep that electricity flowing, kiddies.

Well, this is fine—just what I wanted to know. They're still in place, feeling confident. Chances are, they're not going to move before tomorrow night—and I can walk around with Daniel again tomorrow, just to be sure.

I'm ready to leave, but something keeps me waiting another moment. And I get my reward—the side door slides open and a slightly-built dark-haired man with glasses and an extremely shaggy haircut emerges from the dark. He pulls a skinny cigarette from his breast pocket and lights up. Is this Czinsky? Probably not—probably a licensed specialist surveillance geek.

Regardless, what I want is a look inside the van. The view couldn't be better—all the equipment is arrayed facing the open door. He has the usual test and vectoring equipment, signal strength meters and servos to align the antenna—and *two* live monitors showing the house! He's got *two* cameras!—The one I'd already caught, on the pole by the backdoor, and another on the next pole, from the looks of it, nearer the front. The only reason he didn't see me going out just now was the light from the telephone pole up the block is burned out—otherwise, I'd have been a sitting duck.

But the most important thing is, he has no wireless Internet connection inside. Fine—they're not *that* up-to-date. That's important.

I wait for Hairyman to finish his weed and step back into the van. Then I slip back across the lawn and along the river, carefully carefully through the shadows in front of my neighbor's house and back in my living room window, where Daniel snores like a timber mill.

The next morning, Daniel and I go for our walk again. Up and down the blocks, me searching for him, mostly in vain. The van is still in place, but no motor running this time. Of course not—they knew we were coming.

We head down to the diner for breakfast—when Daniel likes something, he wants to do it every day. Alison is there— somehow, I knew she would be. She has the same stack of newspapers, strewn all over the table. She's tearing out articles—I can't see what the subjects are—and stuffing the pieces in her pockets.

Daniel runs over to her and gives her a hug, and she seems to grow two inches on the spot, her arms around him, her face brightening, the ghost she carries around inside dissolving behind the happy face she finds in his happy face. He immediately picks up the papers on the chair next to her and throws them on the table, sitting there himself.

"Danny, that's not polite."

"Oh please, he's fine," she says. "How are you doing, Daniel?"

"Great!" Daniel says. "I was hiding, and I beat Daddy three times—he couldn't find me."

"Yeah, you got me pretty good," I own.

"I'll bet *I* could find you," she says.

"Could not," he shakes his head.

"Let's find out," she says and instantly we're all headed out the door to the corner.

"Okay, you go hide. I'll make sure she's not watching," I say, "and when you're hidden, I'll send her down after you."

I keep one eye on him as he scampers behind cars and dumpsters, looking for the right place. My other eye is on Alison, whose face is absolutely beatific, leaning against the wall of the diner, waiting happily to play with my little boy.

Then her face grows weary, all at once.

"It didn't work—your plan," she says. "Did you see last night?"

"I saw," I tell her. "You don't know yet that it didn't work. And you don't know all my plans yet."

"Oh really—there's *more*?" she says, sarcastically. "The next part will work better?"

"Ally—I'm not selling happiness pills here, okay? You got to tell her your side of things, and you did a damn nice job, from where I sat. Now we have to let things play out—and yes, I have a few more plans, God help me."

She smiles at me, but it's the echo of a smile, really. Her beautiful face carries so much pain and sadness, so much hope, and hope negated—it's a world, just to look at her.

Up to this point, I've played by the rules, I really have. I've tried to be good, or as good as I can be, sleeping with the daughter of my intended. But now, it seems idiotic. *What* rules? How could anyone have thought of rules for a situation like this?

I lean over and—gently—kiss Alison on the lips.

She's startled, but she kisses me back, for a precious four-and-a-half-hour moment. Then she pulls back.

"Don't do that," she says.

"Why not?"

"You know why not. You're my daughter's lover."

There are those rules again. Maybe they come from the collective unconscious, the distilled product of thousands of years of human evolution. Maybe they're just a vestige of some ancient fears that serve no useful purpose anymore. Maybe they've come from inside us. Maybe they're even *right*, but suddenly I don't care about any of it.

"I can't help it," I tell her, "I love *all* the women in your family."

Somehow, that smartass line feels like letting go of every inhibition I've ever had in my life.

"It's not funny," she says.

"No—what else is it?" I insist, incandescent smile on my face now. "I certainly wouldn't have planned it like this, but here we are, aren't we?"

"We can't do this," she repeats.

"Do what? Kiss?"

"You know it's not just that," she says.

"You're right—it's a lot more," I admit. "So let's stop ignoring it, okay? Let's figure out what to do—or at least admit that we have to do *something*."

She draws herself up tall against the wall.

"No" she says. "Nothing's going to happen between us."

"Okay," I nod. I know I'm smirking, but I can't stop myself anymore. "I think you'd better come up with a better answer than that, 'cause the questions are just flying all around us."

She tries to maintain that resolute look another second; then it falters and fades away.

"Is everything always this complicated with you?" she demands.

"No way," I say, shaking my head. "With Marla, everything was dead normal—emphasis on the word 'dead'. Now I'm just fucking things up every way I can."

"I can see that," she says, and goes to find Daniel.

She can't play hide-and-seek in the usual methodical fashion, not our Alison. She walks into the middle of the block, looks around theatrically and declaims, "Okay—if I were a big smart ten-year-old boy, where would I be?"

She then heads directly for a pile of boxes next to the boatyard shed at the end of the block. And there he is, behind two boxes with a third perched on his head.

And she drags him down the block to me, tickling him madly, the two of them giggling like toddlers. I just take in the picture and try to tuck it away. I know I will never see anything more lovely in my lifetime than two people I've loved for so long sharing so much happiness.

It's a familiar feeling, I realize suddenly—familiar because I always wanted to feel it with Marla and Daniel. It was a feeling I kept tasting, just at the edge of my senses, although it never actually materialized, because Marla could never abandon herself the way Alison just has. The way you have to, to find any happiness in this world.

"Alison's *much* better at hide-and-seek than you are, Daddy," Daniel tells me. Thank you very much.

Allie's beaming. Her face is glowing and grateful and every tenderness I've ever wanted to see in her face is there right now, shimmering out to me.

"Tonight," I tell her, "I'm going to call you and ask you to come to my house. Come immediately—wear Livy's big hat—the one with the big brim and the feather? The My Fair Lady hat?"

"Okay," she says, conspiratorial.

"And a big coat. At that point, don't tell Livy why you're coming over, just that I asked you urgently to come. Tell her you'll call her, so she should definitely wait there. And then give her this map." I put a folded piece of paper in her hand, a page I've drawn with the location of the microwave truck.

"Drive over, park right in front of my garage and come in — make sure you have the hat on the whole time."

"Okay," she says, eyes widening.

"I'm dragging you into my divorce—is that okay?"

She thinks about this for a moment. I see the eyes narrow and then open wide again.

"Okay," she nods.

I grab her hand with both of mine.

"Thanks," I say.

She smiles back to me again.

I lean into her ear. "I've loved you for 25 years," I say.

"I have no idea how this is going to turn out," she says.

"The right way," I say. "What that means, I have no idea, but that's how it'll end up."

"Me too," she says and kisses me lightly on the cheek. Daniel and I end up back home a little while later, but don't ask me how we got there—I can't remember a thing.

A Dark and Stormy Night

As the afternoon wanes, Daniel and I go out on the beach and try the Frisbee again. He's getting better at it—now he can throw it a distance, though aim is going to be a separate effort. So I'm running all over the beach trying to catch it—good for my exercise program. And good for my surveillance program—the van is still in place.

As we head back up over the seawall to the house, the sky is darkening heavily—thick purple clouds and the wind picking up. If it will only hold on until I can get him to sleep—if it's a storm, he'll sit up nervous till all hours.

He wants to go to the diner to eat—as I say, when he likes someplace, he wants to go there constantly. I say no—we'll cook dinner.

"You mean—you and me?" he gulps.

"Uh-huh."

"We could go to McDonalds," he pleads.

Ah, ye of little faith. I pull some turkey burgers from the freezer and start putting coals on the little hibachi on the back porch. He chooses two potatoes from the fridge and I slice them up and put them in a broiler pan on the oven with a little oil and some salt. When the coals have heated whitehot, I station him at the hibachi with the spatula and coach him on turning the burgers. There are four on the grill—if he drops one, there'll be plenty of time for a new one to cook before we're ready for it.

Half an hour later, we have a culinary success— cheeseburgers and home fries that we cooked ourselves. He's shocked that we can cook—maybe he's shocked that *I* can cook even this little bit—and he's thrilled to be dubbed the Chef.

While he's chowing down, I go into my office and log on. After watching a few minutes, I can see the new presence—the Times writer—in the background at Livy's, taking notes and talking into a tape recorder.

I check my email, and there they are—five more messages, one more threatening than the next, from the 'real' Pale Guy. He's putting on the full-court press.

> paleguy@aol.com: Ok, safehouse, you been a good boy. 1 more nite and we both be happy campers. This my nite to howl!!! So stay away from da babe! Or you pay!

Tonight's the night. Bum bum bum bum. Tonights the ni-hi-hi-hight.

After the dishes are done—he washes, I dry; less chance of broken dishes that way—I pull out the couch and pop in Abbott and Costello, who have become the old reliables. Daniel protests—why do we have to go to bed early? We don't have to go to sleep, I say, just relax—we've had a busy day. He's asleep in an hour, just ahead of the blistering snowstorm.

I pop out of bed and rush to the phone.

Walt Evans is the Seaview police chief—we have some history.

We came to an understanding early on that Livy's site wouldn't embarrass him by breaking any existing laws. He agreed not to encourage zoning changes of the kind many towns use to push sites like Livy's out.

He also suggested we pull the shades between the big room in Livy's house and the houses across the street—he felt we could probably get away with the beach side open. There had been a few complaints and we'd dealt with them in a cooperative way.

Without ever saying so, both of us were very aware that Livy's was the most profitable business by half in the town, and she was paying her taxes. I suggested naming the new wing of the police station after her, but the chief felt that was a little much. Anyway, he takes my call right away.

"What's up?" he says.

"Walt, I've got a violation of Federal communications law here."

"What?"

"We haven't spoken about this," I tell him, "but I'm in the process of getting a divorce."

"I don't wonder," he lows.

"Well, anyway," I explain, "there seems to be someone—I'd put money it's a PI—surveilling my house with two microwave cameras attached to telephone poles across the street. And he's sending out the picture on Channel 14 of the broadcast band. That's a violation of Federal communications statutes. I have a lawyer available who can quote you chapter and verse, if necessary."

"I see," he says, letting all this sink in. "You keep a Federal communications lawyer on retainer?"

"I used to work at UBC. He's a friend."

"Okay, so you've done my homework for me," he offers. I can hear the caution in his voice. "And you want me to send a couple of boys down to pick this guy up?"

Uh-oh. Did I miscalculate somewhere?

"Well, isn't that your job?" I ask. "Enforcing the law?"

"Federal communications law isn't exactly my daily bread, old buddy," he says. "I'm not saying we won't do the job, but I get the feeling there's a little more to this than we've discussed so far. So why don't you give me a little more detail?"

I breathe again.

"Okay. My wife's got this guy watching me. Meanwhile, Livy's got a writer from the NY *Times* doing a story about her tonight, following our latest storylines. So sometime in the next hour or two, I think I can catch the detective in an uncomfortable position and you can arrest his helpers in their microwave van on Salisbury Avenue—and all of this'll be live on the internet, and obviously, will get written up in the *Times*. We get a great story and great publicity, and so does your department."

"And that's it?" he asks. "There's no more skeletons in the closet?"

"That's all there is," I say.

"That's more like it," Walt chuckles. "But can you really furnish me chapter and verse on this law? 'Cause I'm not lifting a finger without a real good foundation under me."

"Not a problem," I tell him, and give him the phone number to call. I tell him he'll be speaking to the chief corporate counsel of the UBC Television Network, and that seems to settle any inhibitions *he* has left.

"What time do you want it to go down?" he asks.

"Do you have Livy's site up?"

"I do now," he says.

"Fine—I'm going to call Livy by webcam. You won't be able to miss me. When she leaves with the cameras, give her a few minutes and then go."

"Done deal. You know the correct spelling of my name, right?"

"Got it."

It takes a few minutes to rig the TV set in my house. Abbott and Costello are gone now, replaced by the surveillance camera shot, which I've painstakingly tuned in. I connect a cable to take the picture from the TV to a switcher box; then another cable goes from there to the video capture card on my computer. Once I hit the right button on the switcher, I have a lovely view of the surveillance camera in a window on my desktop. I can switch between my face on the webcam and the surveillance camera by pushing buttons on the switcher.

It's time. I go to the kitchen and get a glass of wine. The wind is howling and the snow is swirling in sheets outside. A few hints of lightning flicker in the distance. 9:50 pm: Showtime.

I call Alison. She's in the middle of her interview—perfect timing.

"It's time," I tell her. "Don't forget the hat."

I watch as she huddles with Livy momentarily and takes off. Livy is clearly confused, but she makes nice with the reporter and continues to work the chat and play the audience.

I switch to the surveillance feed. Alison arrives in a minute. She steps out of the car with the hat on—thank goodness for tall Jeep ceilings. In the low-res security camera picture, no one could tell who it was. All you can see is the shoulder-length blonde hair behind her. Hair just like Livy's.

I meet her in the kitchen and pull her inside, away from the windows, before she removes the hat. Then I shuss her, finger to my lips and we move past Daniel into the office.

I park her alongside the computer, where she can't be seen, station myself in front of the webcam and log on to Livy's site.

"Livy!" I say into the microphone on the desk.

"Hi!" she says, barking at my picture. "What's going on? What do you need my—"

"Livy, listen a second. Actually—*watch* for a second. Look at this—"

I switch my window on her site to the surveillance view. The picture isn't gorgeous, but it's clearly the outside of my house from two angles.

"What the—"

"Livy, I just found this. Someone is watching my house—they've got two cameras mounted on the telephone poles opposite me and they're sending the output over Channel 14 locally. They've got to have a truck someplace near me picking it up—check your map. I just made a phone call—Walt and the boys will be paying them a visit—I think you should come to the party. The radio cameras are on the bar."

Does she get this lightly-disguised code? Ohh yes she does—I see her face light up.

"On our way," she says, and as I switch my webcam permanently to the surveillance cam view, I see her hand the second radio-transmitting camera to the *Times* reporter, who's now *in* the story.

So now Livy's site shows three camera views in separate windows—the surveillance camera view she's getting from me, and the two live cameras carried by Livy and the *Times* reporter, running through the snowstorm toward the microwave truck. All the action coming down clearly for the world to see—all the world *except* the guys in the truck, who have no Web hookup.

"C'mon," I tell Alison. "Put on your hat and let's head to the kitchen."

She follows me in and we begin to smooch in front of the kitchen window. We're clearly visible to both cameras on the telephone poles across the street, but the pictures at that distance won't be clear—not clear enough for identification in court. Just vague enough to be frustrating, I hope.

For a few moments, all I can do is wait—and kiss Alison. And I do that—God, I do. For a moment, I lose track of everything. It's one thing to wait 25 years to kiss a woman—it's another thing for it to be worth the wait. Man, what a family. How did her parents not have 25 kids?

A few minutes later, I hear a bristling outside, and the creaking of the gate. Alison hears it too, but I hold her steady. Not yet. Let him get closer.

We are stationed right by the rear door. The door opens outward, and it's two running steps to the end of the porch. I've practiced the move in my mind twenty times in the past few days.

I wait one more second and then launch myself through the back door. And there, on the lawn in front of me, stands the unlucky detective, camera in hand, staring at me coming like the stalled car at the railroad crossing.

He had to have a clear picture of Livy and I in the house together—at least, that's what he came to get.

I could just grab him and hold him for the cops—surely, the chief will be by to collect accolades as soon as he's arrested the crew in the van. But a story like this one requires at least one image of pointless heroism—and this is it.

As he turns to run toward the gate, I hit the end of the porch and launch myself through the air after him, the leap straight out of my lifetime of adventure movies. Thank God I actually reach him and we land in a heap on the lawn.

When I get up, dizzy, I realize I've at very least twisted my ankle and may have cracked one of my ribs. But he, unlucky sod, landed on his camera and isn't getting up so fast. He's face down, gasping for breath. I grab the camera for effect and hang it around my neck. He gets up slowly now and immediately bolts for the gate, but I grab him and we go down heavily, two middle-aged men grappling and grunting in the dirt and snow.

A moment later, here come the cops. The chief is not with them—he's been watching the action at home and relaying instructions over the radio. They take the detective in for trespassing on private property and his camera as evidence of invasion of privacy. None of us seems entirely sure those are charges that will stick, but it looks good on camera.

The whole thing looks good on camera. Alison and I pile into my computer room and I start remotely rerunning the last fifteen minutes of video on the server. There it all is: Livy and the *Times* woman running through the swirling snow, reaching the van just before the cops arrive, getting the bust in living color as Hairyman and another more elegant-looking fellow are pulled from the van.

I slow down the tape to be sure—Oh God! The dapper gent is my brother-in-law, the middle-aged millionaire husband of my sister-in-law the gold-digger whore. He must've come down to supervise and play hero—they were clearly real confident about Livy visiting me tonight.

Now he would have one phone call, for bail money. I wonder if Marla was watching at home, waiting to see if we took the bait, to see if she'd get her smoking gun. Well, she'd gotten a show, what with the bust and me jumping off the porch like Indiana Jones. I can imagine what she's thinking. It makes it all worthwhile.

"Pretty macho," Ally says, as we watch and clink glasses of red wine.

"I don't like being fucked with," I say.

"Oh, even *more* macho," she needles.

"Okay—my knees are going to collapse and my whole left side is on fire," I admit. "Is that better?"

She comes over and sits on my lap.

"So what the hell are we going to do?" she says.

"You mean tomorrow?" I ask.

"Yeah," she nods, not running from the subject anymore.

"I haven't the slightest idea," I say. "Right now, however? I have a thought..."

And I kiss her, once and again and again and she's kissing me back and it just goes on for a long time like that, a long time.

A long time, until I look up and see the shining red light on my webcam facing us. And, behind it, our live picture in a window on Livy's site. And Alison looks around, following my glance, and sees it too.

Needs

How our picture ended up going out online I'll never know.

Maybe one of us brushed against the switcher while otherwise occupied. It could have been perfectly innocent, although no one, obviously, has even *considered* that possibility since it happened.

I suppose it is possible that one of us wanted Livy to find out about what was happening between us, to find out without us having to *explain* it. Just by pressing that one little button on the switcher, it was all plain as day.

But, as I say, I'll never know how it happened.

Regardless, Alison is beside herself as soon as she sees our pictures on that screen. She shoots up, and runs for her car.

I go after her, of course, but I'm held up by the necessity of attempting to wake Daniel and then half-walking, half-carrying him into *my* car, where he promptly resumes his comatose state.

So I make it to Livy's about thirty seconds behind Alison, and jump out of the car as she heads for the house. I honk the horn to stop her from going in, and I suppose that might have roused

Livy's attention. And, in fact, as I recall the scene in my mind, I can see Livy's silhouette appear in the window above the garage as we speak. But I don't recall being aware of her at the time.

"Alison!" I yell.

"What?" she says, barely turning.

"Hang on. Don't rush in and throw everything away."

"What are you talking about?" she says. She stops now and faces me.

"I'm talking about us—don't go in there and start apologizing to Livy," I tell her. "Don't give us away."

"Are you suggesting I pretend it didn't happen?"

"No—I'm saying don't apologize."

"I swear I don't know you," she says. "I don't know who you are."

"Why? Why shouldn't I want us to be happy?"

She is really upset now. Her eyes are flaming and her voice rises half an octave.

"What are you talking about?" she says, and the hurt in her voice really cuts through me. "So far, we've had a couple of conversations and a few kisses. I'm sorry those happened, but they did. But how on earth can you know that we are going to find any happiness together?"

"The same way *you* do," I return. "I can feel it. I could feel it when you were home a few hours and we'd been speaking for five minutes. We understand each other. We care for each other. We love each other."

"What about all those things you say you learned from your marriage?" She's yelling at me now, really angry. "All those insights that you have to check out against someone new in your life, to make sure you don't make the same mistakes again?"

"Fuck that—this is love. Love is magic. It's the only magic regular people get in their lives. And we've got it."

We're standing close together now, and I'm pressing my case. This is the crucial part of the argument, and I'm mouthing a silent prayer it will go the right way.

"You know it's true," I insist. "This isn't logic or a couple conversations or even the couple kisses, though those were proof, too. We just *know* we have a chance to be happy together."

We're standing heavy-legged, arms extended, like two fighters on the ropes, waiting for the bell to ring, for the twelfth round to end.

"Alright," she admits. "Maybe. Maybe we could be happy. But that doesn't matter."

"What do you mean?" I cry.

"I came back here because I don't have what you have," she tells me. "I left my child. I need that child back in my life. She's the most important thing in my life, and if I walk away from that, I'll never forgive myself."

"But what about us?" I say, like the pretty boy in the Bette Davis movie, standing alone in the driveway with the broken bouquet of flowers.

"You're *my daughter's lover*," she repeats, as though I'm hard of hearing.

"She doesn't love me," I tell her. "She's reminds me of it all the time. And *we* love each other."

"If that's true, things'll sort themselves out with time," she says.

"Let's sort them out *now*," I say. "Go away with me."

"What?" She's stunned.

"Let's run away," I press, grabbing her hands, "the two of us. We'll make up for the time we missed when we should have been together."

She pulls her hands away from me and backs up the driveway toward the house.

"Aren't you listening?" she says, and I'm almost in tears at the conflict roaring on her face.

"I came for *her*," she cries. "I've been running away all my life. I've got to *stop* running. That's the only way I can live with myself. That comes first! *She* comes first!"

"Over us?" I say.

"Yes, over us. A million times over us!" And she turns and heads inside her house. Livy's house.

I hang my head. My shoulders droop. Amazing how easy these social cues can be when you're properly motivated.

I walk back to my car and, as I settle in the seat and fire up the engine again, I see Livy upstairs closing the window, having heard the entire conversation.

Thank you, Lord, I mouth again. Thank you for answering my prayers. No way this could have gone any better than it did.

The Deluge

'The Kiss' was what they called it. Of course, you probably know that, or, as I said at the beginning, you wouldn't have picked this book off the rack. There are so many more interesting volumes—that history of the Peloponnesian war, for example.

Anyway, 'The Kiss' was all anyone was talking about, as far as I could tell, for the next two days. Not only had it all happened where Livy could catch our act, but the *Times* reporter was right there, and filed an article that ran the following day, as well as the Magazine piece that followed a day later.

'Web Poser faces Maternal Rival' was one of the more sedate and tasteful headlines. The fact that I was now making a play for my young lover's mother on camera was just the kind of thing to take us from web hit to scandalous breakthrough entertainment.

Now it was not just respectful articles in the New York *Times*. We hit the big time—the *Star*, the *Enquirer*. We were now in the supermarket checkout lines of America, and of course on *ET* and even *Access: Hollywood*, which didn't seem to care one whit that we were a continent's width away. The hits on the site went up 75% overnight, and the chats on both sites were running so fast you could barely read them.

Running in different directions, however.

The increase in Livy's chat was predominantly women, the group we'd been courting recently—they were now writing mostly to support her against this heartless scumbag who was two-timing her. A sizeable group wrote in, supporting Alison's right to try to find happiness. There was surprisingly little criticism of Alison—a lot of women seemed to agree that I was too old for Livy anyway, mostly with the attitude that she could get somebody a lot cuter.

The chat on *my* site was mostly guys telling me what an idiot I was, giving up the younger girl for the older one, though Alison had her partisans. Most of the guys my age gave me comfort and counsel, speaking the virtues of a wiser, more experienced mate.

Not that any of that mattered. Our sails were set, both 'the girls', and mine, and we were sailing to separate ports now, regardless of what anyone thought about it. Certainly I knew it, even if no one else did.

Livy, never the one to squelch a controversy, let the 'competition with mom' angle go on as long as she could, even though the Sunday *Times* article made it clear that mother and daughter had reconciled completely following the late evening meltdown in the driveway. Alison had finally given up something she really wanted for her daughter—she'd passed the test of admission.

But since not everyone reads the NY *Times*, and because our conversation in the driveway was coincidentally not on camera—that camera, for some reason, seemed to have stopped working a few days earlier—hordes of people kept coming to Livy's site, expecting to see more on the subject. Who knows *what* they expected—catfights, hair-pulling, or maybe all three of us in the sack together, which seemed to be the most popular solution on *my* chat.

I did show up at the house that afternoon, for about twenty minutes, just to reconnect some equipment. The place was incredibly quiet the whole time I was there, everybody going about their business, business which didn't include me. Which was fine. My divorce was next up on my list of priorities, and coming up swiftly.

Luckily, it was accomplished just as swiftly.

I handed my defense to Marla's lawyer as the two of them arrived for the hearing. It included the following:

-email from Marla to me before I left, showing a raise in her salary that she had neglected to mention in her brief,

-copies of the cancelled checks for the money I'd paid her since I left, which she'd also managed to forget,

-a copy of a deposit slip in her handwriting that must have slipped into my pocket when I was at the house waiting to pick up Daniel—a deposit slip from a bank account she'd neglected to list in her brief,

-the police report of Marla putting the car onto the sidewalk in front of me—I figured if fate had conspired to give me such a document, it could only have been intended for our divorce papers,

-The doctor's history of Daniel, showing his disability had been diagnosed years before the recent study—years before I left,

-an email from Marla that stated she'd given me the study two weeks *after* I'd moved out, and another one showing we hadn't seriously discussed it for another month after *that*, and

-the revelation that I'd seen her lawyer for a private consultation about our marriage five months earlier and that I wanted her thrown off the case.

I don't know if Marla grasped the significance of these charges, but, as they scanned the papers, waiting for the court clerk to talk with us, I could see her lawyer did. She sat heavily in her chair, looking a little light-headed all of a sudden.

And that's when I changed my plans. It occurred to me that I absolutely did *not* want to get this lawyer thrown off the case.

First of all, she'd done an incompetent brief, which I'd punched a hundred holes in. The next lawyer would be better prepared, and so would Marla.

Secondly, this lawyer was staring at being humiliated in front of her client and the court, and probably having to return all or most of her fee. She had a vested interest in getting this thing over quickly, and that's what I wanted.

So I came up with a simple plan: Marla gets money; I get my freedom *now*—not four years from now—and liberal visitation.

In the end, it all went in a whimper. I agreed to pay for my son's 'special needs,' and to give her the house, which I wanted Daniel and her to have.

What *I* wanted was a lump sum that I could afford to pay and still have a life. Marla wouldn't have the opportunity to hatch some bright idea to cost me another couple of hundred a week whenever she felt like it. Which she was certainly capable of.

This didn't go down easily. Marla held out, fighting stubbornly, item by item—things came to a head when she insisted I didn't need a car.

The court clerk, who was supposed to be the objective mediator, finally said, "He needs a car because he's going to be driving your son around. You want him to be taking your son to New Jersey on a bus?"

So I got terms I could live with and walked out an hour later with a divorce.

She got custody, of course—I'd checked with a few other lawyers who agreed with Nat Turner's view that it wasn't a winnable battle, and Marla wouldn't agree to joint custody.

But I got my 'liberal visitation,' and in fact, the issue I was so concerned about—unfit parent, pornography site, etc.—never even got raised.

While that was a huge relief to me, it wasn't a complete shock—at that point, her detective was out on bail awaiting trial on charges of theft of the public airwaves, trespassing and public indecency—when the police arrested him, they found his fly open.

My brother-in-law was awaiting trial as an accessory to theft of the public airwaves. I agreed informally to drop the charges as part of the divorce settlement, and really, nobody's heart seemed to be in it, once we'd settled the numbers.

In the end, Marla was about money. Had it always been that way? I don't think so, but 'always' is a long time back. I was someone different then, and so was she. Maybe, now that this was over, we could start remembering the things we *liked* in each other again.

As we were walking out of the courthouse, I held my hand out.

"All square," I said. "Done and done. I'll pick up Daniel Friday."

She shook my hand and we went to our separate cars. I felt five hundred tons, that I didn't know I'd been carrying around, lift off me by the time I got back to the shore, to the waves and the swirling birds and my last few pieces of unfinished business.

The Bill Comes Due

Livy said, "It's time to bring back the Pale Guy."

It had been awfully quiet for a day or two. Not on the site, of course. There, the debates raged about our future, whether either of these women should have anything to do with me and other important issues of western civilization.

But when I showed up at the house, things got real quiet. Nobody—Alison, Livy, even Sylvie—had much to say to me. I knew something was coming—things couldn't go on like this for much longer—but in the meantime, I was just glad when anyone would talk to me at all.

"What do you have in mind?" I asked.

"I think we have to give them something else to think about," Livy said. "We're going to eventually have to work our way out of this storyline, and probably the best way is to have something else starting up again—and the Pale Guy is Old Faithful."

I called Lance.

"I'm willing to do it," he said, "but I need time for auditions."

"Auditions?"

"Yeah. I've been doing some commercials. I got a fabric softener last month—the one with the little gargoyles flying around? Have you seen it?"

"No."

"Anyway, I need to do auditions," he repeated. "And you have to pay me scale—"

"Scale?!"

"I'm a member of the Guild now—I joined when I got the commercial. I can't be a scab."

I found myself looking out at the beach, looking for a tall thin guy who could stand very straight and wear a fright mask. I saw lots of candidates.

"Lance, I'll tell you what—"

"And I need a credit," he interrupted.

"Lance, no one knows you're acting. This is supposed to be for real, remember?"

"You can bury it on the site someplace—"

I exploded.

"Yes, thank you, that's a great thought. 'Java software by Sun, Web hosting by Beachnet, stalker played by Lance the Artist.' That'll go over big."

"It's servitude if I don't get a credit," he persisted.

"Lance, this experience has done you good," I answered after a long pause.

"You think so?" he asked.

"Absolutely," I said. "Now you can pronounce 'servitude,' and use it in a sentence. Goodbye Lance."

And I clicked off. Now I had to find a stalker that would satisfy Livy.

This proved easier said than done. She wasn't satisfied with anyone I found, and I had to admit that most of them were just pathetic. You wouldn't think that acting a stalker would be a taxing job. Hell, all you had to do was stand in a window and look menacing with a mask on.

But suddenly, I began to understand why Lance was getting commercials. He actually had a gift for expressing himself through body movement. These guys were just stumps. They stood in one place and stared, looking stupid instead of scary, or they moved like my Uncle Manny who had to wear rubber pants because his blood pressure would slump every time he stood up (don't get me started)...

Finally, Livy said, "We need to get started. I don't want this to go on indefinitely. We should start tomorrow."

"We don't have anybody yet," I reminded her.

"Why don't *you* do it?" she said finally, inevitably.

"Me? I'm not tall enough, for one thing. And won't it seem odd if I disappear from the house the night the stalker appears?"

"You haven't been on that much lately," she said. "We'll just say you got sick or something."

So, as you surely know from the news accounts, I was out on the deck that night in the Pale Guy's regalia. And I shadowed Livy for less than *one minute* before the police arrived, called by an army of Internet fans who suddenly discovered what town we were in and were panic-stricken by the sight of Livy parading around in front of this dangerous, suddenly foot-and-a-half shorter psycho on the deck behind her.

Now, anyone who knows the Seaview police—and who has taken them on as many wild-goose-chases as I have—knows they couldn't arrive anywhere in one minute if their lives depended on it.

Which leaves the intriguing thought that someone actually called them *before* the Pale Guy appeared.

I know who I'd nominate for that role, but you can decide for yourselves.

The police arrived and took me into custody. I knew both officers, and once they'd bundled me into the squad car, I waited in stupid serenity, waiting for Livy to come tell them what was doing and free me.

Any doubts I might have had about Livy's motivation disappeared when she identified me as the stalker who'd been menacing her and refused my protestations by saying she'd never seen me before in her life.

The officers were mystified—they knew I was Livy's boyfriend; we'd met many times on their courtesy visits—but nonetheless, fifteen minutes later I was occupying a cell at the local clink.

That's about how long I stayed there, too.

The chief let me go immediately—he'd actually been speaking to me on the phone one night *during* a Pale Guy attack. I explained to him how we'd created the Pale Guy a long time ago to juice the ratings. I was concerned this would really piss him off—I was sure we'd broken some kind of statute, if only calling the police under false pretenses.

He shrugged. "Well, thanks for leveling with me, finally," he said. "But you guys weren't real hard to figure out."

Confronted with the fact that there were hundreds of witnesses to the Pale Guy's previous appearances—and that, on almost all those nights, I was either at the house with Livy or online at my own site at the same time, the whole thing evaporated very quickly. Livy never pressed the charges, and I was never even arraigned.

All the news outlets played it up as 'The Internet Riot'. The headline came from the fact that we had such an audience by this time, and they all tried to send emails warning Livy at once, that we burned out a phone switch, taking down part of the Middle Atlantic telephone structure. If I never accomplish anything else in my life—and that's certainly a possibility—I can look back on my crowning achievement: I burnt out a piece of the Bell System. More impressive than sinking the Titanic, I'll tell you.

Anyway, it made a good story on a slow news day. 'Internet Riot' made all the network newscasts, and the supermarket tabloids for weeks after.

What gave the story 'legs' was everyone's initial—and correct—assumption that this was Livy's attempt to get back at me for trying to spirit away her mother. The whole story of the past week got dragged out and relentlessly rehashed—the mother's reappearance, the fact that we'd been lovers (wrong, but endlessly repeated as fact) in high school, the possibility (none, but again repeated endlessly) that Livy was my own daughter, 'The Kiss', the rejection, the reconciliation of mother and daughter, and now daughter's attempt to send me to jail for my transgressions. It played for days.

What sent it over the top—what made us a *cause celebre*—was when the Chief was interviewed and managed to mention that I was actually an employee of Livy's site and so was the Pale Guy. Suddenly, the bigger question was: What was real and what was fiction?

That story ran as the top story of ET that night and took headlines all over the place. Livy made the cover of *Yahoo:Internet Life*, did interviews with Regis, *The View*, Matt Drudge and Ted Koppel, smoothly admitting that yes, some of the content of the site was just a game and it got out of hand, "but I'm a naughty girl and when you're playing on the edge, sometimes those things happen."

Koppel even seemed concerned about disturbing Livy's routine: "And what is your audience watching while you do this interview with us?"

"They're watching me do the interview—I have *my* camera right over here," Livy answered smoothly, pointing to the free-standing camera on the remote-control tripod I built for her. And installed for her. And maintained. And repaired. And replaced. And babied. And virtually invented.

And of course, I was the means by which she cemented her standing as the premiere exhibitionist on the Web, at least for the moment, by the simple expedient of kissing her mother—which I wanted to do anyway—and then by getting arrested.

Her viewership doubled each night for the next week, and she's kept them, by and large. She knows how to keep a man's attention, certainly, and the new, bigger house, with several more women and their boyfriends and suitors, is the biggest hit on the Internet now. This house isn't even in Seaview anymore, though she kept the sitename. The new house is a few miles south, in

Monmouth, where Alison, Marla and I all grew up. That's fitting, I guess.

Livy's new agents called once to inform me of the requests for joint interviews. But the next day, I was told Livy had decided not to do any interviews with me. Ever. Period.

This was not a shock. We'd been headed in that direction for some time—certainly since Alison had shown up, and maybe for a while before that.

But my plans were now all played to conclusion. The ships were set on course, and I was content to let them sail.

The End

In the end, everyone gets what they want.

Alison and Livy are tight as can be. They did the talk shows together, talking about repairing their relationship and how they learned to get along. Oprah loved the story. Alison looks happy whenever I catch her on the tube, really happy and relaxed when I scan her soul on the monitor. She has what she wanted.

I, of course, had that stock certificate Livy gave me in a moment of weakness and generosity. And when Seaviewgirl went public in March, I was the biggest stockholder other than the Queen of the Internet herself.

The shares started at 15 and went to 150. I sold everything I had right there. A month later, when all the web stocks started dropping like flies, Livy was up to 250. Why not? She was one of the only sites on the Web *making* money. I don't care how high it goes—I've got my little pile, and it was time to cut the cord.

But obviously, if you've come this far, you know that's not all I wanted. I didn't wander this long in the desert just to get money. I wandered, for so long, to find out what I wanted. That takes a long time to figure out—the heart just doesn't know the easy way to its natural end.

We no longer have God. Earlier generations knew what to hold dear, because they'd been told by their parents, who'd been told by their parents before them, back to the guy way back at the beginning of the family, who said he'd been told direct by God. But we no longer buy any of that. We believe in television, not God, and television hasn't got a clue what the heart really wants.

It wants to be at peace, that's what it wants. My heart wants to find someone who knows where I'm from, someone I won't have to explain anything to. This is about as much peace as is available for human beings, I think, because life will never be more logical or fair or less painful or cruel than it is at this moment. The most we can go after is peace.

I'm writing now, the way I wanted to when I got out of college. There's no money in it, but it makes me feel *satisfied*. I started working on a heavy dramatic story about a fellow who gets twisted around by unreasonable divorce law. I kept starting it and throwing it out, starting again and throwing it out again, because it just wasn't *funny*, and every day I see the world around me as more and more funny. The interesting thing is, every friend I showed it to thought it was all about me.

Of course, we know better, don't we? I sit here, in my rented house near the beach, the remains of my bridges smoldering around me in every direction. Burned them all myself, and a damned good job of it, too. Each one is the remains of another stab at peace.

A river continues to flow under those bridges. And, in that flow, the pathways remain. It's my river—I've been living on it for a while, and now I'll navigate it best I can. I know how to paddle; I recognize the shallows and the rapids when they come. And sometimes, I'm comfortable enough to lay back on the seat and just let the boat drift on a sunny afternoon.

Marla read the stories of my spectacular breakup with Livy, and knowing the history with Alison, thought it was hysterical. At one point, I called to arrange picking up Daniel and she could barely contain her laughter.

Daniel came over and spent a week with me, during spring break. The weather's getting warmer now, the spring coming on early. He runs in the ocean—I dip a toe in and tell him he's a loony for even considering it, but he runs and splashes happily at the edges of the water.

We walk along the dunes until we hear a crusty voice saying, "Ah, it's my boys—just in time for the painting." And there is Sylvie, lugging cans of varnish over to the side of her deck.

She spends an hour teaching Daniel the proper technique for varnishing old wood. He spreads the varnish in an even coat over a quarter mile of beach all around her deck, and all over his clothes. This leaves him infinitely happy.

At one point, Sylvie and I stand at her door, watching Daniel happily slap brush to wood. And I feel her press something into my hand.

It is a picture, obviously brand-new, of Livy and Alison together. A warm mother-daughter portrait; two people who obviously feel comfortable with one another—now.

On the back, in Alison's elongated hand, is the message, "Thanks for helping me. A crafty and devious god, indeed."

I smile a little—I'm aware of Sylvie watching me and it makes me shy, but I feel a warm wave rising inside. I take a quick breath and hold it, to keep from giggling.

We've waited a long time, I find myself thinking. We're still alive, and not going anywhere for a while. Just keep putting one foot in front of the other, boy—you'll see where you get.

~~~~
~~~~

Read a Preview of
'Swindler & Son,'
The new novel by Ted Krever
On Sale December 2018

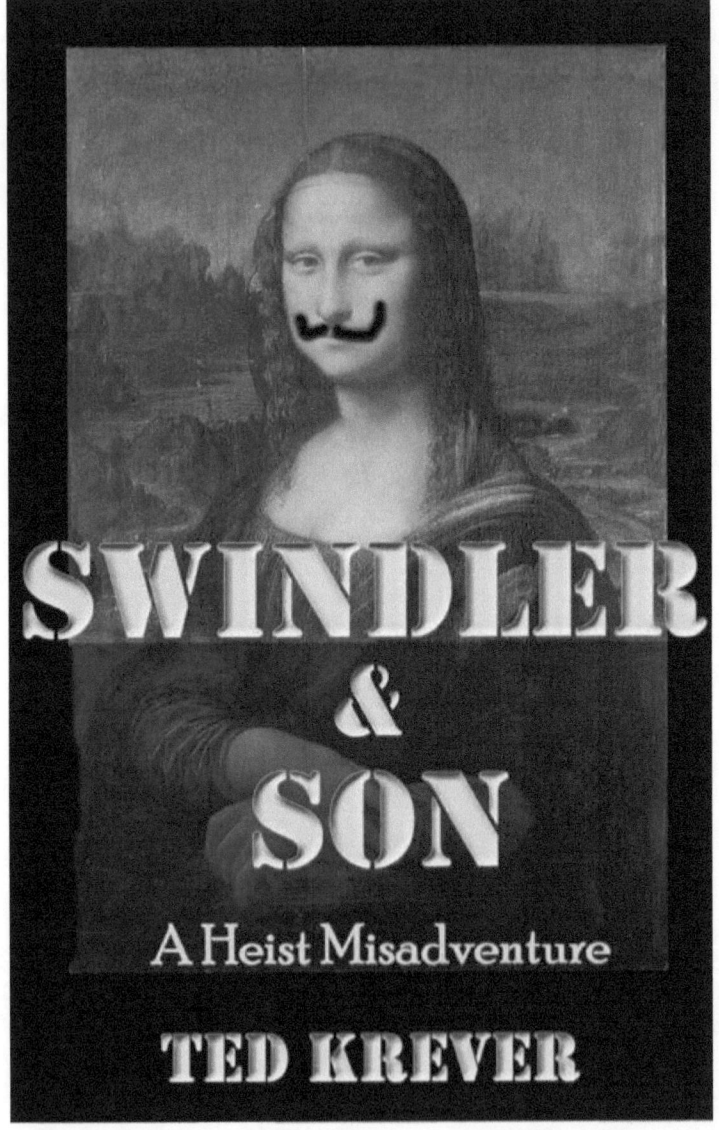

THE START

−So how does it start?

It starts with the sound of my own name spoken aloud.

Call me Nicholas, I'm fine. Nick or Nicky, even better.

But 'Nicholas Marsh' enunciated, first and last, all the way through—when I hear it *that* way, I know I've done something I'm about to pay for.

Hearing it in French, every syllable twisted and slurred and leaking from the earpiece of a Parisian counter-terrorism officer in a Kevlar vest, his back to me and his binoculars trained on my kitchen window—*that's* rock-bottom.

That's how it starts, in the snowy garden of the *Hopital Saint-Louis* in the Tenth Arrondissement, just past sundown on Christmas day, at what I fervently hoped was the end of one of the worst days of my life.

Well, actually, no…

Actually, it started about fifteen minutes earlier, on the other side of the canal, where I was mugged by some twenty-five year-old junkie in a purple-tinted mohawk and a leather jacket. And several nice tats on his neck that distracted my attention when I should have been focusing on his oncoming fist. He took my wallet and phone and left me aching and dizzy, which is why I wandered groggy several blocks out of my way and approached home through the garden.

I love that garden but none of the official exits land anywhere near my apartment. A few years ago, I found a back door, through the *Musee des Moulages* on the hospital grounds, that let me out near a construction gate right across the street from my building.

I'm just opening that back door when I hear my name and see GIGN, French Special Forces, two officers, huddled like Martians in flak suits, gas masks and sniper rifles, peeking through the construction gate at the wide corner, the entrance to my building and, eight floors above, at the dead coleus drooping from my night table.

Frozen in place, I scan the rooftops and find a squad of dark gray uniforms—and, in case I harbor any last doubts, hear my name one more time from the headset hanging from the blonde officer's right ear. I back instinctively into the doorway, sweating and making twenty-five different plans at the same time.

The bus! They won't be checking the bus on the Boulevard de la Villette, that's an answer. Having any sort of answer helps calms the quiver in my legs, brings them back into something like working order.

This is a mistake—it's got to be. If I'd done something to deserve counter-terrorism, I'd remember it, wouldn't I? More importantly, why in hell didn't somebody tip me off? Who do I know at GIGN?

Out through the door and the museum, retracing my steps, back out the far end of the compound, past the *Chapelle* to the *Rue de la Grange aux Belles*. Up toward the roundabout at a regular clip, walking briskly like a Parisian.

Am I thinking of escape? Hell no, I'm just getting pissed. Why hasn't somebody warned me? Why haven't they given me a chance to buy my way out of this?

Oh sure, GIGN makes it look serious but that just raises the price. I know somebody in every department of government and what they cost. Serious things have been undone before.

By the time the bus makes three stops, I know who to talk to—Beltoise, the second man at the *Surete*. He was at our Christmas party just last night.

I *own* him! At least, I should. If I had a middle-class clientele, if I dealt pot or owned a brothel, I could expect a phone call 24 hours in advance of a raid. It's common courtesy!

He'll be at *D'Azur*, of course, charging his dinner to us as usual.

When I arrive, he's tucked into a dim corner. He rises before I can reach him.

"Why is GIGN all around my apartment? You don't warn me?"

His eyes bulge like marbles. "Where's your phone?"

"Phone? Stolen. I got mugged."

He looks *relieved*. "That's why they're not here yet," he mutters and pulls me into the private room in back.

"Nicky, our past history—and the fact that I like you—is why I'll give you a minute's grace before I call you in." He's serious! His face goes cold—not like he doesn't know me, like he's never *seen* me before. "Normal corruption is one thing—but this?"

Normal corruption? Normal corruption is my *specialty*! He's reducing ten thousand years of civilized give-and-take to a catchphrase. Not to mention, it's fed him quite nicely, thank you, over the years.

I look at his face, at the disappointment and condescension there, and realize what a farce it all is. You treat them like princes but the first time you actually need them to put out...they might as well be in insurance.

Faced with this ingratitude, something inside me just gives up.

"Okay," I tell him. "I surrender."

"What?"

"I'll confess, right now. It's the jet ramps, isn't it?"

He looks confused.

"We have this client, a dictator...you know the old joke about, you're not really a country unless you have your own stamps, your own airline and your own beer? Well, he's got commemorative stamps, a brewery, a Mercedes stretch limo and a portrait of himself as Julius Caesar. But he gets embarrassed when his guests have to descend a staircase off the plane.

"There's a staircase on Air Force One' I tell him and he says, 'They could have a ramp if they wanted one.' So when Kumbatta collapsed, we flew a cargo plane in and liberated a couple of jetramps. The guy was so happy, he painted two Cessna's and proclaimed them the national airline. I don't think we *hurt* anybody."

Beltoise settles into the nearest chair, not saying a word.

"That's not it?"

Silence.

"Okay, Napoleon's penis—that was a good deed, I swear."

"*Excusez moi?*"

"It's your Minister of Defence's fault! Not the present Minister, the old one. He had this...thing about Napoleon's penis, that it should be back in France where it belongs."

"It is in France! Napoleon's body is at Les Invalides!"

"The body, sure, but his penis was removed during the autopsy and it's floated around ever since from collector to collector. It's now owned by a urologist, naturally, in Philadelphia."

"Don't be funny."

"It's true. The BBC measured it a few years ago and found it a bit small. Naturally, that outraged the Minister, who insisted the English don't know how to measure. The urologist's price was just *outrageous* so we found a...more generously-sized one around the same age, for a price the Minister could afford. It made him *happy.*"

"You found him another penis?"

"Another *old* penis! You think that was easy? How many three-hundred-year-old penises you think are floating around?"

Beltoise stares at me with—I can't tell if it's respect or concern. The odd thing is, to me, this is actually beginning to feel pretty *righteous.* Confession really *is* good for the soul. "Okay, not the answer. Give me a chance. The eighteen identical one-of-a-kind Moroccan emeralds—"

"No."

"The Van Gogh with the wrong ear missing?"

Beltoise rolls his eyes. "We've never met," he warns, "except for a few state dinners with hundreds of other people I've never met either—but my advice is, you find a quick way out of France now. And don't bother replacing your phone—they'll find you as soon as you do. You understand?"

This is terrifying—Beltoise is a glorified flatfoot with a fancy office. I'm *begging* to be arrested and he's not biting. It's *unnatural.*

"Throw me a bone here," I say. "I don't understand what's happened."

He grimaces. "You know damn well it's the bomb."

"The *BOMB?*"

Of course, I know all about the bomb. I'd arrived back in Paris the day before, just in time for the funerals. Twelve dead, 37 injured, a miracle it wasn't more. A mountain of flowers in plastic sleeves heaped on the rubble, candles arrayed like soldiers in front of the dress shop left somehow intact on the corner.

And a march from the *Place De la Republique* to the *Place de la Nacion*, thousands, orderly and dogged, middle-class families and university students, *Le President* and his rivals, butchers, bakers, artists and computer technicians shuffling through neighborhood streets between broad public squares, solemn and chattering, sombre but fashionable—Paris, formal but somehow intimate. Great buildings and beautiful women dressed in black. Paris is a grand dame, maybe a bit past her prime, but she still knows how to put on a funeral.

'It's an escalation,' they say, the voices that multiply in crowds. Just a few years ago, 'they' were content to shoot up a restaurant or concert hall. Now, somehow, they bring in a bomb the size of a safe to bring down half a block of five-story apartment buildings.

The size of the explosion makes people nervous. Nobody builds a bomb that size to bring down the Rue Breguet. We all sense a grander plan that went awry and the fact that no one claimed responsibility only seems to heighten the tension. You don't even have the consolation of knowing who to be afraid of.

Beltoise, however, has made up his mind.

"It's your shipping certificate!" he yells, no longer caring who hears. "Your company's letterhead! Your *signature* on the bloody thing! You think I will cover for *that*, you're insane!"

I stand frozen for an endless moment, until words I never thought I'd hear myself say come tumbling out of my mouth.

"I didn't do *that*! I'm *innocent*!"

And then, I run.

RUNNING

-You ran?

It's an expression. I know better than to run. I walk at my usual quick pace but not fast enough to attract attention. Okay?

I lose myself in the tangle of back streets, staying off the boulevards, sticking to shorter blocks and parks where I can change direction at will. I stop short in front of angled store windows several times, switch direction several more, take a cab for a short distance and then another to double-back on myself. I'm overdoing it, in truth—if GIGN were really on my tail, they'd just throw on the sirens and take me. Once I'm sure I'm not being followed, I find a thrift shop that's just closing in a church, buy a pair of slacks and a short dark hoodie and wear them out of the store.

-This is tradecraft. Where did you acquire your technique?

Like you don't know. I had a very brief career in—what do you tell strangers at parties? About what you do for a living?

-I don't speak of such things.

We used to call it 'compliance.' I was recruited out of college. They trained me to take in a room or a street, to be invisible when that was useful. Trust no one, calculate the odds, tote up the angles and assume everyone follows their own self-interest.

But they couldn't teach me to be shrewd. I got myself involved in an 'extracurricular' scheme supporting freedom fighters—that is, it became extracurricular once it led to screaming headlines. Next thing I know, I'm getting chewed out in front of a Congressional committee for the exact same things they'd urged us to do in private.

We were thrown out like Big Mac wrappers, three fall guys, small potatoes. A generous severance package—under the table, of course—just go quietly into the night, thank you.

That training comes back to me, now that I'm on the run. Focus! *The bomb! What have I got to do with the fucking bomb?*

I need real information. Somewhere in our files, says Beltoise, is a shipping certificate for a bomb with my signature on it. I can't go home so I almost certainly can't go back to the office. But maybe Harry's apartment is clear.

If this had happened any other time—last week, even!—I could have counted on Harry's counsel, his expertise, his instincts. For fifteen years, he's been there when I needed him.

But that's a huge part of what made this feel like the worst day of my life, even before GIGN's visit. I've no idea if I can count on Harry anymore.

-Explain this please. Who is this Harry and why can't you count on him?

Harry is the majordomo, the ringmaster of our circus, the senior partner in Sandler & Son, affectionately known to staff and select members of the governing elite as Swindler & Son. Everything that isn't about Sara in this story is about Harry.

-And Harry's got problems?

Oh hell no, Harry's got no problems. Harry *is* the problem. Everybody *loves* Harry, *that's* the problem.

And why shouldn't they? Harry makes life a party, a twenty-four-hour Remy Martin and shellfish from the little inlet over *there* and put away your business cards, this isn't some vulgar networking grind, we're here to have *fun*! Remember fun? Harry does.

If you liked the Remy, you must try this cognac—it's Venetian, Dante mentioned it (disparagingly, but he mentioned it) in the *Divine Comedy* and let me introduce you to the Ambassador's wife, she has all the good gossip about the orgies at that other embassy—maybe it was the Czechs but we're not saying. Meanwhile, other groups are discussing 70's film and sex robots and if there's anything else you want to know, the person to speak to is over *there*. The band plays good acoustic jazz, the

Argentine tango couple are giving lessons one-on-one on the terrace and the star of the national football club is kicking balls around with enchanted kids and dazzled grownups on the south lawn.

In Paris, of course. That's our home base. It's one of God's jokes—Harry hated the French so, once we'd been thrown out of every other country in Europe, the only place left to go was Paris. Which, of course, he now loves because how can you not love Paris? It's *Paris*, for God's sake.

And the French love Harry. Big gnarly elegant gay Englishman, what's not to love? He ignores their culture, conducts himself like tenth-generation nobility fallen to trade or maybe a good Savile Row tailor, speaks only enough French to be fed and catered to but laughs and charms so naturally, they can't help themselves. Seduction is the French national pastime; they recognize a Master at work.

I was in Mumbai two years ago, picking up a load of Indian cotton. There was a rash of suicides among cotton farmers in Vidarbha and I was able to pick up several farms' entire crop just by paying off the bank loans. I told myself it was a good deed and a good deal. So I'm in the hotel bar at the end of the day chatting up some girl when a man behind me says, "Oh, you work with Harry Sandler? I was in a steeplechase syndicate with him in Ireland once. Took me for £65,000 quid. Most wonderful time I ever had." He bought us both a drink.

Everybody loves Harry; that's what nearly killed us all. As I watched the Iranian commandos lining up on the deck of the ship three hours ago, in their black stocking caps and their Kalashnikovs aimed at our temples, all I could think was, *Everybody loves Harry*.

Fucking goddamn Harry.

Author Biography

Ted Krever watched the Beatles on Ed Sullivan, went to Woodstock (the *good* one), and graduated Sarah Lawrence College with a useless degree in creative writing.
He spent several decades creating programs for ABC News, CBS, CNN, A&E, Court TV, MTV News, Discovery People and CBS/48 Hours, and as VP/Production of a short-lived dotcom.
He has driven a 16-wheeler across the Rockies, shot overnight news in NY City, managed a revival-house movie theater and married twice, in a triumph of optimism.
He was once accused of attempting to blow up Ethel Kennedy with a Super-8 projector.
Read more at www.tedkrever.com